THE DISTANT
LAUGHTER

BRYAN FORBES

THE DISTANT LAUGHTER

COLLINS
St James's Place, London

William Collins Sons & Co Ltd
London · Glasgow · Sydney · Auckland
Toronto · Johannesburg

First published April 1972
Reprinted May 1972

© John Hargreaves and Michael Leonard Oliver
as Trustees of Bryan Forbes Settlement

ISBN 0 00 221181 5

Set in Monotype Garamond
Made and Printed in Great Britain by
William Collins Sons & Co Ltd Glasgow

AUTHOR'S NOTE

It is no secret that I am a film director married, and happily so, to an actress, but I am not the Warren of this story nor is my wife the Susan. The fiction of the film industry has always been stronger than its fact and my inventions and characters bear no resemblance to living people. Only the insanities are real.

You may take my happiness
to make you happier,
Even though you never
know I gave it to you –
Only let me hear sometimes
all alone,
The distant laughter
of your joy . . .

From Brian Hooker's translation
of Rostand's *Cyrano de Bergerac*

This book is for Nanette
with love

CHAPTER ONE

I flew into London three weeks afterwards, as we had painfully agreed, and the plane was on time, but even so my much publicised wife was not at the airport to greet me.

For minutes after the plane landed I sat motionless in my first-class seat—the model passenger—conscious only of a vague commotion around me: people suddenly familiar with life again after a break: strangers talking to strangers in astonished voices like those of children released after a thunderstorm.

As we taxied towards the parking area it occurred to me that all my boringly careful preparations had led me to this one point, this moment of suspension: as if my mind had been a film projector in which the film had jammed as the climax approached. In moments of terror I invariably translate everything into celluloid—old home movies with the sprocket holes ripped.

Outside the double windows, as the last engine-shudder racked the cabin and the canned music became offensively intelligible, I could see tiny airport vehicles, like Dinky toys, accelerating towards us in wide circles and a few grimed maintenance men trundled their equipment under the mirror-surfaced wings with bored ease.

In the distance, on the spectator balcony, the crowd, that did not contain the face I looked for, shifted expectantly. Even as I looked some remote contact was made. As though carefully rehearsed but not yet fully competent, a small man suddenly detached himself from the main body of the crowd and ran the length of the balcony waving his hat high in the air. Then, as if caught out in some obscene act, he faltered—the run became an over-casual walk, the arm waving the hat dropped to his side. I could almost feel the pain of his embarrassment: the English are always soiled by any excess of public affection. And yet I envied him, envied the humiliation, the luxury of a need nakedly revealed.

9

Only two sheets of stressed plastic sheltered me from the unknown man's reality, and trapped between them was a single tear-drop of condensation. By some freak chance it was positioned beneath the eye of my reflection. Seeing it there and coldly conscious of the irony, I thought how much easier life would be if I stopped believing in love.

I thought, now the anxiety begins. I knew the paths ahead and remembered, mechanically, other arrivals and departures: corruption, like lust, makes its own patterns.

It seemed to me then, at the very beginning, that I had already come far enough. With my eyes open, the tear suspended on the reflected cheek, knowing all the alternatives, I deliberately chose misery. It was a form of relief: happiness is never really so welcome as familiarity.

I sat and waited, prepared and yet powerless, like a man who has paid before delivery for something he does not want.

The prettiest of the three hostesses released the safety-locks on the exit hatch and composed her careful face for the duty-good-byes. My fellow passengers were already on their feet searching for hand luggage, bird-like in their concern to be first away, as though it was at this stage of the journey that the real danger began.

'Anything I can get you, Mr Warren?'

Her cool hands sprang the mechanism on my safety-strap.

'Landings always leave me in a state of shock,' I said.

'Well, if there's anything I can get you. . . .'

Her concern, which I recognised as being only voice-deep, filled me with a sudden desperation. She seemed to represent everything I wanted most to avoid. Her crisp, bright beauty had disturbed me more than once during the actual flight—like nurses, air hostesses put on a layer of sexual mystery with their uniforms: one longs for them to sweat or look ruffled, anything to temper the antiseptic aura of desirability.

This girl's uniform was too tight for her and her heavy breasts were prominent enough to make a Yossarian moan out loud. Her face looked as though it had been sketched in with a fine camel-hair brush, some months ago, passed by the hanging committee, and then faintly varnished. She gave me the impression, echoing so many American women, that she was capable of receiving the wildest erotic compliments without enthusiasm; that it would make little or no difference to her whether she was loved or merely wanted, that the most she intended to take from any man could be forgotten before the vibrator batteries needed replacing.

'I mean, you feel all right, don't you?'

As she bent over me, her tolerance was like some expensive and alarming perfume. It's easy enough, I suppose, to give comfort when your dignity isn't affected.

'It was a great trip,' I said. 'I just don't want it to end.'

She'd heard it all before, of course—the same stale old verbal pass in a score of languages sometimes delivered with the friendly homesick hand on her tight regulation bottom, sometimes with the arm that accidentally brushed the swell of her stipulated breasts as she served the free drinks. I couldn't really blame her when the smile hardened.

'Well, thank you. Fly with us again won't you.'

Another hostess waited to escort us on the three-mile walk to the arrival lounge, taking over the duty-smiles like a relay runner. As I approached her a cold wind rushed at me with that speed peculiar to all things on an airport. This one was young, too, and just as ruefully pretty as her colleague in the cabin. With her darkly outlined eyes and feverish high colour she stared back at me from a dozen future magazine covers. The trouble to-day is that beauty isn't unobtainable.

'Mr Warren?' this one said with generous conviction. 'I have a message for you.' She took my hand luggage from me and the excess weight of it wiped her face clean, but the airline was losing money and she recovered quickly.

'Your wife telephoned from the hotel and left word she couldn't be here. Something about misunderstanding your cable, although I didn't take the message personally. But she sent a Mr Gotten—no, wait a minute, I knew I'd get it wrong—a Mr Grotefend, who has everything arranged.'

'How kind of her,' I said. 'And how kind of Mr Grotefend to have everything arranged. Especially with a name like that. He must have other things on his mind.'

The passport and immigration farce being completed, I stared around at the faces in the luggage hall. They were the same faces I had been living with for the past eleven hours, but here they looked different. A new seriousness had been assumed and every face bore marks of a guilty innocence.

Her Majesty's Preventive Officers were bunched together in maty little groups on their side of the fence, picking out their targets with studied indifference. I reached for a cigarette, having given up smoking forty-eight hours before, but being a regular quitter, still carrying a supply. It was American and tasted foul in the English air. I stubbed it out immediately and one of the Customs boys, noting the act, could hardly contain himself. Just to make his day I pushed back my cuff and looked at my solid white gold Patek Philippe, a gift from a leading actress who always knew what time of day it was.

I remembered past encounters with the enemy—Lowson, my first cameraman, coming back from that location in Berlin with a Leica strapped across his genitals with strips of Elastoplast. It had been January, with snow on the ground when we landed. Lowson was sweating with fear and guilt when we boarded the plane, but by then he had committed himself, he had to see it through, although he made numerous trips to the toilet en route and we laid bets on him. They tumbled him the moment he set foot inside Customs, of course. Despite the sub-zero temperature he was dripping sweat all over his cheap suitcases when they showed him the warning card. 'No, no cameras,' he said, 'just a few cigarettes, the allowance, and a couple of bottles of booze.'

He was taken into a private room and stripped, and, as he told it afterwards, even with his trousers round his ankles, had still tried to bluff it through. It wasn't until they tapped him hard on the vital area that he admitted defeat. The Customs character had had quite a sense of humour from all accounts. 'Who would you like to see first, sir?' he'd asked Lowson politely. 'Your doctor or your solicitor?'

As it happened Lowson did produce a doctor at the trial and pleased everybody except the magistrate by pleading temporary insanity brought about by an acute attack of shingles. He was nothing if not original, even to his choice of lovers, poor old Lowson, and was always good for a laugh.

I was still thinking of him, thinking past the laughter in the snow to the death in a helicopter in Viet Nam, when the girl at my side said,

'Mr Grotefend said he had a car waiting. Just as soon as you clear Customs.' She smiled all the time. 'You've been away quite a time, haven't you, Mr Warren?'

'Two years.'

'I expect you'll find a lot of changes.'

'Yes,' I said. 'Things have a habit of changing.'

'I saw your last film,' she blurted—it was something between a confession and an ultimatum.

'How brave of you,' I said, smiling, being gracious, hating her. I stared past her, looking at a woman suddenly shake a crying child violently, seeing the whole sequence of events to come, thinking: the bitch never intended to be here, she's probably still in bed, she couldn't be bothered.

CHAPTER TWO

I was enjoying American cigarettes again by the time the baggage started to arrive, and as the rubber escalator brought up the remains like a crematorium in reverse, I singled out my cases and had them taken to the Green Customs exit. I saw a Customs officer detach himself from the group.

'Just a spot check, sir. You've nothing to declare, I take it?' he started, rather in the manner of a television interviewer tackling a crippled shop steward during an unofficial strike.

'No, nothing,' I said. 'That's why I came through here.'

'It *is* Mr Warren, isn't it?'

'Yes,' I said. 'Or at least it was when I got on the plane.'

'I thought so. I said to my colleague. You were on the Pan Am Polar flight, weren't you?'

'All the way. I never got off.'

'Ha! And you've got nothing, Mr Warren, you didn't bring anything over this trip?'

'No.'

'No gifts for the wife?'

'Only the gift of companionship.'

'Ha! You know what you ought to have said, of course?'

'No, what ought I to have said?'

'Well, I daresay you've heard it. "I've got nothing to declare but my genius." '

Giving him my undivided surface attention, I suddenly became conscious that he was very young. Uniforms invariably intimidate me at first, and inside every ticket collector there's usually an SS man screaming to get out. This one sported a sparse and embryonic moustache—it looked insecure, a spirit-gum affair for the church hall production of *Journey's End*.

'Oscar Wilde, you know,' he was saying. 'He was in the same game, roughly speaking, as yourself.'

'Roughly speaking.'

'Well, he was connected with acting, if you know what I mean.'

'Yes, that's so. Literally, on occasions, I believe, and of course he was noted for giving himself the best lines.' I tapped one of my suitcases. 'D'you want to open this and make sure?'

'What? Oh, no, that won't be necessary.' He chalked the cases with a flourish and beckoned to the waiting porter. 'You've got somebody waiting for you, I believe. It was put over the P.A.' He made a noise between his teeth and sucked his upper lip as though testing to make sure the moustache was still in place. 'Had your wife through here the other week.'

'Did you catch her with anything? Women can't resist it, you know, and they're so much better at it than we are.'

'Well, I wouldn't say that. I'm a pretty good judge of character, have to be in this job. Size up a face at a distance, make a decision there and then and keep it to yourself. That's the trick.'

'I must try it,' I said. 'My own judgment's always lousy.'

'It's a knack,' he said seriously and I realised I had made another mistake: I can never spot the bores in time. Of course, when officialdom has you on the hook, patience is the only road to freedom. 'Rather like your sort of thing, in a way. You have a few flops—that's the word isn't it?'

'One of the words.'

'I'm not really foolproof yet, but I have my fair share of success.'

'Good. Well, I must try you out with a disguise next time.'

I moved through into the main hall, taking my time, determined not to meet Grotefend if I could help it. I caught sight of myself in a mirror. The face that stared back was blotchy and uneven, something half-finished—as though I'd stayed out in the sun too long on the first really hot day of summer.

'Dick,' the voice boomed, and I turned towards it, knowing that from that moment onwards I was powerless to alter anything.

'Great to see you. Jesus! this crummy airport, d'you realise you've been down forty minutes?'

I thought of the young Customs man as we shook hands and wondered how his knack would have worked here, and if the answer would have been of any value. Weakness was smeared across the face that returned my false smile. Even the professional tan was not up to standard. He's shaved badly, I thought, and wondered where the clue should lead me—nervousness, a late night, love, an ulcer? Or was the answer to be found in the loose mouth, the shred of tobacco on the stained teeth, the glint of sweat on the receding hairline? My imaginary chalk was poised, but I was uncertain as to which mark to make, I couldn't emulate the Customs officer's brave flourish—in the country which Grotefend and I inhabited, duty was not easily defined.

'Sam Grotefend,' he pronounced it Grot-fund in that slightly lisping manner some Americans affect when they want to make a casual good impression. 'Second-hand Sam they call me.' His handshake was clammy, like a butcher who has just touched liver.

'As it happened I used the time. Have I had a morning! You ever tried to teach a spastic kid how to present a bouquet?'

Not trusting my voice, I shook my head.

'I told them, give me a spastic kid who looks like Shirley Temple. I got this premier I'm handling all on my own in aid of one of your British charities, and this would have made space. But nobody gives a damn, there's no showmanship any more.

They give me a kid who's a basket case, how d'you like that?'

I stared at him.

'I just told them over the phone, forget it. They don't know. Say, listen, Bob Daniels said to say he's sorry he couldn't make it himself to the airport, but they got big problems with *The Girls on The Seventeenth Floor*. Big problems.'

'Who's Bob Daniels?'

'Bob? Mr Daniels?' Grotefend looked hurt, as though I had, without warning, done him a personal injury. 'He just took over as Executive Vice President in charge of world-wide publicity.'

'What happened to Wheeler?'

'Wheeler?'

'Yes, wasn't it Wheeler, wasn't that his name? He was in charge last time I was here.'

'Oh, him. There've been two since Wheeler. Wheeler got his six months ago. I don't know who came in after him. See, I've been free-lancing. I just came in with Bob, Mr Daniels.'

'And now he's got troubles, you say?'

I wasn't interested in the newly promoted Mr Daniels or his troubles, but Grotefend was the sort of man one has to bait on sight. I had the feeling that he expected it, that he would be suspicious of anyone who treated him as an instant friend.

'Nothing but. *Girls* opened here last night and got a roasting.'

'What is *Girls*?'

'It was supposed to be the big one, the one that gets them out of the red—you know, you read about it, the one they shot in Rome last year with that big-titted new broad. I said at the time they should've gotten Loren. This all the baggage?'

'Yes. I always arrive light and depart heavy.'

'Well, let's grab a Red Cap.'

'Porter,' I said.

'Yeah. Listen, did they get a picture out at the plane?'

'No.'

'Jesus! They promised me they were going to grab one coming off. What a typical British balls-up. I had it all set.'

'Don't worry about it,' I said.

'No, but, you know, it's the goddamn principle of the thing.'

Just for a second he looked as though he might burst into tears and I had the illusion I could actually see his beard growing.

'Maybe they figured they covered it when your bride came in. She made big space, your bride.'

I have often remarked that for some reason the word 'bride' seems to exercise a peculiar fascination for a certain breed of Americans. At various Beverly Hills parties I have been introduced to elderly women wearing enough fur to defeat the entire conservation movement single-handed, and with such of their own skin remaining visible reminding one of the last turkey hanging in Sainsbury's on Christmas Eve. Their equally improbable escorts invariably induce a feeling of instant horror with the words, 'I'd like you to meet my bride.' To hear Grotefend apply the same term to my own personal situation filled me with panic and I signalled a porter and walked out into the unfinished waste-lands of Heathrow.

'Sensation!' Grotefend screamed over the noise of a departing jet. 'She was a sensation at the opening last night, your bride. I said, I told her—"You should've played it."—They should have been that lucky. Believe me, they got a real dog. Faber. That's the name. Betsy Faber, if you'll pardon the expression. All tits and no talent. But you know who cast her, so who's saying anything? Ever worked with her?'

I shook my head. The sound of the jet rattled close to the threshold of pain and Grotefend, not to be delayed, went into an elaborate piece of mime. Using a grubby finger he spelt out T R O U B L E backwards on his forehead.

'. . . in neon lights,' was all I heard as the sound waves travelled back through low cloud to batter us. 'Still your bride came through, she said all the right things to the old man.'

As the reverberations finally died away I thought, it's the moment of maximum danger—take-off and talking about her. But we can no more determine the length of our passions than we can the span of our years. Like Gatsby, we beat on, boats against the current. . . .

'How is she this morning?' I said.

'I haven't talked with her this morning.' Grotefend looked away. 'She got in pretty late I guess.'

Something other than the immediate had been nagging at me

ever since I stepped off the plane and now I realised what it was: Heathrow no longer reminded me of the war. The Nissen-hut-Naafi-canteen atmosphere that used to envelop the returning traveller had been exchanged for standard marble halls. The British have never really relinquished their affection for the war years, for the blitz, the queues, the privations. I'm guilty of it myself at odd moments. I can never get on a Tube train, for instance, without seeing again the stacked bodies lining the platforms, looking more like Francis Bacon carcasses, to my eye, than the much admired Henry Moore figures. I remember long, regular nights in the fetid, candle-lit vault of the family Anderson shelter in West Ham. There was a kind of comfort there, sitting in a deck chair sipping Thermos tea from a chipped cup, the steel walls sweating close to our anxious cheeks. We kept our voices low for no sane reason (was it that we really believed the Germans droning overhead could hear us and take particular aim?). We had a kind of dreaded peace in the hand-out steel womb, willing ourselves inviolate under the curved, corrugated dome. And when our numbered bomb eventually fell, scoring a direct hit on the house next door and driving our safety-scorning neighbour straight through the springs of his bed so that his body was neatly chunked like the contents of a tin of cat food, it was not fear we experienced so much as the shameful elation at having been missed. A few seconds before the event, anticipating the final screaming descent, my old nanny (who was that in name only, being really a lodger who had helped out when I was a child, but surviving in title to perpetuate my mother's sad snobbery) suddenly gripped my arm above the elbow. An air raid warden had to prise away her fingers one by one and for weeks afterwards I bore the bruised transfer of her hand on my flesh like a tattoo and even now, sometimes, at night, I get a dull ache there and the damp smell of that Anderson shelter crowds back and I can taste again the flying, powdered brick dust.

I turned to Grotefend that morning, wanting to share the remembrance of things past, but he had his back to me, tipping the porter, and the moment passed. A second or two later he had sounded a more contemporary Alert and this time I had no shelter to dive into.

'Just something I want to kick around,' he said, opening the car door for me and ignoring the advancing airport police. 'You want to ride up front so we can talk?'

He got behind the driving wheel and started the engine with that brute ease all Americans have with automobiles. The car was a Lincoln Continental, last year's model, and of course left-hand drive. Officialdom, open-mouthed, flashed by like a commercial with the sound turned off.

'Remind me I gotta great story to tell you about that Faber broad. Great pay-off.' He twirled the wheel with one finger and started following the clustered confusion of signs to the M4. He said, casually, 'How much truth is there in the dirt, by the way?'

'What dirt?'

'Dick, listen, you're sitting next to Second-hand Sam, remember? I'm not your usual white trash, boy, I'm on your side, I'm working for you. I want you to feel we can kick the crap together.'

I stared straight ahead. Listening to Grotefend scrawling his graffiti across the walls of my life, I thought, what a whore I am to remain in this obscene business. I had an enormous wish to believe in justice and peace, those blocked escape routes. Passing hoardings underlined the need. . . . *All of Human life is Here, Love at First Flight*. . . . They seemed to me like those Wayside Pulpit posters I used to be impressed by as a child, begrimed and sometimes crudely mutilated outside Midland chapels: the Church's answer to Wardour Street, comfort in short sentences, with, each week, a coming next attraction. I read them all, desperately, until the tunnel blotted them out and all the time I knew Grotefend was waiting for an answer.

'I don't understand,' I said, ostrich-safe in the half-light.

He had taken the wrong turning as we came out of the tunnel and looked over his shoulder, considering a savage U turn.

'The crap, you know.'

'Don't chance it,' I said. 'Go to the road and make a right.'

'All this driving on the left side. Boy, this country is really screwed up. Look, Dick, I don't want to spell it out. But I'm talking about crap. The stuff you and I walk in. The c-r-a-p that passeth human understanding. That dear old gossip column variety. Break-up, divorce, you know, all the rumours.

I had to head off a few inquiries when your bride got in.'

We waited at the traffic lights. Over to the left I could see the tall tower of the Technicolor plant. It reminded me of long hours spent viewing the first answer prints, of those moments when the private dream becomes a public positive.

'She isn't my bride. She's my wife. There's a difference, you know. We've been married for some time.'

'That's it, that's it. It's unnatural. I mean, it's not unnatural, but that's the way they want to write it.'

He lifted himself in his seat as soon as the lights turned and swung the huge car across the road. Sunlight exposed his face to the bone.

'Don't worry about me. I can play it down, I can play it any way you want.'

'There's nothing to play down.' I felt something approaching panic again. 'As you say, it's unnatural to be married and stay married in our game.'

'Everything's unnatural in our game, starting with my teeth.' He took both hands off the wheel and leant across me to feel in the glove compartment for a battered pack of Marlborough's. 'Look, you've told me, that's it, forget it.' He braked hard and grabbed the wheel just in time to enter the Henlys' roundabout. 'Screw those mothers. I'll plant a paragraph—no truth in the rumours, et cetera, and it's dead. Say, you didn't bring anything for her, did you?'

'How d'you mean?'

'Some little fun thing—a gift?'

'I only left her three weeks ago. I brought myself, the best gift any clean-living girl could have.'

He gave me a sly look.

'I like that, I might use it.'

One of the nightmarish realities of my profession is that one is constantly taken over by strangers. One catches planes, one is met at airports and taken to luxury hotels where the toilet seats are covered in Cellophane and bottles of Chivas Regal, gift-wrapped with stiff silk bows, stand waiting. And while the bell-hop is still hovering for his tip the phone rings and the voice at the end of the line is always a stranger talking with familiar ease. Long before you arrive your name has been circulated on celebrity lists, the modern equivalent of the French Revolution death rosters. At any hour of the day sycophantic executioners are standing by to escort you to the rented tumbrils, and the journey always ends in air-conditioned rooms on a first-name basis. I know strangers intimately in every capital city, and I never arrive anywhere without dread. The only time I feel really safe is on the studio floor, with the red light burning and the film going through the gate at twenty-four frames per second.

That morning, speeding towards yet another hotel room, I knew that given half a chance Grotefend would open, as they say, his heart. It was a revelation I wished devoutly to be spared.

An actress once said to me, 'You entice people in, you half-seduce them and then you slam the door in their faces.' She wasn't being bitchy and for a few months I enjoyed regurgitating the thought in the slow hours of the night and examining it closely. I knew what she meant, and I came to the conclusion that she was right. I've never been afraid of facing the truth about myself in an abstract way. It's putting the truth into practice that presents the real difficulties. My ideal is pleasure without guilt.

Grotefend concentrated on the road until we reached the inevitable traffic jam at Hammersmith, then switched on the car radio momentarily. A voice—I couldn't tell whether it was male or female—screamed 'Power to the People'—and then was swamped by static.

'That's another thing,' Grotefend said, flicking the switch again. 'How come you didn't arrive together?'

'We never fly together for the sake of the children.'

'No, that's sensible. . . . I didn't know you had children.'

'We don't. It's for the sake of children as yet unborn.'

We were stationary for ten minutes, a large piece of Detroit, overheating, surrounded by angry pygmies from Cowley. I remembered happier journeys. In motion one can always fall back on hope, but on dead ground there's nothing left but the return ticket, hope with a hole punched in it. Looking down at a hotted-up Mini-Cooper with a young girl in it, I thought, she got her first ideas here, in London, here is where it all started to go wrong. I felt the skin on my face contract with the effort of control.

The sense of loss grew in me like rice in a starving child's belly.

Progressing in spurts, we finally entered a clear stretch of Cromwell Road and Grotefend pushed down hard for a kick gear shift.

I saw the child blur as the car leapt forward and shouted something, bracing my legs instinctively as Grotefend swung the wheel. The danger was past in a second, but the panic remained and I was afraid to turn my head and look back.

'I didn't see her,' Grotefend said. His relief was as offensive as a body smell. 'I didn't see her, for Christsake!' He gripped the wheel with both hands for the first time. 'That could have made a very nasty story.'

I wasn't able to answer him. Under the Cromwell Road trees the reflection of the sky in the windscreen blackened and dazzled with sickening regularity. I half expected people to pursue us. We kill through indifference as well as through excess of love, and the near-death of that unknown child brought everything into sharp focus. I realised how tired I was and wondered how far pity would stretch. We had only been separated for three weeks, but absence in any form is a kind of murder, something dies every time. I suppose it's the thought of somebody you love, or did love, existing without you. Sitting there on last year's dented springs, I envied Grotefend's facility to endure pain and humiliation.

I thought, with sudden self-hatred, we could have killed that child and saved me.

CHAPTER THREE

The hotel receptionist was quite a pretty girl, but wore a gold brace on her teeth, and she confronted me with the register as though she expected to be insulted.

'Mr Warren is in three fourteen, three fifteen,' Grotefend said. He stole four book matches from a charity display and pocketed two of the hotel postcards.

'Well, I'm sorry, sir,' the girl said, 'but that particular suite's occupied.' She hardly opened her mouth when she spoke.

'What're you talking about?' Grotefend shouted, coming into his own. A fellow American tourist farther down the counter looked towards us and nodded approvingly. 'Miss Hart's in three fourteen. I put her there myself.'

'That's correct, sir. Miss Hart. The suite's taken.'

'Listen, sweetheart . . . this is Mr Hart, I mean this is Mr Warren, Miss Hart's husband.'

'Oh,' the girl said, and she looked at me with interest for the first time. I wondered what it would be like to kiss a girl with a gold brace across her teeth. 'I'm sorry, Mr Hart. Nobody told me.'

'You shouldn't need telling, sweetheart.' Grotefend took my arm and walked me towards the elevator. 'Stupid little jerk.' He bore down heavily on my arm. 'Look you go up and take a shower, grab a bite, and I'll call you in half an hour.'

'I was thinking of taking a rest. That Polar flight always kills me.'

Grotefend swung in towards me. He had totally offensive breath. 'The only thing is, Dick, and believe me I know what a mother that Polar bit is, I've kinda gotten things set up. Not a press conference, just a few of the boys.'

I stood in front of the elevator with head bent, looking at his scuffed shoes.

'The boys?'

'Yeah, you know, the same old gang.'

'Have they matured in the wood?'

'How's that?'

'I don't suppose they've changed much since my last trip, and they were middle-aged boys then.'

'*You've* changed, sweetheart. You two are big news right now. Thirty minutes, huh? Give me thirty minutes in thirty minutes.'

'But why now?'

'I kinda blocked it in—you know how it is, sweetheart.' He leaned heavily again. 'Dick,' he said, 'do it for me, will you? Just this once, get it under the carpet.'

I could smell his fear. It was faintly scented with a cheap, popular cologne: nothing about Grotefend was exclusive. Over the years I have wasted so many valuable hours with the Grotefends of this world, and despite myself, I invariably end up feeling sorry for them. They always ask for transient favours—a drink with some faded columnist, the gulped meal in some fashionable restaurant. It is the fate of film publicists to travel first class on a steerage ticket: paid to observe the élite at close quarters, allowed up on deck to mingle with the famous on a Christian-name basis, but pushed below the water-line again the moment the ship sights land. They have chosen nothing except to go on living at second-hand. Grotefend must have had his own rare moments of perception, hence the self-inflicted nickname.

'Half an hour, then. If you promise.'

'You're prince people, Dick. You have my word.'

'As an English gentleman?'

'Better. As a Jewish publicist. Give my love to your bride.'

He pressed the elevator button and escaped quickly, his reflexes warning him that I could easily change my mind again. The signal light flashed green. I thought, it ought to have been red, permitting myself the ghost of a joke. Behind me I heard Grotefend start to romance the girl with the gold band on her teeth, making her giggle, leading up to the request for the free use of her telephone. Then the elevator arrived and the gates slid open to receive me.

CHAPTER FOUR

I said, 'Hello, darling,' as the door to 314 opened, but it wasn't Susan, it was a maid, and we stared at each other in mutual confusion.

'Excuse me,' I said, and immediately felt guilty, which increased my annoyance.

'Miss Hart's in the bedroom. I'll tell her.'

'Mrs Warren, my wife, not Miss Hart is in the bedroom and I'll tell her, so don't. . .' But I never finished the sentence because at that moment Susan appeared in the bedroom doorway.

She avoided my attempt to embrace her and made a small grimace in the direction of the maid.

'You got here very quickly,' she said.

'I came by jet and Grotefend. There is no quicker way.'

'He met you all right, did he?'

'Yes. It's the only way to arrive in London.' I thought, she's got no idea what she's done, it isn't important to her. The maid hovered in the background, almost as though she was waiting for a signal from Susan to call the house detective.

'We'll ring down when we're ready,' Susan said.

'Or better still we'll move to another hotel.'

We stood like actors waiting for a late cue until the door closed behind her flushed face.

'Well you certainly charmed her.'

'She'll probably enjoy telling it to her fascist boyfriend, and it's another vote for Labour,' I said. 'Anyway, I didn't come seven thousand miles to worry about chambermaids.'

'Why are you in such a bad mood?'

'Am I? Am I in a bad mood?'

'I suppose you're furious because I didn't meet the plane.'

'No. Not furious.'

'Well, what then?'

Our quarrels always started this way. No heavily concentrated bombardment, just the single sniping shots fired across no-man's land until one found flesh.

'I'm toxic from some very nasty airline food, tired and somewhat shop soiled, but otherwise okay. Still, it wasn't a bad idea, even though said in jest. Why don't we move hotels? They always put us in this ghastly suite.'

'We've never stayed here before. It wasn't built the last time we were here.'

'Wasn't it? Well, I'm sure you're right, you always know these things. All I meant was, never ignore first impressions. I didn't like the first take and I'm not going to print it. We could change the location and see if the dialogue sounds better there.'

I heard myself talking, heard myself use the smart professional chat I despised in others.

'We could go to Paris. I'll take you to The Hotel. We'll sleep in the room where Oscar Wilde died.'

'What a macabre suggestion.'

'Not really. I had a long conversation about Oscar in Customs. Shows how far the permissive society has gone. We could stay in bed all day and resist everything except temptation.'

If I'd been directing the scene in a film I would have ended it there. Close up of the wife. Cross cut to the husband, then back to the wife again for the dissolve. I still believe in dissolves, which makes me old fashioned—my films, if they are reviewed at all, never warrant more than a dismissing paragraph in *Sight and Sound*.

Susan said, 'It's an amusing idea, but I've got costume fittings all this week, starting to-morrow.' She went back into the bedroom. I noted with sad satisfaction that she was wearing a new dressing-gown. Susan was famed for her ability to find dress shops open at midnight: I would never have to worry about her going naked in the world. I stood for a moment, undecided, then followed her.

The bedroom appalled me. It was as if I had suddenly come upon the scene of an air crash. There was debris everywhere, expensive debris: dress boxes, hastily ripped, spewing out layers of finely folded tissue paper, and glimpsed between the crumpled cardboard, vivid smears of fabric. Half-unpacked suitcases balanced precariously on chairs, a forest of make-up bottles strewn over one chest of drawers and on the floor the stale breakfast tray surrounded by shoes and handbags. It was all there, down to the last *Daily Mirror* touch—the child's Teddy Bear with one eye missing, the nose rubbed away and a leg grotesquely hanging by a black thread. Remembering recent fears, I felt my ears pop.

'Well, you've done a good job in the time,' I said.

Susan was sitting at the dressing table. She had her head down and I thought at first that she must be crying. Perhaps that's what made me look again at the breakfast tray. Somehow the first impression had registered: there were two coffee cups and floating in the saucer of one of them, obscenely disintegrating, was a cigarette butt.

'I packed all the wrong clothes, so I had to go out and buy a few things.'

'Of course. Life wouldn't be the same without them.'

I looked around for somewhere to sit.

Then she said, so softly I could hardly catch the words, as though she was repeating a lesson to herself, 'It's like a death. You kill everything for me.'

I recognised the dialogue. It was a line I had written myself in an old screenplay, in the days when we discussed things. Pride of authorship never deserts a writer, but I felt an enormous tiredness waiting for what she would say next. I looked at her face in the mirror: pain discovered the lines, pain changed her in seconds: it was like dropping a negative into double-strength developer.

I said, carefully, 'I was disappointed, darling, that's all. I was looking forward to seeing you at the airport. But it's over now.'

I crossed the room to her, treading warily, and sat down on the edge of the stool. I touched her shoulder. The skin felt cold. She was naked under the new dressing-gown.

I said, 'I've always asked you to forgive me in strange hotel bedrooms.'

'It's too easy. You upset me and then it's all right for you and I'm supposed to come round immediately.'

'Is that what I expect?'

'You know it is. I didn't feel well when I woke up.'

27

'Perhaps you drank too much coffee at breakfast.'

'What's that supposed to mean?'

Maybe the anonymity of the hotel room gave me a spurious sort of courage—was it really that?—or maybe because I had lost seven hours in flight my normal caution deserted me—desperation and tiredness are easy partners.

'There are two cups on the tray, but of course I don't want to pry into something as personal as your breakfast.'

'I had breakfast. . . . No, I shared a pot of coffee with Jane Harper who's designing the clothes. She doesn't wear lipstick, that's why the filter tip on the cigarette is unmarked. On the other hand, she does wear men's crêpe-soled desert boots and given half a chance she would have thrown me into bed. Except that she didn't get half a chance. She didn't even get a tape measure round my waist. Satisfied?'

'Yes,' I said.

Susan got up and went into the bathroom. I followed again and stood just inside the doorway. I watched her brush her hair and then pat some lotion into her cheeks. I thought, ten years from now I won't need to humble myself with suspicion, but the thought was devoid of any real comfort—it was as though the All Clear had sounded while the bombs were still falling.

'Susan,' I said. 'I'm sorry.'

She finished with the lotion and capped the bottle before replying. 'I know you're sorry. I just wish it didn't happen so often.'

'Hasn't happened for three weeks. You ought to be grateful for small mercies. Shall I start again? We'll retake it. I'll go outside, come in all bright and bushy-tailed, flirt with the maid and give you this.'

I held out the gift.

She unwrapped it slowly without looking at me.

'Put it on. I always wanted to see a nude woman wearing a single piece of jewellery.'

I was watching her like an enemy, trying to read forgiveness into her face. When she had fastened the clasp I went to her and kissed her. Her lips were soft in the corners, but they seemed to have none of the old pliancy, the first lush eagerness had gone.

She kissed me several times with an urgency that surprised me, tasting my mouth, searching with her tongue, curving in farther and farther towards me.

'I wish we had time,' she said. 'I know you don't believe me, but I've missed you.'

'I do believe you. I'm a very easy person to miss.'

She took one of my hands and opened her dressing-gown and covered my hand with her own, pressing it into her soft body as though seeking to trap there a secret she would never share with anybody else. We stood like that, not moving, but only, as it were, listening for each other.

'I'm sorry I didn't meet you, but I had such a horrible night last night. I meant to get there, but, I don't know, I just didn't.'

Our faces came together in a sort of soft confusion as we kissed again.

'Dear old Sam made a pass last night.'

'Was he the horrible part?'

'He was the most horrible part. He came and knocked on this door twice.'

'Twice? Wouldn't take yes for an answer, eh?'

She said, 'You'll never leave me, will you?'

'I'm here, aren't I?'

'I don't mean that. I mean even though I say and do things that hurt you.'

The extraction of a promise is sometimes more dangerous than making love for the first time. Standing in that clinical hotel bathroom, catching sight of myself in the double mirrors, I saw two strangers, one clothed, the other half naked. It was not a room for promises, it was a place of interrogation. I kissed Susan again, giving myself time to frame a careful answer, but for the first time that day caution wasn't necessary. The phone shrilled in all three rooms and the lie was saved for another time.

'That has to be your midnight caller,' I said.

'You answer it. If it's them, ask them up and give them a drink. I think there's some in the other room. Wait a minute—you've got some of my cream on your face. Didn't you shave on the plane?'

'No.'

'Hope you haven't brought me up in a rash.'

She closed the bathroom door after me and I heard her lock it. I picked up the nearest phone by the bed and there was Grotefend's sincere voice and with it came a return of panic. Listening to the opening clichés I could only think, can I really go on loving her enough to face all this in public? Answering Grotefend, I stared at the crumpled pillows, seeing there a strand of Susan's hair, a faint smudge of mascara. I bent forward and touched the pillow with my cheek—muffling Grotefend like a murderer—and it seemed to me that the linen plumpness still carried a faint warmth and a mystery of scent that belonged to only one person in my life. The wisecracks and the innuendoes crackled in my ear —down below in the lobby Grotefend was earning his keep.

'Fine, Sam,' I said, cutting him short, 'bring everybody up.'

I lay there for a few more moments, knowing that it was as close as I would get to love in the next twelve hours.

CHAPTER FIVE

Grotefend sprang into the room as though he had been sent by the management to quell an orgy. He was followed by three characters I vaguely remembered, two middle-aged and one at the point of no return. The youngest one came in nodding wisely and immediately slumped on to the nearest sofa and put his feet up. I took it for granted that he was acting it up for my benefit.

'You know Bob, of course.' Grotefend was ripping the Cellophane wrapping off the gift whisky supplied by himself and paid for by my employers who in turn would charge it out at an inflated price to the budget of my film. Being entertained by the film industry is rather like bidding against yourself at an auction.

'Dick,' one of the journalists said, 'how goes it?'

'Fine, Bob. You still on the *Express*?'

'I was never on the *Express*,' he said slowly. He fumbled for a cigarette and Grotefend was there like Gunga Din, thrusting a king-size and gold lighter with expert sleight of hand. He gave me one, too, and I noted that the lighter was en̶

Bob had noticed it as well and said, 'Sam, you ̶ putting an ad campaign on french letters? Would hav̶ pull for *Midnight Cowboy*.'

'I didn't work on it. I don't know, though—might no̶ sold. Who wants to bend down to read something? Now a̶ want to say is what're we drinking, we all drinking this?' Grote-fend asked.

'You got any vodka and grapefruit juice?' This request came from the tired man on the sofa.

'You named it.' Grotefend pressed all the buttons he could find and picked up the phone. 'Give me room service. Anything else?'

'Whisky's fine,' Bob said. The other middle-aged man shook his head gloomily, then crossed to the window and stared down at the traffic below.

'Just get in?' Bob said.

'Yes. I came over the Pole.'

'What movie were they showing? One of yours?'

'No, I escaped that.'

'You ever been on a flight where they showed one of yours?'

'Yes. Once. It was billed as a comedy and they screened it while they were serving dinner. Only six people hired the headphones and they never looked up once. It was in colour, that's to say I shot it in colour, but they showed it on those small black and white monitor sets. Suddenly we had an all Negro cast.'

'You've never used Negroes, have you?' Bob said evenly. 'I mean, you've never cast them in a big star role?'

'No. I think you're right.'

'Why's that?'

'How d'you mean?'

'Well, with civil rights and all that stuff.'

'I suppose it's because I've never found the right story.'

'You're not interested in civil rights?'

'I'm very interested. I'm also interested in not making bad civil rights pictures. I mean I wouldn't want to make a coloured *Sound of Music*.'

'You didn't like *Sound of Music*?'

'I didn't see *Sound of Music*.'

...om having a coloured cast?' I said.

...said. 'But you never wanted to work

..., but I've never come across the right

...vould want to work with me, that is.'

...rk with you, Dick,' Grotefend said. I

...d into my hand. Two waiters appeared

...ers at them, the other reporter dragged

...ndow and stood blinking in the middle

'You kn... ...body said to me to-day?'

I shook my head politely.

'I was in Harrods, buying cheese. . . .'

'Where? I missed that,' Grotefend said.

'He was in Harrods,' I said. 'Buying cheese.'

The gloomy man gave him a long, cold stare.

'I was at the cheese counter and this character, sort of vintage Knightsbridge retired Indian Army, is standing beside me and suddenly nudges me and says: "Is that Gruyère?" '

'Says what?' Grotefend asked.

'Gruyère. So I said, "No, it's. . . ." whatever it was, and then he says, "Don't touch Gruyère, it's a killer!" '

'Really?' I said.

'It's worried me,' the gloomy man said. 'What're you over here for,' he continued in the same tone of voice and for a moment I thought his question was still part of the same story.

'I'm just about to start *The Unknown Warrior.*'

He nodded with infinite sadness. His nondescript off-the-peg suit perched on his over-weight frame, and the shoulders of the jacket were limed with dandruff.

'What's the budget?' the man on the sofa said. He only half-opened his eyes.

'It'll probably end up around the three million mark.'

'Dollars or pounds?'

'Dollars.'

'What's the story?' Bob said.

'It's Maxwell's last novel. Did you read it?'

He shook his head and took a large gulp of whisky. 'War story?'

'No, nothing like that, the title's ironic.'

Picking his nose the gloomy man said, 'Oh, one of those. What is it, a message piece?'

'Not really,' I said. 'It's a love story. Everybody gets wounded in bed.'

Bob had taken out a notepad and now he made his first entry. From where I was standing it looked like a single word. He put his felt pen away again immediately.

'Three million dollars,' the man who had come in from Harrods said. 'How much of that finds its way to you?'

'I get my usual fee.'

'What's that?'

'It would keep you in Gruyère,' I said, falling headlong into the oldest trap of all, answering back, hating him. He didn't smile.

That seemed to finish them all as far as I was concerned and it was with a feeling of shared relief that Susan made her long-awaited appearance.

Love and uncertainty had been wiped from her face in the same way that a stain is removed by bleach. I knew her so well and yet I was conscious that I knew nothing of her. The others in the room knew her more intimately, because they had invented her.

The exhausted man had stirred himself as she entered and now, eyes wide open, he was the first to greet her. I suppose, in that motley assembly, he claimed the right of youth.

'Jimmy,' Susan said, and not for the first time I marvelled at her gift for the trivial: she could forget her mother's birthday, but never a name that could advance her cause. 'How lovely to see you again. Did you ever buy that car?'

'Yeah, I did as a matter of fact. Fancy you remembering that.'

'D'you want a drink, sweetheart?' Grotefend was beaming.

'No, thanks, not just now. Hello, Bob.'

She shook hands, looking him straight in the eyes, then turned towards the Harrods cheese counter. 'Mr Golding,' she said. 'I'm honoured.' It was beautifully done, and she knew it.

Mr Golding took a wet cigarette from his lips before shaking hands. I remembered him then. He'd been a theatre critic, an enemy of promise, once, on a now defunct weekly. Now he wrote caustic little pieces which were squeezed in on dull days and only read by the bitchy hordes of the out-of-work. The highlights of his theatrical season now came when he escorted some scrubby, underdressed little starlet to the second night of a new play.

'Miss Hart,' he said gravely, 'always a pleasure to welcome you back.'

'Always a pleasure to be back.'

'Yeah, how's it feel to be back, sweetheart?' Grotefend asked.

'Always a pleasure,' I said.

I could hardly mistake the hostility that followed. I was aware in those uneasy moments of silence before the waiter returned with the special order, that my coffin had been measured and a plot of unconsecrated ground set aside.

All three of them concentrated on Susan after that. I felt like a stoker in a warship going at full speed: below the water-line in the suffocating heated danger without knowledge of the course being steered. The thought carried with it a twinge of self-disgust. It seemed to me that I was capable of everything and nothing, but especially of waiting. I tentatively circled the group, studiously casual. Not for the first time in our life together I listened to Susan's public voice with painful amazement. From the wings an understudy's interpretation of the star part is always superior. Hearing Susan retell our recent life I could prefer the true version but still admire her performance. For performance it was, and because her audience consisted of critics on this occasion the counterfeit was quite safe: critics can seldom or ever differentiate between a bad performance in a good part and a good performance in a bad part.

'It just happened,' she was saying, 'the phone went and it happened.'

'Who was it phoning you?'

'Krutzman. Paul Krutzman.'

'Oh, yeah. The director.'

'The producer.'

'I can never understand the difference between the two.'

'It's something to do with glands,' Grotefend said.

'I thought it was just that producers do the screwing and the directors get screwed.'

'Present company excepted,' Grotefend said, remembering me for the first time in ten minutes.

'But let's get back to this other thing,' Bob said. 'How's it feel being one of the stinking rich?'

'Well, I don't know we are rich,' Susan answered. Talk of money always confused her. She was never one of Nature's bankers. 'You'd have to ask Dick about that.'

'But you have gone non-resident?'

'No,' I said. 'It so happens that we've both worked abroad for two years, but I'm still proud of my National Health teeth.'

'Great,' Grotefend said. 'Great line, Dick.' Then he had immediate second thoughts and refilled their glasses.

'You're going to come back for good then?'

'I imagine we'll stay until we've both finished our respective films.' They were only half listening to me, they sensed that Susan would provide the really damaging quotes.

'Tell me, Susan,' Mr Golding said. 'You've never been directed by your husband, have you? Why's that?'

I waited, fascinated to learn how she would answer. She was careful not to look at me: her best profile forward, she played the ball back to them in a straight line.

'Well, I could say "He's never asked me. . . ." '

'. . . But you won't?'

'No, I won't, because the situation's never come up. When I started I simply wasn't important enough to be considered for any of Dick's films, and since things have happened to me there just hasn't been a suitable role.'

'What about the girl in *Not So Long Ag* ?'

'Oh, I couldn't have played that.'

'Wouldn't you rather work for your husband?'

'Why don't you ask him if he wants to work with me?'

'I couldn't afford her,' I said. 'You know me, I make critical successes that nobody goes to see.'

'Couldn't you have used her in *Stalemate*?'

'I could, yes. It would have given the whole thing a very interesting slant. It was an all male cast.'

'I'd have gone to see that,' Grotefend said.

'What about frontal nudity?'

'What about it?'

'Would you let your wife do a nude scene?'

'Well. put it this way, if she had to take a bath in a film I wouldn't insist on her wearing clothes.'

'That wasn't what I asked you.'

'It's whether the part demands it, if dramatically the only way a thing could work, then I would go along.'

'That wouldn't bother you? Other men seeing your wife naked?'

'It would bother me if they were looking through a keyhole. I'm not in the skin-flick business, nor is Susan.'

'They take money.'

'Yes, let's get back to the money thing,' the cheese purveyor said. Since I last looked at him another layer of dandruff had fallen. 'What d'you earn now, Susan?'

'Oh, I'm hopeless about those sort of things. My agent takes care of all that.'

'How long have you been married?' the youngest one said.

'We're coming up to the classic fence. Seven years next month.'

'It's generally reported that yours is one of the few happy show business marriages, but there were some rumours a while back.'

'Were there? What rumours?'

'About your marriage.'

'Were there any rumours about your marriage? Are you married by the way?'

'Yes.'

'How long since anybody saw your wife in the nude?' I said.

'Look, Dick, nobody wants to write about me. I'm not news.'

'No, that's true. You're certainly not good news.'

'Dick, Dick,' Grotefend said, sweating immediately. 'They're just doing a job.'

'Yes, well when I was a boy I used to chase after the coal horses to pick up the manure. That was a job, too.'

Mr Golding, daintily offended, withdrew to another part of the room, but the other two suddenly came to life and started enjoying it.

'Right now,' I said, 'I'm a film director. That doesn't mean to say I don't still have a working knowledge of horses' arseholes. If you want to talk about my films, I'm very happy. If you want to criticise them, providing you've seen them, I'm happy about that too. I don't mind you coming in here drinking my drink and putting your feet on my rented sofa, and I realise you've got a pathetic job to do until your falling circulation puts you on the bread-line. But if you want to pick up manure, pick it up somewhere else.'

I went back into the bedroom. Tiredness and anger were too dangerously near the surface. The careful insulation of years had worn thin, and I could feel the warning stab of heat. I wasn't proud of my outburst, because it was a battle I had lost.

I could hear Grotefend making the standard speech of apology, for he had a platitude for every occasion. Grotefend, who was doomed to go down through life as his own best friend, never accepted as himself, but only as a mouthpiece for others, entertaining enemies with somebody else's free drink, never quite sure when the blow from without would fall.

Made ill with anger, I realised that Grotefend and the other three men were all people I was fated to remember. Friends would disappear from sight and mind for years on end, but the chance acquaintances of my calling revealed again and again their careless inert power to wound where least I expected. They could bruise me in subtle ways beneath the skin, just like practised secret police, leaving no outward mark. They could dial their way into my life just as surely as I could phone and ask for room service. They were fluent in the language of failure. Somebody ought to publish a phrase book of film journalism and the verb To Envy would head every page.

Alone in that hotel bedroom, sipping a drink I didn't want, I hated them with a director's detachment, an imaginary viewfinder concentrating on each in turn. Even in their seeming innocence, their absolute disarming immobility, I felt a certain menace: a drug injected too often, a kiss given with closed, parched lips. Had they volunteered one gesture of real interest I might have been able to pity them, but there was no spark. That morning the wires of pity were connected to a dead switch.

CHAPTER SIX

One version of the interview appeared the following morning alongside an OXFAM advertisement. The starving child stared without hope at Susan's carefully surprised face. I had read half-way through it before I realised that they were writing about us. It was clever, empty stuff, just this side of libel where I was concerned, and it made us appear like rich, spoilt morons. I dropped the newspaper over the edge of the bath. It fell into a slopped pool of water and a stain spread darkly across the doomed child.

The telephone rang for the fifth time since I had got into the bath and I stood to reach for it, thinking briefly of electrocution.

'Are you taking calls now?' the operator said into my damp ear.

'Well, you've been calling me for the last half hour.'

'Oh. Sir, I just came on and saw the hold over your number.'

'Who's calling me?'

'Just a moment, sir.' I stumbled to pull a towel off the rail. 'A Mr Raven, sir.'

'I'll call him back.'

'It's long distance, sir.'

'I'll still call him back.'

I put the receiver on the hook before she could argue further and immediately it started to ring again, echoing through the three rooms of the suite, but I ignored it. I spurted a glob of shaving cream into my palm. Susan had used my razor and the first slide of the blade across my cheek made me go rigid. I changed the blade, thought briefly of starting a beard, then finished the chore with the minimum of strokes. I had gone back to smoking heavily, of course, and now when I picked up the burning stub from the edge of the wash-basin it slid from my soapy fingers.

I wandered into the bedroom in search of another. Raven, I

thought, what does he want? I hadn't heard from him for about three years, but that meant nothing in the film industry. Producers like Raven often dropped out of circulation for a time, living off somebody else's fat until they could afford the price of a short option. I usually went out of my way to avoid the breed, but I vaguely remembered Raven had done me a good turn once. That didn't give him the right to pluck me from my warm bath from long distance, but once they are back in funds the Ravens of my world live by and for the telephone. He was slipping towards fat, I remembered, the last time we met. Hungarian. Rabovitz, something like that—he'd changed his name the first time he let out his belt a notch. Raven was an inexplicable choice, but he may have once picked up a copy of Edgar Allan Poe by mistake, or been visiting the Tower of London. Perhaps he thought it had an English ring to it, for he was a guttural Anglophile especially when soliciting finance from City merchant bankers, going to absurd lengths, even to the extent of once wearing plus fours (although in fairness it was afterwards reported that an embittered costume designer had in malice convinced him that they were still required wearing for an English country week-end).

Searching for a new pack of cigarettes, I took out my phone book. The entry for Raven looked like a roulette player's system card. Getting the operator back again I discovered that with typical arrogance he hadn't left a number, so I chose the last one in my book and placed the call collect. Raven would expect that. Americans always feel that if they pay for the call it gives them a slight edge. It's a fantasy I'm prepared to nourish.

Susan had gone out to the studio before I was awake. I hadn't slept very well and had taken a pill half-way through the night; it was a mark of my remaining innocence and in my semi-drugged wakefulness I carried with me the last traces of yesterday's anger.

The period between films is a strange one for a director. It isn't as simple as just being out of work. I was restless in that limbo land between the handing over of one film and the start of the next. I seldom take less than eighteen months from script to delivered print, and the act of commitment assumes the proportions of a life sentence.

I had signed the contract for *The Unknown Warrior* over nine months previously but since then there had been three or four false starts. The story demanded a foreign location (the original novel had been set in Russia) but making a film nowadays is a political and economic act before it can dare to have any artistic pretensions. The studio heads talk of frozen currencies before casts and in the early stages a succession of grey-faced accountants sit in on all the planning conferences. If I ever had a son I would insist that he became an accountant, for they are shortly going to inherit what remains of the earth.

When casts are finally discussed another set of financial advisers come in to quote top and bottom prices on every major star, and even tabulate with alarming accuracy the extra liability for drunkenness, normal and abnormal ill health, loss of memory, fornication, marital and extra-marital habits and most known varieties of perversion.

We had a script now, after two changes of writer, and the locale of the film was currently Spain. Cast had been discussed, tentative probing conversations had taken place with agents, but the whole thing still had an air of unreality about it. I had come to London to try and move things along a little faster. And, of course, to be with Susan.

As the phone rang again it occurred to me that I was ringing Raven in the middle of his night. Assuming he was on the West Coast.

'No reply from that number, sir. It's a disconnected line. D'you have an alternative number we could reach Mr Raven on?'

'Alas, yes,' I said. 'Hold on a minute.' I reached for my book again and turned to the B page. I read out the number for the Beverly Hills Hotel: homeless producers with disconnected numbers usually roost in one of three Hollywood nests, and of the three the pink and green Beverly Hills Hotel on Sunset is the most luxurious. The fact that Raven called me at all meant that he had a project of sorts, which in turn meant he would be spending somebody else's money lavishly. Perhaps he had found an obscure cupboard with an old skeleton in it he could rattle for a few months: major careers and come-backs have been started with less.

Curiously, I never mind dealing with types like Raven. Their impure motives are always transparently obvious: the topless waitresses of our industry, they serve inferior fare with a flourish. Better the Ravens than the pseudo-intellectuals. Out and out film crooks usually have a certain charm. They like you to live dangerously with them, but the earnest ones share nothing except their mental halitosis.

It was in that stale, uneasy mood that I greeted Raven seven thousand miles away.

'Baby,' the hoarse voice said, boosted by the transatlantic relay, 'baby, am I calling you or are you calling me?'

'I'm calling you,' I said, 'but you're paying for it.'

'It's the story of my life, darling.' He sounded too happy for a man who wanted nothing from me and the extravagant intimacy of his dialogue was vaguely embarrassing.

'Listen, baby, I'm going to be over there with you later in the week. You still there?'

'Yes,' I said, as the immediate boredom blotted out the loneliness. 'What're you coming over for?'

'We're going to work together, baby. Didn't they tell you?'

'Tell me what?'

'You didn't read *Variety*?'

'No,' I said. 'Should I have done?'

'There's been another palace revolution, darling. The old genius is out and the new genius is in.'

'Chop. Like that?'

'Just like that. Course, it's been coming for some time.'

'But I only spoke to him—when was it?—last Wednesday. We were discussing casting.' It was significant that neither of us felt the need to discuss the deposed man by name.

'That's the way it crumbles, baby. They took his name off the door Wednesday night. But, you know, he didn't go empty handed.'

'Whose name did they put up?'

'You're kidding?'

'No. No, I'm not.'

'You mean you really don't know?' I heard him take the receiver away from his ear and speak to somebody else. Laughter came and went, distorted over the miles, like noises heard in the jungle at night.

'Listen, Dick, baby, go back to sleep. I'll tell you all when I see you.'

'It's morning, I wasn't asleep. You're the one who's supposed to be asleep.'

'I never sleep, baby, you should know that.'

'But tell me now,' I said.

'Me, baby.'

'You?' I realised that I hadn't kept scorn and disbelief out of my voice. 'But that's . . . that's marvellous.'

'I knew you'd be pleased.'

'That's great,' I said.

'So we gotta lot of things to talk about. I gotta lot of ideas, baby, that I know are going to excite you. We're going to be working very close.'

'Marvellous,' I said.

'Just for openers, I got the script licked.'

'Which script?'

'Which script? *The* script. *Warrior.* The only one.' The line went dead for a few seconds and in the pause I thought desperately of something to say in return. In the event he said it for me: 'So that's great news, eh? Say hello to Susan for me and call me at Claridge's. I'll be there Sunday at the latest.'

'Fine.' The line went dead again, abruptly, and this time I was left with what appeared to be the sound of the sea in my ear, but like everything else that morning it wasn't real.

CHAPTER SEVEN

Faithfulness, says La Rochefoucauld, when the Effect of Constraint, is very little better than Unfaithfulness.

It was difficult to reconcile La Rochefoucauld to the King's Road Chelsea, for one is concerned with the bitter taste of truth and the other to perpetrate the myth that youth is attractive in all guises.

We were dining in a new restaurant, so 'in' that the paint wasn't dry on the walls and the artists were still working on the murals. The lighting was so arranged that you couldn't see the food you were eating, but you had the dubious pleasure of being able to recognise faces. And the face closest to mine on that particular evening was on loan to Kitty Raven.

Raven himself still hadn't arrived in London, despite the fact that a week had passed since our phone conversation. I'd had three cables of near novel length, each contradicting the last, giving various explanations and generously embroidered with messages of affection and respect, but the great man had so far failed to materialise. The last cable had included, almost as an afterthought, the suggestion that I meet and take care of Kitty who was arriving ahead of the caravan to organise the interior decorating. When studio executives take over, their first creative act is invariably to remove all traces of the previous king's taste, whether he had any or not. The rules of the game are such that this is strictly the function of wives, not concubines. Kitty Raven enjoyed a reputation for many things, not the least of which was looking too absurd for her age, but she nodded a mean head at Sotheby's and could be relied upon to fill her husband's offices and company-rented apartments with furniture that always increased in value. And when, as inevitably happened, Paul moved out again for the next Crown Prince, Kitty could get removal vans there faster than ambulances. They were her marital perks and I daresay, in her way, she earned them. Her house in Beverly Hills was affectionately known as The Museum of Modern Theft.

Entertaining Kitty was an exhausting process. She had a very simple recipe for social conversation: she liked it to be a personal monopoly and to consist entirely of vitriolic anecdotes about her slightly younger contemporaries. Providing one nodded in her direction from time to time and arranged for the waiters to remove a succession of half-eaten dishes, she was happy and content and for twenty-four hours afterwards would sing your praises as a host. Really young women at her table, like Victorian children, were required to be seen but not heard.

We were four that evening. Kitty's escort was a pleasant middle-aged queen who only interrupted her when he could match or top her bitchiness. He was too rich actually to soil his hands in show business, but he always bought a book of charity tickets and was on first name terms with anybody who had billing above the title. He was a Catholic convert, the worst kind, confessing publicly as well as in church, and it was said of him, I'm sure with justification, that he liked to have his choirboys and eat them too. His name was Sheridan Quigley, but he was always referred to as The Holy Lady in camp circles.

We were a quartet with only one instrument playing that evening, for in the first flush of entry into new territory Kitty only drew breath when she was obliged to sip the low-calorie drink she had brought with her from America and to the restaurant table. She never drank the local water, and wine, she had been told, was not the elixir of eternal youth. She was also on a health kick and had a large Thermos of compost grown vegetables on a spare chair by her side.

'Have you seen Arthur since you got here?' Kitty said.

She was pointing in Susan's direction. Susan shook her head blankly. I knew she had no idea who Arthur was. Nor had I for that matter, but fortunately Sheridan took over.

'He's in the Clinic,' he said, 'having everything out.'

'What's he got, cancer?'

'Oh! Don't say that word,' Sheridan said, stubbing out a cigarette. 'No, you know, he collapsed on the set directing that

44

hideous Sherman child, and they rushed him straight into the Clinic.'

'Well, I'll call on him to-morrow,' Kitty said, making a note on an Asprey pad. 'Just so long as it isn't catching.'

Out of the corner of my eye I could see Susan propping her face open. I ordered coffee.

'D'you have Sanka?' Kitty said to the waiter.

'Of course, Madam.'

'Well, bring it to the table. With some boiling water. Not hot water, boiling water. I'll make it myself.' She swung round on Susan.

'I'm surprised you took that part,' Kitty said. 'Everybody turned that down. What're they paying you?'

'Fifty.'

'Who's your agent?'

'Bill Lumsden.'

'Change him. You know what they're paying that Sherman kid? Two hundred. They must be out of their minds. No wonder Arthur went into hospital. Paul isn't going to pay that sort of money, I can tell you. He's going to make big changes.'

'When d'you think he'll arrive?' I said.

'He's gone to the Springs this week to read a few scripts. What's the one you're doing?'

'*The Unknown Warrior.*'

'Oh, yeah, the Maxwell thing. That's one of the scripts he's reading.'

'So he won't be here this week?'

'Who knows? He's a fast reader. Depends on the gin rummy game. If he's ahead, he'll stay. If not he could be here to-morrow. You know Paul.'

The waiter returned with the equipment for making the Sanka coffee. 'This water boiling?'

'Yes, madam.'

'You know I got a virus in Paris last time? Course, I wasn't about to go into any French hospital, so I took the next plane out with a temperature of a hundred and two. Doctor Kreuger said I got it cleaning my teeth with the tap water. He's so *dear*. You go to Kreuger, don't you?'

45

'I think the studio sent me to him once,' Susan said.

'What'd you go to him for?'

'Oh, nothing. I think it was just an insurance check-up.'

'Did he give you the special shots?'

'No, I didn't really have anything wrong with me.'

'Listen, that's when you *need* the special shots.'

'Oh, I can't wait to take everything.' Sheridan said. 'I'm on K.H.3 at the moment.'

'What're they?'

'They're not for you, Kitty dear. They're the Youth Pill.'

'Injections?'

'No, I take it, as they say, in the mouth.'

'You got to have the injections like the Pope. They say Willie Maugham had them, too, and he was still active, if you know what I mean, the day he died.'

'Next year, dear,' Sheridan said. 'I'll have them next year. I want to see what they do for Ethel first. I hear they're slaughtering whole regiments of sheep for her.'

I wasn't conscious of listening beyond that point. Prolonged exposure to that occupational hazard known as 'the script conference' has left me with the useful facility of being able to separate my mind into many compartments behind the interested mask. From the scattered clues Kitty had thrown I could fill in most of the future crossword puzzle. Raven's reputation for interfering with the creative talent had been legend from his early days, and now that he had one hand on the nettle of real power, I knew I was in for a long struggle. The prospect before me was totally appalling on one level, but it was something I had lived through many times before and I am not without a certain professional resilience. Most of the time it's only a question of patience. The first rule is to appear unruffled. The Ravens of my immediate circle have always been impressed by the quiet, well delivered insincerity.

It was obvious to me that my film would not proceed as previously scheduled. When power changed hands at Raven's level, the game of musical chairs descended all the way to the basement. *The Unknown Warrior* had been his predecessor's decision: therefore it was inevitable that Raven would entertain doubts. Depending on the degree of inherited envy or fear he might even try

46

to persuade me to abandon it altogether, despite the fact that the studio had invested close to a quarter of a million dollars in the original story and various scripts. Nothing impresses so much in Hollywood as expensive economies: costly acts of abortion are always applauded extravagantly.

I comforted myself with the thought that I was going to fight on home ground: in Hollywood the days of the locust are commonplace and I would have been lost from the beginning: in Hollywood, so soon after his ascent to power, Raven couldn't have afforded a defeat.

It was with these thoughts in mind that I presented my engrossed mask to Raven's wife that evening. She waved fleshy arms close to my face as she embarked on another endless story about the talent she despised. She had recently resprayed herself with perfume, going about it like a mechanic touching up the paintwork on a damaged car, now the effect at close range was overpowering.

I tried to blot out memory, but the damage was already done. It was ironic that the only other person I had ever known use that particular perfume should have been a girl I had once loved extravagantly. Ironic and somehow grossly unfair that it should have smelt the same on Kitty Raven's skin.

It was there at that table to the sound of reputations being destroyed in an American accent, that I set about the destruction of my own peace of mind. Smiling, the social mask held firmly in place, I planned the moves ahead. At that time I had no maps, only the need to move out of the present into that unknown country where ghost landmarks have become eroded.

I wasn't to know that, imperceptibly, the past had moved closer to me, like some impenetrable rain forest where the dank vegetation of one's early mistakes remains rotting in remembrance.

When one is editing films the cutting rooms give shelf space to a library of cans labelled 'Trims.' These contain snippets of celluloid, sometimes as small as single frames, culled from the master shots. They are carefully hoarded against the moment when, inevitably, one has second thoughts. With film one cannot afford to lose a single frame: unless consecutive images flow through the projector gate the action jerks, the continuity is distorted.

47

We are never so careful with our own lives. The trims are mislaid, here and there a frame is missing, a mouth opens to speak but no words come, and the action cuts away suddenly to another scene, another time, another place.

'We must go,' Susan said, in an aside to me. Then, louder, 'I'm on early call in the morning.'

'Yes. I'll get the bill,' I said.

'Now don't be boring,' Sheridan said. 'This is my little treat and I don't want any argument.'

'Delicious meal,' Susan said. She had always been able to accept gracefully. Kitty didn't even look up: it was normal for men to pay bills.

'It's a fun place, isn't it?' Sheridan said. 'I shall probably have every single meal here for the next month, then transfer my affections elsewhere. One should never carry fidelity beyond the bounds of possibility,' looking straight at me.

For a moment I had the feeling that he could read my thoughts. Queens often have more perception than women.

He signed without looking at the amount, something which never fails to impress me, and then we threaded our way out. The unhealthy faces of swinging London swung round to observe our exit. Various other couples were also on their way out and I heard a voice shout: 'Watch it! Bunty's going to park the custard' in those strangulated tones still used by young men who are only about town. I had a blurred vision of a girl in white sliding to the floor. A roar of applause went up and waiters hurried to the scene.

Outside the Chelsea pavements were wet from a recent shower and the air was damp and cool. Waiting for the hired limousine to pull across the road, I thought to myself, put this trim in a can all to itself, this is what hope feels like. I knew then that there was no question of going back, that like Gatsby my boats had been launched against the current. I was committed to the deep.

As we drove away the girl in white was escorted out to the gutter. I saw her bend to be sick—a pale suppliant asking for forgiveness.

CHAPTER EIGHT

The rain had turned to a freak bout of snow during the night and I lay in bed wondering why the light outside the window had a different quality. Waiting for breakfast to arrive, I answered the phone to Susan.

'Hello, darling,' I said. 'Has there been much snow?'

'There was quite a lot on the way out to the studio first thing, but it doesn't seem to be settling.'

'Have you worked yet?'

'No. It's the usual chaos. They're still lighting. And there's a union meeting about something.'

'Nothing changes.'

'Still, I don't care how long they take to light as long as I look good. I didn't sleep well.'

'I miss you,' I said.

'Miss you too. Look, what I really rang for, could you be an angel and ring that restaurant—I've lost an earring. One of the turquoise ones you gave me for my birthday. It wasn't in the car because I used the same car this morning and the driver had a good look.'

'Yes, okay, I'll ring them. It'll give me something to do.'

'No news from the black-hearted Raven?'

'No.'

'What will you do all day then?'

'Oh, just potter around. I might come out to the studio and have lunch with you.'

'Well, I wouldn't do that.'

'Why not?'

'George is funny about having people on the set.'

'Well, I won't come on the set. I'll just come for lunch.'

'He likes having lunch with me so he can go over the script.'

'Make sure he turns over the pages with both hands.'

'Oh, darling, it's nothing like that. I can handle George. Will you do that for me, then? Ring the restaurant, I mean?'

'Yes,' I said.

'And will you remember to send flowers to Kitty.'

'Why? She didn't pay for dinner.'

'But you know how she goes on about good manners.'

'What should I do for Sheridan then, send him a brace of choirboys?'

'What? I'm sorry, darling, they're just calling me. That was the second assistant.'

'Give George my love,' I said. 'Tell him I envy him.'

'Tell him what?'

'Nothing,' I said. 'Have a good day.'

I imagined her walking from her dressing room in the Old House at Shepperton, past the cutting rooms to the sound stages. I could visualise her entrance on to the set, hairdressers and make-up men fussing, the sudden flurry of noise and movement before camera rehearsals start. And my envy was real enough, for I had nothing but a vast, useless stretch of time to fill.

The strange thing was, preparing for I knew not what, I hoped that she and George Martin, her current leading man, would betray me. I needed something more than seven years of unease to push me beyond the point of no return. Envy is more implacable than hatred.

There was a cable from Raven, which sat on top of the un-accustomed slenderness of my morning paper on the breakfast tray. I drank two leisurely cups of coffee before opening it, a feeble act of rebellion against the absent Caesar.

The cable merely gave his flight details. He was already in the air and proposed an immediate meeting that afternoon, a few hours after his plane got in. It was signed 'Paul S. Raven, Executive in Charge of World Production.'

I rang the restaurant, but there was no answer and I decided to take some fresh air. Taxis were sliding by in the slush, their occupants smug and upright. I walked across the still virgin white park to Knightsbridge, enjoying the cold and the luxury of walking which two years of living in Beverly Hills had blunted. Everything about London looked foreign and I stopped for fully five minutes to gape at the Kremlin-like red brick walls of the new barracks. The ugliness appalled me. I had grown accustomed to the peeling stucco face of Los Angeles—there, ugliness no longer has the power to surprise, but to find so much of London fouled with the property developer's concrete steps to a life peerage, gave me physical pain. The walk ruined, I over-tipped the commissionaire outside Harrods to find me a taxi for the remainder of the journey.

Even the taxi driver seemed to have absorbed some of the overall resignation. He was young and surly and pulled his flag down like a stabbing knife. He probably took me for a tourist and before I was seated he had swung the cab against the traffic in a savage and unheeding U turn. He then proceeded to rev the engine and drive like a maniac with a reckless disregard for the icy roads. Retribution was swift, for the moment he was forced to observe a red signal another angry face appeared at his window. It belonged to a young van driver who had drawn up alongside.

'You stupid berk,' he shouted. 'Why don't you learn how to drive?'

Through the closed communicating glass I heard the taxi driver make his mocking attempt to save face.

The young van driver hit him very efficiently and very hard. There was a sudden, shocking splash of blood on the windscreen glass and the taxi driver spat a fragment of something white. It was all over in a matter of seconds. The lights turned green, the van driver jumped back into his own vehicle and the traffic moved on. As far as I could see, other witnesses to the scene were supremely indifferent. My own driver proceeded at slower pace, but never looked round.

When we arrived outside the restaurant he merely pointed to the amount on the clock. I paid him and weakly added a generous tip, but he was not looking for sympathy. His mouth was bleeding and swollen.

'Are you all right?' I said.

'Sod you,' he said. And drove away.

The whole episode had a remoteness and unreality, like a badly constructed scene in an underground movie. I felt more of a stranger than ever. It was like returning home after a pleasant party to find that one's house has burnt down.

I needed to share the experience, but the waiter who came towards me in the deserted restaurant was Italian with very little English, and it all became too complicated.

'I was here last night,' I said. 'And I think my wife lost an earring.'

'Yes, last night,' the waiter said, smiling.

'Oh, you found it did you? Marvellous.'

'Please?'

'My wife's earring. Was it found?'

'To-night,' the waiter said. He smiled all the time.

'You want book for to-night. How many please?'

'No,' I said. 'Look, I'm sorry, you haven't understood, and I don't speak Italian. Is there anybody else here?'

'Here,' the waiter repeated. 'Not open now. To-night.'

I could see somebody else moving about in the murky interior, and moved past him.

'Excuse me,' I said, 'is there anybody there who could help me?'

An elderly woman came forward.

'We're not open for lunch,' she said. Her accent, if not her manner, gave me some confidence.

'Yes, I know that, I don't want lunch. I was here last night for dinner and my wife thinks she may have lost a restaurant . . . she may have lost an earring. We were sitting at that table, four of us.'

The woman shook her head. 'No, there was nothing handed in, and the cleaners have been and gone.'

'Oh. Well, if it does turn up perhaps you'd be good enough to call me. I'll leave my name and number.'

I scribbled the information on the back of one of the restaurant cards and handed it to her.

She peered at it as though expecting to read something obscene.

'Warren?' she said. 'Is that the name?'

'Yes.'

'I do have something for you,' she said.

I stared at her. She went to the cash desk and fumbled about, then came back to me with a small piece of folded paper.

'Somebody handed me this last night, but I was busy serving and when I looked for you again, you'd left.'

I examined the piece of paper. The name Richard Warren was written on the outside in thick black lettering, as though by an eyebrow pencil. I opened the double fold. The woman stood waiting.

'You still frown when you're eating. How nice to see you again if only across a crowded room.'

Underneath it was signed *Alison (Osmond)*.

I became conscious that the woman was standing very close to me.

'It is for you, is it?' the woman said.

'Yes.'

I folded the note and put it in my pocket, hoping that when I spoke again my voice would be normal. 'Just a note from an old friend, somebody I haven't seen for some time. I've been away, you see.'

The woman nodded, uninterested, but my anxiety compelled me to be over-confidential.

'Is the lady, the lady who gave you this, is she a regular customer?'

I thought she eyed me suspiciously before answering, but it may have been my imagination, for everything seemed to have gone into slow motion.

'No. No, I don't think so. I don't think I've ever seen her before. We haven't been open that long.'

'So you've no idea where I could contact her to say hello?'

'No, I can't help you I'm afraid.'

'Well, it's very kind of you to have remembered.'

I felt the need to make her like me just in case, by some remote chance, I needed a future go-between. I thanked her again, over-politely, before stumbling outside.

I walked three or four blocks in the slush with my head down, unconscious and uncaring of traffic and passers-by. I felt like a shoplifter must feel: at any moment I expected voices behind me to shout and call me back, ask me to turn out my pockets. I prepared for interrogation, rehearsing meaningless explanations. Turning a corner, I stumbled into a coloured traffic warden and his pinched West Indian face seemed full of menace. Skirting him with a mumbled apology I went inside a nondescript coffee bar. The steamed windows seemed to me at that moment to afford a measure of protection.

I sat at the counter on a level with a machine that had plastic oranges slowly revolving in a streaky orange liquid. There was only one other person in the place, a small man hunched over the first edition of the *Evening Standard*. He was scribbling all over it with a stub of pencil while a cigarette burnt down to his lips.

Eventually a young girl came to take my order. She had a mass of frizzed, dirty hair surrounding a chalk white face devoid of make-up.

'Coffee,' I said.

'Black or white, American or Espresso?'

'American, with cream.'

'No cream.'

'Well, milk will do.'

She was wearing a see-through blouse and the nipples of her full young breasts showed up darkly. I watched her scoop instant coffee from an enormous, anonymous tin, then take the cup to the hot water machine and fill it almost to the rim. She brought it back to the counter and most of the powder lay undissolved on the top.

'Anything to eat?'

'No, thank you,' I said.

'Oh, you said milk, didn't you?'

The addition of the milk slopped the mixture into the saucer. As she emptied the residue into a sink I noticed that her nails were bitten to the quick.

'Have I seen you on the telly?' she said suddenly.

Again the panic returned. It was absurd, but it's a strange thing to discover and to believe still in the existence of an old love, and nothing I did for those first few hours was rational.

'I don't think so,' I said.

She took the money without further comment and I looked round for a table to sit at. I chose the cleanest and sat with my back to the girl and the man. The sugar, damp and congealed, refused to be shaken from the container, and I sipped at the tasteless hot liquid and then glanced around to see if I was observed.

Retelling the sequence of events now I am amazed at my own ludicrous behaviour. The sleazy coffee bar, the watchful nubile girl behind the counter, these are the stock ingredients of a mundane television spy series. There was nothing remotely sinister about the setting or the characters, and yet I remember thinking myself into such a plot, and it was like an atom spy receiving his first microfilm that I took out the piece of paper and laid it close to the saucer, my hand cupped round it. I read and re-read it time and time again, searching for clues. Perhaps there was a sort of schoolgirl code in the second sentence, for the words 'across a crowded room' struck a faint chord of memory. When we had first met the music from *South Pacific* was all the rage, and the lyric of 'Some Enchanted Evening' had a message for new lovers.

Over the years I have trained myself to think in images and the pictures that looped through the gate of my mind that morning were in the gentle colours of remembered pain: the sweet substance of a girl I had once loved to tears and who had loved me, and whom I had thought I would never see again. Now as a single frame lingered I felt once more the agony of her soft gentle mouth on me and the colours grew stronger. I saw the moist lip flesh in close-up, her dark head bobbing below me against a background of field green, and then the searching camera, panning farther back in time, led me to the promise of our first encounter: ankles disappearing into bright red shoes, the young body outlined where it touched the thin summer dress.

I hadn't imagined that remembered pain could be so real, but I felt pain that morning, hunched forward, chilled, my hand clutching the note, in that anonymous café. I suppose in approaching middle age there is always a moment when one stops believing in miracles, and I had lived with jealousy for so long that, like somebody suffering from a chronic illness, the singing relief that comes with the shifting of pain from one part of the body to another, however short-lived, however false in its promise, is something akin to a miracle.

Certainly in those moments when I was learning the note by heart, I was freed from something old and trapped by something new. I could see the pattern of wallpaper above a table where a phone stood, in a house where once she had lived, and there was a cigarette burn on the edge of the table that I had been responsible for. I could see Alison silhouetted against a window in that same room, turning to welcome me, her greeting mouth stopped suddenly by mine. And it was all years before, longer than the seven years I had spent with Susan, and yet that morning she was as real to me as anybody I have ever known.

Who knows what causes any of us to change direction? Some of the strongest swimmers are lost within sight of land, while others know instinctively when to turn back. If I know myself at all, I know that I am not by nature promiscuous. Set down like that, it sounds pompous, but probably any self-judgment contains more than a germ of pomposity. In legal terms, I had been faithful to Susan—such an absurd word really, for 'faith' implies a belief in something and the only belief that Susan and I were left with after seven years of marriage was the efficiency of contraceptive devices.

It seems melodramatic now to write these words, but at the time, living out of suitcases in rented houses and hotel rooms, the gift of permanence was not something I declared automatically going through Customs. I had settled, I suppose, for a sort of unbearable complacency. I sat in strange places, in front of imaginary fireplaces where favourite possessions were always near to hand, but in reality the only possession that travelled with me was the illusion of happiness. Middle-class habits die hard, even when we escape beyond the reach of childhood, and hatred and desire are not middle-class words. Perhaps, in any event, they would have been exaggerated terms to have used to describe my relationship with Susan, for I was out of love with her, but I had not ceased to love her, and this mixture of love and fear troubled me like a meal eaten without real hunger.

That morning I was grateful for the very sleaziness and anonymity of my surroundings.

A torpid fly, lone survivor from the kitchen wastes, suddenly fell from the ceiling and lay, feebly struggling, on its back close to my cup and saucer. The damp wings fluttered it closer to the piece of paper and with a last effort it spun to obliterate Alison's name, leaving only the parenthesis visible. I stared hard at the word contained within the brackets. It was like suddenly discovering the key to the most difficult question on the exam paper.

I left the coffee shop with the paper tightly folded in my palm, and the hand itself buried deep in the pocket of my trenchcoat. The same traffic warden was still outside, waiting beside an expensive foreign car parked on a double yellow line. He looked at me with something approaching pleasure as I went up to him.

'Is there a phone booth around here?'

'Phone booth?'

'Yes, somewhere I can make a call.'

He contemplated his Cellophaned packet of parking tickets before answering me.

'There's one down by the pub, but it ain't usually working.'

I started walking in the direction he had indicated before he could elaborate. Behind me I heard him ask: 'This your car, man?'

The phone booth was occupied when I got to it and I waited impatiently while the old woman inside made a series of abortive attempts to regain her coins. She finally pushed herself out backwards.

'Bleedin' Government,' she said. 'They want to bring old Mosley back.'

I took her place inside and swivelled the tattered directories. The booth reeked of stale urine and amongst the frenzied graffiti on the facing wall the words I WEAR LADIES BLOOMERS I'M 69 YEARS OLD demanded to be read. I found the L-R volume which was dated April 1970 and thumbed through the torn and greasy pages until I found the entries for Osmond. Curiously enough they weren't numerous, perhaps forty in all. There were two entries with the letter A after them, but one was an Alfred. I picked up the receiver, prepared on an impulse to dial the other number, but the line was dead and the mouthpiece wet with some nameless liquid and covered with shreds of tobacco.

The last thing I saw before I crept away to keep my assignment with Raven were the crudely blocked words TREAT ME CAREFULLY I'M SEVEN YEARS BAD LUCK written across the cracked mirror.

CHAPTER NINE

Wardour Street, they say, is shady on both sides. Certainly it was dark in Raven's office that afternoon, but he may have arranged that deliberately. He had his back to the available light and across the acres of newly-installed partner's desk he looked like a shrunken fat dwarf. I wondered again at his undoubted success with women, for one of the great and constant disillusionments of my life is that women, and more especially beautiful girls, are prepared to go to bed with repulsive men. I know that the species has to continue and all that, but I think a line should be drawn somewhere.

I suppose Raven was in his fifties, but it was difficult to imagine that he had ever looked any different. There were very few pictures of him as a young man in newspaper libraries (he was always careful to conceal his origins) and the studio hand-outs were carefully vetted by his personal publicity man. Not that Raven courted publicity. On the contrary he had few of the more blatantly normal conceits of the film industry.

There were three of us, beside Raven, in the office that afternoon. He was a punctual man when he thought it was to his advantage and I had been shown in on the dot and greeted warmly. 'We'll switch the phone off, baby, and go through the whole bit without interruption.'

He was now on his fifth call and in fact had been talking long-distance from the moment his hand clasped mine. The rest of us sat and fingered recent copies of the trade papers: it was like a dentist going about his business in his waiting room. Gerry Blechman, Raven's personal assistant, pushed a trade review across to me: it slated a rival company's top picture for the year. There is a certain type of film executive whose day is ruined unless he reads some bad news about his friends, and Gerry was a perfectionist in disaster.

The other two men were home grown. Cottram, the Managing Director of the British subsidiary, was merely playing the elder statesman until the time came for him to be put out to grass. To my knowledge he had served seven of Raven's predecessors and during all those glorious years he had never had the authority or indeed the inclination to sanction the purchase of toilet paper. His dead hand had signed the minutes of every sub-committee in the history of the British Film Industry and he could always be relied upon to grovel lowest at any Royal Charity Première. His ability to double-deal and offend talent was legendary, but he described himself as a 'simple showman' and wrote letters of such painful hypocrisy that they were xeroxed and circulated to a group of us as collector's items. I used to have one framed and hanging in my lavatory: it was as good a place as any to remind oneself of the existence of Cottram.

Hogarth, the Assistant Managing Director, on the other hand, was not to be dismissed lightly. He had once worked for me as a Production Manager, but it was a period in his life he now preferred to forget. I took malicious pleasure in subtly reminding him every time we met, but it was a dangerous luxury because Mr Hogarth was grooming himself for the day when Cottram bought the knighthood and retired. He was a snob with a very thin veneer of intelligence and his wife's dinner invitations were something to leave town to avoid.

He smiled now, catching my eye: it was his day for pretending that we were both friends sharing a common exasperation. I took another cigarette and he leaned forward to light it for me. He smelt of expensive cologne.

'How d'you mean?' Raven shouted into the phone. 'How d'you mean they're asking five hundred grand? Since when? Charlie . . . Charlie . . . never mind that. Listen to me. You tell the agent to take the deal and shit in his hat. Quick, and then pull it down over his ears. Quote me. Charlie . . . Charlie, let me tell you something. Don't be fucked around by agents. D'you want to know how to handle it? Ring the girl direct and offer her two-fifty. She'll take it.'

He made motions with his hands towards us. Hogarth got up and poured him a glass of Malvern water.

'Charlie, look, tell her to get off the pot or piss in it.'

He slammed the receiver down, then buzzed on the intercom. 'No more calls.

'Dick, I'm sorry,' he said. 'D'you want some tea or something? Shall we have some tea?'

'I'm quite happy at the moment.'

'Right, let's talk about your project then. What was the last budget we had on it?'

Cottram looked predictably blank. 'Two million eight, Paul,' Hogarth said.

'Well, that's not important. I've been giving it a lot of thought, Dick. I mean, the budget can take care of itself. That's horses for courses. What d'you think about it?'

'What do I think about it?'

'Yeah.'

'About the subject itself or the budget?'

'The subject.'

'Well, obviously I think it's very good.'

'You think it's good, huh?'

'We're talking about *The Unknown Warrior*, aren't we?' I had the feeling that possibly I was going mad very early in the game.

'Yeah, that's it. You read it, Arnold?'

'I haven't read the last script,' Cottram said carefully. 'Course, I read the original.' The only reading matter that Cottram studied from cover to cover were the Finance Acts as they appeared.

'Yeah, well there've been a lot of changes since then.' Raven buzzed the intercom again. 'Bring me in the scripts on *Warrior*.' He picked his nose while waiting, and examined his finger afterwards. 'Agents,' he said. 'You know I had the Wilson office barred from the lot?'

'The whole office?' Cottram said.

'All of them.'

'Good for you, Paul,' Hogarth said. I remembered that he had once been represented by Wilson.

The girl came in with a number of scripts, each one with a different coloured binding.

'What's your name?' Raven said.

'Jean, sir,' the girl said.

60

'Well, I want you to stay late to-night, Jean. I gotta pile of letters to get through. And book me a call to the studio in about two hours. Then put in the call to New York. You'd better get me a dinner reservation too. Where we going to eat?'

'I did reserve a table at Les A, Paul,' Hogarth said on cue.

'Okay, fine.' He dismissed the girl, then turned to Blechman. 'You don't have to wait, Gerry. Just fix those other things we discussed.' Gerry nodded and went out.

'I want Gerry to have an office here. Do it up for him and put a girl in.'

'I can put him next to me,' Hogarth said.

Raven sorted through the scripts, selected one, checked the date on the title page, then turned to the end and studied it briefly. He held it in his hand as though judging the content by weight.

'It don't feel like two million eight to me. Look, Dick, we've known each other a long time, long enough to know I never interfere with my creative people. You're the guy who has to make it. I'm just here with Arnold and Robin to help you reach a decision.'

'You mean a casting decision?'

'Yeah, casting, the whole lot. I respect you, Dick, I respect your opinion and you know I respect your talent and integrity. Arnold knows that, don't you, Arnold?'

'Oh, Richard's one of our top directors.'

'That's right. You're one of the best around.'

I stared at the top of the desk with mock humility.

'And because I respect you, I don't want you to make the wrong decision.'

Hogarth took out a gold pencil and clicked the lead into place.

'See, if I can give you a word of advice, you need a commercial picture.'

'Who doesn't?' I said.

Hogarth reached for a notepad.

'That's right. Too many people screwing our industry with crap. What you need is a *Graduate*, or an *Easy Rider*. And I don't think this is it.'

'Well, no, it isn't,' I said. 'I mean, it certainly isn't *Easy Rider*. It's a modern love story, set behind the Iron Curtain.'

'That's right, it's a good ballsy story. Anyway, the point I'm making, Dick—and I've been talking it over with my people—you want to make this script, you've got a deal. But I'm going to try and talk you out of it.'

Raven held an awful fascination for me. When he talked of 'my people' I had a picture of a totally undiscovered race of mental pygmies, interbred to the point where they all resembled scaled-down versions of their master.

'But hasn't the studio got a big investment in it?'

'We'll pay it off, write it off.'

He jogged the script in his hand again. 'It doesn't feel like a love story, Dick.'

I was silent.

'What d'you think, Arnold? I mean, we're trying to arrive at a decision here.'

'Well,' Cottram began slowly. 'I've always liked it, but I can see what you mean, Paul.'

'Look, Dick, I don't mind losing money if it's a good picture. You can't win them all, but why give yourself a hard time for the wrong reasons?'

'Assuming you do cancel,' I said. 'Just assume that for a moment, where does that leave me?'

'I'll find you another. You got a contract, we just switch it. I got twenty subjects, real babies, take your pick. You can do *Roads to Glory*.'

'*Roads to Glory*? You bought that, did you?'

'That's the big one, Dick.'

'It's meaningful in to-day's market,' Hogarth said.

'It's also forty years behind the times,' I said.

'Dick,' Raven said, 'who knows?'

'Anyway I thought I read that Willie was going to direct that?'

'You want to do it, it's yours.'

'I want to do *The Unknown Warrior*. That's what I've been working on for the past nine months, that's what I came over here for. Why should I suddenly want to switch?'

'Dick, we've got no secrets, you and me, right? I want us to have a meaningful relationship. My people in New York have gone cold on it.'

'Your people in New York are in frozen foods. They'd go cold on anything.'

'They're calling the shots right now.'

I wanted to shatter the deadness of this absurd room, these three absurd people. The old guard, monstrous regiment though they were, had at least understood the basic rules of the game. They had robbed and cheated and lied and blustered their way through the halcyon days of Hollywood, carpetbaggers to a man, but they were at least possessed of a buccaneer's sense of humour which redeemed some of their worst excesses and they had nerve. Now they were dead or neutered and in their place we had a succession of faceless corporate men who were usually too busy jet-setting their way across the world in search of new acquisitions to actually view the films they made. What they couldn't understand, they destroyed. What made them money, they squandered. They still robbed, but in cold blood, with not a laugh between them, and the wonder of it was that any of us bothered to return to the arena.

I knew exactly why Raven was trying to talk me out of *The Unknown Warrior*. It was an inheritance from the man whose chair he was now sitting in, and Raven was mean and stupid enough to destroy something just because it wasn't entirely his.

If I had wanted to play the cards that Raven was willing to deal me, I could even increase the stakes: for the pleasure of hearing me agree with him in public, he would put somebody else's money where his mouth was. I knew, that afternoon, that with the minimum of flattery I could walk out of his office minus *The Unknown Warrior* but clutching a brand new contract. Out of perversity more than conviction I decided to deny him such an easy victory. I knew Hogarth was watching to see which way I would go. Since he judged everybody by his own standards he was, I am sure, utterly confident that I would back down.

'Paul,' I said, 'since when have you ever worried what New York thinks? You wouldn't be where you are to-day if you hadn't gone out on a limb for the things you believe in. I mean, I think it's fantastic that you've taken over the studio. I said to Susan, "Thank God at least now I'm going to be working for somebody who talks my language, who understands *film*." '

Even in the half light I could see my crude flattery have immediate effect. He reached for a Ramon Allones.

'It just seems to me that if you and I are going to have any sort of relationship that's meaningful . . .' (I slipped with conscious ease into his painful jargon) . . . 'I have to be totally honest. I can't suddenly say to you that this script I've been working on for nine months is a load of crap. Because you *know*, going in, that I thought it had great potential when I got the studio to buy the option. So for me to turn round now, even for the undoubted pleasure of kissing your arse, would be madness. You'd never believe anything I said ever again.'

'That's right, that's right.'

'Of course you've got reservations on the script as it stands. I've got reservations. But they're script reservations and we can put those right. If we knew the secret in advance we could both phone it in.'

The room seemed to have grown darker since I started talking. Raven's face was in shadow, like a criminal who had been guaranteed anonymity on a television interview.

'Listen, Dick, I appreciate what you're saying. I'm not going to tell you how to make pictures. Your track record speaks for itself. You believe in it, you're right to fight for it. We'll meet up next week and kick it around some more. You thought any more about casting? Who've you got in mind for the girl?'

'I've got one or two ideas. But let's get the script right first.'

'I'll lay one on you for the girl.'

He fished into a drawer and took out a copy of *Playboy*. He opened it at the centre page spread. 'How about playing her?'

Hogarth strained to look at it with me.

'Can she act?'

'Who cares whether she can act. Look at those tits.'

'I suppose you've already signed her?'

'I've got some open options.'

This was a word that Cottram understood and he showed signs of executive restlessness. In his long and undistinguished career his major contribution to the industry had been to perfect a technique of dropping options soundlessly.

Raven flicked the intercom switch. 'Any messages?' He hated a silent phone.

The secretary's voice answered immediately.

'Mr Andrews is waiting to see you, sir.'

'Who?'

'Mr Andrews.'

'He's an agent,' Hogarth said.

'What's he trying to sell?' Raven said with the switch down.

'Talent. He specialises in new talent.' Hogarth stared Raven straight in the eye. Raven flicked the switch again.

'Okay, show him in.'

He turned to me as I started to my feet. 'Don't go. Meet this kid. Say hello.'

The secretary ushered in the agent and his client. The girl was young and over-dressed, her recently adolescent face blotted out with expertly applied make-up. She moved awkwardly and despite her obvious concern to remain unimpressed, fear teetered her and she stumbled in the thick pile of Raven's carpet.

'Bill Andrews, Mr Raven,' the agent said.

'Yeah, hello, Bill. Who's this young lady, who am I shaking hands with?'

'Dawn Stuyvesant, Mr Raven.'

'Well, sit down, Dawn. This is Mr Cottram, Mr Hogarth, and Mr Warren. You know who Mr Warren is, don't you?'

The girl nodded, but looked at Hogarth.

'Mr Warren's a very famous director. Never know, he might put you into one of his pictures. You want to act, do you?'

'Yes, I do.' The accent was newly-buried provincial.

'How old are you?'

'She's eighteen,' the agent said, 'but she can play older.'

He fumbled a large envelope and produced a number of glossy photographs. Raven took them without much enthusiasm. I could see that some of them were nude shots.

'Yeah, these are very cute.' He handed them back.

'You done much acting yet, Dawn?'

'I've done some television.'

'I'm turning down a lot of stuff for her,' the agent said. 'I don't want to rush her.'

'No, that's right,' Raven said.

He stared at the girl. 'That's good advice,' he said.

'Just thought she ought to meet people.'

'Yeah. Important to meet people.'

'Course, if she was lucky enough to work for somebody like Mr Warren here . . .'

The girl looked at me for the first time. She smiled, showing slightly crooked teeth smudged with lipstick. I felt desperately sorry for her, for all of us.

'Yeah, well the important thing is to meet people,' Raven said. 'Meet all the people you can, Dawn. It's good experience. And come and see us again.'

The agent dropped the photographs. Nobody helped him. He made his exit in a half-stooped position. The girl started to shake hands, but lost courage.

'Take care now.' Raven remained seated. 'Where do they find them?' he said before the door was fully shut. 'Jesus! what is this, open house or something? What're you doing, Robin, letting two-bit agents come in here peddling jail bait?'

'I'm sorry, Paul.'

'I mean, keep agents out of this office. I don't deal with agents.'

'No. I'll give instructions.'

'Well do it now.' Hogarth went out immediately. I got no enjoyment from his humiliation: I knew he'd hold me responsible, just for being present.

'Shall we fix another meeting?' I said.

'Yeah. Tell my girl to fix it. And, Dick, do me a favour, will you? Read *Roads to Glory*.'

'I've already read it.'

'Read it again. You might get a new slant. I know you're hooked on the other one, but don't close any doors.'

I shook hands. Cottram gave me his bank manager's smile. Raven seemed to forget me immediately. The switch was down again and he was attempting to make contact with his own world, his own people—the world of the dried imagination where hope could be purchased for ten per cent.

As my taxi turned into Oxford Street I caught a glimpse of Miss Dawn Stuyvesant waiting in a bus queue, and twisted to watch her through the rear window as we passed. The darkened glass framed her neatly for a few seconds: an isolated figure on a dim screen. The taxi pulled away like a camera and I watched her diminish until the rush-hour traffic blotted her from sight. It was like dissolving twenty wasted years.

CHAPTER TEN

Why is it that the death of one poor frightened Pakistani, shot while trussed, his head half-concealed in a ditch, his life cut off in mid-sentence so that he did not even have time to cry out—why is it that this seemed so much more shocking and near than the reported death of 20,000 people in a Persian earthquake, the majority of whom died more horribly in all probability than this one sad man who literally shook with fear as the British ITN reporter told him he had nothing to worry about, he wasn't going to be killed, he was merely going to be taken away and questioned and fed? They all spoke English, the captors and the captured, and the cameraman's instincts never deserted him for a single frame as the bullets delicately perforated the thin, heaving ribs. Then the announcer's face again: a moment's composure before the next commercial break, a newer cat food with still richer chunkier meat, a whiter whiteness to wash away the suburban stains, a more potent and thrilling way to baffle vaginal odours. The last image to fade as I switched off the hotel set was that of a pretty girl about to perform fellatio on a bar of chocolate.

I sat in front of the dead screen trying to examine my feelings. Was it pity I felt, or was it anger and uselessness, or just the conceit of an unwanted involvement? It was like trying to re-read a neglected diary where old intimacies have been recorded in code, the key to which one no longer remembers. I had gone for so long taking my life on trust, as inevitable, that now I was scared to decipher the real meanings. I was ashamed to admit that it wasn't the trussed, dead youth who touched me, but the searing memory of an unknown model's wet, open lips. She reminded me of a time when I had loved obsessively. The imitation act she had just performed so cleanly in soft focus for seven million viewers had once been the secret summit of my private pleasure. Remembering, my body shook in the same way that fear had trembled the stuttering Pakistani. Memory was also a kind of death.

I wanted the past so badly. Jealousy of unknown rivals, senseless, distorted jealousy knotted me like sudden colic. I got up, poured a drink I had no intention of swallowing, walked blindly to the window and rested my head against the coolness of the glass in an actor's pose.

Below, released by changing lights, traffic streaked across glistening tarmac. My madness at that moment was such that I struggled to remember the registration number of her car. Alison had always been an appalling driver, indifferent, like the majority of women, to what was under any bonnet, scornful of the male concern for mechanical perfection. 'It's only a car,' she used to say above the scream of metal curling from mutilated gears. It was a test of love she passed every time we met, for like most Englishmen I had to stifle a keen sense of outrage at such cruelty to and lack of proper feeling for things that go on four wheels.

I remember how impressed, envious even, I was of Lowson on one occasion when he refused to trade in an elderly Riley, but instead drove alone through the night to Dartmoor and there, at dawn, with great compassion, set fire to it. 'I put her down,' he said. 'I didn't want her to fall into the hands of some bloody Steptoe and Son. And I don't mind telling you, mate, I cried in the train coming back.' It seemed extravagant, his grief, but not unreal, I remember.

Alison hadn't liked Lowson, or any of my friends of that period. I think their small talk and endless 'shop' which people in show business take for granted, unnerved her. In those days she wasn't good company in company. Of course in my eyes she had few faults. For her sake I eased away from friendships, avoided certain restaurants, neglected answering mail. Unlike some lovers, I had no desire to share her. I had nothing but the most suffocating, romantic conceptions: endless love-making in remote cottages, the simple life, the shared bed, darkness and the wind and the rain outside. And for a time it worked. We leased the cottage, we spent long week-ends there, making love between damp sheets, bathing each other in a hip bath, like miners, in front of smoking wood fires—all in extreme discomfort, of course, but in the first flood of love we were oblivious.

I never questioned my many betrayals, I didn't care who suffered as long as she was happy. If we were parted for a day I used the time to write long letters to her, letters I did not post but carried with me to our next meeting to deliver by hand, and watched her read them, saturated by my own foolishness.

Her own letters to me were pathetic things, few and far between, scarcely more than schoolgirl pash notes, written on odd pieces of paper in cramped immature handwriting. And yet I used every persuasion to get her to write, bullying her to commit herself. Why is it that, in love, some of us demand more than the other has to give? She hated the actual act of putting pen to paper, yet I demanded my quota as fiercely as I took her body. 'But I'm seeing you every day,' she'd say, not unreasonably, genuinely puzzled. 'Why do you want a letter as well?' My insistence was like a fatal illness. I had to see her love in ink, the trite phrases I am sure she struggled to compose: 'More than anybody in the world, when I awake my first thoughts are of you, I can't imagine anything without you, each day I want you more.'

I used to read her letters in bed, with her lying beside me, holding the single sheet of paper like a child's comic, my other hand curling between her newly-moist thighs. She couldn't understand that either. 'We've just done it,' she'd say, 'isn't that proof enough?' There was no reason why she should have understood, for my compulsion was obscure even to me. That removed clinical part of me would be photographing the scene with the same detached instinct that kept the newsreel cameras turning while the bullets tore into living flesh.

And now I had the first slender clue to her present whereabouts, and I needed to act, I needed to go back to something real.

Susan called from the bedroom. I suddenly became conscious that I was standing in a darkened room.

'I'm sorry,' I said, walking towards the open bedroom door. 'What did you say, darling?'

'Could you hear my lines, please?'

I went and sat on the edge of the bed and picked up her script.

'What were you doing in there?'

'Watching the news.'

The script was already dog-eared and there were various messages and stage directions scrawled across most of the pages. It offended me. I can't bear anybody mutilating a book of any description.

'Which page?' I said.

'The yellow ones. They rewrote it.'

'Again?'

'They never stop. They handed me six new pages in make-up this morning.'

'But you're not in this scene.'

'Yes, I am. Angela.'

'I thought your name was Rachel.'

'They changed that, too.'

'So, it starts here, does it? Are you in the bath?'

'Yes.'

'That wasn't in before, was it?'

'No.'

I read the endless stage directions, always the mark of a third-rate screenwriter, and then gave her the cue.

'He means nothing to me . . . You think this is the first time something like this ever happened to anybody?' Susan waited expectantly. 'Isn't that right?'

'Word perfect. I'm just stunned (a) that anybody could write it and (b) that anybody could learn it.'

'It sounds all right, doesn't it?'

'Well, you said it nicely, I just think it's a cow of a line.'

'All right, we know it isn't one of your scripts.'

'Now don't turn ugly. I didn't say it like that.'

'Don't let's argue about it. I've got to say it, so give me the next cue.'

The man's part was, if anything, worse than her own. I read his lines deliberately and badly.

'Listen, Joe. I love Paul,' Susan went on, 'and we need each other. We've both been hurt deep down. So don't go getting in over your head, because you can get hurt much worse than you think you're hurt now.'

I reached for a cigarette. 'It's unbelievable,' I said. 'Who wrote it?'

'You met him.'

'That character who came to the press reception in a velvet suit?'

'Yes. He's won an Academy Award.'

'I don't doubt it. He's probably on his way to another. This is bad enough.'

'I know it's not very good, but what can I do? I can't ask them to change it now, and I'm first shot in the morning.'

'*Don't go getting in over your head,*' I read aloud.

'Well, read like that . . .'

'Read any way that is unplayable.'

'In your opinion.'

'I do know something about dialogue.'

'But you don't happen to be directing it. If you were, if I had the privilege of working for you, then there might be some point in discussing it. As it is, bloody awful line or not, I've got to learn it and I've got to say it.'

'All I meant was . . . If you'll listen . . . I could tidy it up for you.'

'Darling, it's half past ten. I haven't got the energy to learn the rewrite of the rewrite.'

'Now don't get upset.'

'Just give me the cues so that I get it into my head.'

'You've got to get it in *over* your head.'

She tore the script from me and turned on to her side. Sitting on the edge of the bed, watching her silently mouth the words, guilt for a crime not yet committed filled me with something approaching tenderness. I put out a hand to touch her, feeling her warm clean skin beneath the lawn of her nightdress. She had pinned up her hair to save time in the morning and I stroked her bare neck, but she didn't react.

I said, 'Can I order you something, do you want a hot drink before you go to sleep?'

She shook her head and went on mouthing the dead words. Ash

71

from my cigarette dropped on to the blankets and I got up to search for an ashtray.

'Have you put your call in?'

'Yes,' she said.

I went back to the bed and knelt beside her. I took the script out of her hands. We stared at each other.

'I'm sorry.'

'Yes.'

She allowed herself to be kissed, but her eyes remained open and I suddenly found myself inhibited by her beauty. I haven't mentioned that before, which is revealing, I suppose. There was no escaping it, even at close range, and it was the kind of beauty that still had the power to destroy me. It was hard to accept the obvious fact that we had become strangers; that just as she had no inkling of my real thoughts, I had no knowledge of hers. I could stare into those over-large eyes, the lashes soft now, slightly sheened with oil, and imagine that what I saw there was a reflection of my own transient lust instead of the real and appalling image of guilt. As my lips left hers my hands went with long practised ease to her breasts.

'It's no use,' she said. 'I've got to be up early.'

'And then into the bath. With all those prop men making bubbles.'

'I hate it. It makes your skin go all wrinkly. Like something under a stone.'

She seemed vulnerable then, a little girl again, complaining of something vaguely unpleasant and perhaps in that moment we were closer than we had been for months.

I kissed her again, gently, without passion, taking gratefully the escape route she had offered. I tucked her into the clean hotel sheets and turned off the bedside lamp and left the room.

The drink I had poured earlier was as flat as I felt and I emptied it into the pot of welcoming flowers provided by the management. Not wanting to sleep I started to read my own script, but I was over-familiar with the content and it irritated me. Thinking of the room I had just left, the person sleeping there, and the scene we had just played, it occurred to me that real life is not so far removed from a mediocre screen-play. On the typed page love is reduced to manageable proportions, situations however badly expressed, dovetail, and one can cheat and turn to the final pages to see how it all ends.

CHAPTER ELEVEN

I once came across an entry in an old diary which read: 'To-day I put a deposit on a second-hand suit.' Just that. I looked in vain for a continuation of such a momentous piece of information but with my usual lack of staying power I seem to have abandoned the diary by the first week in February. There were only two further entries in the entire book. On April 11 I developed a *herpes simplex* on my upper lip and then on August 14 I had recorded the fact that Betty, whoever Betty was, had left early. That was 1955, from all accounts one of my duller years.

Walking down Park Lane the following morning the deposit on the second-hand suit seemed to represent a reality in my life that I no longer possessed. It must have been a rational act at the time, probably only arrived at after long fiscal deliberation. After all, to put a *deposit* on a second-hand suit indicates a degree of quiet desperation. I remember a charlady once told me that she always bought her false teeth from a barrow in Stratford market. I thought then, and I haven't lost the nausea, that such a purchase contained the very essence of human tragedy. The idea of eating with somebody else's teeth strikes me as being the end of the road. But at least my old charlady always paid cash on the nail. I doubt if even she would have stooped to a deposit on an upper and lower set.

The company had provided me with pleasant offices at the park end of Curzon Street. I walked in unannounced to find the bare bones of my eventual staff already assembled. I introduced myself to my secretary, Pam, who in turn introduced me to her secretary, Lucy: they could both have been hand-picked by a jealous wife. The production manager Stan Williams had also been put on the pay roll. He had once been my third assistant and I welcomed him back.

'What's happening?' I said.

'We're raring to go, governor.'

'Anybody done a breakdown yet?' I asked, leading him into my office and closing the door.

'Have we got a start date?'

'No. We haven't even got a firm deal, so I wouldn't make the down payment on a new car. But you and I are going to give them a run for our money. What have they got you on?'

'What sort of contract you mean? Weekly, with two weeks' union minimum notice.'

'How much?'

'One fifty.'

'Times are hard,' I said.

'Dick, look, I wanted to work with you, and that's not bullshit. I'd have taken one forty-five.'

Pam came in with a cup of coffee. She knocked first, which was a change from my Hollywood secretary.

'Is this how you like it, Mr Warren?'

'Do you have cream?'

'Only the top of the milk, I'm afraid.'

'I shall live longer,' I said.

'What d'you think of the script?' I asked Williams when the door closed again.

'D'you want me to be frank?'

'Stan,' I said. 'It's a long time since you worked for me, and you've come up in the world, but I dare say you remember that I don't like arselickers.'

'Well, I think it's good and I like the basic story and characters, but it seems curiously old-fashioned.'

'You mean the whole thing seems old-fashioned?'

'Yes. I can't quite put my finger on it, but it's not European. It's as if the writer got it all out of an old guide book.'

'That's a very perceptive remark.'

He wasn't unintelligent, and the guess was a good one, but I also needed to flatter him for other reasons. I needed someone I could trust. There is a unique protective loyalty which nearly

74

always exists between a film director and his crew. Going into a film is rather like entering into a dozen marriages at once. I've been disappointed, but only rarely, in my professional life and there was something about Williams that I remembered from the past that inspired trust.

'I'll think about that when I read it again.' I sipped at the coffee. It was revolting.

'D'you smoke?' I said.

'I'm trying to give it up.'

'D'you want me to encourage you or offer you one?'

'I'll give it up to-morrow.' He took one and offered me a light.

'Can you do something for me?' I said. 'It's not really connected with the film, but it might have some bearing.' I paced the room as I spoke, examining the drawers in my new desk, and I was careful to be turned away from him and to drain my voice of any excitement.

'I want to trace somebody, an old friend, somebody I've lost touch with.'

I glanced at him. He was listening, but only as a production manager. 'I've got the married name, but no address.'

'Are they in the phone book?'

'No. They're probably ex-directory, and I've got nothing else to go on.'

'Well, let's think now,' Williams said. 'Are they in the business?'

'I doubt it. Isn't there something called an Electoral Register that's kept pretty well up to date?'

Williams nodded and reached for a paper and pencil. 'I wouldn't make a note of it,' I said. 'It's quite a simple name to remember.'

'Oh, right,' Williams said and for the first time his face betrayed something.

'The person I'd like to trace is a married woman. Are you married now, Stan?'

'Heavily,' he said, and grinned.

'Well see if you could find somebody called Mrs Alison Osmond.'

'Alison Osmond.' It sounds foolish now but to hear somebody else use her name after a decade made tears come to my eyes and I was grateful for the cigarette. I made myself choke on an inhale.

'We'll both give them up to-morrow,' I said, recovering from the sham and the real thing. 'Try the Chelsea and Kensington areas first, it's just a hunch. And if you draw a blank move on to Westminster and Mayfair.'

'You want me to start now?'

'Seems as good a time as any.'

'How would you like me to play it if anybody asks where I am? I'm looking for locations, I suppose?'

'I suppose you are, Stan,' I said. 'And one in particular.'

'And something we don't want to put into the script just now?'

'No. I don't think we'll give anybody any copies.'

'That's all I wanted to know.'

He passed Pam in the doorway. She looked slightly flustered.

'Mr Hogarth rang, but I didn't think you'd want to be disturbed, so I said you were in a script conference and would call him back. I hope I said the right thing.'

'Perfect. Whenever Mr Hogarth rings I'm always in a script conference.' I felt the old stirrings of warmth that I always get in the early days of a film. There is something of the frontier, pioneering spirit when a unit first starts to take shape. 'What did he want?'

'He wondered whether you could have dinner with him to-night?'

'What d'you think?'

'I don't know, Mr Warren. I haven't got your diary.'

'Yes, all right. Ring him back. Where did he suggest?'

'He mentioned the Playboy Club, sir.'

'Did he now? Now how does that affect you? D'you think I should change my mind?'

It was cruel to bait her, but I felt strangely elated for no good reason.

'I'm sure Mr Hogarth wouldn't suggest anywhere that wasn't absolutely right. You ring him back and say yes. What time?'

'He said eight o'clock, sir.'

'Fine. And get my wife, too. Try the studio first.'

I picked up a fresh copy of the script when she left the room and sat with it at my desk. Opening the pages I thought about what Williams had said, and then I thought about what Williams was

76

doing on my behalf. And when the phone rang and an apologetic assistant told me that Susan had already left to get back to the hotel I felt cheated, for at the outset deceit makes us anxious to cross the frontier of the first lie.

CHAPTER TWELVE

I caught sight of myself on the closed circuit television monitor as I entered the Playboy Club. I looked like a guilty man who has escaped identification in a police line-up.

The Bunny on the door had rather sad ears; one was bent at a curious angle and it gave her a quizzical look. I behaved well and scrupulously avoided looking at her platformed breasts. Instead I stared straight at her razored-edged, satin groin where the rosette bearing her name looked like a target for all the lonely to aim at but never hit.

Passing the souvenir counter I wandered into the first roulette room. I was a quarter of an hour early for Hogarth, quite deliberately, for I intended to take chances early in the evening.

Four Bunny croupiers worked the two tables and with the exception of a crumpled young man and his equally crumpled girlfriend, the players were all Oriental. Which just goes to prove, I suppose, that art seldom imitates reality. I found myself thinking that if I had been directing the scene I would have fired my assistant for giving me such an appalling bunch of extras. There was absolutely no dialogue, no pleasure. Just a bunch of short, dedicated men and four pretty but distorted girls.

I lost the price of a few second-hand suits with consummate ease, exchanged a friendless look with one of the Orientals and then went on a tour of the building.

Most of the other club members I met seemed to be trying to give the impression that they were not there by design, but had merely wandered in off the streets in the mistaken belief that it was a place of worship. Certainly I have encountered more evidence of intent to sin in the choir changing rooms of my childhood. In the bars there seemed to be a fair sprinkling of married couples, the wives noting every wobble of the Bunny waitresses while the husbands dipped studiously bored faces into over-large drinks. Of course the whole conception of the *Playboy* dream—taking the girl next door to the far side of paradise and stripping her—was an act of sexual genius beyond parody.

Hogarth was waiting for me in the downstairs bar when I returned to my starting point. I strolled towards him with a racy, adventurous feeling, difficult to explain—perhaps we wear so many disguises before others that in the end we appear disguised before ourselves. An old instinct prodded me that Hogarth was planning a palace coup himself, that he was in the process of secreting his weapons all over town.

He was wearing a flamboyant Mr Fish shirt and had his back to me, studying the past Playmates enshrined in their back-lit niches behind the bar.

'I'll take out a year's subscription for you,' I said.

I was delighted to see him betray guilt. He was a careful man, Hogarth, careful about his clothes, his accent, his opinions; and most of all he was careful about the face he let you see.

'I hope I haven't kept you waiting?'

'No, no. Just arrived. Where do they find them, d'you suppose?' indicating the Playmates.

'Ask Paul,' I said. 'I'm sure he has a telephone number for where the rainbow ends.'

'Poor old Paul,' Hogarth said. 'He told me to-day he takes pollen capsules. What'll you have to drink?'

'Scotch, I think. On the rocks.'

He ordered the most expensive brand in a voice he had cultivated especially for waiters.

'How's Susan?'

'Very tired,' I said. 'She had a rough day at the studio. She never got out of the bath.'

'Give her my love.'

'I will. She sends you hers, and thanks you for the flowers. And how's the delectable Mrs Hogarth?'

'Complaining that she never sees me.'

'Ah, you executives, you work too hard.'

He looked at me sideways, then smiled and pushed my drink towards me. 'Cheers,' he said. Having been away from London for two years the toast seemed false—it was rather like looking at an old movie and hearing the young subaltern address C. Aubrey Smith in the Warner Brothers officers' mess.

'I thought we'd eat here,' he said. 'The food's very good and one doesn't see too many of the same faces one sees all day.'

'Fine,' I said.

'Well, it's nice to welcome you back.'

Over a second and a third drink he embarked upon a detailed and nostalgic digest of mutual friends, barbed and witty, and, I detected, faintly envious on occasions. It was almost possible, lulled by the generous doubles, to warm towards him: his ambitions were as vivid as his shirt and, like his cuffs, he allowed too much of them to show. From time to time, content to let him have the monologue, I found myself thinking about Williams; I think I half-expected to look up and see him advancing towards us bringing the news that would transform the sweet agony of waiting.

When finally we made our way into the restaurant the head waiter piloted us immediately to a sheltered table. I looked around and saw that Hogarth had plotted well, for he had nothing to fear from the other diners. For the most part they were young men seriously on the make, their eyes flitting from the untouchable to the possible. Nobody paid us so much as a glance as we took our seats.

I timed him and he took exactly two hours to get to the real point of the meeting. He had a certain subtlety, he didn't wait for the traditional moment of coffee and brandy, but slipped in the opening gambit with the first spoonful of out-of-season raspberries. Being a comparatively new wine snob he enthused too anxiously over his choices. He had ordered Chateau d'Yquem '62 with the dessert and was drinking it like Coca-Cola.

'I think the scene over dinner in *The Unknown Warrior* is masterly. I mean, it really excited me,' he said. 'You know the one where the man teaches the girl how to appreciate wine.'

'Yes, it is an effective scene.'

'Paul doesn't see it, but I was explaining to him, that's what it's all about. It says everything, it sets the relationship.'

I let him wait. The sort of avarice that drove Hogarth almost always miscalculates and I was content that evening to let him remove his own masks.

'Of course it's difficult for him at the moment.'

I sipped my Chateau d'Yquem: I am a more experienced wine snob. 'How?' I said.

'Well, the politics, it's always politics, isn't it?'

'Is it?' I said. 'I wouldn't know, I've never aspired to your heights.'

'Oh, I'm not involved at Paul's level and in any event you know where my loyalties lie. I've always been on the side of the creative talent.'

I nodded, my glass still raised, seeing him through the richness of the wine in his true colour.

'The point is New York's running scared at the moment and they're putting a lot of pressure on Paul. I mean, don't misunderstand me, I think, I know Paul's on your side too, but they're giving him a hard time.'

'Is what you're trying to tell me, and I appreciate it if you are, that Paul is the fat red line between the film—my film—and New York?'

'That's roughly it.'

'How roughly?'

'I think they'd like to cancel.'

'Yes,' I said slowly, giving the impression that I was choosing my words with great care. 'I sensed that at yesterday's meeting.'

'You see, Paul's got a very unenviable task. I don't envy him. He's been put in, between you and me—and I really would like you to keep this under your hat—on a sort of caretaker basis. I've got my own contacts in New York, and the bottom line is that if Paul doesn't come up with the answers, he'll have to make compromises.'

'Does he know that?'

If the question took him unawares he covered well. 'He knows he has to deliver or else.'

'That's interesting,' I said. 'I'm always fascinated by the workings of large corporations. How about Cottram, where does he fit in?'

'Where did he ever? They have to have somebody on the letter-heading, and why keep lamb when mutton's so cheap?'

'You really enjoy it, don't you?'

'It's a game, Dick. It's all a game.'

'Except for those who make the actual films.'

'That's the point I'm making. I want you to know you've got a friend at court.'

I thanked him and the subject was dropped. I had to admire his technique, for having sown the first mine he turned the conversation away from the danger area. He ordered brandy and became expansive in a more predictable way. In Hogarth's private exchange there was a direct line between power and sex. He gave a long slow smile to the Playmate who bent to serve us and she returned the smile in Bunny Mother textbook style.

'Thank you, Mandy,' he said and watched her teeter away.

'Are you ever tempted?'

'Specifically or in general?' I said.

'Both.'

'It crosses my mind.'

'Our trouble is, Dick, we're too particular.' I knew I was now going to be treated to a performance by Hogarth the sexual sage. I knew his tastes so well. He had married well, his wife was the Honourable something and had a face that needed diffusion above and beyond *Tatler* standards. They maintained two houses and his and her Bentleys. But Hogarth needed to return to his origins at frequent intervals and I knew that his snobbery stopped at the bedroom door. When in New York or Beverly Hills he was discreetly promiscuous, with a marked preference for putting his hands inside jeans rather than under Hartnell skirts.

'There's a film we ran yesterday which you ought to see. Swedish. Quite incredible. If they can get a certificate for it, it'll take a fortune.'

'I've always been put off by the nude films I've seen. The people are so unattractive—all those pimply bottoms and Brillo pad genitals.'

'Oh, this is quite different. It's not one of those out-of-focus quickies.'

'Does the hero take his socks off? That's another thing that always makes me squirm. They take everything else off but leave their socks on.'

'Well, I'll run it for you. Believe you me the little girl to whom all things happen is really something. I mean, I'm not a tit man myself, but she could convert me.'

'Does she speak English?'

'I'm checking on that.'

'What a varied life you lead, Robin.'

'We also serve who only sit and make deals.' He spoke as to an equal and I found myself withdrawing farther and farther as the evening ground on. Somebody once said that society can only exist if the slightly deceitful flourish. Well, Hogarth had a head start on most of his fellow plotters for he had already selected the doors he wanted to open in the corridors of power. But then, I don't like society much. And I no longer care if the Hogarths of my world flourish, for their brief candles don't light my particular path. Whenever I think of them, if I think of them at all, I'm reminded of something I once saw cut into the wall of a Spanish prison. The unknown inmate of the cell had written 'Is there a life before death?' and that night, sitting opposite Hogarth in the neutered eroticism of the Playboy Club, our every whim catered for by near-naked girls as impersonal as nuns giving enemas to wounded soldiers, enjoying vintage brandy that neither of us were paying for, I tasted the bile of my own deceit. I wanted desperately to believe that love transformed, that my search for the past was different from Hogarth's future lusts. Although he never suspected it, he was closer to being a friend that night than ever before. But I was sober enough to realise that anybody who needed to make a friend of Robin Hogarth was committed to a murder of the heart.

When we finally left, he put an arm round my shoulder as we walked to the street and gave me his private office number. I refused his offer of a lift and walked back to my hotel, back to the shared room where Conscience waited.

CHAPTER THIRTEEN

I was in my office before the secretaries arrived the next morning. I made myself a cup of coffee which tasted marginally better than the one Pam had served and then opened the mail. It consisted mainly of cries for help from out of work actors and because I was unfamiliar with the British scene I read each one carefully. They were pretty evenly divided between the sexes but they shared a common note of hopelessness. Most of them enclosed photographs, the bent edges betraying the fact that they had faced rejection before, but there was one, all too obviously enlarged from a snapshot, which carried with it a credit of sad originality. The author of the letter, a middle-aged actress whose major experiences were confined to tours with ENSA during the war years, wrote touchingly of a daughter's recent death in a car accident, then added as a postscript, 'the enclosed likeness was taken only a week ago by the ex-mayor of Worthing.'

News of my arrival and impending production seemed to have escaped the notice of all the major agents, but there was a parcel of photographs from somebody calling herself Bunty Jane (Personal Management) Limited who not only offered me her entire list of exclusively nubile pin-ups but also, for good measure, threw in a semi-nude shot of herself. She was, I regret to say, the pick of her bunch.

Out of curiosity I rang Hogarth's private number. It went unanswered for fully half a minute and then a girl's voice came on the line.

'Mr Hogarth, please,' I said.

'Who is that, please?'

'Mr Warren, Mr Dick Warren.'

'Oh, yes, Mr Warren, I'm afraid Mr Hogarth is taking a meeting out of the office this morning. Would you like to leave a message?'

'Yes, just tell him I rang and tell him to eat lettuce for lunch.'

'Lettuce for lunch?'

'Yes, to get in training.'

'I see, Mr Warren. Right, thank you for calling.'

I was still grinning feebly to myself, with Bunty's photograph in my hand when a somewhat reproachful Pam knocked on my open door.

'I'm sorry, Mr Warren, I'd no idea you wanted to start work early this morning.'

'I didn't,' I said. 'But I have a wife who gets up at six and I hate being alone in hotel bedrooms.'

'Would you like a fresh cup of coffee?'

'No, and we must have a very serious talk about the future of coffee in this office. Neither of us has burst my taste buds yet. Go to Fortnum's and get some American and a Cona. You got some petty cash?'

'Yes, Mr Warren.'

'Well, charge it to the picture. And get me the latest *Spotlight*. Both volumes.'

'They're in the top drawer, sir.'

The phone on her desk rang and she hurried to answer it. She put her hand over the receiver and whispered through the open door.

'Mr Raven, sir.'

'Okay, don't be frightened of him, just put him through.'

I was forced to listen to a prolonged bout of coughing before Raven's voice became intelligible.

'Dick, where are you?'

'In the office.'

'You in the building?'

'No, I'm in my own office.'

'Far as I can see it's you and me against the rest. I'm the only person in this goddamn place.' He coughed and choked again. 'You happy where you are?'

'Fine, but I'll be happier when I start working.'

'That's right. But we can't rush it, Dick. Just so long as you're happy. I like to be sure my people are happy. You done any thinking about casting?'

'I'm looking at *Spotlight* now.'

'Let me try something on you. How about Mitchum for the father?'

'Can we afford him?'

'Look, you want Mitchum I'll get him for you.'

'Well, it's an interesting idea. I'll think about it.'

'That's right, you think about it. That's a great idea, eh, Mitchum?'

'You should get up early every morning,' I said.

'You want to have dinner with me and Kitty this evening?'

'Let me check the diary.' I put the phone close to the copy of *Spotlight* and leafed through the pages.

'No,' I said. 'I'm sorry, we can't to-night.'

'That's too bad. I'll have Kitty call Susan and fix a date. Anything else you want? My people taking care of you?'

'I'm just fine,' I said.

'Anything you want just call me. And give Robin a call. Keep him in the picture.'

I heard another phone ring in the background, and he was coughing again when he rang off to take it.

I spent the rest of the morning studying *Spotlight*, reminding myself of familiar faces and noting new ones. Casting a picture is not something I enjoy. Actors are too vulnerable and there's never enough work to go round.

Williams rang me just before lunch.

'I think I might have found the location you want.'

Smothering the excitement in my voice I asked him for more details.

'Governor, I don't want to raise your hopes, but the name checks out. I'd just like to make a few more enquiries.'

'How long will that take you?'

'Not long. It's not far away.'

'I'll wait in. Would you like to have lunch here, I'll send out for something.'

'Great. Anything'll do me.'

I sat chain-smoking, waiting for the past to catch up with me. I tried to think what I would do next if Williams's information proved correct. We think we lead when we are being led, and we make promises to ourselves to the extent that we hope. I warned myself, she's married, what makes you think you can go back and disturb somebody else's life? And I have to be honest, the idea that I would be hurt was more vivid to me than the possibility that I might hurt others. In love, they say, victory goes to the man who runs away, but hope is a ticket from the pawnbroker, and I was anxious to redeem it. When Pam brought in the sandwiches and the new Cona machine I scarcely saw her and she had to ask twice whether there was anything else I needed before I answered her.

Williams arrived after an interval of an hour, enjoying the role of private detective and betraying nothing as he entered the room.

'I never knew so many people had the vote,' he said. 'Those suffragettes did a marvellous job.'

'Tell me.'

'Well, I found a couple in Chelsea, but they were living in one of those big blocks of council houses and I didn't somehow think that was your scene.'

I munched on a sandwich, but didn't offer him one.

'So when I'd checked out all your suggestions, I just worked on one of my own hunches. I tried Hampstead. I don't know why, but I've always been lucky with locations in Hampstead.' He really was a very nice character. 'So I tried up there and came up with this.'

He handed me a piece of paper with an address on it.

'It's just behind Mount Vernon, near Frognal. Quite a nice looking pad. I checked with a few of the local shops, very casual, you know and always asking for the husband, not the female talent. Finally drew a full house at the newsagent.'

I noticed that in his excitement to impart the good news he had lapsed into a Cockney accent.

'And you think this could be it?' I said.

'Well I'd be very surprised if you didn't take the pot. I made out the husband was an old army mate whom I'd lost touch with, bought twenty Rothman, two Mars bars and a copy of *House and Garden*, all of which I put down to petty cash . . .'

'. . . Good thinking,' I said.

'Once a first assistant, always a grafter. Told him I was a

Tottenham fan, which is a lie, but a lucky shot in the dark, and I was in.'

'What did he tell you?'

'Been married about nine years, one child, a daughter, wife is apparently a good-looking bird, got a cook and a chauffeur, drives a Mini-Cooper she does, don't know about him, and answers to the name you gave me.'

He picked up a sandwich and munched happily.

'Well, that's marvellous, Stan, thanks a lot.'

I don't know why, but the mention of a child came as a shock to me. I had never considered such a possibility. Having a child was something we had often talked about, and for a time we had stopped taking precautions, willing ourselves to take deliberate chances, but it never happened. The fact that now she was the mother of somebody else's child chipped something away from hope.

'How much was the petty cash?' I said.

'Nothing, I was kidding. I enjoyed myself. Williams of the Yard.'

I stared at the piece of paper, then folded it carefully and inserted it into the back of a notebook.

'Well, I suggest you take the rest of the day off.'

'Nothing happening?'

'No. We're between takes at the moment, Stan. As you know there's been a change of management, and that always means aggravation. At the moment I don't rate our chances very high, but I could be wrong. The natives are a little restless, and the jungle drums are active. But I shall play *Sanders of the River*, keep out of the sun, and sweat it out.'

'Good picture, *Sanders of the River*. Leslie Banks and Paul Robeson.' I nodded.

'Nothing else you want me to do then?' he said, finishing his coffee.

'You can start work on the breakdown, but you don't have to come in to do that. Work from home and I'll call you when I need you.'

When he left I took out the piece of paper and stared at it for a long time. I had broken the code and now I had to sell the secrets.

CHAPTER FOURTEEN

That night I made love to Susan. I can't be clever where she and I were concerned, I can only describe things as they happened. In the impersonal loneliness of a hotel bedroom, the telephone—that savage destroyer—kept silent by instruction, a man who has shared nearly seven years with a woman does not need to counterfeit. We slid between cool sheets, our bodies damp from the bath and we made love. It was no more and no less than that.

Perhaps now, looking back, I can find darker reasons that I am not proud of, but that evening and that night it was more like the start of an affair than an expiation. Who was it who said 'such are the inexplicable workings of our hearts that it is with horrible anguish we leave those by whose side we have lived without pleasure'?

I understand Susan now and previous convictions have been shredded. For in many ways the end of a marriage resembles the last days of a beleaguered city when the occupants seek to destroy all the evidence. As the smoke rises, the good things are lost with the bad, but if ever one returns to poke through the cold ashes we can discern sometimes the faint outline of a single word that has somehow escaped the flames. And if I could put a word to Susan, it would be vulnerable.

'Such are the inexplicable workings of our hearts . . .' I wish I could remember what came before the quotation. So much of my life has been left on the cutting room floor, the images creased by indifference and yet now, when I want to remember, to straighten out the crumpled single frames that would give continuity and meaning to the remembrance of things past, I find I have lost the knack. Held up against a cold light the colours have faded, as if by some alchemy the process has gone into reverse, relentlessly annulling both shadow and substance until not even the negative remains, but only a transparent piece of film.

We made love. I have to believe that. Perhaps Susan had her reasons which were different from mine. Perhaps we shared the common guilt of familiarity, who knows? There are worse reasons in a marriage. I can describe my feelings now because I have forced myself to go back and sift through the ashes, but at the time I suppose I wanted to believe in a miracle, one last act of desperate tenderness that would somehow relieve me of guilt to come.

Lifting my head from the scented dampness of her throat I half expected her to read my thoughts, but she lay with her eyes closed, for in the aftermath of contentment Susan had no consciousness of love or sex, pleasure or pain, but only a sort of pliant innocence.

It was Raven who decided for me in the end. The telephone rang with that peculiar insistence one only finds in hotels. I let it ring for fully two minutes, elbowed above a sleeping, uncaring Susan, before anger made me reach across her to pull the receiver off the hook. Susan turned and curled out from under me while near the floor the timid voice of the girl operator spoke into the discarded bath towels. I reached down and lifted her apologies to my ear.

'I thought I gave instructions that we weren't to be disturbed?'

'I know, sir, I realise that, but the gentleman wouldn't take no for an answer. He insisted it was a matter of extreme urgency and said he'd take the responsibility.'

'What gentleman?'

'Just a minute, sir, I'll put him on.' She sounded close to tears.

'Dick, were you asleep?'

'Who is it?'

'Sam.'

'Sam who?'

'Sam Grotefend. Look, I'm sorry I disturbed you.'

'So am I,' I said. 'But you've disturbed me, so what is it?'

'Mr Raven wants to talk to you.'

The phone grated in my ear as it changed hands at the other end of the line. I heard a glass crash to the floor.

'Dick, we've been trying for an hour, what happened? You sick or something?'

'No,' I said. 'I just went to bed early.'

'Oh. Well, listen, I have to talk to you.'

I fumbled to find a cigarette, but my lighter was somewhere on the floor.

'What time is it?' I said.

'It's late, but not all that late. Look, I'm sorry to do this to you, but I have to see you to-night.'

'See me?'

'Yeah, I can't talk over the phone. I'll come over, what's your room number?'

'Look, is it that important? Susan's asleep.'

'It's that important. Give me the room number.'

'Three fourteen.'

'I'll be right over.'

I was ashamed of my own weakness when the line went dead. I turned back to Susan, hoping she would share my outrage, but she didn't stir. I groped for my lighter, lit the cigarette and stumbled to the bathroom to find a dressing-gown. My wrist-watch, still on the edge of the wash-basin, showed the time as one thirty. I found myself combing my hair and then wondered at the vanity that even anger doesn't totally destroy. The evidence of what I had wanted to call love plum-stained my neck and I pulled at the dressing-gown to conceal it. Then I went into the sitting room to await Raven's arrival.

He must have had his chauffeur standing by because he was pressing the doorbell less than eight minutes after he had hung up. When I opened the door he strode straight past me into the room without a greeting.

'Well, it'd better be important,' I said.

'I'll tell you how important it is—I'm fighting for my fucking life.'

'Is anybody else coming?'

'No, just you and me.'

'I thought the great Sam was with you.'

'Sam who?'

'That's the story of his life, everybody says Sam who?'

'Oh, him. I left him taking messages.'

He picked up the phone.

'Listen . . . Never mind that! Listen, I may get a transfer call long distance. Put it through, on this extension. This is Paul Raven. Ray-ven. You got that? Well, don't make any mistakes.'

I closed the communicating door to the bedroom and when I turned he was pouring himself a stiff drink.

'You want one?' he said.

'I might as well.'

He sloshed it into the glass and took a handful of ice which he seemed to crumble into both glasses. I took mine from him and sat down.

'Those assholes,' he said.

I knew him well enough to know it was a time for listening.

'D'you know what those assholes did in New York? They got themselves in a proxy fight. I told them, I warned them before I left, stay away from it. So what happened? They blew it, that's what happened. The shares dropped ten points to-day.'

'Well, they're greedy boys,' I said.

'They're not greedy, they're just four star idiots. D'you know what they did? They went into a proxy fight without counting. They ain't got enough stock, they don't control it.'

'So what's going to happen?'

'It's cold turkey time, they're going to be knocked out of the box, right through the ropes and into the street and what I've got to do is make sure they don't take me with them. Because my deal ain't signed. Well, it's signed but they got an out. I tell you, what with that and your goddamned telephone system over here I've been going out of my mind. What's this, Scotch? I don't drink Scotch. Who do you know in this town?'

'What d'you mean?' I said.

'D'you know any bankers?'

'I keep a couple of accounts, but I wouldn't say I know the chairman.'

'I've got to work fast before the Stock Market opens to-morrow.'

'Couldn't Cottram help?'

'Cottram? Are you kidding? He'd turn in his own mother if he thought she'd increase his golden handshake. I need money and I need it fast.'

'How much?' I said.

'I'm waiting to hear. Ten, maybe twenty million.'

'Oh, that sort of money,' I said.

The phone rang and he grabbed it.

'Stay off the line,' he screamed. 'Of course I'm here, where else would I be? So stay off the line.'

He slammed the receiver down again.

'Whoever hired him?'

'Who?'

'That publicity prick.'

'Oh, Sam Who you mean?'

'Ringing to see if I'm here. New York just called.'

He picked up the phone again.

'Listen, operator. You got New York for me? Raven, I told you. Well, I told somebody. They're just transferring it from Claridge's. What d'you mean, hang up? I want the goddamned call. All right, but you lose it and you're out of a job.'

He replaced the receiver yet again, but his hand hovered over it. I got the impression that it was hairier than usual. The receiver was to his ear again before it had rung once.

'Yes, speaking, put him on. Charlie?'

'Charlie, go ahead, I'm listening. Yeah, yeah, forget that, just give me the bottom line . . . What d'you mean they wouldn't talk to you? Who wouldn't talk to you? . . . Listen, you go back and tell those apes . . . What d'you think I'm paying you for? . . . Don't phone, go in there, kick the door off the hinges . . . Lay it on them . . . Charlie, don't give me advice, just do as I tell you.'

I turned to find Susan standing in the doorway.

'Who's shouting?' she said, half asleep. 'I heard somebody shouting.'

I steered her back into the bedroom. Raven seemed unaware of the interruption or Susan's nakedness. 'It's all right,' I said. 'Paul on the phone to New York and it's a bad line.'

I took her back to bed and tucked her in. She was asleep again before I left the room.

'Charlie,' Raven was shouting, 'you want for me to get another lawyer? Then get in there and sort it out.'

He listened for a few moments, gulping at the Scotch he

didn't want. 'Right. Right. That's what I'm saying. Okay, I don't care what it does to them. And call me back.'

He slammed the phone down.

'I don't trust that bastard, either. He's probably taking it from them on the side.'

'Anything new happened?' I said.

'No, they're all going ape-shit.'

'What d'you think'll be the next move?'

'They haven't got a chance, that bunch of amateurs. Why did I ever get into this situation?'

'Why did you?' I said.

He paced the room, ignoring me for a time. He even bit off the end of a monstrous cigar in approved B Picture fashion.

'I tell you one thing we're going to do—we're going to go ahead with your picture.'

'Well, that's good news.'

'It ain't going to be good news for them. How much did you say the budget was?'

'I've been aiming at just under three.'

'Right, you've got a deal at three. How soon can you start shooting?'

'As soon as you've okayed the script.'

'Who cares about the script, shoot what you like. Shoot Macy's Christmas Catalogue for all I care. You on a pay or play deal?'

'Yes,' I said.

'So you should worry, because I tell you how I'm going to get even with those mothers. They think they're so smart. I'm going to commit them to three pictures straight off.'

He picked up the phone again. 'Get me Claridge's,' he said. 'Paul Raven's suite.

'They're going to be in for twelve million dollars before I'm through. They won't know what time of day it is.'

The phone answered. 'Who's that?' I imagined the hapless Sam on the other end of the line presenting his tattered credentials yet again.

'Listen, first thing in the morning set up a press conference . . . Send telegrams to-night signed with my name. Tell them we've got an important announcement to make. And have the trades come in first, set up a breakfast with me. Don't worry what it's about, what d'you need to know for, just do it . . . No, you don't have to ask Bob Daniels, I'm telling you. You take your orders from me.'

And so it went on. He made half a dozen other calls, his language degenerating back to his slum origins. I watched with awful fascination, wide-awake now and in a way, against my better judgment, impressed with his naked drive. He was relentless, scattering any hint of rebellion like a madman at a ten-pin bowling alley. He got Cottram out of bed and tongue-lashed him like an office boy, but I was interested to note, as a war correspondent out of the line of fire, that the only person to whom he tempered his language was Hogarth. Old campaigners like Raven scent the young Turks. Purely by luck of circumstance, because I was in a position to further his plan of battle, I escaped that night. He unrolled the maps, pointed to the soft underbelly of the enemy and outlined where he was going to attack and why. He was Patton and he slapped the cry-babies unmercifully.

'Start taking on a crew to-morrow,' he said. 'And get a cast together. Sign everybody you can. Book studio space and make it firm, no pencil deals. I want it in dry ink.'

He suddenly and surprisingly relaxed and started to laugh.

'Dick,' he said, 'I just remembered something.'

'What?'

'When I got Cottram out of bed. He was so confused he thought he was talking to them. When I said Paul, he said "Have you told him yet?" So he's in the act, too—but not for long. I'll announce his retirement at the Press Conference.'

CHAPTER FIFTEEN

Mr Daniels and the hapless Grotefend had somehow managed to summon and assemble a representative selection of the London and Provincial press by eleven o'clock the following morning. One of the conference rooms in the Hilton had been made available, and despite a practically sleepless night I entered it with bright eyes—my hangover dispersed by anticipation.

I made my way to the small platform. Cottram, Hogarth and Daniels were waiting behind it. I had seen Grotefend on the way in, anxiously reassuring the Press that the bar would be opened immediately following the announcement.

Cottram was blandly good humoured: puzzled but not dismayed before the event. He greeted me warmly. 'Well, quite a turn-out,' he said.

'It always is,' I said, 'for Peace in Our Time.'

'Quite.'

The innuendo, feeble though it was for that time of morning, had sailed right over his balding head. I noticed he was even wearing a carnation. Hogarth presented his Gioconda smile and his handshake lacked muscle.

'I trust you slept well?' I said.

'Me? Yes. I appear to be the only person in London who did.'

I turned to Daniels. He seemed reasonably presentable for a gentleman of his humble calling.

'We've never been introduced officially, have we?'

'No, Bob Daniels.'

'Oh, sorry,' Cottram said.

'You obviously made some profit for the GPO during the night.'

'Yeah.'

He exuded a prophylactic lack of interest in the whole proceedings and was obviously miffed at having lost the initiative.

Grotefend came up to the platform and started tapping the microphone. 'Testing, testing, testing,' he said.

'Okay,' Daniels said. 'It's not a moonshot. Relax. Everybody here?'

'Just one or two of the magazines missing.'

'Any sign of the great man yet?'

'No,' Cottram said. 'I believe he's still having breakfast, isn't he?'

'Yeah.'

Daniels turned to Grotefend, who was unravelling the microphone cord. 'Check and see if he's left.'

'Any idea,' Cottram said, 'what he's going to say?'

I looked him straight in the eyes: something told me not to be too innocent before the event. 'You know Paul better than me. He's one of the great ad libbers. The only thing he told me was he was going to announce some pictures.'

'Pictures?' Cottram looked offended.

'So I gathered.'

'You mean *pictures*?'

'Seems a reasonable proposition,' Hogarth said. 'After all we are a motion picture company.' He allowed me to see his smile, and I wondered how much he had found out. To have Raven do his work for him was, I suspected, a windfall ahead of its time.

Cottram looked at his watch and I guessed at his thoughts. But Raven, who lived by the phone, always knew when the rest of the world was sleeping, and Cottram was lost before he started.

A few flashbulbs went off at the back of the room and we all took our places on the seats at the back of the platform as Raven walked like royalty to the microphone. He looked remarkably spruce and affable. I glanced at Cottram: he was sitting upright in his chair, staring straight ahead at the broad back of his one-man firing squad. Hogarth, on the other hand, was being studiously casual. Daniels was waiting to introduce Raven, but was waved aside.

'If I need introductions at my time of life,' Raven said into the microphone, 'then I guess show business is in a bad way.' He got his first laugh from the back of the room, and I knew we were in for a performance. Even his voice was different, slightly humble, pitched lower than usual and with most of the grosser American accents flattened out.

'Ladies and gentlemen,' he began, 'firstly let me thank you for taking the trouble to attend at such short notice. It's much appreciated. I'm not going to keep you long, but I hope I'm going to give you some good copy. As you can see I'm speaking off the cuff . . . but not, I hasten to add, off the record. Please feel free to quote me, because if you don't I may not open the bar.'

I found myself admiring the technique, for the British Press pride themselves on being hard to seduce, and yet I could see quite a few smiling faces in the front row and already people were taking notes.

'One thing I like about the English Press, and that is they only get smashed . . . drunk, I should have said . . . *after* they've filed the story. In New York they prefer to arrive crocked . . . sorry, smashed . . . and sober up during the interview.'

This drew a small round of applause. Cottram's face (and I angled myself to keep it in view) was a study in discontent. His own conversations with the Press were invariably monosyllabic and I could see that he was already regretting the fact that he didn't have an interpreter.

'But to be serious and to get down to the nitty gritty, I'm talking to you to-day as somebody who is not only proud to be the head of a global company totally committed to the conception of entertainment, but as a showman who has gone through a few hoops in his time. We read a lot about the fortunes, or lack of them, of our industry and there's no point in pretending that we haven't been going through a rough patch. But that's yesterday's news as far as I'm concerned. The company I represent not only believes in the continuing future of the motion picture industry, but they've sent me over to put my mouth where their money is. We're in films and we're going to stay in films. We're in films and we're in Britain making films.'

I am not going to say that his speech was riveting, because it wasn't. The film industry has a thesaurus of platitudes that it refers to on every public occasion. The results fool nobody, but for reasons I can never fully comprehend, they inevitably command space. Raven's performance that morning—and it was a carefully calculated performance—was larger than life, and yet he fooled enough of his audience enough of the time. He threw a bone here and a bone there, and everybody got something according to their needs and went away happy. It had passed a morning, filled the odd paragraph, and aided the destruction of a few livers.

'I'm not going to give you good people the usual publicity handout,' he said, using the well-tried reversal technique. 'You wouldn't believe it, and I couldn't say it. I've been on the outside, too, remember? and this isn't a revival meeting, I'm not trying to convert anybody. All I'm saying to you is that this company is going to make pictures. Some of them will be good pictures that nobody'll go and see, some of them will be lousy and they'll be standing in queues. Who knows? we might even get lucky and turn in a great picture, but you can't win 'em all going in, you can only try. We're going to do more than try, and we're content to leave the verdict to you.'

He stopped there and looked round for me, and my blood froze. I have a horror of public compliments, especially from somebody like Raven.

'Now I don't make pictures personally,' he said. 'I just sign the cheques. I leave the creative part of it to the creative people, and we're proud to-day to be associated with one of the finest talents this industry has ever produced. He's a great picture maker and he's a native of your country and he needs no introduction from me. I refer, of course, to Mr Richard Warren.'

I stood up briefly and nodded, acutely embarrassed.

'Mr Warren will shortly start shooting on a multi-million dollar film entitled *The Unknown Warrior* from the best selling novel of the same name by Charles Maxwell. This will be the first of three pictures, to be made in this country, with British technicians, British know-how, and is intended to be positive proof that my company thinks that the scene is still right here. They'll be international films aimed at the world market. Now any questions so far?'

'How much did you say the budget was?' a voice shouted.

'Three million. Yes?'

'Have you cast anybody yet?'

'Mr Warren is having conversations with top talent. Don't press me to name them yet because they'll ask for more money. You have a question, young lady?'

A woman got up wearing peace beads.

'Yes, Mr Raven. Could you tell us why your company, which previously announced that they were cutting back on European production has suddenly had a change of heart?'

'They didn't have a change of heart, they had a change of studio head.' Raven was enjoying himself now. 'Next?'

'Are your films going to follow any particular trend?'

'Such as?'

'Well a lot of people over here are concerned with the emphasis on sex.'

'It's here to stay,' Raven said. 'But if you mean are we in business to make a cheap buck on pornography, the answer is no.'

'Can you give us the names of the other films?'

'*Roads to Glory* and *The Brickman Affair*.'

Cottram was looking at his watch again. I saw him lean over and whisper something to Daniels, who shook his head. It was impossible to tell what Hogarth was thinking.

Raven survived the questioning with something approaching honour, never revealing any specific facts that could later be used to reduce his own case, but at the same time spinning a web of half-truths and convincing possibilities that could only embarrass New York. He was careful to flatter the company without naming any names, treading, as they say, on eggs, without ever once cracking the shells.

And he timed it to perfection. When he felt that he had gone far enough to hang everybody but himself, he skilfully withdrew behind his humble, sincere mask, using the lower registers of his voice.

'Now, ladies and gentlemen, just before we repeal prohibition, I have one other announcement which I have deliberately kept until now because I wanted to pay tribute to one man who is with us to-day and without whom this industry would have been the poorer.'

It took a conscious effort of will for me not to look at Cottram. I didn't even trust myself to light a cigarette.

'He's always been a modest man, but he's served this industry and my company well over the years and his contribution has been invaluable.

'We're an emotional industry, because we deal in emotions, and you must forgive me if my words to-day strike you as being a little . . . what shall we say? . . . sentimental. But I feel sentimental. And at the risk of embarrassing you and him, I want to take time out to tell you a few things about Arnold Cottram, our present Managing Director.'

It was safe to look at Cottram at this point. If he had any premonition, then he concealed it well. I would like to give him credit for masterly self-control, but I suspect that his life-long devotion to complacency did not desert him in the seconds before the blow fell. He had sat at the top table at so many charity luncheons when the pickings were ripe, listening through a haze of cigar smoke to his meandering band of equals murder the English language whilst evoking his name. He deserved what he got, but perhaps not the way he got it. It was his misfortune to be dealt his last hand of cards by a professional. Unbandaged, unprepared, with no priest close enough to give comfort, he met his public death with the same incomprehension he had always brought to the boardroom.

'Arnold has not only given a lifetime of service to our industry, but he has always found enough room in his heart and in his pocketbook to embrace other causes. I've known him a long time and I respect him greatly. I respect him and I shall miss him, we all will.'

Turning round, he squeezed the trigger with a smile.

'Arnold, your retirement as Managing Director will come as a shock to a great number of people, all of whom are your friends. But as you have often said, this is a young industry and age has to make way for youth. You're stepping down, but if I know you, you'll still be around to give freely and generously—as you've always done—of your advice and wide experience to those who come after. I thank you and I say God Bless you.'

If I had been shooting the scene, I would have asked the actor playing Cottram for a second take. His disbelief was too real. He sat motionless while Raven led the applause. He managed to acknowledge the applause, but he was like the understudy suddenly forced to take over in the middle of the play, and there was no prompter in the corner.

Raven even succeeded in surprising me with the *coup de grâce*. 'I know Arnold joins me in wishing his successor Mr Robin Hogarth, who has come up the hard way, every possible good luck. Ladies and gentlemen the bar is now open.'

A few journalists made their way forward to the platform to get the few stuttered quotes that Cottram was capable of, but the majority of them made straight for the drinks. Raven posed for photographs, standing between Cottram and Hogarth and clasping their hands. He didn't miss a trick.

Grotefend found his way to me.

'Jesus,' he said, 'did you know that was coming?'

'No,' I lied. Daniels appeared at his elbow and hurried him away. I found myself shaking hands with Hogarth.

'Congratulations,' I said.

'Well, thank you. I'm as amazed as you are.'

'I'm not amazed. I always knew you'd make it.'

It was a slip and he was on to it immediately.

'Did Paul tell you last night?'

'No, I didn't mean that. I was just being genuine.'

'I don't think Arnold knew,' he said, 'or if he did he didn't let on to me.'

I escaped as soon as I could, having avoided less skilfully than Raven the questions put to me, at the bar. I had no real sympathy for Cottram, but even as a spectator I felt soiled. Hogarth came up to me once more and said that Raven wanted a production meeting after lunch; he had already slipped into the emperor's new clothes and decided they fitted him and his manner hinted at condescension to come. I knew he could dispense bread, but I wondered how he would distribute the cake.

CHAPTER SIXTEEN

Susan was avid for the full gory details when she arrived home from the studio that evening and I dutifully acted out Raven's speech for her further amusement. Apparently the news had been received on her set with refreshing cynicism and one wit had asked for two minutes' silence.

The evening papers had given some space to the announcements, concentrating mostly on the financial implications for the home industry. Poor Cottram had been ignored in one and given two lines in the other, but doubtless the eulogies for him over the open grave would be given proper prominence in the Trades.

I had spent the entire afternoon in Raven's office. The production meeting had progressed fitfully, interrupted by a constant stream of incoming long distance calls. I wasn't privileged to hear all of them, and retired to Hogarth's new quarters. All traces of Cottram's previous occupancy had been removed whilst the Press conference was in progress, for Raven was not a man to do things by half measures.

Gerry Blechman joined Hogarth and me to swop obituaries and not for the first time I found myself impressed by his ability to remain indifferent to the sight of blood.

'When Paul moves, he moves fast, you know.'

'How are New York taking it,' Hogarth asked.

'Well, with New York you got to figure the odds. I mean, it wasn't kosher, maybe, but on the other hand, they ain't going to lose any sleep about Cottram. Where Paul has boxed them in is on the pictures. Now they got to make up their minds one way or the other.'

'Yes, I see,' Hogarth said, but he didn't, he was still fishing

'See if they cancel out now they gotta hit bottom, but on the other hand who's going to bid for a company that just committed to twelve million dollars?'

'It's clever,' Hogarth said. 'Don't you think so, Dick?'

'I don't know,' I said. 'It's too clever for me.'

'It'll all be over soon,' Blechman said. 'It's chopped chicken liver.'

I could sense Hogarth trying to decipher Blechman's culinary code. I was familiar with the that-and-two-cents-will-get-you-on-the-subway-type of dialogue affected by Hollywood con men, but to Hogarth it was still another world, a world he was desperate to enter.

'Has anybody seen Arnold since this morning?' he said.

'He's taken care of,' Blechman said. 'Nobody walks for nothing. Listen, Arnold Cottram was a well meaning prick, that's all. Paul made it easy for him, he gave him a nice little pat on the back in front of all your newspaper people, and now the lawyers'll go in and he'll end up with some bread in the bank. We should be that lucky when our time comes.'

We were pondering this simple approach to life when Raven called us back. He had reverted to type by now, presumably because of his various shouted exchanges with New York, and the secretaries looked close to tears.

'How soon can you go, Dick?'

'Well, if I burn the midnight oil, I suppose I could start shooting second unit in six weeks.'

'Right. Has he got a production account open?'

'No, but I'll take care of that,' Hogarth said.

'And get on to the casting.'

'D'you still want to me to investigate Mitchum?'

'Mitchum?'

'Yes, that's who we were discussing the other day.'

'You may have been discussing him, I wasn't. Go with some new kids. Check with Kitty, she's got some ideas. The important thing is to get the show on the road.'

He picked up the phone the moment it rang. 'No, tell them to go screw,' he said. 'And bring that letter in, I want to sign it.

'Gerry, you and me we got to take a trip to New York. Find out what pictures are playing and book the flight.'

'You want Jumbo?'

'I'll take the best picture.'

'That makes sense,' Gerry said. He disappeared. The phone rang again.

'Has to be New York,' Raven said, then waved us to stay.

'Yes, Sol,' he said patiently. 'Sol . . . we've been through it. You don't want to stay in the ball game you shouldn't have made the first pitch . . . What're you talking about? How was I to know you're in the middle of a take-over? Did you tell me? . . . Sol, I'm asking you a question . . . Did you pick up the phone and tell me you were going to sell the company? Right. So what's your beef? Sol, don't talk to me like a man with a paper asshole. Get off the pot or piss in it.'

He put the phone down, vastly amused. 'That's the best day's work I ever did.'

Hogarth was smiling and nodding, but his thoughts were elsewhere and I wondered if Raven had made his first mistake. Demanding no loyalties, Hogarth gave none. His career as Crown Prince had just ended, and he wanted to keep the throne. I had no doubt that the moment Raven was safely in the air, Hogarth would be making his own calls to New York.

'So, we're all set then?' Raven said, looking in my direction.

'Yes, I'll get the thing rolling.'

'Keep Robin posted.'

'Of course.'

'I'll only be over there a couple of days.'

The girl came in with some letters for him to sign and I edged to the door.

'What sort of story is *The Unknown Warrior*?'

I stopped.

'Well, you read it, didn't you?'

'Sure, but it was some time ago and I just need a refresher.'

'It's a love story.'

'Well, what would you say? Give me another picture it's like.'

Hogarth was looking at his shoes. 'I don't know how you'd tell it in *Reader's Digest*, but I suppose the nearest comparison would be *The Spy Who Came in From the Cold*.'

'That was a good picture. Burton and Taylor . . . No, not Taylor.'

'Claire Bloom,' I said.

'Right. So, if I said it was another *Spy* I wouldn't be too far out?'

'It has certain vague similarities, but I was really talking about the mood. The plot is entirely different.'

'Okay, Dick, have a good time and I'll see you when I get back. Take Kitty out to dinner.'

I walked away from that room trembling with my own lack of courage. I was living in a world inhabited by neolithic madmen and I was committed to make a film costing three million dollars for a man who patently had never read a word of the script and who had only allowed it to go forward to satisfy some predatory feeling of revenge. We had all become so conditioned to the asylum that such acts were not only tolerated, but in varying degrees, encouraged. My own craven acceptance was a case in point. I despised myself. I stood by the lift shaft wondering what slow erosion had brought me to this cave in my life, where such talents as I possessed could be bought in such debased coinage. Self-justification hung like a button from a single thread. I wanted to make that film for a variety of reasons, and since I want this to be an honest account, I might as well admit that one of those reasons—perhaps, at that moment, the only one worthy of examination—was that it would keep me in London. We think we are consumed with lofty ideals, but when we believe we know our minds best, that is the moment that our hearts betray us. Isn't the real answer that in the very moment when we cannot be reconciled to the actions of those we most despise, we still have the capacity to deceive and betray ourselves?

CHAPTER SEVENTEEN

When eventually I saw Alison again after an interval of ten years I was with Susan.

I can't remember in any detail the frenzy of the week that followed Raven's announcement and departure. True, my diary shows a secretary's list of appointments and meetings every quarter of an hour, but there is nothing on the page to indicate what I really felt, how I reacted to the scores of faces that came and went. I interviewed crew and actors, pored over budgets and schedules (which are mysteries indeed to the uninitiated; I can read them like shorthand when my professional life demands and I have often wished that I could plot my emotional life with like accuracy, for one is often compelled to shoot a film out of continuity, beginning at the middle, progressing to the end and leaving the opening shots until last. It seems unnecessarily complicated to the outsider, but it has a logic as complex as a chess game, it is a challenge I welcome and if, as sometimes happens, I am permitted the luxury of shooting every scene in its correct order, then the major part of the excitement is denied me and I feel cheated).

So I must tell this part of the story as I would approach a sequence in one of my films. I existed on a diet of coffee and cigarettes. I approved sketches for the costume designs before I had put an actor's face to the role those designs were intended to embellish. I was clinical towards some, compassionate towards others, wet-nurse, dictator, family doctor, religious maniac. Events and decisions were jumbled, threaded together by other willing fellow-maniacs infected by the common needle. It's no use trying to explain how a film is put together, for it doesn't make sense even to those who perpetrate the many acts of chaos. The urgency is fabricated and yet necessary, the emotions generated are flamboyantly phoney and yet sincere and the general disorder is in fact a scrupulous attention to detail.

As always my band of fanatics included several characters of startling originality. The Art Director I finally selected, a man called Jimmy Wellard, could only work if his pet parrot was allowed the freedom of his drawing board. 'When she craps on a design, I know I'm getting somewhere,' he said. A homosexual, he lived quite openly and happily with a postman. 'My dear,' he would say, 'I've always been potent first thing in the morning. We met over a registered letter and the marriage was consummated three special deliveries later. It was the uniform that attracted me.' His friend, whom the parrot hated, would sometimes come and sit in his office, consuming endless mugs of tea and sweating profusely. 'He advises me on doors,' Jimmy said. 'He's infallible on doors.'

My first assistant, a Cockney, George Murdock, seduced the continuity girl the first day they both started work. 'I can't concentrate if I'm not getting it regularly,' he said, 'and I'm too old to chase it, so I put it under personal contract. Besides which, it means the call sheets'll be accurate, because if they aren't I can ruck her in bed.' Like most real Cockneys he could switch personalities to fit every occasion and was totally content with his lot, having reached the peak of his ambition. Stories about him were legendary. He was reputed once to have gone up to a member of the Royal Family who had been visiting a studio set, handed the guest a chipped mug of tea and a cheese roll and stage-whispered, 'Do anything you like Your Royal Highness but don't rabbit while the red light's up.' He was tireless and brilliant at his job.

I had also collected a lighting cameraman the size of Toulouse Lautrec whose first requirement on any new film was a pair of antique library steps to enable him to look through the camera. Like most of his breed he derided weather reports, child actors and sound crews, in that order. His name was Bill Mason.

We shared a much-needed fatalism during that first week of pre-production. So much of what we planned and plotted into the early hours of every morning seemed hopelessly beyond our collective reach.

For people who are accustomed to long periods of unemployment, film technicians, surprisingly and loyally, never 'work to rule' or connive at delaying tactics when an actual job comes their way. Fired by Raven's urgency, I was able to infect them with it and we swarmed across the virgin breakdown charts like demented locusts.

I saw little or nothing of Susan for days on end, for she was usually asleep when my sessions ended and had departed for the studio before I was awake in the mornings. So when I awoke one day, the day I had intended to use to search for London locations (for by now we had decided to switch the locale of the film from one of the Iron Curtain countries because of lack of preparation time) and found Susan's head on the next pillow, I stared at her without comprehension. I suppose the hotel room contributed to the general unreality of my existence during that period, but I swear to you that I had the feeling for a few moments that I had been sleeping next to a complete stranger. It was like the remembered nightmare of a youthful sexual encounter when, after a beery party, you fight back to consciousness in a room you have never seen before to find you have shared a bed with your best friend's mistress. I am told that such things are commonplace today and that to actually make the girl you take to the party is considered very old-fashioned and dull. I'm sure I am old-fashioned, but I am glad I didn't by-pass the thrill of the chase in my own youth, for it seems to me that raw sex in a drugged state without any semblance of tenderness or concern before or after the act is a more squalid form of dullness.

Susan opened her eyes to find me propped over her on my elbows.

'What is it?' she said.

'Nothing. I didn't know where I was, that's all.'

'What time is it?'

I groped for my wristwatch and traced the hour and minute hands like a child learning the basic rules.

'Well, my watch says nine thirty, but it must have stopped.'

I rang down, but the girl on the switchboard confirmed it—it was nine thirty.

'My God!' I said, 'you've overslept. What time was your call?'

'I'm not on call.'

'What?'

'I've got the day off.'

'You've got what?'

'Look, go back to sleep, darling, and I'll tell you later.'

'I can't go back to sleep,' I said indignantly. 'I've got to go location hunting.'

I staggered into the bathroom and shaved my fatigue-swollen face while Susan ordered breakfast. I actually sprayed hair lacquer on my cheeks instead of cologne and it took three cups of coffee to restore me to anything approaching coherence.

'I thought I'd come with you,' Susan said.

'Where?'

'Wherever you're going.'

'I don't know where we're going yet, we're just looking, that's the whole point of a location hunt.'

'You must have some idea.'

'Yes, of course, we've got some idea, the general area.'

'Well, I don't mind, I'd just like to be with you.'

The innocent words, repeated here, seem totally devoid of any sinister significance, and indeed, to be fair to Susan, I believe that when she spoke them she had no inkling of my deceit. Why should she? At that time my betrayal was all in the mind, but I remember hearing those words with a sense of monstrous distortion, as though somebody had suddenly turned the volume knob to the limit. My mind was instantly cleared of everything except an instinct for self-preservation.

'Wouldn't you like to do that?' Susan said.

'Do what?'

'See something of me.'

'Yes, of course. I'm sorry, you've just broken my dream, I was thinking of something quite different.'

'Well, don't tell me about it. I hate hearing other people's dreams.'

'I've got to leave almost immediately,' I said.

'I'll be ready.'

I thought with sudden panic, she suspects, she knows something, but reason returned to dismiss the fear immediately. I realised that my stumbled invention of the broken dream was not a lie, that my waking thoughts had contained the start of the affair. I had gone to sleep with a plan half-formed and during some portion of the night the virus had incubated. Now the fever raged. I remembered that I intended to use the location hunt as a cover to seek out the house where Alison was reported to live.

As I said before, my actions had little or no continuity. Like some exaggerated club-sandwich, my life contained a variety of conflicting emotions; in order to satisfy one hunger, I had to swallow the whole concoction. Consumed with the need to advance the film, I had still found time to plan the order of my own release. One urgency counterbalanced the other, and I had merely been waiting with the cunning of a prospective lover to find the perfect excuse.

Now Susan threatened to upset everything. I thought. I've got to begin again, and it was like a child's annoyance, containing more fear than hate. Set down here, so long after the event, it all seems so petty and unreal, but I was in the first grips of an illness and reason was not uppermost in my mind. For of course had I reasoned it out, my knowledge of Susan, that special knowledge that comes with any relationship which has survived that strange intimacy called marriage, would have told me my fears were exaggerated. She had no reason to suspect me of anything. On the contrary, I now realise that her offer to accompany me that morning was probably nothing more than an expression of her own guilt. I had forgotten that in marriage we hurt through weakness more often than through calculation.

CHAPTER EIGHTEEN

We set off in convoy, Susan, Jimmy Wellard, the parrot and I in the leading hire car, with George Murdock following under his own steam, and Bill Mason and Stan Williams behind him in another hire car. There was a festive air about the whole proceedings in contrast with the weather which was overcast.

Wellard had already done a preliminary reconnaissance and sat in the front seat, the parrot perched on his shoulder, consulting his maps and pointing out possibilities. The parrot fixed a judicial eye on Susan and from time to time gave a Fascist salute with one leg.

'I hope you like parrots,' Wellard said when greeting Susan outside the hotel, 'because she's very sensitive to atmosphere.'

We made a series of choices, Susan and I remaining in the car while Wellard and George went to haggle terms with the various owners. They were gifted salesmen, obtaining permissions by a mixture of blatant flattery, cheerful lies and cynical exaggeration, and we left several bewildered householders in our wake.

'I always give them something to look forward to,' George said. 'If I'm up against a bloke I tell him there's a fair chance that Liz Taylor will be in it, and if it's a bird then I throw in Cary Grant. You'd be surprised at the number of pictures they haven't made. Course, when you're dealing with the Law a few oncers is favourite.'

We had lunch by the river at Hammersmith where the parrot influenced people but failed to make friends. 'She's very useful when I'm in the mood for a little rough trade,' Wellard confided. 'Lorry drivers, for instance, are always very curious for parrots.' Susan listened, fascinated, for like most women I know she was attracted to amusing queers and they sensed this and relaxed. She was soon discussing clothes with Wellard, and he made sketches for her on the pub menu, signing one she said she wanted to keep.

Stan and I wandered off to relieve ourselves and stood blinking in the acrid stench of stale urine which is still a feature of so many English pub loos.

'Where next, governor?' he said.

'What's next on the list?'

'Well, we've more or less exhausted the list, but I thought perhaps you had some ideas of your own.'

'We might take a look at Hampstead. Around there anyway.'

'Funny you should say that, governor,' he said, concentrating on the task in hand.

I thought, the setting's right for conspiracy, furtive talk of adultery and, in the distance, a church bell tolling: the sacred and the profane. Perhaps men are compelled to turn inwards in such places, seeking the comfort of crudeness which sometimes can make life tolerable. A virgin whitewashed wall in a pub lavatory is too much for some, they have to scar it with a written offering to the priapic god. In the war years it was always Kilroy who admitted to the majority of prodigious sexual feats, and despite the inevitable genital elephantiasis, he managed to retain an engaging personality. But we have moved on from Kilroy and now the writing on the wall has a bleaker despair: even obscenity has become violent. The unknown artists share a common need to mutilate; the absurdly voluptuous females are violated time and time again as the anonymous Biro rapists superimpose their fantasies until the sadism at eye level becomes a running sore in the brickwork. There is no compassion, no humour, just a phallic dagger plunged into the suppurating womb.

'I'll lead them in my car,' Stan said, as we rejoined the others. Susan took my arm. 'He's just told me something incredible,' she said. 'Did you know he lives with a *postman*? Isn't it incredible? I think he's so funny. Is he any good at his job?'

'Brilliant.'

'Not so sure about the parrot, though.'

We drove off again and on the way to Hampstead I started to discuss graffiti with Wellard. He claimed to have once known a screenwriter who had collected actual specimens, literally chipping out sections of walls and tiles and carting them home. I remarked that I had never actaully caught a graffiti artist at work, but Wellard countered with a second anecdote.

'I was once in a cottage in Sloane Square . . .'

'Cottage?' Susan said.

'Men's loo, dear, vernacular for, not the cottages with roses round the door. Anyway, I was going about me legitimate business for once, just dying to spend a penny in fact, and as I went down the steps I saw this old character—and I mean he was ancient enough to be my grandfather—in the act of putting pen to plaster. Well, he heard the tread of my heavy feet and must have thought it was Lily Law, and was out the other end before you could say "consenting adult". Naturally, Mrs Wellard being a curious girl, I went to see what sonnet he had conjured up. And what do you think he'd written?'

Susan shook her head.

'Well half-written, because it was unfinished. He had started to write "I am an eighteen year old guardsman . . ."'

The parrot gave its Fascist salute and hissed.

'That story always offends her. She likes happy endings. Where are we going by the way? Does our fearless Production Manager know where we're heading for?'

'I thought we'd look around Hampstead.'

'British Occupied Hampstead, or the Vale of Health?'

'I'm not quite sure,' I said. 'Stan seemed to have some ideas.'

'Probably ideas above his station,' Wellard said. 'What're you looking for in particular?'

'Well we still haven't found a house for Carson, the art dealer.'

'You see him as Hampstead, do you? I would have thought it was a bit beneath Carson, unless of course you're playing him as a Socialist art dealer.'

Susan had her arm through mine and was holding my hand. I felt I was taking an insurance cardiograph, that moment when the contact pads have been fixed into place and you hold your breath hoping that the fear won't register on the machine.

'It's a long time since I've been up there, but there used to be some splendid houses in Spaniard's Row.'

Wellard shrugged. 'Been used, dear. They crop up so often in British films that the critics are getting confused. Still, I mean, it's up to you, you're the director. I can only be responsible for my own bad taste.'

Susan gripped my hand. I stared hard at the back of the chauffeur's neck and we both suppressed our amusement. We were close at that moment, closer than we had been for many a month.

'What d'you feed your parrot on, Jimmy?' Susan said.

'Gossip, dear.'

'How old is he?'

'She dear. She. And she doesn't give her age, like me.'

We had been halted at the lights at Swiss Cottage. I couldn't recognise any of the old landmarks, the name over the Underground Station was the only positive clue. Was it fear or excitement that made me relinquish Susan's hand and reach for a cigarette as we accelerated up the hill—or the sudden lurching uncertainty as to what lay ahead? As though reading my thoughts the ageless parrot crossed Wellard's shoulders deliberately and fixed me with an accusing eye. I blew smoke towards it and it ruffled its feathers and defecated.

In the leading car, Stan played the role of accomplice with some skill. Perhaps he had done the same thing, in some form or another, for a succession of visiting directors—one should never suppose that any situation is unique. We travelled to the Heath first and looked at various houses bordering it, then went to Highgate before returning to the fashionable part of Hampstead proper.

'Useless,' Jimmy kept murmuring, but we ignored him.

I knew the address off by heart and as we got closer I felt more and more a stranger to myself. It's easy enough, I suppose, to put fictitious characters into such an episode; the dramatist and the novelist can manipulate shadow and substance to suit the plot. But in real life the plot is never apparent, we are like small part actors not important enough to be given the entire script; all we get is the cue sheet for one scene at a time. Sitting there with the warmth of Susan's thigh against my own as the last seconds of security ticked away on the hired-car's clock, it occurred to me that perhaps it would have been better to have let love stay stationary in my mind.

There is always a laziness about a street full of rich houses, and as we turned the corner and I caught my first glimpse, looking past the unblinking parrot through the dusty windscreen, the only person I saw was a chauffeur standing by a new Rolls wringing out a chamois leather. The image suggested a deserted film set because I cannot avoid my own visual shop. We travelled slowly, for Stan was dictating the pace of the convoy. It was like the schoolboy trick of walking against the movement of an escalator. It probably sounds callous, unbelievable almost, but I realised that what wounded me most as a man, nourished me as an artist. The mind works on so many levels at once. In pain of childbirth a woman can remember how the midwife has combed her hair, during a soliloquy the actor playing Hamlet can note a bored face three rows back and sandwich in a sigh of hate. So we lingered, so we might have passed, sealed figures moving through a landscape of well-kept brick which effectively blocked out the limitations of human love. The profane memory was jumbled with the sacred, for I said a prayer, silently pleading for self-deception to end. As if in answer, Susan leant forward as we passed the Rolls and my first sight of Alison after ten whole years was through the strands of my wife's hair—a tenuous net of safety to mask my fall.

One cannot improvise upon reality itself. She seemed to have become very much thinner. If she was beautiful still I was not to be convinced in those brief moments. She had a child with her that I took to be her own, and she paused at the gate of the house to remonstrate with a reluctant dog. I photographed everything from a rigid camera angle, for I found myself incapable of moving my head. As we drew level the child noticed the parrot inside our car and pointed. The shutter jammed; I was conscious of nothing, I dared not look and it was a child's laughter that pushed me farther back into the past, a sound without a face, for by now they were behind us and Wellard was saying, 'Have you seen enough?' as though by malicious chance he shared my secret.

Filled with a good enough substitute for hate, I did not trust myself to answer him. He found nothing unusual in this, for directors are by tradition enigmatic and difficult.

'We ought to have a Rolls,' Susan said. 'Wouldn't you like a Rolls, Jimmy?'

'Are you offering me one, darling?'

'I'm not, no.'

'Then don't let's talk about it. The only time I shall have a Rolls to call my own is when they take me out in the oblong box.'

I felt Susan make an involuntary movement, for any talk of death, however vague, troubled her. She moved her hand to find mine again and the stone on her engagement ring caught in the cloth of my jacket. It reminded me, more forcibly than anything else that had happened that day, how much, out of habit, she depended on me.

CHAPTER NINETEEN

One remembers a past love affair only to confirm one's present loneliness. God knows, to an outsider, the idea of presenting myself as a lonely man during the next week or so would have seemed ludicrous. My every waking hour was spent in contact with other people, many of them physically attractive people, for I was interviewing actors and actresses. The cartoonist's standby for an otherwise dull day is often the casting couch. It is not an article of furniture I have ever depended upon for sexual success, but there is no escaping the fact that in an overcrowded profession talent and good looks are not synonymous, and afternoon pleasures are exchanged for a few days work, sometimes not even that, just the promise of further consideration. Perhaps I've seen the reflection of the firing squad in too many eyes advancing towards my desk to want to pull that particular trigger, or perhaps it's because I find most actors sad, living as they do between to-morrow's hope and yesterday's scrap book. To fail without talent is the price of arrogance, but to struggle against the odds when talent is there is wormwood.

My public face betrayed little. I was even photographed for the gossip columns. I came across a faded cutting the other day, book-marked between the pages of an unfinished novel, and it was like looking at somebody who never existed—a war-time snapshot of a dead airman on the mantelpiece in a stranger's house. I remember thinking at the time that such transient exposure would advance my cause. I thought, she'll see this and seek me out again. But she must have noted other comings and goings during the decade since the end of the affair and done nothing, and my expectations were short-lived.

I went back and dined at the same restaurant on three occasions, but they didn't play their part in the conspiracy: the menu never changed, the first opening flush of politeness had gone from the waiters and I could not counter Susan's puzzled complaint—only new lovers can tolerate a combination of noise and indifferent food.

One morning, I remember, in what I thought was a sudden flash of inspiration, I invented a toothache and demanded an urgent appointment with a dentist Alison and I had once shared. I suppose I imagined that the voluntary submission to pain would bring me some sort of perverted luck. I found only seediness, and lay back at an angle staring open-mouthed into the prematurely aged face of a man I recalled as a contemporary. The ironic thing was he found a cavity my monstrously expensive Beverly Hills dentist had overlooked and filled it carelessly. The only thing that hadn't changed was his equipment. When he dropped the pink pellet of mouth-wash into the glass I was reminded of the judicial gas chamber, for he seemed the sort of ineffectual character who peers out at you from the pages of a war-crimes book. I couldn't waste the pain and bending over the spittoon I pronounced Alison's name through frozen lips. He remembered her but only vaguely and shuffled to trace her card in the file. I remembered all too late that I had given him her married name, and of course he returned empty-handed. It was as if, like an undetected war criminal, he was doing his best to conceal all traces of the past.

And then again I had Kitty Raven to help replace loneliness, imagined or real, with her own particular brand of tolerance. Denied ringside seats in New York, she collected blow by blow eyewitness accounts from her network of grass widows and was on the phone to me at all hours to relate her own embellished versions of Paul's negotiations.

She had bullied my secretaries into accepting her interruptions and the only person to call her bluff was George. A skilful judge of his director's every mood, he grabbed the phone before I could weaken on one occasion. 'Sorry, darling,' he said, 'Mr Warren's on the other line. Leave your name with the casting director and we'll see you as soon as we can.'

But there was no George to save me from taking her to dinner alone, for she turned up at the hotel suite unannounced, told Susan she ought to get an early night, and informed me she had made a booking for two in my name.

I was too familiar with Kitty's repertoire not to suspect something beyond the privilege of paying the bill. Kitty never drank for pleasure, only to intensify a satisfaction already achieved, so when she sank a vodka-tonic before I had stirred the ice in my Scotch I knew it was to be a night of revelation.

Her technique, which she brought straight from the meanest gin-rummy school on the Bel Air circuit, was to make you discard first. I didn't have long to wait.

'You and Susan getting along better now?' she said.

'Never happier.'

'That's not what I hear. She shouldn't be married anyway. Does nothing for her career. What's she like in the picture?'

'I don't know. I haven't seen anything.'

'That's your second mistake. The first mistake was letting her near that drek. Don't eat so many peanuts, they're bad for you.'

'I'm nervous,' I said.

'What're you nervous about?'

'I always get up-tight when I'm starting a picture.'

'Have you cast it yet?'

'Most of it.'

'Who've you got for the girl?'

'Monika Lehmann.'

'Oh, that Kraut broad. Yeah, I know her. Well . . . What made you take her?'

'The part's supposed to be German, and I like what I've seen of her.'

'Well, if you saw her last film, you saw all of her. She was stark naked most of the time. If you want my opinion, you could do better. Is she over here yet?'

'Not yet. We don't need her until about the fourth week.'

Surprisingly, she dropped the subject, and something should have warned me then. But we went to our table in what, for Kitty, was a relaxed mood.

When the Head Waiter presented the elaborate menu she lost no time in redressing the balance.

'You can take that away,' she said, 'because I know exactly what I want. Bring me a piece of melon, and afterwards I want a green salad with thousand island dressing.'

'Would you like something with your salad, Mrs Raven?'

'Just the salad.'

'Very good, Madam.'

He noted the order carefully, but my trained eye detected something beyond the evidence. He turned to me.

'How about you, Mr Warren?'

Not to be intimidated I ordered the sort of dinner that put health farms in business. I made a point of consulting him on all the specialities and ignored Kitty's growing impatience.

'Shall I send the wine waiter, sir?'

'Yes, send him, we're celebrating to-night.'

'I'm delighted to hear it, sir,' he said gravely.

I spent an equal length of time studying the wine list.

'Does Madam have any preference?' the waiter said.

'Madam isn't with the little foxes to-night,' I said. 'She's having salad.'

Like his predecessor, he concealed his pain well. He poured her a glass of iced water before leaving in search of my choice.

'I can't be bothered with all that performance,' Kitty said before he was out of earshot.

'I've heard you diet for Paul as well as yourself. How is he, by the way? Have you talked to him to-day?'

'Yeah, he came through just before I left.'

'And how goes it?'

'You shouldn't under-estimate Paul.'

'What makes you think I do?'

'I'm not saying you, but there are a lot of people in this town go around saying he's a back number.'

'It's only envy. That's all it ever is in our business.'

'He'll survive.'

'He'll survive because he's got talent, and he's got you behind him.'

'Bullshit. Who're you trying to impress?'

'Well, not you, Kitty. I know better than that.'

'You know what Paul's talent is, his only talent? He knows just when to doublecross the doublecrossers.'

'That's quite a talent.'

'It's the name of this game. As for me, I don't influence Paul, and you know something? I don't want to influence him.'

'What happens when he uses his talent, his one talent, on you?'

'You trying to amaze me?'

'No, I'm just curious, that's all.'

'Oh, bullshit.'

'That's the second time you've said that. You must have been to see *Love Story*.'

'Listen, don't knock success. You think Paul hasn't doublecrossed me? He started with me. I'm the one he practised on. D'you know how long we've been married? Twenty-six years. D'you know when we stopped sharing a bed? Twenty-five years.'

She waited until her melon and my Quiche Lorraine had been served, then had to wait again while I accepted the wine.

'That's such a big deal,' she said, 'd'you know what happens if you send it back? They bring the same bottle out.'

'I believe you,' I said. 'I just happen to like tradition.'

'So do I. That's why Paul and me have still got a joint bank account. That's the greatest tradition of all.'

'Made America what it is to-day,' I said.

'You British are so piss elegant.'

'Ah! now I know you've had good news. How's the melon?'

'It's kosher. You want me to tell you the good news?'

'Is it secret?'

'Until you go to work in the morning. And when you get there you'll find you're working for somebody else. Paul quit. As of this afternoon he quit.'

My fork never wavered.

'And he quit for one reason. Because they paid him to quit.'

'Is that good news to me, too? What happens to my little picture that Paul was fathering?'

'You should care.'

'Oh, but I do care.'

'Listen, they either make it or they'll shelve it. Either way, it's just another film. You want to take my tip, let them shelve it. I read the script. It's not going to win any Academy Awards.'

'Who are "they" now?'

'Who are they ever?'

'I'd like to know what genius I'm going to be bored by next.'

I knew I was walking on the proverbial thin ice and that if it broke I would be out of my depth. One should never under-estimate the power of an American executive's estranged wife. The less they sleep together the more she will defend his right to whore with others. Divorce is messy, and besides it interferes with your social life, plays havoc with the community property, and offends your friendly neighbourhood cardinal. Some couples I know are so sophisticated that the wife recommends the gynæcologist to the mistress. The matrons of Beverly Hills, swathed in mink to their restored necks, alight from the most grotesque obscenities of Detroit at lunch-time and gather to-gether in the Polo Lounge of the Beverly Hills Hotel. A passing male could be forgiven for believing he had stumbled upon the vultures' Shangri La. Rising above the noise of distant police sirens, the thin cacophony of the female cabal shredding reputa-tions would put the fear of God into everybody but a fashionable lawyer. The widow carrion relate gruesome tales of coronaries, while their still-married sisters cluck a mixture of sympathy and expectation. Their plumage stiffened by the latest queer hair-dresser, they peer and peck at each other with a dedication only matched by a French concierge. Outside it is high noon and in other parts of the sprawling city their menfolk are munching raw protein and girding themselves for the return home. The girls, growing sleeker on Chef's salads, waste nothing, and when they rise from their perches they leave only the scarlet smears from their beaks on the glasses of iced water—every scrap of garbage has been picked clean.

Kitty, I knew, could be a dangerous enemy. She had charted

where the bodies were buried, just as surely as she had filed every miscarriage, stock option and Swiss numbered account. To know her you had to hate her.

'You reckon you're so smart,' she said.

'Do I?'

'All you directors and writers and faggot he-men actors, you all think you can outsmart the Pauls of this world.'

'Kitty, dear, if you can be bitchy on iced water, think how you'd go on wine. And vintage wine at that.'

'Like I said, smart.'

'I was just kidding,' I said. 'Isn't that what you're doing?'

'I'll tell you what I'm doing, I'm sitting here plotting who Paul's going to take next. You can have your creative integrity, just give me a checking account with the Bank of America. You and your lot think you've opened the oyster and found the pearl. You get yourselves a fast agent, a percentage of the profits and artistic control and you're all set to take over the industry. Well, I've got news for you, you ain't going to lick 'em and you ain't going to join 'em.'

What scant pleasure I had derived from goading her vanished in that moment. The iris of my conscience closed, and I was suddenly sickened and weary of her vulgar blood-soaked world. I lacked the courage to tip my dinner into her lap, but I wanted desperately to shatter her complacency, her Chanel-saturated reek of success. Perhaps I was close to the truth when I described this story as a chronicle of hate, for I did hate, and I shall hate again, whenever the sunless shadow of a Kitty Raven darkens my page.

Sitting across from Kitty that evening I had a premonition of my own artistic end but I was still convinced that I could outrun the pack. More than that, I wanted to buy time.

'That's all the free advice I'm giving to-night,' Kitty said. She stared across the restaurant in search of fresh targets.

'Who's Betsy Faber sitting with? I can't see without my glasses and I'm too vain to put them on for that tramp.'

I looked, but couldn't recognise the vaguely Arabic face.

'I don't know,' I said. I signalled the waiter for the bill.

'A few weeks ago she was giving it to Bill Golding. I often wondered what he did for sex until I saw Betsy Faber eating corn on the cob in the Caprice.'

I signed hurriedly and over-tipped.

'You want to go on someplace?' Kitty said.

'I don't think so,' I said.

'D'you still gamble?'

'I have a flutter now and again.'

'Let's gamble.'

'I'll drop you there if you like, but if you'll excuse me I don't think I'll join you.'

'There's no fun winning on your own,' Kitty said, and in a way it was an epitaph that fitted us all.

CHAPTER TWENTY

Even if I had still been a good Catholic I doubt whether I would have confessed my lie to Kitty, although I made my own act of contrition. I did gamble that night when I left her. As the taxi I declined to share put a welcome distance between us I started to walk back to the hotel, then changed my mind, hailed another taxi and told him to take me to Hampstead. I had no clear idea of what I wanted to achieve, I just knew that I had to challenge my own vulnerability.

I stopped the taxi in Church Row and paid it off. Three leather-encased motor-cyclists rattled the Georgian façade, searing past me like something out of Cocteau. I walked with head down, taking the short cut past the gravestones in Mount Vernon until I came to the street where Alison lived. I crossed to the opposite side of the road, glancing only once at the house to see if any lights were burning. A wall obscured the downstairs, and those portions of the house that were visible were in total darkness.

When I reached the end of the road I behaved like the true amateur fugitive, miming being lost for the pointless benefit of anybody who might have been watching. I hesitated, looked around, consulted a cigarette packet for an imaginary address, then crossed to the other side and retraced my steps. It was adolescent stuff, the remembered subterfuge of the schoolboy suffering from unrequited love after the cricket club dance; with fearful indifference one followed the rival home at a distance, praying all the time the route would not end in lovers meeting.

I was a lamp-post gap from the house when a shaft of light mottled the pavement ahead. I heard a man's voice and then a dog bolted across the road in erratic search.

'Come here, you idiot!' the voice said, as I walked forward. I was nearly level with the gate when the owner of the voice appeared and had to check my pace to avoid collision. He glanced at me, but was intent on the dog.

'Come here when you're told,' he said, crossing to where the dog was cocking its leg.

It seems fatuous now, but I think I half expected him to be made over in my own image. There is a conceit in all of us that wants to believe that those we leave will seek some likeness in others. Although I am sure he could not have described me in any detail following our brief encounter, I had photographed him with Polaroid accuracy. He was of shorter build, with an embryonic paunch, fine sparse hair allowed to grow long in the neck and with the sort of face that never seems clean-shaven.

I realise that I have so far avoided giving him a name: the defence mechanism, although rusty, still operates. His name was Cyril and he was Alison's husband. I remember that when she first told me I could hardly suppress my delight. We all have pet names that prompt immediate scorn, and Cyril had long been my Pavlovian control. It eased my deception to think I was betraying anybody with such a shrill absurdity.

I forced myself not to look again, but I heard his voice behind me and later was able to recognise it when he picked up the phone. It wasn't until I was alongside the graveyard again that fear overtook me. Association unleashed the fear of time lost, the wasted years, the needs we are driven to share. I half ran the last few yards, believing, like a child, that the breath of something nameless was close behind.

In the lighted sanctuary of the High Street, I stood and waited for a passing taxi, but none came, and in the end I walked to the Tube station. I bought a ticket at the machine and then, on an impulse, entered a phone booth and called Stan.

'Did I get you out of bed?'

'No,' he lied.

'Look, I'm sorry, but I've just been told that Raven's out.'

'Jesus!'

'It may mean the picture's off.'

'Yes. I see.'

'We'll have to wait and see what to-morrow brings.'

'Well, I'm sorry for you, governor.'

'I'm sorry for all of us.'

'Is there anything you want me to do to-night?'

'No, nothing. Come to think of it, I don't know why I called you. I suppose I just had to tell somebody.'

'Yes, of course. That's all right. Who's taking over?'

'I have my guesses . . . well, my guess. But it's academic. The faces change, but the philosophy's the same.'

'Well, you know, anything we can do . . .'

'Yes, thank you Stan. Go back to sleep.' Even when he was in the act of hanging up I delayed telling him my real reason for calling.

'Stan,' I said hurriedly, 'there is something you can do. Are you alone, by the way?'

'No, but nobody's listening.'

'That location, the one in Hampstead, could you go back and do something for me?'

'Sure.'

'I don't really want to use it, but I want to find out more.'

'Understood.'

'D'you think you could go through the motions, just make enquiries . . . I mean I don't have to tell you what to say. The point I'm trying to make is, I want the phone number.'

'Fine, no sweat. I'll do that, I'll do it first thing.'

I didn't know how to thank him, so I just rang off. Then I decided to catch the last train back to London.

It was reasonably crowded and I had to stand for the first part of the journey. When eventually I found a vacant seat, I was myself sandwiched between two placid drunks. One fell asleep immediately afterwards and rolled towards me with the motion of the train until his head was on my shoulder. He was young and his hair smelt of cheap brilliantine. I let him sleep undisturbed until I had to get out. I sat there with a stranger's head human on my faithless arm, wondering whether I was journeying to a new point of departure or merely back to the same place where it had ended before.

CHAPTER TWENTY-ONE

In one of my blackest moments, a friend attempted to give comfort by bending me to the view that although most artists are forced to defend their own work after the event, only the film director faces the humiliating necessity of having to justify himself in advance. The friend was Lowson, of course, I've remembered now; I can even recall the flat where the conversation took place, behind Victoria Station, in a now demolished mews. Lowson and I shared the rent and the same girl. 'Look,' he said. 'You're beating your bloody head against the Stone Age cave wall. If you're a novelist they can read your manuscript, right? They know what you're saying and whether they want to buy it. Supposing you're a painter—well no painter's so broke he can't find a bare surface and a piece of charcoal. And if you're a composer, you can hum the tune. But you, you've chosen a way of life that's not only unreal from start to finish, it's also bloody unworkable. You're struggling to impose a creative act on an industrial process.'

I was starting then, script in hand, begging, lying, ad-libbing my way up and down Wardour Street, willing to work for nothing, possessed, intolerant, fake-humble, angry but above all convinced that the images I carried in my head were capable of attaining immortality. I got my chance in the end, through the death of one man and the near-insolvency of another. It was a second feature, totally devoid of any merit, but I attacked it with the passion of Griffith in his heyday. I was not allowed the privilege of visiting my own cutting rooms, and such footage as I managed on the poverty-stricken budget and three week schedule was assembled before the prints were dry by my repulsively untalented producer. It was exposed to the trade in six weeks from start to finish, and for once the booking agents had the intelligence to recognise a bad film when they saw one, and committed it to that section of the deep known as The Programme Filler. Shown to the unsuspecting public without benefit of prior announcement on the bills, it mercifully sank without trace and I lived not only to lick my wounds but to fight another day.

Such early experiences breed a certain resilience to the continuity of insanity and injustice which my calling offers. I may not enjoy, but I am no longer surprised by the worst excesses of my profession, and when I turned up at my office the following morning to find that Hogarth had already phoned three times I greeted the news with more relief than suspicion.

Politics demanded that I call him back immediately, but morality made me passing courageous, and I sat it out until he called again.

'Dick,' he said, 'I've been leaving messages, didn't you get them?'

'I was looking at some film. I just got in.'

'Have you heard the news?'

'What news?'

'Paul's got the chop.'

'Oh, that. Yes, Kitty told me.'

'When?'

'Last night. I had dinner with her.'

'Well, I knew last night too, of course, but I didn't want to ruin your night's sleep.'

'How thoughtful of you,' I said. 'Well, what now?'

'Well, for the moment they've asked me to assume full responsibility.'

'Do you want me to congratulate you?'

He was trapped into giving a forced laugh. It had all the warmth of congealed tinned soup.

'So of course I'm in the unhappy position of taking immediate decisions with regard to current production. I don't think we should sign any more firm deals until I give the okay. Do you have any idea what we're in for at the moment?'

'I've got more or less a full crew,' I said, 'and we've done deals with quite a few actors.'

'Is Monika signed?'

'Not signed, but we're on the hook.'

'Well, stall everybody else until you hear from me.'

'What about set construction, do we go ahead?'

He hesitated. 'No,' he said finally.

'You don't mind the rumours flying?'

'Dick,' he said, 'you appreciate I can't tell you everything at the moment. The whole thing's being decided right now in New York.'

'Are you trying to tell me that the film's been killed?'

'I'm not trying to tell you anything, Dick. I realise your feelings, and believe me I understand, because I'm not just a desk man. I can't say more and I can't say less. The film's not on or off, it's in abeyance. That's the word, abeyance.'

'That's the word all right,' I said.

'As soon as I have any news I'll call you. I've got New York on the line now.'

'Don't keep them waiting,' I said, but he had gone, with presumably a sudden rush of executive blood to the head.

I called Wellard and the others in and explained the situation briefly. They received the news in stoic silence.

'I'll finish the breakdown, shall I, guv? May as well work out me notice,' George said, being the first to recover.

'Pity,' Wellard said, 'but one cannot kick against the pricks, alas, though of course I have spent the greater part of my life trying to perfect a technique.'

My continuity girl looked close to tears; it was her first job in seven months.

'It isn't the end of the road,' I said. 'I'm not giving up,' but even as I said it, I wondered if I had the staying power. I could see beyond the dreary boardroom struggles in New York to the endless vista of meetings and shouting matches that I would have to attend. Once again there was a curious war-time flavour about it all, a feeling of being isolated in a battle.

'There's only one thing to do in these circumstances,' Wellard said. 'I shall go home, feed the parrot, put a generous supply of sand in the bottom of her cage and round my bed, retire clutching a full bottle of claret and await my lover.'

'That's quite a good plot,' George said. 'It's got suspense, romance and an X Certificate. I'd pay to see that.'

'Don't be too bold, dear,' Wellard said. 'I might take you at your word.'

They had drifted away to discuss it further by the time Stan returned. He put a piece of paper in front of me. On it was written a telephone number.

'Piece of cake,' he said. 'Nobody in but the *au pair* girl. I chatted her up in my impeccable German, got a foot in the door by the time I had mentioned the word film company, was given coffee and a large portion of chocolate cake.'

'You didn't promise her a film test, did you?'

'No, too old a hand, governor. She wasn't my type, anyway. But I said I'd take her phone number just in case.'

'What d'you think she'll tell her employers?'

'I left no fingerprints. No, I just said we were looking around in the area, making up our minds and if I was interested I'd write to her boss. She could only speak about three words of English, and the story I told her, even I lost track of it.'

'Well, you're a good friend.'

'Pleasure. What's the latest on our situation?'

I told him what I knew and he reacted with typical fortitude. We discussed various possibilities, exchanged reminiscences of similar happenings in the past, and then he left me alone.

Half an hour later I was still sitting in the same position staring at the telephone, the number, by now, committed to memory. Once again I rehearsed a dozen opening speeches, only to reject them immediately. The hidden meanings of our lives are concealed in such mundane wrappings. Because, I suppose, I am what I am, I related my predicament to old films, casting myself for the role Kirk Douglas played in *Strangers When We Meet*. I found I could recall every twist of that plot, and the more I remembered the more I felt the cancer of doubt stirring in my blood. Even Kirk Douglas had found it difficult to telephone Kim Novak, but at least they had their lines written for them.

So it was with second-hand anguish that I finally lifted the receiver and dialled the seven digits. I gave myself a last escape route, dialling deliberately, like somebody playing Russian roulette in slow motion. If he answers, I thought, or if it's the German *au pair* girl, I'll just hang up.

But the voice that answered was Alison's. I forgot everything I had intended to say as the remembrance of things past became the reality of a living familiar person once again, the sound of her enquiring voice so close she could have been in the same room watching my humbled confusion.

I finally said, 'It's Richard, I got the note you left in the restaurant.'

There was a pause then she said, 'I think you must have the wrong number,' very carefully.

'Can't you talk?'

'No, I'm sorry, I can't help you.'

'When can I ring you?'

There was another silence.

'Can I ring you to-morrow?'

'Yes.'

'To-morrow morning?'

'Yes, I should try that.'

'What's a safe time? No, wait a minute, you can't answer that. Ten thirty?'

'Yes, no trouble, thank you.'

'I'll ring you at ten thirty.' Before I rang off I said in a louder voice, 'I'm sorry to have troubled you.'

For a brief moment afterwards I had the illusion of complete happiness. But it was only an illusion. Love joins and then separates with suspicion. I tried to imagine what had happened at her end of the line, whether her explanation of the wrong number had been accepted without question. I thought, supposing Stan pressed his luck too far with the German *au pair*? If the girl had mentioned his visit, would Osmond now be putting two and two together? The trouble is that the inexperienced sinner cannot resist self-dramatisation, and after a decade I was making a journey without maps in a country that some cross with ease. I half expected the phone to ring at my end and to have to be exposed to Osmond's cold questioning. The really inexperienced players always make the mistake of listening for the echo of their own fears.

In the event, nothing happened and my self-confidence returned. It was with a sense of elation that I flicked the intercom switch.

'Pam,' I said. 'I've had sitting around waiting for the axe to fall. Get me a self-drive hire car. I'm going to take a trip in the country to-morrow.'

'Yes, Mr Warren. What kind d'you prefer? Automatic?'

'I think so. The thrill of the gear-shift is something I can live without.'

'Any particular make?'

'Yes,' I said. 'If we're going to go, let's go with a bang, not a whimper. Hire me a Bentley.'

CHAPTER TWENTY-TWO

'I really think we should meet this morning,' Hogarth said. 'There are certain things I have to tell New York when they come to life.'

A mixture of irritation and panic hardened my resolve. 'I can't make it this morning,' I said. 'I have to see this location. The appointment's been made with the owner and I can't break it at this short notice, it's too bloody rude.'

'Will it take all morning?'

'I imagine so, it's about an hour's run out of town. But, look, New York won't be in the office until two o'clock our time. I'll come straight to you, and be with you by two.' My watch showed three minutes to ten.

'All right,' he said, 'but please don't be any later. I have very heavy responsibilities.'

'Don't we all. I'm only trying to make a picture for you.' This time I didn't give him the satisfaction of hanging up first.

The hired Bentley was waiting for me outside the hotel. I grabbed the keys from the salesman, signed the insurance papers on the bonnet and declined his refresher course on the dashboard controls—something I regretted immediately, and I had the humiliation of calling him back to tell me how to start the thing. By the time I eased out into the traffic it was ten fifteen. For some reason it's always easier to go from right hand to left hand drive, than the other way round. Arriving back in Los Angeles I can step straight into some huge American monster, gun the absurdly over-powerful engine and take off in a scream of protesting rubber without a qualm. But to face the unfamiliar London traffic after an absence, sitting on what seems to be patently the wrong side of the car, is to know opening moments of real terror. I hadn't gone a hundred yards before I provoked a bitter cry of 'You stupid Tory berk' from a passing delivery van driver, and I was sweating by the time I attempted the rapids at Hyde Park Corner.

The clock was against me and that added to my panic as I gave the wrong indicator signal and headed for Knightsbridge. I had shaved and dressed myself with extra care that morning with an adolescent's concern for his appearance, but the face that glanced back at me in the driving mirror belonged to somebody too old for intrigue.

I drove straight for the Air Terminal in Brompton Road, and made fairly good time, for most of the traffic was coming into London at that hour, but I hadn't allowed for the new one-way systems and No Right Turns that had sprung up since my last visit, and it had gone ten thirty before I parked the car and entered the building.

I had chosen the location carefully. After deliberation in the small hours, with Susan asleep by my side, I had finally opted for somewhere plausible but public. I convinced myself that, if by chance, I bumped into somebody I knew, I had the choice of a dozen reasonable explanations that I could play by ear.

There was one final moment of hysteria when I got to the phone booths, for one digit of Alison's number had vanished from memory. I lit a cigarette and leant with my head against the glass in an agony of concentration. I had come prepared with a pocketful of small change, and I talked to myself, urging calm like a quiet madman, as I dialled. The call mis-routed the first time, but at the second and more deliberate attempt I heard the peculiar ringing tone that even in those early days had something familiar about it.

She answered before it had rung three times, which I took to mean she had been close and waiting, but with her own fears and doubts.

'I'm sorry,' I said, 'I tried to be on the dot, but everything went wrong. How are you?'

'I'm fine,' she said.

'Was it all right last night? I gathered you couldn't talk.'

'No. Cyril was in the room.'

'Cyril?'

'My husband.'

The dog barked in the background.

'I saw you the other day, you were walking the dog with your daughter.'

'Where?'

Her voice was still guarded.

'Outside your house. I was passing in a car.'

'Outside here? What were you doing up here?'

'Looking for you,' I said.

'Oh, I see.'

'Do you?' She didn't answer.

'Well, your daughter will remember,' I said. 'We had a parrot in the car, and she spotted it and pointed. I don't think you saw it.'

'No,' she said. 'I'm glad I didn't, I should have been panic-stricken.'

'Seeing me or the parrot?'

'Both. What were you doing with a parrot?'

'Oh, it isn't mine. It belongs to a friend of mine. I was with some people at the time.' For some reason I found myself unable to mention Susan, and I envied her having crossed that particular bridge where Osmond was concerned.

'I want to see you,' I said. 'Is that going to be possible?'

I waited.

'You mean now, you mean to-day?'

'Yes. If that's possible.'

'Well, where could we meet? It isn't easy for me.'

'No, I'm sure. I thought of that. But, I've sort of got it worked out if you want to listen. Is it all right to talk as long as this?'

'Yes, there's nobody here. The girl's taken Lucy to the zoo.'

'Well, I'm at Brompton Road Air Terminal. I chose this because I thought it was fairly safe for both of us. I've got a car and I thought if you came here we could go somewhere. Is that possible?'

'I couldn't stay long,' she said. 'I'd have to be back by lunch.'

'Yes, well that's fine because I've got appointments after lunch.'

I waited again.

'I've just got to see you,' I said.

'All right,' she said finally. 'I'll come to you.'

'Do you mind? I just think it's safer than the other way round.'

'No, I don't mind. It'll take me about half an hour.'

'I won't go away. I'll be by the bookstall. Will you recognise me?'

'I expect so,' she said.

When I stepped from the smoky booth I realised that for the first time in many years I was completely free from anxiety, jealousy, hate; it was as if I had been handed a blank cheque and told to fill in the amount.

CHAPTER TWENTY-THREE

Perhaps it was the surroundings, for everything connected with air travel seems a negation of the advertisements—in the air everything goes slowly at speed, and on the ground it just goes slowly. Certainly I don't think I have ever lived through a longer thirty minutes. Caution made me save the bookstall, so I denied myself even a daily paper, and sat with a cup of slopped tea and a curled cheese sandwich, stupidly scanning every fresh face from the first minute. After fifteen I got up and paced, stifled the urge to use the men's room for fear of missing her, consulted the departure board with the concentration of a failed punter, then circled the lounge to my starting point. By now I was convinced that all the clocks in the building had suffered a power cut. I checked and double-checked them against my own wrist-watch—behaving, in fact, like somebody out of a badly written play slavishly trying to give the author's description 'worried expression' full value.

Stationed at the bookstall with five full minutes still to go, I bought all the latest and most expensive women's magazines, plus a copy of *Men Only* to give some balance to the choice, and it was with an anonymous nude tucked under my arm that I turned to find Alison standing beside me for the first time in ten years.

'Fancy seeing you here,' I said, inadequate, as always, to the major occasions in my life.

'Yes, what a coincidence,' she said, with something approaching a smile. I thought, it's going to be all right providing we both have a sense of humour. For one moment I am sure she thought I was going to shake hands, but I offered her the bunch of magazines.

'Would you like a present?' I said. 'I found them in a waiting room.'

'I'm not that late, am I?'

I moved her away from the bookstall and started to walk her towards the exit.

'Where are we going?'

'In my car. Have you parked yours?'

'Yes, I got on a meter across the road.'

'How long?'

'Two hours, but I mustn't be that long.'

'Don't look so worried,' I said.

We were walking slightly apart, instinct making us cautious and I approached the wrong Bentley at first, not realising my mistake until the key failed to open the door.

'You can see I'm used to this sort of thing,' I said.

'You are funny. How long have you had it?'

'I hired it for the day.'

'You're mad.'

'Mad and funny,' I said. 'In that order.'

I settled her in the car and she fastened her seat belt.

'D'you always do that?'

'Yes, I got into the habit with Lucy.'

The magazines were still in her lap.

'Did you buy *Men Only* for me, too?'

'No, I just thought it looked better. I thought the girl was beginning to give me strange looks.'

I started the engine with reasonable expertise this time.

'Well now,' I said. 'Where shall we drive to?'

'I don't mind. You choose.'

'Is Richmond Park still there? I mean, they haven't built on it?'

'All around it, but not on it.'

'Shall we go there then?'

She nodded and grinned straight at me, and I suddenly saw her down the years and was totally destroyed by both the rekindled memory of those halcyon days and the reality of the present moment. I hunched myself over the wheel as we entered the traffic and without looking at her I said, 'I still love you, you know,' and we drove in silence all the way until we reached the park.

CHAPTER TWENTY-FOUR

Until I sat down to write this book I had no idea that the conscious act of remembering still has the power to revive old pain. It's like the first steps one takes after a long illness. The stitches have been removed and the flesh one touches with such tentative fingers seems healed, but beneath the faintly scarred surface we present to the world, the lesions remain, and when we test them they remind us that nothing will ever be quite the same again.

Now, when it's too late to alter anything, I wish I knew what it was that impelled me to embark on that particular sea. Did we really have extraordinary things to share with each other? Did we have anything to gain by loving one another a second time?

We were so easy and careless in those early moments, walking through tall burnt grass towards the grazing herd of deer, stupid with our quickening discoveries, believing that every doubt could be resolved, every unspoken fear set aside.

It's only in the city, in rooms, that the actuality of sin bites sufficiently deep to draw conscience to the surface. Elsewhere, the awareness of sin has no more substance than the passing cloud which blots out the sun.

At that first meeting I squandered what remained of caution. To convince myself, I reminded her of everything that had been perfect in the past, deliberately choosing to forget we had ever given each other the gift of misery. It was like a child holding a single raffle ticket who is totally convinced that the prize, when drawn, must be his, that no other solution is possible.

That old thief, Time, cheated me many ways that day. I forced the pace, I had such a need to infect her with my own disease. And most of all, like any anxious lover before or since, I wanted her to re-infect me. I willed her to return my confession, as though the mere repetition of a few words would somehow solve every-thing. And when at last she surrendered to my insistence, I covered her open mouth with doubt, bruising her lips between fresh demands. Hardly breathing, we clutched each other like Sunday lovers in the grass, my hands finding again the soft contours of her breasts which then I bent to kiss through expensive fabric. That was all she would allow, though I was mad enough to have attempted all. We lay as though buried together, every part of our bodies touching and punishing and when eventually the anguish receded and we moved apart the dazzling sun seared our blotched faces. We sat up to pick grass seed from our hair, and I blotted my mouth with a handkerchief, time and reality nudging us, and the deer moving closer. There was a shyness then that always comes when the body still lives in expectation, and just to touch her neck with my hand was pain. I stood up first, unsure on my feet like a foal, and she had to support me for a few seconds before we walked hand in hand towards the plantation of trees and the parked car.

On the journey back she left her seat belt loose, sitting as close as possible, and I drove with one hand, the other cupped on her warm lap.

'What does your husband do?' I said.

'He makes things. Or rather, he makes one thing in particular. He makes money.'

'How long have you been married?'

'Nine years, almost to the day. It was our anniversary dinner the night I saw you in the restaurant.'

'Had you thought about me before then? I thought of you, you know.'

'Yes. Well, of course it was easier for me. I was always reading about you and your wife.'

'Does Cyril know about me, about the past I mean?'

'I said I'd met you. He admires your films.'

'Well, he shares my taste in women, doesn't he?'

'Your wife is very beautiful.'

'Yes,' I said.

We were getting closer to Hammersmith by now and for some maddening reason every traffic light was in our favour.

'When will I see you again?' I said.

'I don't know . . . I don't know what to say.'

'Please.'

'We'd drown each other.'

The loudest noise in the car was not the much quoted clock, but the sound of my heart.

'I have to see you once more.' I was willing to place my bets one chip at a time, just to stay in the game.

'What good would it do?'

'I love you,' I said.

'But once it's over, you can't go back, you said that yourself.'

'When? When did I say that?'

'Oh, I don't know, years ago, when everything was different. But I remember it, I remember thinking at the time, if it ends, he's right. But it never seemed like ending then.'

'It never did end, that's the trouble. If we'd parted in bitterness, after some great soul-destroying row . . . You were always the one, and now I don't know what to do with the rest of my life.'

'That's silly. You're married, I'm married, I've got a daughter, you've got a career.'

'But you're not happy. You wouldn't have agreed to see me to-day if you were perfectly happy.'

'What's happiness got to do with it? I don't know anybody who's happy.'

I took her hand and brought it to my lips, which was rather an old world gesture, trite and courtly. Physically, I ached for her; I was growing ever more desperate to extract a further promise, I would have settled on any terms at that moment. The road was running out and I deliberately slowed down, but we were in the midst of thick traffic and immediately the cars behind started to hoot. She withdrew her hand and edged farther towards her window. She pulled the sun visor down and studied her face, searching, I am sure, for any marks that could possibly betray.

'Well, all right,' I said. 'I agree, we're both in the same boat, but just see me once more and I won't bother you again.'

The lie came so easily.

'You'd better drop me here,' she said. 'Otherwise you'll have to go all round the world because of the No-Right Turns. I'm parked in one of those back streets.'

'You haven't answered me.'

I kept driving.

'Don't spoil it,' she said.

I pulled in to the kerb. She gathered up the magazines.

'Thank you for these.'

'You can't thank me for a few magazines and then go out of my life again. What about back there in the park, are you going to thank me for that too?'

'That's not fair,' she said.

'Of course it's not fair. I don't feel fair. All I know is I have to see you again. I'll see you on any terms. I'll be funny, I'll be humble, I'll be anything you want, but just say yes. I can't let you go without some hope. I know this is a hire car, but I'm not a chauffeur looking for a tip.'

The absurdity of my dialogue made us both laugh, and perhaps that was the saving of me.

'Well, I'm not,' I said, laughing. 'But if you want me to, I'll wear a peaked cap next time. And you can sit in the back and I'll leer at you in the driving mirror.'

'I'm all for that—it sounds very depraved.'

She had her hand on the door. 'All right,' she said. 'Phone me.'

'When, to-morrow?'

'No, not to-morrow. I have to take Lucy to the dentist.'

'The day after, then? The same time?'

'Yes.'

She opened the door and stepped on to the pavement. Two passing workmen gave her an appreciative look, and I envied them their freedom.

'Drive carefully.'

'You too. Good-bye.'

'Good-bye,' I said. I sat and watched her cross the road and disappear down a side turning on the opposite side. She never looked back. Had she been a stranger I could still have fallen in love with the back of her legs.

CHAPTER TWENTY-FIVE

I found Kitty sitting with an uneasy Hogarth when I kept my two o'clock appointment. She was wearing the big ring, a topaz large enough to receive BBC2 on, and I knew from her expression that the new Pope had been chosen.

'For a genius,' she said, 'you're remarkably punctual.'

'Something my mother taught me,' I said. 'That and telling the truth is the best course in the long run.'

'She sounds a real bore,' Kitty said.

'Well, don't worry about her. She was your age when she died.'

Although he made no sign or move, I felt Hogarth warm towards me and I guessed that he had just paid for lunch. I had a feeling of lightheadedness, something that Kitty could not touch or corrupt.

'So what's new?'

'I haven't spoken to New York yet,' Hogarth said, 'but I had a long telex in this morning.'

'I spoke to Paul,' Kitty interrupted, 'tell him what happened.'

'Well, apparently Mr Raven is giving up his executive position, but continuing his association with the company as an independent producer. I gather it was a very satisfactory agreement for all concerned.'

'Who's taking over?'

'Norbert Quarry.'

I used my handkerchief to conceal a grin; Alison's scent was still on it and I missed her.

'He's a new one,' I said. 'I haven't heard of him before. Where did he come from?'

'Television, real estate and mortuaries.'

'Did he work his way up to mortuaries from television, or the other way round?'

'I don't know,' Hogarth said warily. He looked to Kitty.

'He originated *Macey's Midgets*,' Kitty said. 'He's a rich boy just got richer.'

'Course that was a very successful series,' Hogarth volunteered. 'Ran four years on network.'

I thought of somebody with the improbable name of Norbert Quarry listening to and looking at *Macey's Midgets*, the most nauseating television programme of the last decade, for four straight years, and kept the handkerchief under my nose. I needed something to sweeten the air.

'It seems a natural progression to mortuaries.'

'You don't want to big-mouth your opinions all over town,' Kitty said. 'What makes you think you're so secure?'

'Kitty,' I said, 'the day I start feeling secure in this rat race I'll take a full page ad in *Variety*. I'm delighted for Mr Quarry, I'm sure he's a man of perception and integrity, and he can have my business all the way down the line to the grave. Literally.'

'Speak for yourself,' Kitty said. 'He's not getting me. I'm booked into Forest Lawn. When I go I want to go first class.'

'Oh, I remember him now. Didn't he make a killing—if you'll pardon the expression—shipping the boys home from Viet Nam?'

'That's the one.'

'And now he's in films. What a riches to rags story.'

Hogarth coughed. He switched his intercom self-consciously. 'Let me know when you get New York,' he said.

'Does he intend to have a mass burial, or is it all going to be done discreetly?'

'Do you mean as far as your own situation is concerned?' Again I intercepted a look between Hogarth and Kitty.

'Mine, yours, anybody's.'

'Well, I gather that Mr Quarry is prepared to confirm my own appointment as far as Europe is concerned.'

'That must make you happy.'

'Yes, thank you. And, as far as I know, your own film is going ahead.'

I was surprised and I expect I showed it. From the moment I had entered the room and found Kitty sharing Hogarth with me,

I had anticipated disaster: I felt that my quota of luck had been used in Richmond Park.

'Paul did you a good turn,' Kitty said. 'As part of his settlement he insisted they let you go ahead. He's always liked you, I can't think why.'

'It takes a genius to know a genius.' I was conscious that my personality changed whenever I was in Kitty's company. For some reason I always felt compelled to give more than I had to take and this inevitably meant that my dialogue slipped into a slick carbon copy of all I most despised.

Kitty looked at me steadily. I saw Hogarth bring his manicured finger tips together: he looked like an ageing Christopher Robin just about to say his prayers.

'So he brought the property away with him. He's going to produce it for you. It's going to be a personal production of Paul Raven.'

I might have known she would trump my one trick. I might have suspected earlier had I not been so lulled by the changes in my personal fortunes.

'Some people get all the breaks,' Kitty went on, 'you might even make some money with it now.'

I recovered sufficiently to say, 'I thought you hated the script.'

'Paul'll tell you how to put the script right.'

'I must say, it's obviously going to be an important picture now,' Hogarth said.

'I thought it was always an important picture.'

'Yes, but you know, I mean let's be honest, Paul Raven is Paul Raven and he's been associated with some pretty big grossers.'

I nodded. 'So it looks as though the only fatal casualty was dear old Cottram.'

'I wouldn't say that, the company have been very generous in my opinion. I don't think he's got any complaints.'

'Too damn, right,' Kitty said.

'Then I'd better get back to work. When's Paul arriving back?'

'He'll probably get a plane out to-night.'

'Good,' I said. I got up. 'Doubtless we shall all be in touch in the very near future.'

'Yes, if you check in, Dick, we'll let you know what's happening.'

'Can I go ahead and confirm the various deals?'

'Well, I think you'd better wait and discuss them with Paul.'

Kitty smiled at me and Hogarth showed me to the door: the interview was over.

I went back to my own office to rally the troops and by the time I had made Monty's speech to the Eighth Army I was feeling guilty towards Susan.

CHAPTER TWENTY-SIX

Like most wives Susan prided herself that she knew me better than most. 'I can always tell what you're thinking,' she used to say, and as in the childhood game sometimes she was warm, sometimes she was burning her feet, and sometimes she was very cold.

I never intended this book to be a confession, a mere setting down of the evidence, for there is always something beyond the evidence, and it is that we shield from those we live with. To know everything about another person would be intolerable. I didn't *know* Susan then, and now I shall never know her—then I was married to her. I knew what she liked to eat, and what toothpaste she preferred, and the position she enjoyed most in lovemaking. When we went on holiday I knew what books to pack, and even when the choice was right I knew to the page when she would grow bored and stop reading. I was in love with her once, but she didn't want love, she wanted a career, which in her case meant the transient fame of yesterday's headlines. She had always had money, her family were second-generation gentry who looked down on Jaguar owners and sent their daughter to Heathfield. She was seduced by a cousin when she was seventeen, on Daddy's side of the family, which sent Mummy into a state of self-righteous shock, but it was Mummy who arranged matters and accompanied her on the round-the-world cruise afterwards. Unfortunately, Mummy's success was complete and Susan was never able to conceive another child. Perhaps if we had had children, this story might never have been written—but I can't believe it would have altered anything, that is just my middle-class reasoning. It's easier, perhaps, to believe that Susan did the best she could with what she had been given—for prolonged exposure to Mummy, especially in the vintage years that I was privileged to taste, would have warped anybody's judgment of human nature. Daddy, when I knew him, had been reduced, as they say, to a shadow of his former shadow and succumbed to a single bee sting during Ascot week two years after we were married—a piece of timing which saddened the bookmakers as much as it infuriated his widow. To understand Susan one had to visit her mother's bathroom.

We had been married in church with Susan dressed by Dior, and the guests, all four hundred of them, by Moss Bros. The congregation reminded me of nothing so much as a superior crowd call on a day when the make-up man has only had time to attend to those closest to camera. The first ceremony was notable for its bored hypocrisy and interminable length, and we had to endure a shorter, Roman Catholic, version immediately afterwards, playing to a much smaller house, before joining the red-necked well-wishers under the marquee on the lawn. It has always been a source of amazement to me what the British will tolerate at a tribal rite like marriage. They will drink inferior champagne out of shallow glass ashtrays and consume quantities of wilting smoked salmon until the sun sets on the last drunken guest. One cannot exaggerate the banality of the basic below-the-navel humour, which at any other function would be regarded as totally offensive. We departed with kippers Scotch-taped beneath the bonnet of the car and french letters inserted in the exhaust, and when eventually we reached Le Touquet a bland Customs official raised tolerant eyebrows at the discovery of a chamber pot with the words CLOSE YOUR EYES AND THINK OF ENGLAND painted round the rim, and asked for a translation. We gave him the literal translation, but the significance still escaped him. 'Ah,' he said, 'the wogs begin at Dover.'

Had Susan been the innocent that legend still demands and the majority of family guests perpetuate, the crudity of the initiation might well have deflowered her mind, but she was no stranger to my bed and in fact, on the actual pre-wedding night, we made love in Mummy's lounge while she was out flogging the caterers.

But those were halcyon days which even the combined blessings of two churches could not sustain. I have often wondered why, separately and together, Susan and I agreed to the religious charades. Susan was all too familiar with God working in mysterious ways from a very early age, and was cheerfully agnostic and free from guilt. I had the guilt that passeth human understanding except to born Catholics, but it was something I had learnt to live with. I suppose I was fortunate in that, all my working life, I have been on the move, seldom staying more than a couple of years in any one location. So I never had to fear that the church could salvage me at will. Some relic of childhood, a love of ceremony, a sense of the dramatic, demanded that I made token amends once a year, and I usually went to midnight Mass at Christmas. In Hollywood, naturally, where such things are as organised as IBM, I could not avoid the visiting salesmen altogether, but even there I managed to keep them at a distance by making a couple of C rated films. The caressing confidence that the church gives to so many was never something I could surrender to without question and I have always found the financial know-how of its priests superior to their theological arguments. So I have floundered between the cult of hope and the reality of human misery. If God wants to stand up and take an encore for His successes, then he must also face his audience for the child born with hereditary syphilis.

I have come a long way in thought and in deed from the first stirring of guilt towards Susan that hot evening in June, in London, when it all began in earnest. I have said before that I want to understand myself, then and now, and to achieve that I must be ruthless with us all. It isn't one of those easy crosswords that Surrey commuters finish between Guildford and Waterloo: there are so many blanks to fill, and the Clues Across make nonsense of many of the Clues Down. How easy it would be if all our actions had a meaning at the time we make them, but so much of life is tawdry chance and we have no more perception of the universe than the drowned kittens in the sack in the bucket of water.

I left Hogarth's office with mixed feelings: granted a stay of execution, but still in Death Row, and somehow I had to organise my own petitions. Was I really honest at that point? Did I want the film to go forward whatever the cost? Or did I seek to strike that unhappy compromise between ambition and love? The world I inhabited was grotesque enough, I argued, what difference would one isolated act of defiance make? I was cynical enough about my own profession to know that Raven could easily find another director to take my place—indeed, knowing Raven, he had probably asked somebody to stand by in readiness. Walking between Hogarth's office and my own I rehearsed several speeches and in the event delivered none of them.

I am being dishonest even now, for I never seriously entertained making the great self-righteous gesture of resignation. It was a pleasant salve to flirt with, but it had no substance beside the reality of Alison recently encountered, and the only guilt I felt was not towards my own conscience but Susan, for at the very moment we make up our minds to deceive another person we draw closer.

Guilt wears so many masks, and the temptation is to select the most flattering. I don't want to give anybody the impression that my falling out of love with Susan had any connection with Alison. That had happened long before. I can conjecture many things—if we hadn't gone to that restaurant with Kitty Raven, if Susan hadn't lost an ear-ring, and so on, the list is endless, would the end of this story have been any different? Or would I have kept alive the memory of Alison in somebody else?

Perhaps I played the childhood game with too much conviction that night, for Susan said to me, 'Why the sudden affection?' and later, 'What have I done to merit all this?' and some of her old pliancy returned, and for moments on that hotel bed it was possible to believe that guilt was only an illusion. But the lust was simulated, the tenderness was really fatigue in another guise, and afterwards we were strangers again, trapped by an old intimacy. She went to sleep easily, her naked body contoured beneath the single sheet, while I lay there listening for the man calling the dog, seeing him walk back inside that house in Hampstead and claiming, in his way and with his rights, that body which even in the aftermath of lovemaking I could still desire.

CHAPTER TWENTY-SEVEN

If only it were possible, just once, to love without injury.

Susan was on later call the following morning and we had breakfast together for the first time in weeks. I never cease to take pleasure in a well-served hotel breakfast; there is something to be said for a pot of good coffee that you haven't had to make yourself, an abundance of hot rolls and croissants and buttered toast kept almost liquid under a silver dish. I even enjoy my first cigarette of the day.

'They're so ghastly,' Susan said, when I had told her of the latest developments in New York and Raven's imminent return. 'Why don't you tell them all to get lost?'

'Yes, it's an attractive thought.'

'You could do something else, you're always being offered scripts.'

'Not really.'

'Well, do nothing then.'

'I'm not very good at doing nothing.'

'You'd see more of me.'

'Would I? You're still working. You've always said you hated me being around when you're working.'

'Well, I don't mean hanging about the set.'

'Maybe it'll work out,' I said. 'Maybe I'll be able to handle Raven. He's always got his fat fingers in a dozen pies, perhaps he'll leave me to get on with it.'

She gave a small grimace of displeasure as I stubbed a cigarette out in the saucer.

'Oh, I'm sure you can handle Raven, that's not what I'm

worried about — I just hate to see you depressed.'

She held my hand across the table: it seemed curiously old-fashioned and formal, like some tableau.

'Least things are better between you and me,' I said.

We shared a conscience that morning, and because I was expecting to be hurt from another direction, I had forgotten with what ease Susan and I could injure each other. I wondered who had taught us the technique.

I fussed over her, watching her dress and apply her make-up, generous with my overdrawn affections, and she allowed herself to be pampered because she felt she owed it to me. It was like a scene from one of those slick American comedies of the thirties that crop up now on the late, late show. And when our floor waiter came to clear away the breakfast debris he witnessed a tender farewell, and yet within minutes of the door closing I was phoning Alison, dialling conscience again seven times to share it with somebody else.

Osmond answered. Even in those early days my instincts for self-preservation were swift.

'Mr Talbot, please,' I said, giving the floor waiter's surname in a normal voice.

'Who?'

'Mr Bill Talbot.'

'What number are you calling?'

'Well, I thought I was ringing the Highgate Garage,' I said.

'You've got the wrong number,' he said irritably. 'This is a private house.'

He rang off before I could apologise. Curiously enough the incident did not depress me. I felt, with little enough justification, that time was on my side. I had made the decision and it was enough to know that Alison and I were both in the same city. At that time I had no jealousy for Osmond, only a kind of superior tolerance.

I listened to the radio while shaving, something I hadn't done for years. Raven and the film suddenly held no fears for me, it was as if I had shot the whole thing and read the first rave notices and was dressing to go to the première. I had affection enough to spare, enough even to embrace Hogarth and all the others who inhabited the world of deceit.

CHAPTER TWENTY-EIGHT

Grotefend was waiting in my outer office and he looked like something escaped from the Battersea Dogs Home. I think if I had thrown him a rolled-up copy of *Variety* from the door, he would have caught it in his mouth and carried it to my desk.

'Hi, Dick,' he said, 'are you busy?'

'I don't know yet, I'm not even inside the room.'

'Can you give me a moment?'

'Come right in. D'you want coffee?'

'Mr Grotefend's had coffee,' Pam said, 'and Mr Wellard is waiting to see you urgently.'

'I won't be long, honey,' Grotefend said.

We went into my office and he closed the door carefully. His manner was immediately servile.

'Dick, I know you're a busy man, so I'll lay it on the line. I'd like to handle your picture.'

'D'you know something more than I do?'

'Know something?'

'Well, events in the last two or three days haven't exactly induced a feeling of permanence.'

'Oh, that. Well, that's more or less why I'm asking. You see, things haven't exactly worked out for me. You know my track record, so I don't have to sell myself. I think you and I have gotten along pretty well in the past, and there's something to show for it.'

I spoke his foreign language fluently, and I knew from past experience that it would be unnecessary cruelty to correct him on questions of fact. That sort of thing merely prompts a longer monologue where the Grotefends of my world are concerned. Our working relationship was confined to four unenjoyable meetings at most, and there was nothing to show for it—nothing except the sweating man in the office pleading for his life.

'You'll have the minimum of crap, that I promise you. I mean,

I'm used to working with artists of your calibre, and I'm a family man, like you. My family is important to me.'

I looked through the morning mail, neatly set out in piles before me. I noted that I had become honorary member of three more gambling clubs.

'I've read your script and I think I know what you're after. You just say the word and I'm your boy.'

'What about your present job?' I said.

'Dick, you might as well be the first to know. Bob Daniels just broke a few eggs in my lap. There's going to be changes, big changes with the new set-up. You're looking at one of them.'

'I'm sorry.'

'Listen, who needs them? I never was a front office man, I've always been out in the field running. That's where I started and that's where I'm happiest. I understand *The Unknown War.*'

'*Warrior,*' I said.

'What?'

'*The Unknown Warrior.*'

'Yeah, I understand it, it's going to be a fine picture and I just want to leave you with a thought—I know you're a busy man—this is the sort of picture that needs international publicity from the word off. Put in a word for me, will you, with Raven?'

'Well, he isn't back yet.'

'He gets in to-night. Do it for me, will you, Dick?'

At any other time his fear would have been contagious. But that morning I felt reasonably secure.

'I'll mention it to him, yes.'

'That's all I'm asking. Mention it to him, lay it on him strong. Coming from you, he'll take it.'

'Of course we might have a local union problem.'

'He'll get round that.'

'Well, I'll certainly mention it to him.'

'You didn't mind me asking?'

'Not at all.'

'That's wonderful, just wonderful. I'll get out of your hair now. You got everything you want?'

'I've got half a script, half a cast and a new producer,' I said. 'I'm in great shape.'

'You look great, Dick. Can I buy you lunch?'

'No, I'm having a working lunch.'

'Don't overdo it now.'

He was backing to the door.

'Say hello to Susan for me,' he said. 'I got a paragraph about her in this week's *What's On*. I'll send her a copy.'

I saw Wellard next, who brought in some superb sketches for me to okay. Then I spoke to some agents, dictated replies to those letters which didn't go into my waste-paper basket, and arranged to interview an editor after lunch. Then I told Pam I wanted to do some work on the script and the moment she was out of the room I dialled Alison's number again on my private line.

This time she answered. 'Did you ring earlier?' she said.

'Yes.'

'I thought it was you. Cyril wasn't feeling very good this morning. That's why he was still in the house. At one point I didn't think he was going to go to work.'

'Did he suspect anything?'

'No. Why should he?'

'Am I going to see you soon?'

'Oh, Dick,' she said, 'I want to see you, but what's the point? I'm such a bad liar and we'd have to lie all the time.'

'That depends.'

'No, it doesn't. People always say that, just to fool themselves. That's only in films. In real life, lies destroy you. I didn't promise, did I?'

'No, you didn't promise.'

'I've got Lucy, you see. Children trust you.'

'Yes.'

Pam put her head round the door and I waved her away.

'What's the matter?' Alison said.

'Nothing. Somebody just came in.'

'Who?'

'Nobody. A secretary.'

'Where're you phoning from?'

'My office. It's all right. The next noise you'll hear is my cigarette lighter. I'm lighting a cigarette.'

'You should give it up.'

'I should give a lot of things up, you included, but I doubt if I will. You mustn't be too unfair, you know. You sent me the note.'

'Yes, I know. Don't think I haven't thought about that.'

'Don't sound so sad. That isn't in the plot. The last thing I want to do is make you sad.'

'You don't.'

'No, of course not. This is one of those happy phone conversations I have every day of my life. I read all those new GPO ads. Use your friendly telephone more often and phone somebody you love. And I do love you,' I said.

I heard her dog bark and, more than her silences, it reminded me that she had a sort of security without me. She had a husband who was good at making money, and a child who trusted her, and when the phone went dead there would be things to do and life would go on.

'Because I love you,' I said, 'I'll do what you want me to do. I'm not being brave and self-sacrificing, because I don't feel brave. I feel dead. If you tell me never to phone you again, I won't phone. I won't bother you any more, but I won't stop loving you.'

'You know I won't ask that.' Her voice sounded very far away.

'You have to. One of us has to.'

'Well, I can't say it now.'

'D'you want me to say it for you?'

'No. I don't know what I want.'

I said, 'Darling, you can't have it all ways,' knowing her well enough to be hard at that moment. The responsibility as well as the guilt was mine: I knew what I wanted and what I would have to do to get it. We are seldom completely generous in love. We may deceive others, we may even pretend to ourselves that our every action is motivated by the highest ideals, but the inexplicable workings of the heart demand satisfaction at any cost.

'If you want to throw everything away again for a second time, then I won't stop you. I love you enough to understand why.'

'Love,' she said. 'Why did God invent love?'

'Perhaps He didn't,' I said. 'Anyway, you don't have to decide now. I'll make it easier for you. Take this number, it's my private line, nobody else has it, not even Susan.' I read the numbers off the dial and made her repeat them. 'Put it on your shopping list, under Chemist.' I thought, I'm even teaching her the rules of the game. 'Then if you feel like a prescription, ring me. If you don't ring I'll know you're cured.'

'I'll never be cured,' she said.

CHAPTER TWENTY-NINE

In any other profession, I honestly believe Raven would have been behind bars.

Just as in the old vaudeville days every failed comedian had his unfavourite town and said of it, 'they don't bury the dead in this place, they put 'em in front row on Monday night,' so my profession does not bury its grosser villains, but instead gives them endless opportunities to disguise their lack of talent and applauds their more blatant acts of dishonesty.

He returned from New York with his podgy fingers still tingling from the golden handshake. For just under a month in office, during which time, his only executive act—and that one taken in spite—was to remove Cottram, he was rewarded with $75,000 in cash, future stock options, generous and untabulated expenses, and the right to make my life a misery.

You might ask, why did I tolerate him, why did any of us tolerate him? But to understand the reasons behind our lack of courage, you have to appreciate that for every Raven who finally has his bluff called, there are a dozen more standing, literally, in the wings. There is never a shortage of understudies and they never throw away the mould.

That doesn't excuse me, it doesn't excuse any of us. I suppose, each in our different ways, we want to make films whatever the cost.

He returned in good humour and full of third-hand ideas.

'It was the only way, baby,' he said. 'I protected you, I saved the film. Now you don't have to consult those bums. What do they know? Eh, tell me, when did they ever make a film? I got everything you wanted.'

'Who has the final cut?'

'You do, baby.' He put his arm round me, but it only reached the middle of my back. 'I never interfere with my creative people, you should know that. We don't even have to talk to them. All right, maybe I have to talk to them—occasionally, when we want more money.'

'What about Hogarth, where does he fit in?'

'He's a joke, baby. I invented him, remember? I gave him the job. Important directors like you don't talk with Hogarth. I can take care of him. One word from me and New York would cut off his balls, if he's got any.'

'Well, it all sounds too good to be true,' I said.

'Dick, we're going to clean up with this picture by the time I'm through with it. Clean up! Now, how far you got? You got a schedule yet?'

'Practically. I'm still working on the final version of the script, but it's in pretty good shape.'

'Listen, before I forget—your idea of Mitchum, it's not going to work.'

'I don't think it was my idea.'

'Sure, sure it was. You mentioned it the first time we met. He's unavailable. So we've got to come up with another idea. How about Nicolson?'

'Which one?'

'The guy in that, you know, that motor-bike thing.'

'Yes, very good actor. One of the best.'

'How about him?'

'Well, he's very American, the character's supposed to be a Foreign Office type, ex-Eton and all that.'

'Think about it. He's pretty good box office at the moment.'

Despair got a foot in the door. I knew I was walking in a cut-price store.

'Think about it,' Raven repeated. He munched a handful of salted peanuts.

'Well, I don't know that there's much point in thinking about it. He's totally wrong.'

'You said yourself he's a good actor.'

'Yes, I'm not disputing that, but he could never be Foreign Office, not in a thousand years.'

'It's a big budget picture, Dick. They got four million dollars riding on it.'

'Three,' I said. 'We think we can bring it in for three.'

'Is that all? These nuts are stale.' He spat them into a tissue. 'I want to talk to you about the budget. I think it'll be nearer four.'

'Why?'

'Because.' He flicked the intercom. 'You got any nuts in there?'

'I'm sorry, Mr Raven?' the girl answered.

'Nuts, peanuts, salted nuts.'

'No, sir. I thought there were some in your drink cabinet.'

'They've been here since the war. Get the whole thing re-stocked.'

He cut off the machine and returned to me.

'The budget's going up, Dick, because for one reason, they've got to take care of me. Now, don't misunderstand me, I'm not getting a million dollars. But everything's relative. When I decide to make a picture, agents ask more—don't ask me why, they just do. The sets cost more, everything costs more right down the line. And listen, why should you care what it costs. The important thing is we're going to make a great picture.'

'It's not worth four million,' I said. 'At four, it won't get its money back.'

'Dick, you want to know something? If it doesn't make it at four, it won't make it at three.'

He smiled and spread his hands. I noticed he was wearing a copper band on one wrist.

'Do me a favour, let me worry about the budget. You got the girl here yet?'

'Monika? She's due to come in for costume fittings at the end of this week.'

'You met the husband?'

'I've spoken to him over the phone.'

'A number one prick. D'you know what he was before he found her? A number two prick. He promoted himself.'

'Well, I've met the type before. She's all right, she won't give us any trouble.'

'Take my tip, keep him off the set.'

I tried to recall any part of our conversation which didn't contain some germ of disaster.

'Forgetting the husband for the moment, you're quite happy about the choice of Monika?'

'She's all right. Those Kraut broads all look alike. Don't photograph her legs and keep her monosyllabic. Give her any long speeches and you'll empty the theatre.'

I started to laugh.

'What did I say?' Raven asked. He liked to be told when he'd made a joke.

'I was just thinking about something Kitty said about you.'

'What? What'd she say?'

'She said you always knew when to doublecross the double-crossers.'

He liked that. He smiled broadly.

'She should know,' he said. 'Did you take her out?'

'Yes, we saw each other.'

'Who else has she been seeing?'

'I don't know,' I said. 'She holds her gin cards very close to the chest.'

'I'd better call her. She still at the same hotel?'

'As far as I know.'

He grabbed a phone. 'Get me Claridge's,' he said. I had no doubt that Kitty's hotel bill would find its way into my budget.

'Where's the action?' he said. 'You come across any new action?'

'I don't know what your type is these days, Paul.'

'I'm a knee man. I like them on their knees.'

'That narrows the field of course.'

'I forgot—you're a happily married man, aren't you?'

'That's right,' I said.

'Me, too. I was never divorced.'

The phone rang and he was smiling for once as he spoke into it.

'Give me Mrs Raven, will you? Mrs Paul Raven, yeah.'

He waved the receiver about while waiting. 'I hear they had a bomb scare at Claridge's last week. They should keep all those foreign kings out.' I heard a polite voice at the other end of the line trying to attract his attention. 'No answer from the room. Well, leave a message, will you? Say her husband just got back and where the hell was she.'

There was a knock at the door and two secretaries entered with fresh supplies of drink and a carton of nuts.

'Give me one of those,' Raven said. He examined the label on the bottle. 'Only eight years old. Okay, it'll do. Put the rest there and fix it later.' The girls trooped out again. Paul splashed two generous tots on to ice. He handed me one and raised his glass.

'Is this part of the four million?' I said.

That was the best joke he had heard since New York.

'Dick,' he said, 'if you're going to steal, never steal for peanuts.'

CHAPTER THIRTY

It was eight days before Alison phoned me.

I won't cheat and pretend that I thought of nothing else during those eight days, but I was taking Nembutal by the third day. I was somebody living a triple life. I saw little of Susan, far too much of Raven, and in every free moment I thought about Alison. It's strange how the human mind swings back and forth. Once, alone at my desk, seeking for the hundredth time to perfect the screenplay, I found myself beginning a letter to her which later I destroyed—but traces of it remained in the dialogue I subsequently wrote for my fictitious characters, and in subtle ways the girl in the film began to assume those characteristics which, in Alison, I admired and missed. I thought, if I never see her again she'll see this film and remember my hurt. In a way it was a form of hate, for there were moments when I despised my own weakness and lashed out through my characters. I could imagine her going to the Swiss Cottage Odeon and seeing pieces of our love up there on the screen. Lacking the present, I wanted to make her uneasy in the future.

Raven, on the other hand, gave of himself freely: I never had to worry whether he would phone me. He seemed determined to win my confidence. Nothing was too much trouble and he insisted that he take all the major worries on his own shoulders. I must say he kept Hogarth and the rest of the front office at a safe distance and his concern for my well-being bordered, at times, on tenderness—for he had charm when he wanted to use it. Now I blame myself for being put off guard. Had I been living my usual hermit-like existence which I have always found works best for me in those uneasy final weeks before shooting starts, I daresay I would have suspected more. From time to time I did have suspicions, but I never acted on them; I was too possessed.

Once again I had cause to be thankful for Stan's loyalty. It couldn't have been an easy decision for him to take. I was a transient friend, good for the duration of the film—but beyond that the chances were that we would part completely. End of picture parties promote drunken exchanges of undying affection, but it is rare to work with the same crew again.

He came to my office after lunch one day. I was working on the script and vaguely irritated by the interruption because most of the queries he put to me could have been answered by George. He fumbled around and seemed unwilling to bring the conversation to an end, something out of character for him, for he knew my working habits by now and in any case was, by nature, decisive.

'What else?' I said. 'Anything else?'

'No, that answers me, I think. Just wanted to double-check on those locations.'

I picked up my pencil again, but he made no move to go.

'How's the script going, d'you think?'

'I'm reasonably happy. No, that's a modest lie. I think it's bloody good.'

'The new pages I read seemed much better. Tighter.'

'D'you like the way the girl's coming out?'

'Yes, I've got sympathy for her now, something I never felt in the earlier versions.'

He hesitated again. 'Look, don't take this the wrong way, will you? Because it may be nothing, and I don't usually repeat gossip. And that's all it might be. Gossip.'

I suddenly felt sick. My mind immediately began to frame excuses for Susan, racing ahead to those moments I dreaded most.

'What're you trying to tell me?'

'Well, I was chatting one of the girls in Raven's office this morning. Nothing much, just the usual stuff while I was waiting. And I asked her if she'd read any of our script. I saw a copy there on her desk, and I just said it for something to say really.'

'And?'

'Well, she said she had read it, and that she liked parts of it. I mean, she's not a critic or anything, naturally. Then she said something I didn't take in at first—it was only said casually.'

He looked up at me and met my eyes.

'She said they were expecting the next batch of pages in from the States this afternoon.'

I stared at him and as one panic receded it was replaced by another, and with it came anger.

'In from the States?'

He nodded. 'That's what she said.'

'The bastard,' I said. 'He's got somebody else working on it behind my back. Did you get a copy?'

'No. As I say it didn't register at the time, and then he called me in. When I got through I went looking for the one on her desk, but it had disappeared. It might be nothing, of course.'

'Not with Raven.'

'You didn't mind me telling you?'

'Well, I mind, but not your telling me. That fat slobby bastard. He knows I'm slaving away here. Okay, Stan, thanks. Let me think about it, I've got to think how to handle it. Don't worry, he won't trace it back to you.'

'Oh, that doesn't matter.'

'Don't be Jack Armstrong. Of course it matters. With the fat boy you have to be very careful—he's the only one permitted to roul. If he ever finds out you were the one, you're going to be looking for another job.'

'Okay, but I don't want you to feel embarrassed if it does come out. I mean, I'll understand, if it does.'

He left the room hurriedly and once he had gone I indulged in some solitary childish tantrums—hurling pencils and script across the room in a frenzy of frustrated rage, and then, when I had calmed down sufficiently, picking them all up again.

Having made the promise to Stan, I had to think about how to present my opening remarks to Raven. I had seen him operate with other people, and a shouting match was something he would win hands down. I needed to be more subtle, it was important that I put him on the defensive. But at the same time speed was of the essence. Now that I was in possession of the information I had to act upon it immediately. Still pacing, I opened the communicating door and shouted to Pam to get Raven on the phone.

I went back to my desk, arranged cigarettes, ashtray and lighter conveniently near and waited for the phone to buzz.

It went after a few seconds' delay and I picked it up like a hand grenade with the pin removed.

'Paul?' I said.

'Who's Paul?' a voice said, 'I thought you'd be expecting me.'

Nothing registered for a moment.

'You must be a very busy chemist's shop.'

'Yes, I am,' I said foolishly.

'Are you too busy to take my order?'

'Darling, I'm sorry, I was waiting for somebody else to come through and when the phone went I picked up the wrong one. That doesn't sound right, either, does it?'

'You're in a bad way.'

'Yes, I am. I've missed you.'

'I missed you too, that's why I'm ringing.'

My other phone buzzed. I juggled with the two receivers, putting one hand over the private mouthpiece.

'Pam,' I said. 'I'm on the other line, I'll have to call back.'

'He says he wants to see you anyway.'

'Tell him I'll be right over.'

I put the phone back and returned to Alison in time to hear her say, '. . . but don't if you don't mean it.'

'What don't I mean?'

The line seemed to go dead suddenly.

'Darling?' I said, 'what is it, what's the matter?'

'Nothing. I'm just being stupid, that's all. I suppose I'm not very good at it yet. I just want to see you. When can I see you, can I see you now, this afternoon?'

'Not this afternoon, I can't.'

'This evening then? He's out at some convention all evening, I could meet you somewhere and we could drive again. I've thought of somewhere this time.'

'I don't think this evening's possible either. Look, it would take too long to explain and it's nothing to do with us, that I promise you. I want to see you, too.'

I waited for a reply, but it never came.

'Darling, don't be miserable, please.'

'I'm not,' she said.

'My life's too bloody complicated—not with you, with everything except you, and when we do see each other I'll explain it all. I'll ring you back this evening, as soon as I can. Will you be in?'

'Yes, I'll be in.'

'I do love you, you know.'

'Do you?'

'Well, don't say it like that, you know I do.'

'I don't know anything any more. I'll wait for your call then.'

'Don't be sad. I'll make it up to you.'

'I'm not sad,' she said, and with that she disconnected misery. My first thought was to call her back immediately, but some part of me had already begun to look beyond love towards survival, and I got up from the desk and left the room to meet another betrayal.

CHAPTER THIRTY-ONE

Raven's office was in darkness when I arrived. Kitty and her interior decorator had concealed the largest colour television set on the market in a very expensive Chinese lacquer cabinet—the result destroyed both the functional and the traditional, but I don't suppose Raven noticed. He had always bought taste at second-hand and let somebody else pay for it.

He was watching one of the moonshots.

'Our boys have done it again,' he said, 'pour yourself a drink.'

He fiddled with the control knobs and succeeded in making an already distorted picture more obscure. What seemed to be a swollen piece of ectoplasm floated in the top left hand corner of the screen, and a muffled American voice came and went. I caught two or three words clear of static and I think the astronaut said, 'Chuck told me if we get out of this one he'll thank God.' I had the impression that I was present at a séance; Raven, crouched in his seat, concentrated on every out of focus detail.

'They're in one hell of a spot,' he said. 'But they're going to come through. Houston and American know-how are going to pull them through.' He sounded like a parent telling a fairy story to a child nearly asleep.

'Did you get a drink? Pour me another, will you?'

The screen suddenly went blank, then an announcer was hurriedly faded in, and in tones normally reserved for Royal funerals, informed us that they had temporarily lost the picture. Raven turned the sound down, but left vision on.

'Well, baby, did you want to see me, or did I want to see you?'

'I called you, Paul, because something came up which disturbed me.'

'That's right, you called me.'

'And I thought I'd better discuss it with you right away.'

'Before you get started, I've got something for you, something I know you'll like.'

He opened the centre drawer in his desk and took out a small package.

'Go ahead, open it.'

He sipped his drink and regarded me paternally, pleasure spreading over his face. I put a finger nail under the gift-wrapping and tore open the package.

'I had it sent over for you.'

I studied the object inside the box without comprehension, turning it over in my hands several times before I could decide whether I was holding it the right way up. It was made of clear plastic in parts and was in the shape of an intricate box. Turning it again, I discovered that there was a small piece of gold metal on the base which carried the words 'Survival Kit'.

'Let me show you,' Raven said. He took it from me and put it on the desk. Then he pressed the small plaque. The thing started to make noises which after a few seconds I recognised as the sound of an old-fashioned toilet requiring several attempts to get it to flush. The thing was programmed to produce the sound of gushing water finally, then there was a pause, and then a particularly ripe fart. The thing then switched itself off and became an inanimate and obscenely useless object once again.

Raven choked over his drink.

'Isn't that cute? Put it on the table at a dinner party and watch the reactions.'

'They should have one on the moon,' I said, 'it might give them a few laughs.'

'I knew you'd like it. Try it on Susan to-night.'

He topped up his drink again and pushed the bottle towards me.

'Sorry, I interrupted you then. Go ahead.'

'Well, it concerns the script.'

'How's it going, by the way?'

'I think it's going well. I've done a lot of work since you last read it.'

'Great, can't wait to read it.'

'I hoped you'd say that, because what disturbed me this afternoon was something I couldn't really believe. Now, you and I have got no secrets, right?'

'Right.'

'So, don't take what I'm going to say now the wrong way.'

'Dick, before you go any further, let me give you the bottom line. You're running the show. You're in charge of the shop.'

'I got a call this afternoon, from the Coast. Never mind who, that's not important. But somebody I trust, right?'

He nodded, leaning back in his chair, so that the reflected light from the television screen obscured his features.

'And the purpose of the call was to warn me that another writer was working on the script. Now, it's quite expensive to call long distance, and I don't think my friend wastes his money.'

He leaned forward again and toyed with the Survival Kit on the desk. His fingers prodded at it, but he resisted setting it off again.

'Dick,' he said deliberately, 'I'm going to level with you. We're partners and I owe it to you, otherwise our relationship is not very meaningful. If you hadn't come to me, I was going to come to you. You ask Kitty. You're quite right, your friend, whoever he is, is quite right. I am having a little extra work done on the script.'

'But why?'

'Hear me out, will you? You gotta understand, Dick, that the situation in New York's not good. The new boys are feeling their way, they need a little security, they want a little insurance. Look, I wasn't going to tell you this, but since we've opened this can of peas I may as well give you the whole thing. When I got over there they wanted out. But I mean, out. They were going to cancel the picture, pay you off, out. Well, I used a little friendly persuasion, did a little horse trading, and talked my ass off, with the result that we're sitting here to-day. Okay, I'm talking to you as a friend now, remember. What do they know about the business, do they know Dick Warren? Sure they know of you, but to them you're just a name on the balance sheet. I had to sell you. I don't mind telling you, I had to give them a hard sell. Now part of their concern was they didn't go for the story, and I had to admit that one or two of their ideas made sense. So I had to go along with them, you know you can't win them all. In the end I got the deal, but I had to do a little trading. And part of the trading was a few changes in the script.'

'But why didn't you tell me? You could have told me as soon as you got back.'

'I didn't want to bother you.'

'You don't think finding out like this bothers me?'

'Dick, I thought it was a risk worth taking.'

'Who's doing the revisions?'

'Murdock.'

'But he's third rate.'

'You're right. He's fifth rate. That's why I hired him. I ain't going to use his script.'

He poured me another drink without asking.

'I've got too much self-respect,' he said. 'They ain't going to read it either. And I tell you something else, they ain't going to read your script. What goes on the screen is between you and me, we're the ones.'

'I still don't know why you didn't tell me.'

'You don't? Well, I'm sorry. You know what you mean to me, Dick.'

'Do I?'

'Yeah, sure you do. You're all upset now and I appreciate that. Murdock's nothing, forget Murdock. They wanted a new writer. I gave them a new writer. Screw Murdock, he's just a name pulled out of the hat. But you represent to me something I'd like to be. What do I do? I make deals, right? I go to New York and meet these jerks and I keep one hand on my balls. They're pretty smart, but I'm a little smarter. They think they're screwing me, and I took them to the cleaners. I can't write scripts, I can't direct pictures, I can't do any of those creative things, but I pick the ones who can. I picked you, Dick. Now you tell me I made a mistake.'

I couldn't see his eyes all the time, but I swear there were tears in his voice when he finished. It was the moment of maximum danger for me. I suppose I wanted to be convinced against my better judgment.

'I think you made a mistake in not telling me immediately.'

'I admit that. I did what I did because I thought it was for your good, but if you tell me I made a mistake, then I apologise. I had to play the cards I was dealt. But I thought I knew you pretty well, and there didn't seem any sense in upsetting you. You see, you're an artist, Dick, you're too emotional, too close. That's what a producer's for—to stay objective and call the shots. I give you my word, Murdock's pages are going to end up in the men's room.'

After a pause I said, 'Can I see them?'

'If you want.'

'Yes, I'd like to see them.'

'Take a copy with you. But, Dick, first of all, you and I have got to understand each other. You want to make this picture, right?'

I nodded.

'It's something you believe in.'

'I believe in my own script.'

'Then that's the one we're going to shoot.'

I believed him then, because I wanted to believe him, I wanted to buy time. He gave me a copy of the other script and again emphasised that it had only been commissioned to placate New York, and told me to read it if I must and then forget it. Like so many others before me I convinced myself that I alone could beat the system. After all, I still played roulette!

We had a final drink together, and then contact with the moon was re-established and he turned up the sound. I excused myself. When I was half-way to the door he called me back.

'Hey!' he said, 'you forgot your gift.' I took his senseless bribe with the same smile I had used to accept his duplicity. The two men on the moon seemed as remote and as unreal as the rest of my life.

CHAPTER THIRTY-TWO

My memories of what happened next are like disjointed pieces of film, out-takes from somebody else's life assembled by a madman.

There is a first sequence in black and white when I left Raven's office and collected my car from the underground garage. I placed the offending script and the gift on the passenger seat beside me and drove automatically, not dangerously but without any comprehension. Later—how much later I have no idea—I found myself heading north on the Edgware Road and it was an unfamiliar traffic sign, the green figure of a man walking that caused me to brake and take note of my surroundings. I looked for a phone box, turning off to search side-streets and when I found one I got out and left the engine running. I phoned Alison. There the film is ripped, it no longer runs through the projector of my mind, and the sound track has been erased. I suppose we talked in urgency, with that desperate kind of love that always precedes a doomed meeting, but for the life of me I can recall nothing of what we said, and yet curiously I can remember staring through the small squared windows of the phone booth and seeing a woman in a nightdress come out on to a balcony to brush her long hair. Then blank frames again, until Alison's car comes into sight behind me in my driving mirror, and I keep her small headlights in view as we move farther and farther out of London, driving in orange light, and memory slowly assumes colours even though it was night. City streets give way to suburbs, and then green hedges side-sliding past and behind me the night-sky glowing as though London was on fire and we were fleeing to safety. Once a shock cut, by the cats' eyes in the centre of the twisting road, the blood-splattered fur of a night animal killed at speed and I glanced up in my mirror to see Alison swerve to avoid something beyond care. After that the black green of the countryside, the street lighting spaced at longer intervals until finally we were driving into a wall of darkness.

A different sound track, the hiss of rubber on tarmac giving way to the muffled squeal of grass as we left the road and bumped across the soft verge to come to rest under waiting trees. Silence first, and then the unfamiliar silence of the countryside at night and we got out and embraced in the damp air and I felt the whole length of her body against mine, remaining there like waxworks kissed into life until longing overcame fear.

Then the smell of leather in the back of the Bentley, the feel of leather cold against my naked skin as we fumbled like children in a nursery cupboard, my hands ice-cold on her remembered breasts, tracing her blind skin until my fingers found warmth. She cried out for times remembered, her body arched beneath mine and one hand flung against the misted window. Single frames, the frozen familiarity of the act of love, blurred in the same featureless expressions of sudden death. Like the animal on the road, obliterated. A sudden rush in darkness to gain the safety of the other side which ends in a burst of light and pain.

Consciousness returned in slow motion, the madman finally quieted, and we slept for fitful tender minutes until the cramped reality of our surroundings demanded that we parted, the warm flesh relinquishing its hold by degrees.

I draped my jacket around her shoulders and we sat side by side like lovers on a park bench, her head across my chest, her hair gloving my lips. Her breast beat in my palm ever more slowly and I eased my fingers to touch the nipple.

'They've grown,' I said.

'That was Lucy.'

'Did you feed her?'

'I tried. I tried for about a month, but I wasn't any good at it.'

She slid farther down until her head rested in my lap.

'Don't we make a fuss about it all,' she said. 'Why d'you think that is?'

'I don't know,' I said, 'I've often thought the same thing.'

'Ever since I wrote you that note I've thought of nothing else. It was my fault, wasn't it?'

'What're you talking about?'

169

'Now you're all conscience stricken. I can feel it.'

'Course I'm not. I'm just sleepy.'

'I know you, you haven't changed. I was always guilt-ridden before, but you saved yours till after the event.'

'That's nothing out of the ordinary. Come here,' I said. I lifted her head and searched for her mouth. 'Are you wearing lipstick?'

'You see! No, I took it off before I left the house. That just proves how guilt-ridden you are.'

'Caution isn't guilt.'

'It's the beginning.'

'You're not going to be convinced, are you?'

'No,' she said. 'But it won't make any difference to my loving you.'

We listened to one another then, for I could not trust myself to speak. Much later she buried her face against my neck and whispered: 'We're mad, you and me, we always were mad. There was always too much love.'

'Did you used to think about me?'

'I thought about you at the altar when I was marrying him. Does that shock you?'

'No.'

'It terrified me. It stayed with me all the time. It was always you I was making love to. When I was pregnant with Lucy he was away out of the country on business a lot of the time, and I pretended it was your child and that you were dead. Once I drove myself to your old flat and sat outside in the car for hours until it was quite dark. A woman came out of the house next door and asked me if I was all right. She wasn't anybody we'd ever known, all the people were different. I remember telling her my husband was dead, and she took me in and gave me a cup of tea.'

'My dear,' I said, 'you make me feel very humble.'

'No, I'm not telling you because I want to hurt you, it isn't that. I'm only saying it because now it all seems so far away. As if it happened to another person. You see, I never understood why we ended. That's really what I could never explain to myself. It all stopped, but it didn't end, did it? and that doesn't make sense either.'

'I used to have the same trouble.'

170

'Did you?'

'Yes, asking myself why.'

'But we both got married, to people we didn't love . . . No, that's not fair, I've got no right to say that.'

I knew she expected something from me at that moment, but it wasn't that easy for she was too near the truth and I despised myself for recognising it. Does it sound too far fetched to say that I could betray Susan with my body but not with my mind?

'It's not even the whole truth for me,' she said when she had waited. 'I'm not that awful. It's just that it was never the same. That's not so bad, is it?'

'I'm not the right person to ask,' I said.

'Tell me something else . . . No, you don't have to.'

'What?'

'No, I mustn't start on that. That really is madness, and I want it to be perfect this time.'

'What? You must say it now.' I wanted the first confession to be hers. Even dreading what she might say, I needed to know what those ten lost years contained. The body is so much more important to men, we think that faithfulness begins and ends between the thighs. But it was a question she asked, not a secret she surrendered.

'I was going to say did you have other women. Apart from your wife.'

'You know me,' I said lightly, 'I'm boringly faithful in my fashion.'

And so we started again and as we talked, as we promised and probed, I remembered all, I remembered what it had been like to love her before. In that parked car on a road I could never again locate on the map, we began the slow process of opening old wounds. I thought, Oh, God, can You once let it happen without hurt? Repeating too many promises to keep, squandering the remaining moments before we dressed in desperate suffocating embraces, we excused both the past and the future.

Later, our actual parting under the swollen, dripping trees had a remoteness I would not dare put in a film. I opened her car door and she slid into the driving seat and out of habit fastened her strap, while I stood there for all the world like a driving instructor watching a successful pupil move off alone for the first time.

I followed her for most of the journey, but when we reached the outskirts of London the late night traffic suddenly thickened and gradually the distance between us lengthened until I lost her at the lights. From that moment I drove with extra care, preparing myself for innocence.

CHAPTER THIRTY-THREE

She was never jealous of Susan in the conventional sense, at least not in the way that I came to resent Osmond, but she laid siege to the rest of my life—part incredulous, part genuine interest, but always underlying the questions, a need to be reassured. It was as if the physical possession of my body (for after that first evening our demands upon each other became obsessive) was but a first step upon a long road. Sometimes I could hardly recognise the past in her, and in telling the story now there is no point in concealing anything. I have nobody to spare and my own feelings count for little. Just to describe those days is pain enough.

She had changed, we both had. In reading the map of physical love, I could chart the valleys and the peaks like any avid schoolboy—and the comparison is not too distorted, for often we behaved like adolescents, taking the appalling risks without thought, the need to slake a sexual thirst overwhelming all caution.

There is no hurt to compare with the careless wounds that lovers inflict—they are covered easily enough at the time, but the flesh never heals completely beneath the dressings. They seep (I believe that is the medical term), they constantly remind us that we are fallible, the edges fester.

The distorted face of love does not only surprise us on the pillow; it is in those moments when, all passion spent and we least expect it, that the game of make-believe shatters with sad ease.

I remember once, when we lay stupefied by that mysterious damp aftermath of love in Stan's characterless Bayswater bed-sitter (for by now I had drawn him into the net), watching life outside at pavement level through a gap in the drawn curtains. Her arm lay cramped beneath my head and as she withdrew it to reach for her Cartier wrist-watch—that expensive referee—on the bedside table, her groping fingers picked up an old Call Sheet.

'I thought you said you hadn't started shooting,' she said.

'I haven't yet. That was just for make-up tests.'

'Do they still do those?'

'Some cameramen insist.'

She studied the sheet intently.

'Is that her understudy?'

'Stand-in.'

'What's the difference?'

'Stand-in's don't talk. They just stand.'

'I could be a stand-in.'

'You could, but you wouldn't like it.'

'I might. I'd see more of you.'

'Then everyone would say, why is that pretty girl a stand-in, why isn't she playing the part?'

'Would you like to direct me?'

'I should hate it. What's the time?'

'I don't know. Early. Why wouldn't you direct me?'

'Because I never sleep with leading ladies.'

'Never?'

'Well, not any longer. What time is it?'

'There's ages yet. At least twenty minutes.'

All our meetings were as carefully plotted as a Monte Carlo rally; there were regular check points and penalty marks to be awarded if we failed.

'Is that why you've never directed your wife?'

'Sort of,' I said. I was trying in a slow, subtle way to read my own watch without her being aware.

She studied the Call Sheet again. 'All those people,' she said, 'just to look after one German girl.'

'She can't help being German,' I said.

'She's very attractive, isn't she? Men find her sexy.'

'Do they?'

'I read in a magazine that she's had her nose altered.'

'Did you?' I said, edgy now, but wanting to humour her.

'I'd never have my nose altered.'

'You don't need to.'

'Do you find her sexy?'

'Darling,' I said, 'I do believe you're jealous.'

'No, I'm just interested. It's another world to me. I don't understand how somebody like you can spend time with Miss Lehmann without being attracted to her. Or she to you for that matter.'

'Well,' I said, 'that's a very interesting question, and one I would like to answer in depth. Unfortunately, despite the fact that I'm very comfortable here in bed with you, and find you at least two hundred times more attractive and sexually desirable than Miss Lehmann—with or without a nose job—we both have to get up and dress.'

'I love it when you get all pompous,' she said.

I managed to swing myself out of the bed, but she put both arms around me and held me there in a sitting position.

'Now in the old days, before full frontal nudity, you could show two people in bed in films, providing one of them had two feet on the floor. Or it might have been just one foot, I'm not sure. It was before my time.'

'So we could have got away with this?'

'No. We would have been wearing pyjamas.'

'But adultery was all right with one foot on the floor?'

'Again, no. That was another set of rules.'

'Tell me about those,' she said.

'I can see through you. You're just trying to prolong the moment. And, as my mother never stopped telling me, it'll all end in tears.'

But I turned round, and she kept me there while the penalty marks mounted, and we made love again. I don't want to give the impression that I was a sexual athlete: most novels I read to-day endow the leading characters with powers beyond the ordinary, and life, I have found, does not emulate Mr Harold Robbins with any degree of accuracy in the bedroom. But sometimes we are driven by a common need and in the first flush of any passion we find that we can surprise ourselves. I had become such a stranger to love, that each time we met I needed to explore myself through her, and at such moments I could smother guilt with tenderness.

And when we weren't making love in a borrowed bed, we probed each other endlessly. And whereas Alison showed little or no interest in my life with Susan, I was drawn more and more to explore the web of her own life with Osmond. I had to put the questions, even though I learned to fear the answers. Having possessed Alison, I now needed to possess him; I felt in some obscure way that I could not fully explain to myself, that his claim on her was still greater than mine.

'Do you and Cyril still share a double bed?' I said once.

'Yes.'

'Which side do you sleep on?'

'Like we are now.'

A lover's success brings no comfort. Trust, which we built so instantly at every fresh meeting, was watered the moment we parted.

I was once driven to ask whether she and Osmond still made love regularly.

'Yes,' she said, 'he's very highly sexed.'

'And you?'

'I'm his wife.'

'What a very British answer,' I said, regretting the words the moment they left my mouth.

'Well, I am, just as Susan's still your wife. I could ask you the same question.'

'Ask it,' I said.

'Darling, we're not children, we are both married and so far you haven't suggested we have a double divorce.'

It was the first time she had mentioned the possibility. Until that moment we had both avoided the subject, not, I think, for any conventional reason—my own feelings went deeper than that: like a child I had tied a cotton to the loose tooth, but I hadn't found the will to fasten the other end to the door knob.

'I'm always reading about those. Couples living next door

who suddenly up and exchange—it's the staple diet of the Sunday papers now that clergymen on grave charges no longer increase the circulation.'

She smiled, but her mood, which I could now recognise with an old skill, remained serious.

'I'm not a total bitch,' she said, 'I still care for him.'

'Fine.'

'Shouldn't I care for him? I don't love him any more, I'm in love with you, I've never stopped loving you, so he hasn't had much of a bargain.'

It was the start of our first quarrel, there, in the rumpled bed in the basement flat, and it seemed that we exhausted ourselves in public, for the bedroom was in the front of the house and there was an endless procession of people passing at almost eye-level. The perfect setting, I suppose, for adultery, a constant reminder that we had to go back into the real world.

We patched it up, but the skin had been broken for the first time; unlike the bruise made by those kisses we give in the act of love, it was not something to cherish. We wanted too much of each other, that was the trouble. The body remembers too much, and when one is in the grip of a hopeless passion, when that happens there is no telling into what quicksands the mind will lead us. I ached for the touch of her flesh, the sweet scent of her, the feel of her hair passing through my loving fingers. Away from her I was prey to every anguish that has ever been attributed to lovers. I longed to write her letters, as before, but we had changed, life had changed us, we weren't the same people, we were only pretending to be the same people. She said once, 'I can lie to Cyril, but I can't lie to her' meaning her daughter, and she explained to me the devastating innocence of the very young, the absolute trust they place in those they love. I was a stranger in that country, but she pointed out the landmarks and I could believe in them.

Sometimes I didn't recognise the face that stared back at me from the shaving mirror. It was like going back to school, to the memory of a first love—a fragment of a long lost summer, when innocence had a tennis whiteness and the extent of love was a crumpled note hidden beneath the lid of a desk. Then the world could end with the pimple discovered in the cold wash-rooms—above the lead basin, in the mottled mirror, the face that stared back was deformed beyond belief. I remembered crying in 'the bogs' as we called them, grey flannel trousers round the ankles, a patch of daylight beneath the door, and in the distance the laughter of those who had not yet tasted the bile of unrequited love. It was this remembered pain that crowded the hours when I was absent from Alison.

I was lucky that I had plenty to occupy me, for left alone I would have resorted to desperate measures. As it was I was desperate enough, but with a kind of justice, love gave an impetus to my normal life, and preparations for the start of the film were urged forward relentlessly. I took quick decisions, and on those days when we were going to meet, the crew, I know, noted a change in me: I was kinder to people, I was tolerant of mistakes, I had love enough to spare.

CHAPTER THIRTY-FOUR

I hadn't lied to Alison about Monika Lehmann: I wasn't attracted to her sexually.

In the flesh she was rather a sad girl, and gave me the impression that everything was an effort. I suppose the language barrier had something to do with it; my own German was on a schoolboy level, and although she had obviously made efforts and was word perfect on the actual script, her conversations in English were desultory.

Her husband on the other hand spoke fluent English with an American accent, which made him doubly irritating.

For once Raven had been totally accurate in his assessment. Herr Toller (immediately known to the crew as Herr-Not-To-Be-Tolerated) combined all the worst exported characteristics of his race with an assumed international brashness. He ate too much, talked too much and held a definitive opinion on everything.

At the introductory luncheon we gave them both in the studio, he conducted monologue post-mortems on The World Cup Final, The Berlin Air Lift and Raven's last two films and succeeded in giving instant and consistent offence. I discovered that he had originally been a car salesman in Dresden. When he met Monika he decided to sell himself first, married her and embarked on what was, from a show business point of view, a double success story. His methods in the beginning were very conventional: he entered his wife for various beauty and talent contests, taught himself how to use a stills camera, showed much but not all of his wife's considerable physical endowments and was careful never to part with the negatives.

Monika had a certain photogenic rise to fame in a series of grubby little Continental films, but her acting talents seemed destined to take second place to her bust measurements. Having tasted his idea of the high life, Herr Toller was not prepared to suffer defeat, however, and worked with renewed dedication. Working on the well-tested theory that in films most of the people in a position to help can be fooled most of the time provided you are crude enough, he lowered his wife's neckline, took her to Rome, changed her name and the colour of her hair and arranged to have her photographed trying to enter St Peter's in a bikini. After that he refused all offers, displaying a degree of patience which must have strained his natural greed to the limits. His nerve held and the gamble paid off, for she eventually landed the second lead in a costly American epic about the early Christian martyrs which converted nobody to religion but established Miss Lehmann as somebody who might, in the immortal words of Raymond Chandler, provoke Bishops to kick holes in stained glass windows. It was at that point that Herr Toller invested his wife's salary in some acting lessons and made her wear dresses so modest they practically covered her forehead. While Monika studied under some local Lee Strasberg, Toller took a crash course in film contracts, committing to memory every clause that had ever been set in fine print, and inventing a few himself for good measure.

He complained endlessly about everything. In my world one learns to live with the tape-measure mentality: dressing rooms, caravans, even the comparative sizes of leading players are all subjected to serious scrutiny worthy of the Ascot Stewards. I once directed a film where the leading man insisted on having a trench dug on location so that he could walk on higher ground alongside a less exalted colleague. He wasn't the least embarrassed by the fact that half the countryside had to be dug up to bolster his ego, and in fact supervised the excavations with more animation than he gave to his actual screen performance.

Out of sheer malice I played the innocent with him and referred most of his more insane complaints to Raven. Toller had, of course, arrived armed with a translated script and knew it backwards. He had counted every line that his wife had to say and compared the total with that of the leading actor's.

'Richard,' he would say, 'I've been thinking,' and the preface inevitably meant a degrading, exhausting hour.

'I don't somehow see how Miss Lehmann can possibly play the scene in the restaurant the way it is written.'

'How's that, Kurt?'

'For one thing, it is written from the wrong point of view. The audience at this point, if you don't mind me saying so, is not concerned with the man, they are thinking only of the woman. And yet she says nothing. It's a nothing scene.'

I would begin patiently enough. 'Kurt, on film, as you well know, lines count for nothing. They're always the first thing to go when you're looking for cuts. It's situations, Kurt. I agree with you, it's the girl's scene—and when you see the way I intend to shoot it, you'll understand. I shall be on Monika most of the time, looking into her face, in big close-up—and although she says nothing, we'll know what she's thinking.'

He remained unconvinced, pulling at his lower lip and grimacing. 'I think we should try a re-write. I've even jotted down a few ideas which I think are worthy of consideration.'

'Show them to Mr Raven,' I said, 'he's already having some re-writes done.'

'He is? Since when?'

'Didn't he tell you?' I said innocently.

'Nothing, he told me nothing. When is he having these done?'

'I think some weeks ago, I'm not sure.'

'But it's in the contract, script approval.'

'Well, you'd better argue it out with Raven, he's the producer.'

'I am going now.'

The ploy misfired, and a few hours later Raven rang me.

'You prick,' he started, but his voice contained some sacred and profane remains of humour. 'You sent the Kraut to me.'

'Did I?'

'You know you did. He comes screaming into my office about re-writes.'

'Oh, that.'

'Listen, I hate the Kraut so much I wouldn't take a free ride in his Mercedes if I was stranded in the Sahara. Keep him out of my hair, baby, otherwise we're going to recast.'

'Oh, I'm sorry, Paul, I thought you could handle him.'

'Look, do us all a favour, throw a little something into his wife. You go for tits, don't you?'

'Not me,' I said. 'I'm happily married, remember?'

'Well, get somebody to ball her, or have you got a whole mess of English faggots down there?'

'No, but they're well trained,' I said. 'They've been taught that such things are the producer's prerogative.'

'Thank you, baby, thank you. I need to have that aggravation. I'm married too, in case you don't remember.'

'Of course I remember. I've bought your wife more meals than you have.'

'I'll leave you with this thought, baby: if that Nazi husband gives me any more, Lufthansa are in for a profit year.'

When I retold the story that night Susan found little humour in it.

'He's done very well for her so far,' she said. 'After all, he made her, so presumably he knows what he's talking about.'

'Have you ever met him?'

'No, but I know people who have. Robin, for example, thinks he's very bright.'

'Robin?'

'Robin Hogarth.'

'Oh, that Robin. Well, of course, he would. It takes a pimp to know a pimp.'

'I don't see anything wrong in a husband protecting his wife's best interests.'

She turned back to the bathroom mirror to finish brushing her teeth with the electric toothbrush. The batteries were dead and she flung it down.

'Use mine,' I said.

'I can't use yours.'

'Why not? You won't catch anything, I haven't been anywhere.'

She stared at me in the mirror. I thought, there isn't any topic that doesn't bring me back to Alison, and then I thought of another bathroom, the one I had never seen but imagined so vividly where perhaps at that very same moment two other people were preparing for bed. I turned away first.

'The bristles are too hard for my gums.'

'Well, eat an apple. Just as good.'

'I hate going to bed without cleaning my teeth.'

She ripped off her dressing-gown and the lushness of her body suddenly troubled me. With that practised familiarity marriage alone allows, I set about the softening of her anger. I could trace the equation of her weakness—the hidden crib at an exam I did not need to pass. The slow flattery of my quickening demands would, I knew, bring about her pleasure first, for I could afford to be generous: there was no wrist-watch on the bedside table, no passers-by to fear, only the shared loneliness and the pain of love under the mouth.

CHAPTER THIRTY-FIVE

As I see it now, safe from them all until the next time, there was a moment when I might have won hands down. Raven put a price on everything, and I should have turned the ticket round. I might have forgiven him then and been free of evil done once and for all. But the moment passed, perhaps it passed without my knowing and only hindsight brings perception. Either way, it would have been all the same to Raven, he would have retreated back into his money or vast carelessness, like Gatsby's Tom and Daisy, and boasted about it to his next paid audience. I suppose if I met him now, he'd greet me like a friend, but he can afford forgiveness and I can't.

I came across a photograph the other day, hidden between the pages of an old script. It was a standard ten by eight glossy and everybody was in focus. That's one of the more grotesque tricks that our profession plays on us: our failures are as generously documented as our successes. There we all are—Raven with his arm on my shoulder, Wellard, George, Bill Mason and his operator, even the ghastly Toller—all smiling broadly for the publicity cameras. It was taken on one of the sound stages and I can see portions of the half-finished set in the background. I remember the morning well. Wellard was worried about the budget he had been given for his designs and with typical courage had demanded that Raven see for himself.

In a weak moment I had found enough pity to put Grotefend back on the payroll, and he repaid me with slavish sycophancy. 'By the time I'm through, Dick,' he said, 'they'll know who made the picture. I'm going to do a slap-up job on you.' Now years later, his stills honour his promise, and the irony of it is it's the only evidence that remains. Of the film itself, I haven't a trace.

'It's like everything else,' Wellard said that morning, 'you get what you pay for, Mr Raven.'

'That's right,' Raven said. 'Who's arguing?'

'It's your picture, and if you want a set this size, I'll build it, but I'll need another twenty thousand.'

'No way.'

'Look, Mr Raven, I haven't had the undoubted pleasure and privilege of working for you before, but Mr Warren here will tell you that I'm not particularly fond of my own voice outside the bedroom. If I wanted to impress you for five glorious minutes I could pretend it can be done for less. Now when I say I want another twenty thousand pounds, I'm not guessing. I've calculated it down to the last bent nail.'

Raven ignored him and turned to me.

'Can you save it anywhere else?'

'That's begging the question,' I said. 'We either want the sets or we don't want them.'

'We want them.'

'Then the rest is academic. I have to find the saving somewhere else. I'll cut down on the crowd budget or something.'

'If I might be allowed to add one final, tiny scream of protest,' Wellard said, 'the point I'm trying to make is that I have been designing sets for a script which I gather is being re-written on both sides of the Atlantic, which started out as a reasonably modest thriller. Greater minds than mine have now decided in their wisdom that a small, back-street café should be replaced by something approaching the ballroom at the Dorchester.'

'It's a very good scene,' Toller interrupted. 'Very important to the character of the girl.'

'Yeah, it's a good scene, but it needs production value,' Raven said. He fumbled with some book-matches to relight his cigar, but Grotefend was there with an Olympic flame.

'Sorry, sorry, sir,' he said. 'I just refilled it.'

'Well, watch it, for Christsake! Could have taken off my eyebrows.'

'I think what Jimmy is saying, Paul . . .'

'I know what Jimmy's saying.'

'Well, hear me out. Jimmy's point is that we're going to waste money building something we could just as well shoot for real.'

'Is this it here?' Raven turned to survey the almost bare stage.

'Yes,' Wellard said, 'I've had the area marked out for you and just put a few flats up at the end to show you the height.'

Raven paced into the distance. Toller followed him.

'Stupid old closet queen,' Wellard said.

'That he isn't,' I said.

'Don't be so sure, dear.'

We stood and waited until Raven had finished his deliberations. Grotefend continued to instruct his cameramen to take shots. The flashbulbs blinded me so that when Raven was close enough to talk again I studied his face through a series of black dots.

'Dick, I've said it before, and I'll say it now in front of these gentlemen, you're the creative guy. You make the decision. All I want to spell out is this: don't give 'em something they can see on television for free. I'm not cutting corners at this stage of the game. But don't anybody come to me at the preview and say why did we shoot it all in a toilet.'

I heard Wellard sigh.

'Well, I'd better get back to the old drawing board then, if that's the decision.'

'We're waiting on you, Dick,' Raven said.

'I'll go over it with Stan and Jimmy. We'll find a way.'

'That's all I'm asking.'

Wellard was already marching through the big doors. Raven stared after him through cigar smoke.

'Would you like any copies of these photographs, Mr Raven?' Grotefend said, 'For your personal use.'

Raven walked through him. 'Let's you and me drive back to town together.'

'I'd like to come with you,' Toller said, 'there are one or two things I'm not happy about.'

'Later, I'll talk to you later,' Raven said. He put his arm through mine and we walked past the bored carpenters into the dusty sunlight. Behind me I heard Toller attempt to regain face. 'One thing we must be sure about,' he said to Bill Mason. 'Miss Lehmann can only be photographed from one side in close-up.'

Looking at Grotefend's souvenir now, I wish we'd all had someone to care as much about us.

CHAPTER THIRTY-SIX

Looking at bearded hitch-hikers through the darkened glass of a large Rolls limousine is not something I enjoy, and when I am driving alone I invariably stop, but with Raven that day there was a generation gap both inside and outside the car, and we glided to London leaving a trail of raised fists in our wake, like so many mock crucifixions.

With the glass division between ourselves and the chauffeur electrically raised, we were isolated in the most expensive cocoon ever made.

'Why do you employ faggots?' Raven said, before we had gone half a mile.

'I don't. I employ talent.'

'You think he's talented?'

'Yes, I do. I think he's one of the best.'

'Fags are always unreliable. I think you should get rid of him.'

'I'd need a better excuse than that,' I said.

'Okay. I don't like his designs. That good enough for you?'

I knew that it was an occasion for bravery. Raven was too experienced, and too dirty a fighter to risk sparring in public. He had always done his training for the big event behind closed doors, and I suppose the black glass of the Rolls gave him a feeling of confidence. The Queensberry Rules were a closed book to him: you came out of the corner and you tried to open the cut on the forehead, you butted, you wiped the sweaty laces of your gloves across your opponent's eyes when you broke from the clinch.

'Well, I'm not going to fire him,' I said.

'That's okay.'

'And if you fire him just because you don't like the way he talks, then you'd better look for another director too.'

He was slumped in his corner of the car and his cigar had gone out. He operated the window switch and cold air rushed in to ruffle his sparse hair as he threw four inches of hand-rolled Havana leaf into the passing gutter. The window was closed again and the sudden vacuum made my ears hum.

'Oh, we're going to play that game, are we?' he said.

'I'm not playing any game. I'm trying to make a film the best way I know how. And before we settle Wellard's future, he made one good point. When do we finalise the script? I've read the forty pages of shit you commissioned.'

He nodded, switching to the Statesman role for a second.

'You're not serious about shooting any of that, with or without me? Unless of course, you don't care any more. Because I'll make it easy for you, I'd rather wait until Susan's dying of leukemia before I shoot a page of that junk.'

'What if I told you that nobody likes your script?'

'You're entitled to your opinion.'

'New York didn't even understand it.'

'That encourages me. It is written in English, of course.'

'You fucking directors, you think you know it all.'

'No, we don't. Some of us have just decided to turn round and trade a few punches, that's all.'

'I could replace you to-morrow.'

I nodded. 'Ten times over. Or I've got a better idea—why don't you direct it yourself? Take that other script, it's just about on your level.'

'Whatever script anybody shoots, it'll be my decision.'

'But nobody's arguing that point. You are, as they say, the final words.'

I turned from him and looked out of my side window. I suddenly felt capable of throwing in my towel, not from cowardice, but from a terrible rage to live. And it was in that mood I stared past my own reflection towards the country that Alison inhabited—for coincidence once again dictated the geography of both my lives: we were just entering the outskirts of Hampstead.

Raven said, 'Don't make an enemy of me, Dick.'

'You want me to treat you as a friend?'

'I want you to be smart. Walking off the picture isn't going to do you any good.'

'Oh, you'll have to do better than that,' I said. 'I've got some money in the bank. Don't rely on me selling boot laces immediately.'

His expression never changed. He took a fresh cigar from his case and toyed with it.

'What's your objection to the script?'

'Your script?' He nodded. 'Well, how shall I put it? I mean, I'll try and be honest. I won't overstate the case by saying that it's unshootable. You could find somebody to shoot it, and I guess you're mean enough to try. But if you really want my opinion, what you'd end up with would be third rate. There are quite a lot of directors who can improve on a bad script, but nobody can lick a bad script. You ought to know that by now, you've made a few bombs in your time.'

'And you think yours is the answer?'

'I think it's nearer, and if we could stop circling round each other and take a few decisions, we could still pull something out of the fire. You see, curiously enough, I'm not looking for a fight. You started this, not me.'

'What did I start? You're the one. Jesus, all I did was make a suggestion concerning some fag art director and you hit the roof.'

'Oh, no,' I said. 'That's too convenient, too simple—and you're not a simple man.'

He grinned at me, the thin compliment slipping under his guard.

'You don't think so?'

'No.'

'Well, you could be right. I'm not looking for a fight either, I just want my own way. You can't blame me for that. You knew that going in.'

'Yes, the only difference is that I didn't choose you, you chose me. I could produce this picture without you.'

'Not any longer.'

'So we're back to square one. Now, empty threats are a waste of everybody's time. True?'

'I guess so.'

'So I'll say it very calmly. I am not going to shoot one word of that other script. I am not going to fire Wellard unless he falls down on the job. And finally I don't want you on the set while I'm shooting.'

The stage directions would have read 'Long pause' at this point. Raven lit the new cigar with care, then blew on the tip to get an even glow.

'I'm going to surprise you,' he said at last. 'I was just testing you out to see how much you cared. You're quite right about me not being simple. I like to do everything the hard way. I can be a mean bastard if I put my mind to it; you don't know how mean, though you may get a chance to find out later on.'

If this all sounds like dialogue from some melodrama, I can't help it. That was the way he spoke. He had cast himself long ago and perhaps because he knew no other life, he remembered too many old movies and believed in them implicitly. He had other performances to give and when he thought the occasion warranted would switch from the old-time heavy, enigmatic behind the cigar smoke, to the equally bogus humanitarian ready to be seen dining with fashionable Negro actors and send large donations to the safer Liberal causes, always ensuring that his charity began at home but ended up in the gossip columns.

When he turned on the charm that was the time to make sure your gum shield was in place.

'Why spoil a beautiful friendship?' I said.

'Have you cast the boy yet?'

'No, not yet. I gave you my short list.'

'Well, I'll surprise you again, you can take an unknown, take the kid who's just been at the National Theatre.'

'Nethercott, you mean? John Nethercott.'

'Yeah, that's the name. D'you think he'd change it?'

'Ask him,' I said, 'you've got a way with men.'

'To hell with it, they don't queue for names any more. Well, does that make you happy?'

'I'm delighted, he was always the one I wanted. I don't know about Toller, though. He won't be too keen.'

'Who did he want?'

'Oh, he just wanted the part cut out.'

'Well, he's made his last territorial claim, I tell you. But I can handle Toller. I've done a little digging around and Herr Toller is getting careless. He got a little girl friend of mine pregnant the other day. I know, because I paid for the abortion. So, if Herr Toller steps too far out of line, I'm going to have to break the news to Monika, and that's his meal ticket gone out of the window. Without Monika he couldn't get himself arrested.'

I had no sympathy for Toller, and in fact disliked him as much as Raven, but I couldn't help thinking of him as a fellow sufferer at that moment. There is a fraternity of guilt.

'I may get away for a few days,' I said, 'just to concentrate on the script.'

'Good. Let me know where you are.'

'I thought I'd go down to one of the fat farms. I can work there with no temptations.'

'That's right,' Raven said, 'take the script into the sauna and sweat it off.'

CHAPTER THIRTY-SEVEN

Of course, the seemingly casual suggestion I made to Raven, with its hint of total dedication, was the result of much midnight planning. For some time now I had been aware that Alison was growing disenchanted with love in a basement. We are all so spoilt: hopelessly saturated with the ad-man's slick, we lie stranded on a beach of discontent if our material toys are not constantly to hand. Love, they used to say, will always find a way, but love between somebody else's used sheets in the stolen afternoon hours had become suspect.

We stayed as late as we dared one afternoon, our bodies just touching, sunlight making sliced bread patterns on the wall, and the heat of the streets outside pressing into the room. She wouldn't have the windows open, you could hear people's voices she said, and it made her feel too exposed.

I turned my head on the hot pillow to look at her. She had her eyes open.

'I thought you were asleep.'

'No. Is it time?'

'Nearly,' I said, 'we've got a few more minutes.'

'I was thinking, you can't go back unless you go completely back. I can't sleep any longer, at home. I lie awake all night wanting you.'

'You just think you lie awake all night. Nobody does.'

I kissed her damp eyes and my hands smoothed its way down to her breasts. She didn't move.

'When finally I do go to sleep, I have the most erotic dreams about you. Wounding dreams.'

'Poor darling,' I said.

'I don't think,' she said slowly. 'I don't think I can take much more of this.'

I propped myself on an elbow and leaned over her. Something approaching an old panic chilled me in that stifling room.

'What? What's wrong?'

'Nothing's wrong, it's nothing to do with you and me, it's just this.' Her eyes swept round the walls, and I suddenly saw the room for the first time. 'This' was the land of the bed-sitter, last year's *House and Garden* colours faded by damp, the washbasin in the cupboard, the deodorant stick on the mantelpiece beside the Pools coupons and the unpaid telephone bill.

'Well, we'll find somewhere else,' I said. 'I'll take a flat.'

'No, I don't want a flat. We'll start making it into a home, and homes are places where people go to sleep at night.'

'Darling,' I said, 'what else is there? We can't go to hotels. That would be disaster.'

She pushed her head into the pillow.

'Don't cry,' I said. 'Darling, don't cry. I don't like it any more than you do, but the alternatives are worse.'

'I'm not crying. I'm just tired.'

'I'll think of something.'

'No, it's no use. I'm just being greedy, it's my own stupid fault. I suppose it's because he's going away on a business trip.'

'Cyril?'

'Yes.'

'When?'

'The fourteenth.'

'What's to-day? To-day's the sixth. That's to-morrow week.'

'Yes, but it's pointless, as you say. There's nothing we can do about it.'

'There might be.'

'You couldn't get away in any case, so let's forget it.'

We got up and dressed then, and kissed good-bye beside a Playboy Calendar, and she left first, as per custom, and I waited until I heard the roar of her Mini before remaking the bed and washing up the coffee cups. All the time my mind was searching for some solution. For a few minutes I seriously entertained the idea of moving into the Hampstead house when Osmond left, but it was fantasy, nothing more.

It wasn't until much later that same evening, reading the papers, that I found the answer. I turned a page and there was a large advertisement of a pretty girl apparently trying to transform herself into the Michelin Tyre Man. She was wearing shiny pneumatic Bermuda shorts which inflated. 'Reduce your waist-line this new easy way in the privacy of your own home,' the copy said. Perhaps it was the words privacy and home that first caught my eye.

I phoned her from the office the next morning.

'Darling,' I said, 'I've solved it.'

She listened in silence as I outlined the scheme. We would both book into one of the fashionable health farms, perfectly legitimately, under our own names. I suggested one I had been to before, since familiarity breeds innocence as well as contempt. We could have a whole week together.

'And get healthy at the same time,' I said. 'Don't you think it's brilliant?'

'Yes,' she said, but doubt remained. 'I've got to think of Lucy.'

I'd forgotten Lucy. 'Would she miss you for a week? You could phone her every day.'

'Children don't think phones are real,' she said. 'But I'll arrange something. She can probably go and stay with a cousin.'

I got Pam to make my own booking a few minutes after we had rung up. I wanted the arrangements to be as public as possible and blamed Pam for feeding me too many sandwiches at lunchtimes. Wellard was in the office when the call was made.

'My dear,' he said, 'you *must* have the underwater massage. It's the equivalent of being had by the *entire* company of the Ballet Russe at once.'

'God,' I said, 'you go back a bit.'

'I'd always go back for that, dear. There are some things in life worth repeating.'

In fact it all went too smoothly. In the bathroom that night I indulged in some exaggerated despair on the scales. 'I've got to take some of this off before the picture starts,' I said, 'otherwise my brain won't function.'

'What are you?' Susan said.

'Well, without lying, about eleven pounds over my previous best. I think I'd better pay a return visit to Buxted.'

'I should,' Susan said. 'If I wasn't working every day I'd join you.'

CHAPTER THIRTY-EIGHT

On the morning of the fourteenth I had answered all my mail by nine o'clock, having arranged for Pam to come in early. Then I went out for a haircut, and bought a couple of new shirts, some perfume and bath oil, returning to the office to meet Nethercott and Monika to discuss their roles together and read through their major scenes. I had carefully excluded Toller from the meeting, finding, somewhat to my surprise, that Monika was a willing partner to the deception. It was like preparing for a long-awaited summer holiday.

The reading went well. Nethercott was an instinctive actor, not too self-confident (usually the mark of an indifferent performer) and had obviously given a great deal of prior thought to the role. It's always gratifying for a director to have his Svengali-impulses vindicated.

I noted an immediate improvement in Monika, too. She could not, by any stretch of the imagination, be called a great actress, but she had taught herself the rudiments, and she possessed a predatory, animal grace. She reminded me greatly of the early Monroe: some women have that quality which is not discernible to the naked eye, but which the lens of the camera photographs and brings to life.

She and Nethercott looked good together and as I walked round them in the office, studying their faces as they went through the lines, I could see how and where I could fuse their personalities. Whether it was the general excitement of the day, or whether at that point I suddenly felt the film beginning to stir in me, I don't know—but certainly I felt happier and I relaxed for the first time since arriving back in London.

Hearing the lines spoken I could spot the remaining weaknesses in the script: there was a sense of adventure in the air, something infectious which they caught from me. Studying Monika's face as she laughed at some feeble joke Nethercott made in broken German, I caught a glimpse of what she might be, given the chance, given a little patience and understanding. I had no doubt that she had received little or no help along the route, that most producers and directors had hired her for her body, relying on the fact that they could always re-dub her voice afterwards. Without make-up, her hair loosely held back by a ribbon, her exquisite breasts just glimpsed beneath the man's sweater she was wearing, she seemed a totally different person from the glossy publicity stills that adorned the covers of a dozen magazines every week.

She and Nethercott left arm in arm to continue their conversations over lunch, and even Pam raised an admiring eyebrow as they walked through the office. I collected up my portable typewriter, a couple of reams of paper and copies of all versions of the script as Pam brought in my usual lunch of sandwiches and coffee.

'I bequeath it to you,' I said. 'My régime starts now.'

'I don't know how you've got the will power. If I was going to one of those places I should have one last super tuck-in, and smuggle in a few bars of chocolate.'

'How d'you know I haven't? Hold the fort for me, won't you? And don't give anybody the number unless you have to.'

'Does that include Mr Raven?'

'Unfortunately, no, but he has it anyway.'

'Do you want me to ring you, Mr Warren?'

'Yes. You ring . . . No, I'll ring you every morning, because I've no idea what times my treatments will be until I get there.'

'Well, good luck.'

'Thanks.'

'With the script I meant,' she said, and then got confused. I kissed her lightly on both cheeks. 'Watch out for the return of the Thin Man,' I said.

CHAPTER THIRTY-NINE

I suppose to most people, fat or thin, the thought of paying a hundred guineas a week to starve yourself is only one step from total madness. Passing the Oxfam posters on the way down to Sussex, I pondered the apparent insanity myself. The answer is, I fear, that self-denial is harder than writing out a cheque for charity, and self-discipline in the comfort of one's own home, impossible. Practically everybody I know is fighting through some diet or another. I've tried them all for twenty-four hours. I have existed on nothing but bananas, I have made dedicated forays into the darkest recesses of compost-grown food shops and come away loaded with enough wheat-germ, herb teas and vitamin pills to sustain me on a desert island for a year; I have swallowed the royal jelly of queen bees, even pollen in capsules which you are required to place beneath the tongue the second your eyes open in the morning; and I have spent hours discussing the common problem with friends of either sex, all of whom have, at one time or another, in the full exaltation of seeing a few transient inches slide from their hips, claimed to have found the ultimate panacea. I once met a woman in the Ritz Hotel, Madrid, who told me quite seriously and in embarrassing detail that she had undergone a series of frightening injections of donkey urine, and assured me that the results had been staggering. She drank three very large vodka-tonics during the description, and said that she had not eaten breakfast or lunch for fifteen years. Another friend, who was a compulsive and secret chocolate-biscuit eater, took colonic irrigations three times a week, and deliberately had his suits made a size too large in order to maintain the façade of progress. I knew one actress who literally starved herself to death.

Perhaps it is only right that one half of the Western world caters exclusively to human greed, while the other half preaches and propagates the necessity of moderation in all things. We are, I do believe, what we eat. And what we eat, for the most part, does not bear very close examination.

I don't want to give the impression that Buxted Park, my destination that afternoon, was some bogus holiday camp for cranks. On the contrary, it provided, in the utmost comfort, the pleasures of a large English country house with the discreet and unobtrusive attention of a well-run hospital. The rooms were delightful, the food, when one was allowed to eat, pure nectar, and the treatments gentle and relaxing. One could spend exactly the same amount of money enduring a totally hideous holiday in some four-star hotel, and come away, bloated and irritable, and more exhausted than when one arrived.

Even without the added attraction of Alison, I would have driven away from London with a quickening sense of anticipated pleasure—just as in the old days, just after the war, the journey to the South of France by car was an experience without parallel.

I arrived about four o'clock and checked in. I had booked one of the named suites, the Churchill Room, which sat in the middle of the original house and overlooked the lake and deer park.

I knew the form, and after unpacking my bags and arranging my typewriter and papers on a table by the open window, I took a shower and waited to be seen by the resident medical staff.

My incoming weight, blood pressure and pulse having been duly noted, I was asked whether I wanted to go on the full or light diet. I opted for lunch on the light régime, remembering the great bowls of salad that had sustained me on previous visits. The formalities being over I was free to wander the gardens, or take a swim in the vast outdoor pool. My treatments did not begin until the following morning.

Alison and I had agreed that she should not arrive until the evening. As carefully as any team of thriller-writers, we had plotted a trail of seeming innocence. There was to be no contact during the days, and we intended to get our money's worth of treatment and abide by the rules. That, at least, was the original plan.

I did some work on the script, the enthusiasm from the morning session with Monika and Nethercott carrying over, and I sat there, looking across the well-kept gardens to where the deer grazed, feeling vaguely weak, like someone recovering from a long illness who has been allowed up for the first time.

CHAPTER FORTY

Alison arrived just after I had finished my evening meal (a bowl of vegetable soup, and an apple). We met, but did not acknowledge each other, in the Reception Hall, and I busied myself sorting through picture postcards until I had heard the Receptionist giving the number of her room. Wearing the towelling dressing-gown provided by the management, I already gave the appearance of an old-established inmate, for there is something faintly intimidating about entering a health farm for the first time and encountering the already initiated. We both played our parts to perfection, and gave no indication that we had ever met before, or that we found each other remotely interesting. I said good night loudly to the Telephone Operator after registering my breakfast call, and proceeded to my room.

The next three hours were difficult. I found I couldn't settle to any work, read a little, took a long bath, then watched the news on television. In the dining-room an enormously fat fellow-resident had volunteered the somewhat daunting information that after a week on the full starvation diet, 'you're too weak to turn the knobs, old chap,' and therefore I was suitably self-impressed when I managed to tune into BBC 2 without feeling any pain in the wrists. The news was the usual chapter of disasters on a world-wide scale and I tried to recall when it was that we had listened to any good tidings.

I left my room when the building was quiet, taking a book with me so that if, by chance, I ran into anybody I could volunteer the explanation that I was on my way to the library to change it. I am sure it seems absurd now, like an escapade from a story by Frank Richards—Vernon Smith, the Bounder of the Remove, sneaking out of the dorm after lights out to keep some assignation on the tow path. Except that none of the students of Greyfriars School ever kept an appointment in Samarra with sex. Although I read every episode as it appeared, I don't remember the subject cropping up, and I doubt whether even Vernon Smith, rotter though he was, ever contemplated betraying a woman.

Frank Richards would, I am sure, have devised a dozen mishaps *en route*, but I encountered none and it was with a sense of anti-climax that I finally arrived outside Alison's room. I knocked gently, then tried the handle of the door. It was open and I went inside, locking it after me.

I realise that I have never fully described Alison. Perhaps my reasons, even now, are more complex than I care to acknowledge, or perhaps the sin of omission stems from nothing more than a sense of inadequacy. I have always been attracted to physical beauty in either sex, but even in my screenplays I have never relied upon elaborate character details before the event. The most unlikely people find each other attractive; there is, as they say, no accounting for taste, and in any case my memory is too biased to attempt to bring her to life for strangers. I loved her. More than anybody I have ever met, she had the power to make me vulnerable.

I remember that I stood at the door of that unfamiliar room looking across ten years towards a woman who had never once been out of my thoughts. She grinned at me from the bed.

'You're thinner already,' she said.

'It's worry.'

'Have you had any treatments yet?'

'Not yet.'

She fished around for a piece of paper on the bedside table.

'Mine are all written out for to-morrow,' she said. 'After a light breakfast—what's that?'

'China tea and a slice of lemon.'

'Oh. Well, after that I start off with a sauna, then I have a massage, and then at twelve o'clock I have the hot and cold foot bath. Is that fun?'

'Excruciating. I can't take it.'

I slipped into bed beside her. It was like the Christmas Eves of childhood, when the house is full and you share a small bed with a visiting cousin. Alison got the giggles immediately.

'Maybe it'll be better when you've lost a few pounds,' she said wickedly.

'They don't specify this treatment in their brochure, but I'm told it works wonders for men of my age.'

'I'm glad,' she said, 'because I don't want to share you with anybody.'

'Are we going to be able to sleep in this?'

'I hope not.'

'You're not only fat,' I said, 'you're shameless.'

It was the sort of dialogue I would never dare put into a serious screenplay. In films love affairs are always conducted in writhing close-up, and when the characters converse, if they converse, the audience has come to expect self-analysis and long, turgid passages of regret.

'Have you taken your herbs?'

'No, I didn't like the look of them. Have you?'

'No.'

'We're going to be a big disappointment to them.'

'Did you have dinner?'

'No, I was very strong. I had a bar of chocolate on the way down though.'

'Well, I had dinner, but I didn't have any lunch.'

'My friend was right.'

'What friend?'

'Oh, a girl friend. She told me that the moment you enter these places your entire conversation is about food. She didn't last the week, she broke out after three days and went down to the village and had three helpings of fish and chips.'

'Ah, but there was a difference, you see, she didn't have me.'

'That's true.'

'Did you tell many people you were coming?'

'Not many, just those I bumped into. I mean, we agreed, didn't we, that it wouldn't be a secret?'

'Yes,' I said. 'Did you tell Cyril?'

'Why do you pronounce it like that?'

'Like what?'

'See-rill.'

'Do I?'

'Always.'

'I don't know why. Did you?'

'Yes, he knows I'm here. After all, he's paying the bill.'

'Will he phone you?'

'He might. He does sometimes. Just depends.'

'What would you do if he phoned now?'

'I've told them I don't want any calls to-night, unless it's an emergency. You know, unless it was Lucy.'

I listened to my own heartbeat. She started to unbutton my pyjamas.

'You're so formal,' she said. 'All buttoned up to the neck.'

'Well, I had to cross no-man's-land to get here.' I reached down for my dressing-gown. 'I even brought my own props.'

'What?'

'An alarm clock.'

This brought on another fit of giggles and I put a hand over her mouth. When she was quiet I kissed her, but she started to laugh again.

'Are you going to laugh all night?'

'I don't know. I'm sorry, I just thought of something. When you reached down for the alarm clock I thought for one awful moment you were going to produce something else.'

'Do they still make them?' I said.

'Well, don't ask me.'

'That's what you were laughing at, is it?'

'Just then. But before I was just laughing. At us. At this place, this bed, the whole bit. We're funny really. It's a long dirty week-end without food. Not like those romantic stories I used to read, where the hero and heroine always consumed champagne and caviar.'

'I could try and drink herb tea out of your slipper.'

'They haven't got any backs to them.'

'What I can't get over is why you should think I was reaching for one of those.'

'See, you can't even say it.'

'French letter then.'

'One that chimes the hours.'

'Now don't start laughing again, you'll wake the whole place. I was relying on the Women's Lib. I take it that you are suitably liberated and on the Pill?'

'Yes and no.'

'What does that mean?'

'I forget. I'm not very good at remembering to take things. I've got more half empty bottles of medicine than anybody I know.'

'You realise what we're doing, don't you?'

'No, what?'

'We're lying here talking like an old married couple.'

'Are we?' she said.

'Yes.'

'Wouldn't you have bought me a bigger bed if we'd been married?'

'I might not. I might have wanted to stay this close to you.'

'Actually, I prefer Stan's bed.'

'Ah! That's what I call perversity.'

'Yes, well I am perverse, you ought to know that. What's he like, Stan?'

'He's a very nice bloke.'

'Will you give him my love, and thank him?'

'I'll thank him, I have already.'

'From me?'

'From both of us.'

'Seems funny to lend your bed to people like us.'

I started to wind the alarm clock.

'Have you put the cat out?' Alison said.

'If you start to laugh again, I shan't be able to make love to you.'

'What time have you set it for?'

'Six.'

'Why can't you make love to somebody who's laughing?'

'It's just impossible.'

I put the clock down again. It had a very loud tick.

'Well, it's not impossible, but it's sort of deflating.'

She thought about that. 'Do lots of men say that?'

'How d'you mean?'

'Well, for instance, do you think that to-morrow morning there'll be trainloads of bank clerks and that sitting close together reading *The Times*, all thinking I was deflated last night, my wife laughed when I made love to her?'

'Probably.'

'Isn't that sad,' she said. 'Something so happy and we all take it so seriously.'

CHAPTER FORTY-ONE

Even by the standards of my world, we led a bizarre existence that week: strangers by day and a married couple by night. I suppose that most of human love is a mixture of the sacred and the profane, ridiculous, sometimes obscene, sometimes tender, periods of calm alternating with frenzy, often painful, occasionally humbling, and more often than not a dark revelation.

In a way, it was the perfect existence. We were starved of everything but love for each other. Our bodies were steamed, kneaded, plunged into hot and cold baths, massaged, vibrated, oiled—as though everybody we came in contact with was part of the conspiracy, preparing us, like slaves of old, during the day for the pleasures of the night. Segregated during the treatment hours, glimpsing each other in corridors, or at meal times, it was as if we were actors in some superbly cross-plotted thriller where all the suspects were guests in a large house and things only happened when the lights went out.

We slept, even in that narrow single bed, and woke before the much derided alarm clock went off. Once, in the very early hours, when the mist sat on the lawns like dumped cotton waste and the deer came and went jerkily as though animated in some old-fashioned movie, we stole downstairs in the silent house and raided the kitchens. Undetected, suppressing excitement like guilty children, we came back to Alison's room and feasted on two packets of lactic cheese, one peach and a bottle of unfermented grape juice. I had never felt so well or so rested.

'You look as though you could be pregnant,' I said.

Peach juice glistened on her chin and I licked it away.

'Perhaps I am,' she said.

'It wouldn't happen so soon, though, would it?' The joke had trapped me and as I passed the bottle of grape juice to her and she drank from it, I sensed something move away from me, like a ghost. I had a sudden premonition.

'*Are* you pregnant?'

'Not that I know of.'

'But could you be?'

'By you?'

'By him.' Somehow it was not the moment for pronouncing his name.

She finished off what was left in the bottle. 'Oh, I'm sorry, did you want some more?'

I shook my head, wanting only the answer.

'Could you be?' I repeated.

'No, silly.'

'But you said you don't always remember.'

'It doesn't make all that difference.'

'What does that mean?'

'We don't do it all that often.'

She fed me the last pieces of crumbling cheese.

'When they put you on the scales to-day you'll get a black mark.'

'How are we going to get rid of the evidence, the bottle?'

'I don't know,' she stage-whispered.

We looked around the room for a suitable hiding place. 'I'll have to smuggle it out,' I said.

'But then what will you do with it?'

'I'll put it outside somebody else's door.'

Somewhere in the building we heard a vacuum-cleaner start up. It was our cock crow.

'I might go for a walk this afternoon,' I said. 'I haven't got any treatments.'

'Let me check. No, neither have I.'

'If I go for a walk, is there any remote chance that I might bump into you?'

'What an immoral suggestion to make to a married woman.'

'It's made,' I said, 'by a married man, while the balance of his mind is disturbed by prolonged starvation.'

'You must go. The cleaners'll be outside.'

'Will I see you?'

'You ought to work.'

'Will I see you?'

'Yes,' she said. 'Yes.'

I missed lunch that day and worked on the script. I felt capable of anything, but habit warned me to suspect peace, and I phoned Pam to find out what was happening behind the lines. I had heard nothing from Raven for over three days, a silence so alien to his character that it could only betoken menace.

'As far as I know, he's gone to Paris,' Pam said.

'Paris?'

'Yes, he went the day after you left. I know, because we booked the tickets.'

'Tickets? Plural?'

'Yes, we had to get two tickets.'

'Who went with him?'

'I've no idea, they were both booked in his name.'

'Well, check whether Mrs Raven went with him. Nothing else?'

'No, it's all very quiet. Oh, a message from Stan that you're not to take anything off your hips.'

'Cheeky sod,' I said. 'Give him my regards and tell him he's got a fortnight's notice.'

I thought about Raven and the possible permutations of his Paris trip, but I could not arrive at any definite conclusion. There was always the chance, of course, that he was using my absence to get a replacement for Monika, but I had cast approval written into my contract and it seemed unlikely.

I rang the studio next and spoke to Susan.

'Your voice sounds weak,' she said. 'Have you lost pounds and pounds?'

'You won't recognise me.'

'Well, I'm eating for both of us, I might tell you. I had two cheese rolls during the break this morning, and lunch and now I'm eating a whole bag of toffees.'

'Sadist,' I said.

'And last night, we went out and had a simply gigantic Italian meal.'

'Who's we?'

'Oh, George and a few of the cast. Robin very sweetly took us all out for a treat.'

'Was Mrs Robin with him?'

'Yes.'

'That must have been a treat.'

'She was very nice.'

'She's poison.'

'Well, I didn't sit next to her. She seemed terribly nice.'

'Anyway,' I said, duty and fear receding, 'you enjoyed yourself, that's the main thing. How's the film going?'

'Difficult,' she said.

'How?'

'Difficult to talk. I'm on the set.'

'Oh, it's like that, is it?'

'Very much so, that's why I'm eating. How's the script coming?'

'Slowly, that's why I'm starving. Take care of yourself.'

'You too, darling. Miss you.'

For a moment I wanted to believe her, for guilt is often overtaken by pity. She promised to ring me later if she got a chance to leave the set.

'Well, don't do that,' I said, 'because I shall be having a treatment. I'll ring you to-night.' And immediately after she rang off, the sense of well-being disappeared. I stared at what I had written that day: it seemed facile, the sort of writing I despised in others and I crumpled the pages, consumed with doubt. I began to wonder if any part of my life was real. Something, some echo back to my school days perhaps; perhaps the room itself which reminded me of a house I used to spend holidays in, took me back to an awareness of sin. I did something I had not done for years. I went into the over-large bathroom and locked the door and knelt in the centre of the room. I was like an actor returning after a long period away, to a role he had once been word-perfect in: I could remember the gestures, but the dialogue eluded me. Facing the mirror over the bath, I said, 'Oh, God, help me,' without believing that He could, but there was nothing else to ask for. I knelt there, and when I raised my eyes the mirror only reflected despair. I thought, you can't even pray without locking the door. It was as if the act of prayer was something shameful.

I walked down into the garden and smiled acknowledgments as my shadow caused some of the other inmates, sitting in deckchairs, to look up. The sun was shining, but there was a bite in the air, and I remembered something I had once read in that wise fragment of Connolly's that he published in wartime under the pseudonym of Palinurus. I remember I took it with me when we crossed to the D-Day beaches and for months it was the only book I had so that, even to this day, I can recall whole passages by heart. He wrote, 'We only love once, for once only are we perfectly equipped for loving: we may appear to ourselves to be as much in love at other times—so does a day in early September, though it is six hours shorter, seem as hot as one in June.' The sun was hot on my face as I walked the well-kept paths towards the distant rose garden, remembering the last words of the quotation. 'And on how that first true love-affair shapes itself depends the pattern of our lives.'

Does an author ever know, I wonder, how far his words reach? To have come that far, to have survived the war, to have met somebody and have lost them carelessly, only to find them again when it was all too late.

I had time to retrace my steps, time to think back in more agonising detail, before Alison appeared in the distance, walking towards me. I stopped by the fence which separated the formal garden from the landscaped pasture and after a few moments she stopped beside me and to a casual observer our encounter must have seemed a matter of chance.

'Do you ever think what it must have been like in the old days?' she said.

I did not turn my head. The herd of deer suddenly froze as one, listening for an enemy that never appeared.

'It was different,' I said, 'that's all you can be sure of.'

'What's the matter?'

'Nothing.'

'Yes, there is. What's happened?'

'Nothing. The work didn't go well, that's all.'

'I wish I understood,' she said. 'If I understood anything about that side of your life, I could help. But it's always been a foreign country to me.'

'Yes,' I said, 'I remember.'

'I was only thinking, on the way down here, the arguments we used to have. Your friend Lowson, he always used to take your side against me. What's he doing now?'

'He's dead,' I said. 'He was shot down in a helicopter photographing Viet Nam.'

'I'm sorry, I didn't know.'

'It was in some of the papers.'

'I'm really sorry,' she said.

'You don't have to be. He wasn't your friend. You didn't really like him, did you?'

'No, not if I'm honest. He always claimed you.'

I turned round and leant against the fence. Facing me were half a dozen small gravestones, some of them sunk into the mossy ground. I walked across the path and studied them more closely. They commemorated dead pets.

'They're like children's graves,' Alison said. She took my arm and urged me away.

'We shouldn't be so intimate in public,' I said. 'We can be seen from the windows over there.'

She said, 'I can't pretend all the time,' but took her arm out of mine and walked slightly behind. The sun was blotted out by gigantic rhododendrons which stretched to meet above our heads. Where once there had been a profusion of exotic and un-English flowers, there were now only blackened clusters; they reminded me of the fingers of corpses burnt in agony. It was suddenly not a place to remember love.

We walked on until we came to a ruined tennis court. Traces of the netting remained, rusted to dust, and weeds grew through the weathered surface.

'Anyone for tennis?' I said, unable to resist a joke that repertory actors are weaned on. But Alison took it for a literal comment: as she had just said, my life was a foreign country.

'Imagine the parties they must have had here. Playing until it was too dark to score. I always think tennis courts are romantic places.'

'You were probably good at it,' I said.

'Yes, I was. I used to play every day.'

'All in white.'

'Now who's being romantic?'

'I am,' I said, turning away again. Then we walked to the walled kitchen garden and entered it through a small door. The scent was different here, a smell of herbs and tomatoes by the long greenhouses. Safe behind the wall, we held hands, and I broke a small tomato from the stalk and fed it to her.

'That's twice we've cheated to-day,' she said.

'Three times,' I said. 'We made love, remember?'

CHAPTER FORTY-TWO

I threw some pine water on the sullen rocks in the stove and immediately regretted it for the heat spat back at me. The only other occupant of the sauna that morning, a newcomer of indeterminate age, raised his eyes and we both gasped as the hot vapour rasped our unhealthy lungs.

'Sorry,' I said, 'I overdid it.'

The other man nodded, then let his head sag forward again. I wondered why it is that one's forehead is always the first part of the body to drip sweat.

'Your first time?' I said.

He nodded again. 'I think you're sitting too high up, if you haven't done it before. Come down to the bottom layer.'

He heaved himself down and collapsed again and it was obvious that he hadn't the energy to converse. But for some reason I felt compelled to keep a dialogue going, in the same way that some people are incapable of remaining silent on a train journey.

I studied him more closely. By accident and not design I was on a level with his partially exposed genitals. His skin was smooth, pink now, but not naturally so and the layers of fat started just below his nipples. He was sweating profusely and large droplets of it left his chin and bounced on the first rounded projection: it was like watching mountaineers falling off the cliff face. His hands were clasped below his belly and from time to time he shook them. I noticed that his nails were even and well kept. He was obviously not somebody who lived by manual labour and yet he did not suggest the jaded tycoon. Nakedness in the sauna is a great leveller, but he seemed completely different from the other guests I had encountered, and he intrigued me.

'How long are you staying?' I asked.

'Not long,' he said, 'a few days, that's all.'

'To do any good you need at least three,' I volunteered with the smugness of an old hand.

'Depends how much you want to lose.'

'Yes, I suppose so.'

I could detect the remains of an accent, but his voice was low and it was difficult to place with any accuracy.

'The first day's a bit rough, but after that you really begin to feel the benefit. You get rid of all the toxins.'

'I doubt that,' he said.

'Well most of them, until the next time.'

'Oh, yes. Did you say sins?'

'Toxins.'

'Oh, yes.'

He wiped his face with a corner of his towel. The way he did it reminded me of something else, but I was too hot to search for the origin. Then he staggered out to take a cold plunge. Left to myself I felt compelled to increase the heat again, ladling the oily green water on to the stove for the sheer pleasure of hearing it hiss. I am always slightly amazed that the stones don't shatter. I heard my companion gasping and splashing in the tiled room outside, but I was determined to show my superiority by remaining put for at least my daily quota of twenty minutes. I didn't expect to see him again, but he reappeared, dripping wet, his skin blotchy, and clambered to the second level.

'It's the devil and the deep blue sea.'

'It is that,' he said. 'I'm getting the hang of it now.'

'I feel we ought to introduce ourselves. My name's Dick Warren.'

'Father Lawrence,' he said.

His reply took me totally by surprise and it must have shown on my face. He didn't grin or extend a hand, but he watched my reaction in a way that made me believe he must be short-sighted.

'You're a priest?'

'Yes,' he said. 'I'm sorry if it shocks you.'

'No, not at all. Why should it shock me?'

'I just thought maybe. I admit I'm a bit out of me element.'

The accent came through the heat now. I found myself studying him with fresh interest. For reasons I couldn't fully explain, his answer had in fact shocked me. Whether he guessed I was being polite, or whether he wanted to confide, reversing his usual role, he suddenly came to life.

'You see, by way of explanation, even though you didn't ask for one, I'm really quite a young man. And I've got a lot I want to do in life, but I eat too much. I'm not a great one for liquids, but I eat a powerful amount and it's beginning to slow me down. I heard of these places, so I thought I'd spend me holiday here.'

'Why not?'

'Well now, that's a good question and it's one I've asked meself. There's nothing actually against it, as far as I could find out, except that it's not done a great deal in my line of business. Would you like to put a bit more on the fire, please?'

I ladled some more pine essence and the sudden heat pierced us both.

'There's nothing like the hell of your own making,' he said, tentatively wafting the joke towards me.

'What's your line of business?'

'I direct films. I'm a film director.'

'Is that so? I used to enjoy a good film. I don't go often, I'm afraid to say.'

'That makes me feel better,' I said, 'because I don't go to church often.'

'Are you Catholic?'

'Not a very good one.'

'Well, that makes two of us.'

He surrendered to the heat, leaning back against the hot wood and closing his eyes. His towel had slipped and once again I found myself compelled to contemplate what I could see below his navel. Unused (one assumed), his genitals had those acorn-like proportions favoured by Victorian sculptors. I felt vaguely alarmed by the whole situation; there seemed something faintly ludicrous, yet disturbing, about the chance encounter. One part of my mind worked to reject coincidence, and I put my bare feet to the scorching floor and groped for the door.

The cold of the pool went right through me and I submerged quickly, seeking to produce the maximum shock. I stayed in the icy water longer than usual, trying to sort out my thoughts. The rest room was deserted, as I allowed the idea to form in my suddenly cleared head and when I entered the sauna again I had taken a decision.

Father Lawrence opened his eyes briefly as I took my place on the shelf opposite him. I willed him to keep them closed, for in a way it was a form of relief not to be observed. I was conscious of the absurdity, and yet compelled to act.

'Father,' I said, 'can I ask a great favour? I want help.'

He had said he was a young man, and I guessed his age to be below forty, perhaps the right side of thirty-five. Liquid with sweat, his face seemed unformed, only the eyes gave me the courage to continue.

'Just ordinary help. I need to talk to somebody.'

'Are you trying to say you need to confess?'

'If you like. Does that seem out of place?'

'No more than me, I daresay.'

His tolerance of the situation attacked my reason like the heat. Having brought myself to that point, I wanted nothing so much as condemnation. It was like attempting to rouse a sleeping doctor in the middle of the night and urging him to meet an emergency. My need grew, pushing towards him over the heated rocks. Perhaps he sensed this and he licked the sweat from his lips and wiped the ghost of his smile.

'When did you last go to Mass?' he said.

I had forgotten the pattern, but I recognised the note in his voice, that impersonal note which habit imposes.

'Last Christmas. I go on Christmas Eve.'

Even as I laid bare my past, the spirit emulating the flesh, I could not escape what life had made of me. That cold and detached part of me which can anticipate an actor's loss of memory from the darkness behind the camera before the actor himself is aware of anything untoward, remained critically aloof, observing and despising my weakness so that I was never unaware of the surroundings and the two characters playing the scene. I could see the man, myself, bent forward as though there was still a need to whisper, and the priest, naked except for the sodden towel across his lap, listening as though for the first time to the sameness of human frailty. But the dialogue once begun had to continue and in the end the sameness grew into originality.

'How many times?'

I told him, dragging the past to the present, listening to my own voice admitting what I had guarded so carefully for ten long years.

'Do you intend to go on with this mortal sin?' he said. 'I can't help you unless there is a real longing to repent.'

'But can't you understand what love does, Father? You're part of the world, this room we're in now, that's part of the world, too. Priests marry now and don't leave the Church,' I said, my argument striking out in different directions, 'surely you can understand some part of it.'

'What I understand is no consequence, it's what God is prepared to understand.'

'But if He gave us Love, how can He blame us for using it?'

'You can't have love and the loss of God at the same time—that isn't love,' he said, sadly, sweat falling down his face like tears giving the appearance that he was begging for my forgiveness. 'It's only lust,' he said.

'All right, I'll give you that in the beginning, but what if lust turns into love, that's possible, too? That's behind me, I can repent that, but what I need to understand is what comes next.'

He raised the towel to his face again, but I never heard his answer, for at that moment the masseur opened the door and reminded me that my time was up and I followed him without looking back, going to another soundproofed room where, under artificial sunlight, his expert fingers brought another kind of truth to the surface. I lay there, my eyes protected from the glare, listening, like the priest, to just a man talking.

CHAPTER FORTY-THREE

On the day of departure guests are permitted a heartier breakfast and encouraged to sample the generous salad lunch. It could be described as instant rehabilitation, preparing us, like prisoners, for the return to the outside world and the temptation of new white bread, strong coffee and the menace of potatoes. Just as an assistant prison governor once said to me after I had given a lecture, 'They always come back, rehabilitation's a joke, sir,' so the inmates of health farms, their bowels and pores cleansed, go forth at the end of a self-imposed sentence determined to stay straight and avoid their old fattening haunts. But if they fail, as fail they must, there is always the comfort of the cell to return to, the friendly staff nodding knowingly, the old lags who are seldom absent for more than a few weeks, hopelessly committed to the capital crime of obesity. There is a sort of religion of fat which unlike the orthodox churches never has to tout for business. Believers take communion together at the *Caprice* and *Mirabelle* if they are high church, but it is something one can practise equally well at home and it allows for all humbler variations. The British read avidly from the great Book of Stodge, while the Americans grovel before the altar of Synthetic Cream. Of such, I suppose, is the Kingdom of Heaven until the neck thickens, the arteries clog, the heart misses a beat.

Such depressing thoughts were not uppermost in my mind as I stole from Alison's bedroom for the last time, our week at an end. True lovers, they say, never look back, but I dared challenge the superstition, seeking to fix every detail in my mind against the time when loneliness would crowd back, walking under the ladder of our happiness, back to my own room.

There was a feeling of being back in wartime. Lovers parted more often in those days, there was always a train to catch somewhere. We hadn't slept that last night, keeping watch for the morning light like fire-watchers huddled together on the improvised bunk bed. So many promises given again, the whispered repetitions that human love demands when we fear the worst. Our lovemaking was uneasy, and for the first time it failed her so that the cry she smothered in the pillow betrayed only sadness. Perhaps our minds were so awake to the thought of separation that we could not bring ourselves to unwrap the gift of the body with our usual care.

I don't suppose I shall ever think of Alison again without seeing her in the context of that hired room. Even now I can trace every detail of her naked body as the first light revealed it; it was like a well-loved snapshot, framed behind glass, that has been exposed to the sun for too long; the translucence faded, the shadows and the substance merged as one. The dawn was brighter than the rest of the day and as the shared sheet slipped to the floor, I bent to kiss her breasts, and then tasted the warm tenderness of her tongue upon mine, and was filled suddenly with an intolerable depression.

She said, 'For the first time I know it's got to end. I never seriously thought of it until now.'

Later, alone in my own room, examining my unshaven face in the mirror, those words began to assume a wider and more terrifying significance, the present made future, and I had a glimpse of what the end would be like.

The easily acquired habit of a week made me use my own bed, and I lay there between the cool sheets, desperate for a second chance. It was like the agony of the schoolboy who leaves the examination room and hands in a blank paper, only to find once he is outside that he knew all the answers.

But, when the maids arrived to prepare the room for the next inhabitant, my belongings were neatly packed, there was nothing to show, the evidence of suffering was out of sight.

Alison was already seated in the dining-room when I made my

appearance. I took a plate and helped myself to everything, glad of an opportunity for greed to reassert itself. I stood in the middle of the room and gave a passable imitation of a man undecided as to where to sit. I advanced towards Alison, hesitated, then smiled.

'Is anybody sitting here?' I asked, loud enough to satisfy the onlookers.

'No. Help yourself.'

'Thank you.'

I sat down. I noticed that she was eating slowly and carefully. I took my first mouthful. It was sheer bliss. When I looked up she avoided my eyes, concentrating on her food.

'This makes it all worth it,' I said.

Lovers can always break a code.

'Yes,' she said. 'How long have you been here?'

'Just the week.'

'It's been a week to remember then.'

'Yes,' I said, 'I've never spent one like it.'

I reached out to take the oil and vinegar, allowing the backs of our hands to touch. When I looked at her again I knew that she was close to tears, but before I could whisper any comfort a voice behind me said, 'My God, have you been eating like that every day?' and I turned to find Kitty Raven standing by the table.

'Kitty,' I said, 'don't tell me you've been sent to bring me home?'

'Are you kidding? I just checked in. What sort of diet's that?'

'Oh, this is just the going-away present.'

I was conscious that Kitty was looking past me to Alison. I turned back.

'I'm so sorry,' I said, 'this is an old friend of mine, but I can't introduce you because I don't know your name.'

'Osmond,' Alison said. 'Mrs Osmond.'

'Mrs Osmond, Kitty Raven.'

'Hello,' Kitty said. 'Is everybody allowed that?'

'It depends what your diet sheet says,' Alison said.

'To hell with that, I've never gone by the rules yet. Dick, get

215

me a plate like that. Not too much beetroot though, and no mushrooms.'

I went to the serving table, conscious that Kitty immediately took my seat. I served her as quickly as possible and when I returned to the table I looked around for a third chair.

'Have mine,' Alison said, 'I've finished.'

'No, I'm sure you're just saying that.'

'Really. You stay and have it with your friend.'

She picked up her handbag. I hoped the panic did not show in my face.

'I hope you lose what you came to lose, Mrs Raven.'

'That'll be the day,' Kitty said, and started eating.

Alison turned and walked out of the room. I took my place in her chair and picked at the remains of my meal. I did not trust myself to speak first.

'Well,' Kitty said, evenly, 'who was she?'

'No idea,' I said, 'I'd just met her when you came in.'

'You're slipping,' Kitty said, 'she looked your type.'

CHAPTER FORTY-FOUR

The first thing I saw on my desk when I got back to the office that day was the front cover of a Trade magazine. Under some fifth-rate art work some sixth-rate typography proclaimed TEENAGERS ZOOM!—SEE THEM BURST OUT OF THEIR CLOTHES AND BUST UP A TOWN. I put my own script down on the desk and stared at the headlines for fully ten minutes. I thought, what is it all about, why do you care? You kill yourself to make a film you believe in, you take the insults, you fight the Ravens, you surround yourself with talented people and in the end all the industry cares about is some piece of shit that makes some easy money.

Stan and Wellard came into the office and I immediately went off the wagon and put back a few of those lost ounces. I told them to look at the offending front cover while I poured the drinks.

'I don't care much for the leading man,' Jimmy said. 'He needn't bother to burst out of his clothes for me.'

'But you see who made it,' Stan said. 'I worked for that outfit. They are, without doubt, the cheapest, lousiest pair of crooks in the business.'

'Cheers,' Jimmy said.

'What I don't understand—maybe I'm weak from starvation— is how do they stay in the business?'

'They make money, dear. They make crap and crap makes money.'

'Then why do we go on pretending?'

'I don't, dear.'

'All right, why do I go on pretending?'

'Well, you're very perverse, dear, everybody knows that.'

I gave us all another drink. I could feel new fat forming around my middle.

'I mean, I've finished the script . . . Get it run off, will you, Stan?'

'How many copies?'

'The usual, plus half a dozen extra, and mark it Final.'

'You've come back very aggressive,' Jimmy said.

'I feel aggressive. As I was saying, I've finished the script, and I intend to shoot it as well as I know how, and you're going to give me great sets, and Stan's going to ensure that we come in on budget, and for what?'

'Do you want me to answer that, dear?' Jimmy said.

'By all means.'

'Well, dear, let's start with the facts of life. Your trouble is you should never have resigned from the Boy Scouts. All that rubbing together of twigs before the age of puberty has disastrous effects in approaching middle-age.'

'Thank you for the approaching.'

'And, if I may say so, for reasons best known to your old scoutmaster—'

I turned to Stan. 'He's making all this up, I was never in the scouts.'

'Dear, you're one of Nature's Boy Scouts if ever I saw one, so let me continue. For reasons best known etcetera you still believe that there is justice in the world. There is none. Therefore, when we come to that startling innovation known as the motion picture industry, you labour under a grave disadvantage. Because you care, and because you're talented, you rather naïvely assume that the people for whom you make your films share your ideals and convictions.'

'I don't assume that for one moment.'

'Yes, you do, otherwise you couldn't have survived this far. Where was I? Give me the continuity somebody.'

'You had one hand on your left hip,' Stan said, 'with a half-smoked fag between the first two fingers, and your lips were pursed.'

'I didn't ask for a copy of my official police photograph, dear. Ah, yes, now I remember.' He swivelled back to me, grinning. 'Two of your drinks, dear, and I'm Vanessa Redgrave in Trafalgar Square. Now, then, as I was saying when my friend killed my act, you are naïve. Rebecca of Wardour Street. You think that when you turn in one of your masterpieces everybody on the other side of the business is going to recognise and applaud your genius. Whereas, in actual fact, most of them still think Ingmar Bergman married Rossellini, and therefore you are wasting your time.' He swallowed the rest of his drink. 'Fill me up.'

'Have you finished?'

'I'm not sure.'

'Let me ask you something then. Why are you in the business?'

'Do you want the unabridged version?'

'Absolutely.'

He accepted another large drink. 'Thank you. I am in this business, because . . . my talents, such as they are, do not extend to the building of council houses, and I have a parrot and a postman to support. I like to eat well, and I like to pick and choose who I work for. I mean, it's easier for me, dear. When they sound the Last Post, if you'll pardon the expression, there are no infant Wellards destined for the orphanage, and I've left a small donation for the R.S.P.C.A. to take care of my feathered friend, and there it is. If my other friend goes first, then, dear, it's Gettie Gas Oven and no flowers please.'

His face was flushed from the drink and the monologue, and the honesty of his answer, masked as it was by a veneer of self-mocking camp, was strangely humbling. Looking back, it was that drunken evening we spent together (for we continued over dinner and beyond) that saved my sanity. Perhaps the best parties are the unplanned ones as people say, but certainly had I been left alone that evening I would have done something desperate and irrevocable. As it was I left the dinner table and fumbled around in a public phone booth to phone Alison. When a somewhat sleepy Osmond answered my nerve failed and I put the receiver down without a word and went back to the table slightly sobered. I hadn't been so drunk since VE Day and I seem to remember that we composed an obscene telegram to send to Raven, and that the desk clerk at Leicester Square all-night post office refused to accept it.

We ended up by going back to Jimmy's house which was somewhere off the Fulham Road, a beautifully proportioned Georgian cottage that he had carefully and exquisitely restored. His friend was asleep when we crashed in, but got up perfectly good humoured and made quantities of extremely good coffee. Inside, the house was furnished with great taste, the sort of taste that cannot be bought but stems from a rare instinct.

I remember that Stan stood in front of a particular painting and peered at it for a long time before exclaiming, 'I've got that in my loo!'

'What's that, dear?'

'This painting, I've got that.'

'Not that one, dear. That's the original.'

It was my turn to stare at it, my turn to wonder, and I thought back to the afternoons in Stan's flat, to that other counterfeit that we had shared. I think I envied Jimmy for coming to terms with and accepting love where he could find it—love, if you like, which had outdistanced fear.

CHAPTER FORTY-FIVE

I wasn't to see Alison again before the film started. We spoke on the phone but somehow the time was never right and for days after we parted at Buxted our conversations were strained and edgy. I know it sounds unlikely, but we didn't seem to have much to say to each other—it was as if the long nights we had spent together had emptied us of pretence. There could be no return to the casual, flitting relationship that had existed before and neither of us ever mentioned going back to Stan's flat to take up where we left off. Those days had gone for ever. Once, during a particularly acrimonious production meeting I forgot to ring her as arranged, something previously unthinkable and when eventually I remembered and got to a phone it was her charlady who answered and listened to my lies, and our whole time-table collapsed. There had to be a continuity between calls or else the fabric of our deception rotted, and it was three days before we were able to mend it.

I remember saying to her, 'Have you kept up the diet?'

'No,' she said. 'I went off it immediately.'

'Are you on your own?'

'Lucy's here,' she said.

'How is Lucy?'

'Fine.'

'Darling, what's the matter?'

'I don't know, I just feel empty, I suppose.'

'I miss you,' I said.

'Are you very busy?'

'I said I miss you.'

'Do you?'

'Why d'you say it like that?'

'Oh, don't take any notice of me. Darling, I'm sorry. I'm just no good on the phone. It never seems you on the phone.'

'This is a recorded announcement,' I said. 'If you wish to leave a message, please start speaking after you hear three pips. Please speak clearly and say after me, I miss you and I love you.'

I waited.

'That was a recorded joke. Please smile now.'

I waited.

'Are you smiling?'

'Yes,' she said.

'When will I see you?'

'I've got Lucy,' she said. 'I'm on my own to-day.'

'To-morrow then? Meet me at the usual place to-morrow. You say the time.'

'Oh, darling, we can't do that, not any more.'

'Why not? It's better than nothing.'

'Is it?'

'Well, of course it is. Unless of course, you don't want to see me.'

'That's unfair.'

'Yes,' I said, 'the whole thing's unfair. I don't love that many people.'

'It's just me,' she said. 'I just feel low to-day, you mustn't take any notice. Ring me to-morrow and I'll be different.'

'I don't want you any different.'

But when I rang the next day, timing the call to the second almost, there was no reply. I checked every hour for the next three hours, but there was never any reply. That afternoon I took the first of many risks, driving to Hampstead and parking the car at the corner of her road, keeping the house under observation. I stayed there for a whole hour until a Traffic Warden got out his notepad and pencil.

The following day I rang again and when she answered relief coloured my voice with anger.

'Where were you?' I said.

'We went out for the whole day.'

'But I rang you when I said I would. You must have known I'd ring.'

'What could I do?' she said. 'He took us out for the day.'

'I see.'

'I couldn't get away to ring you.'

'No.'

'Now you're all upset.'

'I was just worried, that's all. Did you have a nice day?'

'I didn't plan it, you know. He just took a day off from work and said we were going out.'

'Yes, I understand.'

'No, you don't. You're all hurt. Well, I've got some other bad news for you. We're going away.'

My anger went immediately. A new panic set in.

'What d'you mean?'

'We're going on holiday.'

'How long for?'

'A month, I think.'

'Where?'

'Where we usually go. Spain. He's got business friends there, and we rent a villa. Darling, I'm sorry.'

'Will I see you before you go?'

She didn't answer immediately.

'I've got to see you before you go. Please.'

'Yes, yes, I was just thinking.'

'I was only upset about yesterday because I love you so much. If I didn't care, I wouldn't worry, would I? Do you know I love you?'

'Yes,' she said, 'of course I do. But don't make it any more awful.'

'How long have you known about the holiday?'

'Not long.'

'Did you know at Buxted?'

'No, not the actual date. I knew we'd be going some time or another. But he always makes up his mind on the spur of the moment.'

'It's soon then?'

I waited.

'Is it soon?'

'Yes,' she said, miserably.

'How soon?'

'To-morrow,' she said.

'And I'm not going to see you before you go?'

'Darling, how can I? I can't see you to-day.'

'Couldn't you make some excuse to get out of the house? Just half an hour, that's all I ask.'

'What good's half an hour?'

'Well, at least we'd see each other.'

'I can remember you,' she said.

I pleaded with her several times and in the end she cried, and that destroyed me. She promised to find a way to write to me and in return I arranged a *poste restante* address, and there we left it.

How remote it all seems now. The agony and the longing, like something out of an elegant French novel, Constant's *Adolphe* perhaps, except that we had no Madame de Stael to keep us apart. But this part of the story has a curiously old-fashioned feel to it; writing it down I am more than conscious of how sedate and correct we were, as though we consulted a book of etiquette for adultery before making a move. Remote and unreal. People do such awful things to each other out of politeness. Were we too loving, too concerned for others? The price of buying your own happiness at the expense of somebody else's unhappiness has always seemed too high to me, though in the supermarket atmosphere of to-day's sexual scene I suppose I am considered an outsider. You're supposed to pick up the bargains as and when you see them.

I don't know any more. Loneliness is a difficult emotion to re-capture in words, and as I try to remember the days that followed, it isn't the negatives of loneliness that my mind develops, the images that form show only a man going about his normal life, and outwardly nothing has changed—the features are the same, and the heart of the matter remains resolutely hidden.

What did I do in the days that followed her departure? I wrote the first letter to her and posted it myself to the foreign address, walking to my office in order to find a post box and hesitating before it, placing the envelope deep into the slot as though con-vinced that the moment I walked on it would somehow slide out and lie exposed on the wet London pavement for all to see. And that lunchtime on the first day, going to the studio to view some camera tests, the midday placards carried scare headlines of an air crash. I made the driver get out and buy both editions. The stop press released me from fear at the expense of thirty-eight passengers and crew killed on a mountainside in Argentina.

I submerged myself in work, accelerating the pace, partly from anguish and partly from professional necessity. The period immediately before the start of a film is, at best, a time of doubt. But even if I could turn the pain on and off as my work schedule demanded, equally I could not prevent it returning suddenly when I least expected it. Curiously, it was Monika and not Susan who caused most of the worst moments. There was no physical similarity, but she had a quality of softness when she was relaxed and through her I found my way back to Alison.

Herr Toller seemed to have been tamed. I suspected that Raven had read the riot act and achieved the uneasy peace. I was sure that Toller was merely waiting until the film was under way before reverting to his normal unattractive self. Nethercott, on the other hand, I liked more and more, and it did not escape my notice that Monika shared my enthusiasm for her leading man. If Toller suspected anything beyond a professional relationship, he concealed it well, but perhaps the instincts of a pimp are too ingrained; perhaps he couldn't resist the publicity that such a convenient romance would inevitably produce.

Jimmy had his own theory about Toller's marriage.

'That's a closet queen, dear.'

'You say that about everybody,' Stan said.

'If the closet fits, get into it, dear.'

Certainly, for a man married to a sex symbol, Herr Toller exhibited none of the classic symptoms of possessiveness. He cared more for what his wife was said to represent than for what she actually was.

And just as the mounting pressure of work insulated me against the loss of Alison, so it also protected me from deceiving Susan. We were leading completely separate lives, only coming together to share a bed at night, and although in many ways our relationship was calmer than it had been for years, there was never any danger that the calmness would be misunderstood. Susan's film was not going well: it was over budget and over schedule and she had too much temperament during the working day, to want to seek it with me after hours. She seemed to be very fond of me, which fed my guilt, and in return I was tender and understanding towards her.

'Darling,' she said, 'I'm sorry we haven't made love recently, and it's nothing to do with you, truly, it's just this bloody film which is wearing me out. There was some talk to-day that we'll finish it off back in Hollywood.'

'Who thought that one up?'

Perhaps I wasn't quick enough to keep all the excitement out of my voice, because she looked at me sharply before answering.

'Oh, I don't know, we seem to have about twenty-eight producers all telling a different story.'

'But what would they shoot in Hollywood?'

'The beach scenes. Apparently they think they've left it too late to do them over here.'

'So you may have to go back before I've finished shooting?'

'Well, it's not definite,' she said. 'I mean, I don't want to go without you, but what can I do?'

With hindsight, I can still give her the benefit of the doubt, and yet the maze of our lives at that time wound about us like a Proustian sentence, so that now I have completely lost the map I thought I once possessed. There is no going back. Did she mean it when she said she would miss me? Guilt doesn't remove every trace of an old need: we want, as they say, to have our cake and eat it too. Because I had so much to hide myself, I didn't look for other escape routes.

'You can't do anything,' I said, 'it's just this lousy business we're in.'

'But you're excited about your film, aren't you? You said the other night that it was all coming together. For the first time, you seemed really excited.'

'I am, but that's nothing to do with you going away.'

'Will you miss me?'

'Of course I will.'

'I'll fly back the moment we've got the last shot.'

'You think it's definite then?'

'No, nothing's definite.'

'But you're talking as though it's bound to happen.'

I shall never know if she was being deliberately casual, but I suppose we judge others by our own capacity to deceive.

'Well, if it happens, if I have to go, I'll fly back. Will you come and meet me at the airport?'

'You know me,' I said, 'I'm very sentimental about airports.'

CHAPTER FORTY-SIX

The subject wasn't mentioned again until the day before I began shooting the picture. That afternoon I met Norbert Quarry for the first time, and I disliked him on sight. The dislike was mutual.

Quarry flew in that day and after giving the usual meaningless interview to the Trade Papers, in which he made it transparently obvious that he had lost none of his original skill as a mortician, he summoned me to his hotel suite. He seemed to have taken a whole floor at the Dorchester and when I arrived the various inter-communicating rooms were festering with acolytes. The great man himself was closeted with some merchant bankers, all apparently anxious to sip the heady waters of film finance, but word was eventually got to him that I had arrived and after an interval word was passed out again for me to wait. I waited. Somebody had ordered vast quantities of club sandwiches which the faithful munched without interest, swilling them down with iced Coke. From time to time a new arrival would join the throng. I was the stranger in their midst, for they all seemed to know each other. A few girls wandered through the suite with the assumed nonchalance of seasoned day-trippers. Fresh supplies of food and drink continued to be brought to the rooms, and in one corner of a foreign field a poker game developed for very high stakes.

I was asked to eat and drink, but otherwise the entourage

showed little interest in me. Just as I was on the point of open revolt, Raven arrived. He greeted the assembly with easy familiarity.

'How long's he been in there?' he asked.

'Norbert's in with the money,' one of the henchmen said.

'I knew that, I said how long?'

'Oh, he's been in there quite a while, I guess.'

'Well, tell him I'm here and get him out.'

He took my arm and led me into one of the bedrooms. There was a girl sitting at the dressing table, spraying herself with perfume from a giant bottle.

'Hi,' she said.

'What's your name, honey?'

'Barbara.'

'Well, Barbara, Mr Warren and I want to borrow this room, so why don't you go and play a little strip poker.'

She pouted, gave herself one last spray, and minced out.

'If it moves, he lays it,' Raven said. 'If it doesn't move, he buries it.'

'What's he want to see me for?'

'He wants to meet you, he's anxious to meet you.'

'So anxious, I've been waiting for an hour.'

'Well, he's a busy man. He's got a lot of fingers in a lot of pies.'

'I just hope you're not trying to pull a last-minute stunt.'

'Dick, relax. He owns the company, he's paying the bills, he just wants to meet you.'

The henchman put his unshaven face round the door.

'Norbert'll be right with you. Can I fix you a drink?'

'Yeah, I'll have a vodka tonic. No, I won't, I'll have a bullshot. How about you, Dick?'

I nodded refusal.

'He's all right,' Raven said. 'Listen, he's a new boy. He's feeling his way.'

'All my life I've been meeting new boys feeling their way.'

'You'll like him. He's on the ball.'

But I didn't like him. He came through the door about five minutes later, smooth and apologetic, a man with pale eyes and a strong handshake.

'Mr Warren,' he said, 'I'm so sorry. You have to blame your City gentlemen, they take a long time to say no.'

'Who'd you see?' Raven said.

'Sir Charles, is it? I can't figure out their titles. Is he an Earl or something?'

'No,' Raven said, 'he just got it from the last Government. I didn't know you were seeing him. You're lucky he said no. He's nothing.'

'I thought he had a certain style.'

'Last year's style, maybe.'

The henchman returned with Raven's drink.

'Get everybody out, will you,' Quarry said. 'The place is like Forest Lawn out there.' The man started to go. 'Wait a minute. Where are we eating to-night? Have you made a booking?'

'No, sir,' the man said.

'Well, make a booking. Where shall we eat, Paul, you tell me.'

'*Les A* or the *Mirabelle*, they're both good.'

'You say.'

'Are you paying?'

'That's my station in life.'

'Make it the *Mirabelle* then.'

Quarry turned to me. 'I hope you and Mrs Warren will join me.'

'Well, my wife's working and as you know I start our picture to-morrow.'

'What could be better?' Quarry said. 'We'll celebrate. Get me a table for six or eight at the *Mirabelle*.'

Before I could think of another excuse the man had disappeared.

'I don't know what we're all doing in a bedroom,' Quarry said. 'As soon as the mob have gone we'll move out.'

'I like bedrooms,' Raven said.

'Yes, but Dick and I haven't got your memories.' I could almost see him working to gain my confidence. I want to be honest. He was impressive. Immaculately turned out, clean shaven, with a boyish face beneath well-groomed hair, worn fashionably long. He spoke quietly and with only the faintest of accents. If his reputation hadn't preceded him, he would have passed for a respectable, ultra-conservative Boston banker. He epitomised the new-style film executive: bland, with none of Raven's extrovert crudeness of manner or language. And yet the image was suspect. It didn't go with the motley collection in the rooms outside. There was a past which the Savile Row suits and the Jermyn Street shirts could not conceal. And I knew that he could read my thoughts.

'I was hoping you'd be free for dinner, because it'll give us an opportunity of discussing things. I'm sure Paul has told you that we're very excited about our relationship with you.'

'Yeah, I told him,' Raven answered.

'For my part, I'm learning, I'm learning all the time, and now that we're in business together I hope it's going to be a long and fruitful association. Excuse me, I just must use the can.'

He went through into the bathroom. Raven downed his bull-shot. He raised his eyebrows at me.

'I can't make it a late evening,' I said. 'I've got to do my home-work.'

Raven waved a hand in my direction. 'Relax, enjoy your-self.'

When Quarry reappeared he walked through to the main room. It was empty except for Barbara, who was biting her way round the last of the club sandwiches.

'Have you met Miss Nevers?' Quarry said.

'Yes, we met.'

'Could you excuse us a moment, darling, I just have to talk to these gentlemen.'

Miss Nevers gave us another version of her pout. It didn't have quite the same impact as the first time because her chin was covered with mayonnaise, but she took her meal and her sug-gestive body back into the bedroom and slammed the door. Quarry shrugged.

'She's had a rough time. We've flown thirteen thousand miles in the last week. Look, Dick, I don't want to keep you. We're going to be seeing each other for dinner and we can talk then in a relaxed way and straighten out anything that's worrying you.'

'I'm not particularly worried,' I said.

'No, I must say you don't look like a worried man. Well, that's fine. I look forward to meeting your wife. What time shall we say?'

'Make it eight,' Raven said, 'we'll meet around eight. I'll pick you up.'

Quarry put out his well-manicured hand. 'I like your picture, Dick. As you know I came in cold and I had to take a lot of decisions in a hurry, but I know I made the right one with you. I've read both the scripts and I understand from Paul you've done a great job with them. We'll drink to it to-night.'

Going down in the lift I said to Raven, 'Who gave him the other script to read?'

'I knew you'd say that.'

'Why did you give it to him?'

'Dick, he's paying for it and he keeps tabs on things. But he's not going to interfere. Believe me.'

'I don't believe you,' I said. 'I don't believe you and I don't trust you.'

'Well, I'll tell you one thing you can believe. Things are changing. Whatever you think of Quarry he's the coming thing. In two years' time you're going to be making pictures for him or you're not going to be making pictures.'

We sank to the ground with that comforting thought.

CHAPTER FORTY-SEVEN

As it turned out there were eight of us for dinner at the *Mirabelle*. Susan and I were the last to arrive and we found that the party now included Kitty and Hogarth and his wife. I'd heard it vaguely rumoured that Mrs Hogarth had once been a Deb, but it was hard to believe that anybody had ever swooned at her coming out. She was a transparent snob, the sort of woman who always ensures that you see the Dior label when you help her off with her coat, and every year sent out hand-made Christmas cards of surpassing vulgarity. She greeted Susan with tolerant condescension: actresses, especially screen actresses, were, you felt, just above staff in her book. I kissed her before she could re-compose her face.

'Audrey,' I said, 'how lovely to see you.' Then I kissed Kitty, since patriotism was plainly not enough. 'How ravishing you look, Mrs Raven. I'm sorry we're late, but Susan didn't get back from the studio until seven thirty.'

'Oh, are you making a film?' Audrey said.

'Darling, you know she is,' Robin said.

Kitty exchanged a look with me.

'Is it a new film?'

'It started out that way,' Susan said, 'but I've been on it so long it feels like last year's model.'

The monosyllabic Miss Nevers stopped eating olives and stared hard at Susan, opening her eyes wide.

'Are you Susan Hart?' she said.

'Yes, I am.'

'But you're a film star!'

'Let's go in to dinner,' Quarry said. He took the last olive out of Miss Nevers's hand and gripped her firmly by the arm. He led the way and Kitty lingered behind the others.

'Boy!' she said, 'between that freak and darling Audrey we're in for a scintillating evening.'

'Is there a Mrs Quarry anywhere?'

'Two. Both of them stiff with alimony.'

We took our places at the best table in the room. Champagne was waiting and was served immediately. I found myself sitting between Audrey and Miss Nevers, while Susan, on the other side of the round table, was flanked by Hogarth and Raven. For tactical reasons Quarry had put himself between Kitty and Miss Nevers.

We studied the celebrated menu with the seriousness it deserved, but the effort quickly exhausted Miss Nevers.

'Do they have hamburgers?' she said, 'I don't see it here.'

'We could make you a hamburger, certainly, Madam. Or else there's the duck, to-night, or the Chateaubriand . . .'

'No, I'll take a hamburger.'

'Certainly, Madam. And how do you like it done?'

'Kinda burnt. With onion rings.'

'No onion rings,' Quarry said. 'You're sure that's what you want?'

'Yeah, I can't read all that stuff. Puts me off my appetite.'

'How about you, Kitty?'

'She'll have what she always has,' Raven said. 'The chef knows she's been on a seven-year diet.'

I looked across to Susan. 'What're you having, darling?'

'Oh, just something light. Can I have a plain grilled Dover sole, off the bone, and melon to start with.'

'Yeah, that sounds good. I'll have that, too,' Miss Nevers said.

'But you already ordered hamburger.'

'I can change my mind, can't I?'

'That's two Dover soles, is it?' the Head Waiter said.

'No, just the one, same as her.'

'I think half the fun of eating is choosing, don't you?' Audrey said to me.

'Yes,' I said, 'but large menus tend to intimidate me.'

'Oh, I think they're such fun. When we're in France I always insist on going to the *Tour d'Argent*. I wept when they lost one of their stars that year. Course, it's got so touristy now.'

She questioned the Head Waiter in her best Heathfield French while everybody else listened patiently, and then ordered one of the more exotic specialities.

'Darling,' Robin said, 'that'll keep everybody waiting, it takes half an hour.'

'Oh, will it?'

'Would you care to take half of a Chateaubriand with me, Mrs Hogarth?' Quarry said.

'I'm afraid I don't quite share your American love for very large steaks. But thank you so much. Oh, dear, I'll have to start all over again, won't I?'

'Why don't you have the Chicken Kiev, darling, you like that.'

'No, it's not one of my chicken nights.'

Hogarth shot an anxious glance at Quarry. 'Well, don't take too long, darling.'

'Oh, am I holding everybody up? We're not in any hurry, are we?'

The Head Waiter tactfully moved on to take Quarry's and Raven's orders, and Hogarth rattled off his in an obvious attempt to restore the family fortunes, I gave mine and then we were back to Audrey again.

'I think that if I'm not to be allowed to have my first choice, I shall have to ask the chef to do me a piece of paper-thin veal with his special sauce. Tell him who it's for.'

'And to start with, Madam?'

'Well, now . . .

I heard Kitty murmur, 'Oh, Jesus!' and Hogarth sank his second glass of champagne so quickly he made himself splutter.

Audrey finally settled for some *pâté*, and then there was a further pause while Quarry selected the most expensive wines on the list, and by the time conversation was resumed even Miss Nevers was aware of the atmosphere.

'What do you do?' she said to me.

'Mr Warren directs pictures, honey. I told you.'

'Oh.'

'He's just about to start one for me. I think we ought to drink to it, Dick.'

'Yes, here's to Dick,' Hogarth said.

'How's the Lehmann girl behaving?' Kitty said after we lowered glasses.

'Fine.'

'You wait.'

'I think she's going to surprise a lot of people,' I said.

'The day she surprises me,' Kitty said, 'I'll take out German papers.'

'My mother's German,' Miss Nevers said, and again the conversation stopped dead.

'I'm ashamed to say I don't go to films very often,' Audrey said. 'Unless it's a première or something.'

'Of course you do, darling,' Hogarth said.

'Is it going to be one of those frightfully daring films?'

'In what way?' I said.

'Well, you know, where everybody takes their clothes off?'

'No, I don't think so.'

'I always think that's so ghastly, don't you? I was only saying to my hairdresser the other day, where's it all going to end? I mean, he sees everything, and he was telling me that some of the films you can see in the West End now are simply not to be believed.'

'Yeah, the trouble is,' Quarry said, 'those are the ones that are taking the dough.'

'Did you see the grosses on *Restless Virgin*?' Raven said.

'Unbelievable.'

'I saw that,' Miss Nevers chipped in. 'We ran it at the beach house.'

'Did you like it?' I said.

'Yeah, I thought it was kinda freaky in a cute sort of way.'

I was so fascinated by the way she moved her mouth when she framed any word of more than two syllables that I failed to hear the next question that Quarry directed at me, and had to ask him to repeat it.

'You thought any more about the alternative ending?'

'Is there an alternative ending?'

'Yes, the one where the boy doesn't die.'

'I don't think I ever seriously considered it. He certainly dies in the script I'm going to shoot.'

'I don't think unhappy endings bring them in any more.'

'We haven't thrown it out yet,' Raven said. 'But we're thinking about it.'

'I'm not thinking about it,' I said. I heard the edge in my own voice.

'You see, Dick, forgive me putting in my two cents, but the feeling I've got is you've got more going for you if the boy's still on his feet at the end. I mean, I don't see it as a problem.'

'But the whole point of the story is that the girl has to betray him. If she betrays him, they have to kill him.'

'That's the way you've got it now, but I'm saying you can go another route. Supposing the girl doesn't betray him?'

I stared hard at my plate.

'Have you ever thought of that, that's quite a twist?'

I still didn't answer.

'See one of the first things I did when I took over the company was to get a breakdown of the top ten grossers and my people came up with some pretty interesting data which we put in the computer. I'd like to show it to you.'

'Interesting,' Hogarth said, 'you're using computers, are you?'

'We use computers on everything.'

'Fascinating.'

'Those little babies have got the answers.'

'Can they tell you what people are going to pay to see next year?' I said.

'Within a certain margin, yes.'

He was so reasonable, so polite, so much the gracious host, that I knew my mounting anger would destroy me. I was caught in the trap. I had to believe that the script I was about to shoot made sense, or I would be impotent before the first foot of film was exposed. I knew that I had to put up a defence, but it's not easy to defend the unknown. Convictions are not enough. You can't argue for something intangible. The dedicated exploration that is painstakingly achieved on any film is not something that can be anticipated for third parties. There is no *Michelin Guide* to consult: you set out for a destination that isn't even on the map and you have to have a blind faith that your nose will take you to it.

From that moment onwards it required an effort for me to remain at the table. I can only liken my feelings to those of a dedicated jigsaw puzzler. Attempting the most complicated puzzle available to him, he reaches that point when he has fitted together most of the pictorial pieces, and now he is left with a vast expanse of sky. So many of the pieces look alike, and there is no graduation of colour to assist him. And he faces the fact that even when he has solved it, the puzzle isn't his: somebody else will come along and break it down again.

Several times I looked to Susan for support, but it was not her evening for being brave for me. Perhaps, in view of what I know now, she had already decided that the events of my life must take their own course or perhaps being more generous, the real implications of the dialogue escaped her. It is possible that she had no real inkling of my despair: the politeness of the dinner table conceals more than nausea.

It was odd that my only ally proved to be Kitty, though I don't flatter myself that her defence was prompted by a sudden rush of affection for me. Generosity for others was not one of Kitty's failings; what funds she had, she spent on herself. No, I think what spurred her that evening was a vindictive urge to get at Paul through Quarry. She liked her husband to be the protagonist at all times, and Raven was curiously silent for most of the evening. They were all too complicated for me. Audrey epitomised the very meal she was eating—she never came out into the light. Hogarth was too busy polishing his own future to risk venturing an opinion either way and Susan . . . well, Susan, was no longer in love with me and that explains much. I was left with Miss Nevers who gulped the red wine with the fish (which made Audrey frown and then smile secretly) and from time to time struggled to comprehend and got no thanks for it. At one point, when Quarry slapped her down, his mounting irritation with me slipping momentarily out of control, she pressed her leg against mine and kept it there. Had I not been so vulnerable, I might have enjoyed the possibilities of a brief flirtation, for Quarry looked the sort of man who over-valued his sexual vanity, but the heat of her body

236

prompted only an automatic reflex, and after that evening she went out of my life for ever.

Quarry was quietly persistent, and refused to allow the conversation to drift away from his main purpose. I tried to match him in conviction and he listened with every outward appearance of understanding but never gave an inch.

'You see, basically, we're saying the same thing, Dick. You're arguing from the creative sense, and I respect that, but what I'm trying to put across is that in to-day's climate you have to approach it from a different way. You've got to use marketing techniques if this industry's going to survive. Everything's in the packaging. We've got to rationalise.'

'Is that how you tackled the mortician business?' Kitty said. She stubbed her cigarette out on her salad plate.

'Yeah. We're selling things, Kitty. One day we're selling wooden boxes and the next day we're selling cans of film. It's the same thing.'

'How do you rationalise selling boxes?'

'Simple. You find out what people want and you give it to them.'

'Does this fish come from Dover?' Miss Nevers interrupted.

'Er, probably,' I said.

'I saw that once in a film. *Mrs Miniver*. It was on the late show.'

'Listen, honey, it's Dover Sole, that's the name on the label. You see, Kitty, Dick, that's what I'm trying to say. You tell people what they're eating, and they believe you. You tell them how they're going to look when they're buried and they believe you. People don't want to think for themselves.'

'You're not going to make pictures that make people think?'

'Not if I can help it.'

'How well have you read my script?'

'I read a script like I read a balance sheet. I want to know if the two columns add up. See, let me ask you a question. What d'you want? D'you want to win the New York Critics Award or do you want some money in the bank?'

'I wouldn't turn my nose up at either.'

'Okay, which is more important to you?'

'Nobody goes into a film hoping it's going to lose money.'

'You're not answering my question.'

'Well, obviously I want a successful picture.'

'What makes you think you've got all the answers?' Kitty asked Quarry.

'Did I say that?'

'From where I'm sitting, yes.'

'Kitty, I don't have all the answers, but I got more than most. I didn't go into this with my eyes closed. And I'm either going to make it work my way, or I'm going to get out and into something else. I want a return on my money, I got stockholders to think about.'

'I think this is something we can take a rain-check on,' Raven said. 'What time's your call in the morning, Dick?'

'You're the producer,' I said, 'you tell me.'

'Well, I don't know about Dick,' Susan said, 'but I have to be up at the crack.'

'Are you starting on location?' Quarry said.

'Yes.'

'I may look in on my way to the airport.'

'Oh, are we going to-morrow?' Miss Nevers said. 'Where we going?'

'Rome.'

'But we just got back from there.'

Quarry ignored her. To comfort herself she started to eat quantities of coffee sugar.

'Well, a very pleasant evening,' Audrey said.

Quarry walked away from the table. He didn't even look at the check when it was presented to him by the grateful management, and told the Head Waiter to sign it for him and add fifteen per cent.

'I don't want to go to Rome,' Miss Nevers said. 'I might just miss the plane,' but it was said without conviction. Quarry had uncorked the sweet smell of success for her, and she had to inhale it or be left behind.

We said good-bye on the pavement in Curzon Street and went our separate ways. Quarry shook my hand warmly. 'It'll work out, Dick,' he said. 'You'll see. Good luck in the morning.'

He got into the waiting Rolls ahead of Miss Nevers. 'Nice meeting you,' she said to me, and to Susan, 'What's the name of your film?' Susan told her. She nodded. 'I might do a film myself one of these days. Everybody tells me that's what I oughta do. But we never stay long enough in one place.'

Quarry called her from the car and she got inside. It drove off before her door was fully closed.

'Is she his wife?' Audrey said. 'Nobody introduced us.'

'No, dear,' Kitty said. 'They're not even good friends.'

'I thought she was very amusing. Well, good night, Mrs Warren.'

Hogarth kissed Susan, but I could not bring myself to taste Audrey's cold cheek twice in one evening. I refused Raven's offer of a lift and we took a taxi instead.

'God! what a depressing evening,' I said.

'What was wrong?'

'Didn't you listen to any of it?'

'I listened, yes, but I couldn't follow what he was getting at.'

'Well, it was quite simple. Raven's obviously made some deal. Maybe the whole thing's just a tax loss, who knows?'

'He didn't seem quite so bad as some of the others you've worked for.'

'Just another pretty face.'

'Perhaps they'll all leave you alone when you get started.'

'Perhaps. I doubt it.'

'The girl friend was something, wasn't she?'

'Sad.'

'I didn't think she was particularly sad. And I thought you were rather taken with her.'

'She gave me a little hot thigh during the evening.'

'Perhaps she thought you'd put her in the film.'

'Yes, that's all I need. Did the charming Robin tell you anything riveting?'

'Not really. I don't know why you don't like him, he's always terribly nice about you. He admires you tremendously.'

'While it suits him. Didn't he say anything to you? You were deep in conversation at one point.'

'No, he just mentioned he might be sent to Hollywood, that's all.'

'Do you think Hollywood is ready for the lovely Audrey?'

'I don't think he's taking her. She hates America apparently. I feel sorry for him. It can't be any fun living with that *Tatler* accent and dirty bra straps. She was exactly the same at school.'

'You went to school with her?'

'Yes, you know that. I told you ages ago.'

'You never told me.'

'Well, I did, but it doesn't matter. She wouldn't acknowledge it, of course.'

'But she looks years older than you.'

'She is years older. We weren't in the same class or anything.'

I had a sudden vision of them both as schoolgirls with every possibility of innocence left to them. Then I thought of what we had all become. I reached for Susan's hand.

'I wish I'd known you then.'

'You wouldn't have cared for me then.'

'Have you changed so much?'

I could not see her eyes in the darkness of the taxi, but she took her hand out of mine and raised it to her cheek and for a second I could have believed she was crying in that instantaneous way women have. Perhaps I was imagining it, for her voice was quite steady when she said, 'Nothing ever stays the same. That's the only thing I ever learnt at school.'

CHAPTER FORTY-EIGHT

I spent a sleepless night, hardly the best omen for the start of a new film, but it wasn't the uncertainties surrounding that part of my life which kept me from closing my eyes. Lying awkwardly in the sheet sandwich, it seemed to me that I was no longer capable of all the plotting and lies which until then I had thought my affair with Alison could not do without. I even explored the fantasy of what it would be like to exchange everything for the undemanding compliance of Miss Nevers. Her nubile, erotic stupidity at least had the attraction of being passive and I conjured up variations on a theme until they eventually resembled the frantic and improbable excesses of a Victorian pornographic novel.

I got up and went into the sitting-room to use the house phone, managing to charm the night porter into bringing me a cup of his thin instant coffee. I sat reading the script, staring at the scenes I had shortly to bring to life, and the next thing I knew it was morning and Susan was bending over me and I saw her face at a tilt, imagining for a moment that it was framed in my viewfinder, that the film had already begun.

I shaved my tender skin while she took a bath. My chest felt constricted from too many night cigarettes, but surprisingly enough, by the time I had taken a shower fatigue had vanished. I had a quick look out of the window while dressing: the sky seemed bright. We took a hasty cup of coffee each and then we left the suite. When we said good-bye and departed in our separate cars I was filled with an unreasonable amount of optimism.

We were starting the film in a great derelict house off Regent's Park which Jimmy had found and transformed. It was a difficult opening sequence but I had planned the schedule so as to shoot in continuity as far as possible, for the script was a complex one and began with a long and savage dialogue between the boy and the girl, which I intended to re-use in fragments throughout the rest of the film, as a recapitulation. I had pared it down in successive re-writes until only the essentials remained. I wanted to come in on two people at a crossroads in their relationship, take it to a certain point, and then break off abruptly and start their story farther back. Then, when I used a fragmented flashback device at intervals I would progress the opening scene by a few lines until, in the closing moments of the film, the audience were given the last pieces of the puzzle.

Over the years I have developed a very necessary technique of visual improvisation. Thus, even though I have carefully familiar-ised myself with the chosen locations, I don't approach each new day's work with any visual rigidity. Film is light, and light changes, and a location you have okayed perhaps only a few days before is totally different when the cameras are in position.

I jumped out of the car on arrival and ran up the stairs to the open entrance. I had a schoolboy's disappointment when I found that I was not, after all, the first on the scene. Jimmy, Stan, George and Bill Mason, the cameraman, had all beaten me to it and were sitting at a breakfast table laid with silver, napkins, and a Georgian coffee set. They held the tableau as I stopped in the doorway.

'What kept you, dear?' Jimmy said.

'You cheeky bastards!'

Jimmy lifted the cover of a silver salver to reveal buttered toast surrounding my viewfinder.

'I suppose you were here all night?'

'More or less,' said Jimmy and I believed him, for everything was beautifully prepared, and my confidence accelerated as I went through the house examining all the rooms we were going to shoot in.

'Are the toilets working?'

'Like a dream,' Stan said. 'And we got the hot water system to work at midnight.'

I turned to Bill. 'How d'you think we're going to be for light?'

'No problems. The weather report was lousy, which always encourages me. But I'm all set to give you anything you want. We've rigged sun guns in most of the rooms and I can get a good balance for interior, exterior. No problems.'

'I thought the light in the hallway was sensational when we came through. How long d'you think we've got that?'

'At least an hour.'

'Let's get set-up there then.'

'What are you starting with, Governor?' George said.

'Scene five.'

'That's just the boy.'

'Yes,' I said. 'Is he here yet?'

'He should be,' George said. 'I checked his home and he'd left on time.'

'Where's Monika making up?'

'In the third-floor bathroom.'

'Tell me when she's here.'

'She's here.'

'Is the Stormtrooper with her?'

'*Nein.*'

'It's all too good to be true,' I said. 'Where's it all going to go wrong?'

'I'll let you know in an hour's time,' George said.

By now the rest of the crew had arrived and the ground floor of the house was orderly chaos as the equipment was placed into position. As I walked through the house future shots began to suggest themselves and memories of Quarry faded farther and farther into the distance. I didn't bother to enquire whether Raven had shown up: I was certain that he would time his first appearance to just before the lunch break. He liked to keep his crews guessing.

I climbed the stairs to the third floor and knocked at Monika's door. She was in the improvised make-up chair, wearing a towelling dressing-gown. The make-up man was fussing with eyeshadow brushes. I kissed her on the forehead.

'Relax,' I said, 'you're not in the first shot.'

'Do I look awful? I didn't sleep all night, I was so nervous.'

'You should have joined me. I slept in a chair.'

I studied her face in the mirror.

'Don't go mad, Rembrandt,' I said, 'you can't improve on Nature.'

'Well, I thought just a little highlight here and there, sir.'

'Is that her own lipstick?'

'Yes, I haven't worked on the mouth yet.'

'Well, don't, it's fine as it is.'

I bent and kissed her again. 'Trust me,' I said.

'I do.'

'You're going to be very good.'

I left the room and bumped into Nethercott on the stairs. He was carrying a bunch of flowers, and he obviously hadn't slept either.

'You shouldn't have,' I said.

'I can't believe it's actually happening.'

He embraced me awkwardly, holding the flowers away from my back.

'All those people downstairs. They're not waiting for me, are they?'

'You're first shot.'

'Oh, Christ, which scene?'

'Five. But it's nothing. Just two words.'

'I'll just drop these in to Monika.'

'That door there.'

He bounded up the last few stairs. Twenty minutes later the clapper boy slapped the first slate in front of his strained face, and twenty seconds after that I said 'Cut and print' just to give him confidence. He wasn't that perfect, but it was a shot I could pick up again any morning first thing, and I knew the whole unit needed a fillip right at the beginning to set the mood for what I was determined would be a good day.

And so it proved. You have good days and you have disasters, and you learn to live with them all. The good days aren't necessarily the ones that produce the best results on the screen, and I have returned home in near despair on occasions only to find, when viewing the rushes the following morning, that some sort of magic has been trapped between the lens and the celluloid.

My instincts had been right about Monika. She wasn't a great actress, but she could be moulded and she responded to kindness. The crew liked her, and because they showed it she didn't come, as George put it, any of the old acid. The prop men mothered her and Nethercott praised her after every take. I had no real worries about him. His initial hesitation was purely nerves, but my unoriginal trick of printing his very first take had worked the necessary calming miracle. He was a beautiful young actor, in the sense that we use the word beautiful. The camera photographs thoughts and his performance had depth from the word go. By lunch-time we had over two minutes in the can, and it was my turn to be worried since it was not a pace any of us could maintain and we were in danger of running out of scheduled scenes.

Raven arrived as I had predicted, but there was no sign of Quarry.

'He got tied up with phone calls,' Raven said. 'But he sent you this and said not to worry.' He handed me a magnum of champagne, which I immediately passed on to the camera and sound crews. Raven had already sent flowers to Monika, and to Nethercott he gave a gold wrist-watch. 'If you're any good in the picture, I'll buy you a strap to match,' he said with what, for him, was a display of charm.

He suggested going out to lunch in a restaurant, but I didn't want anything to shatter the mood I had created, and I insisted that we all take the tray lunch provided by the location caterers. Raven was put out and showed it, and he only stayed for the first shot after lunch and then said he had to get back to take a call from New York. He couldn't resist an artistic contribution, however. 'I don't think the broad is wearing enough make-up,' he said. 'Check it, will you?'

'Of course,' I said. 'I'm glad you spotted it.'

'I don't miss much.'

'What did he say?' Monika asked the moment he was through the door.

'Nothing. He said you looked great.'

Later, when I dismissed her, I noticed that she only took Nethercott's flowers with her—Raven's she gave to her stand-in.

I did one final shot with Nethercott and then we called it a day. I checked the progress report with the continuity girl and found that we had exceeded the scheduled work by two scenes and three pages.

'When do we start the sequel?' George asked.

'Don't worry,' I said, 'you're in for a bad day to-morrow.'

Exhaustion caught up with me the moment I stepped into my car for the journey back to the hotel. I dreamt about Alison and when my driver nudged me awake at journey's end, I remembered that I had intended to stop off at the office to see if a letter had arrived. I realised, shamefully, that for the first time since our reunion I hadn't thought about her all day.

CHAPTER FORTY-NINE

At the end of the first week we were a day ahead of schedule, something which Raven greeted with more enthusiasm than he viewed the daily 'rushes'. For some reason he concentrated most of his criticism around Nethercott's performance. He accepted Monika without comment, but he seemed determined to withhold any praise from the boy.

'What exactly do you object to?' I asked him.

'It's a gut reaction.'

'What does that mean?'

'I don't get a feeling in my balls.'

'Well, your balls aren't your guts, for one thing.'

'Okay, I'll come out with it. He hasn't got it.'

'What d'you mean by "it"?'

'He's dull.'

'I've deliberately kept him down in these early scenes, so that's my fault.'

'I don't care whose fault it is, I'm just telling you that what we're seeing on the screen isn't going to set the world on fire.'

'Look,' I said, patiently, 'I agree with you that on the first week's work you haven't seen him pull out any stops. But, that's me. That's how I'm directing him. I want him low key. The performance has got to build, dramatically he's got to hold it all in

246

reserve, because otherwise there's no story climax and there's no performance climax.'

'Okay,' he said. 'You think he's great, I think he's dull. Anyway, we'd better let New York see it and they can decide.'

'Decide what?'

'Decide whether they like him.'

'And if they don't?'

'Well, we'll cross that bridge when we come to it.'

'No, let's you and me cross it now. If they don't?'

'Then they'll recast.'

'They can't recast.'

'Who says?'

'If they recast him, they can also look for another director.'

'They can do that too.'

'Fine. Long as we know where we are.'

We had this enlightening conversation in the sound truck outside the location, the sound crew having vacated it to give us privacy. I opened a window to let in some much-needed air, because quite apart from his opinions, Raven's cigar smoke was fugging the atmosphere.

'For Christ'sake, I'm only telling you for your own good. If they don't like him they ain't going to get behind the picture. You must see that.'

'I'm saying that nobody, certainly not those morons in New York, has the right to judge a performance on half a dozen scenes. I do know something about acting, you know. I haven't made many mistakes with actors in my time.'

'Listen, I got the message. You like him. I'm saying you're wrong.'

'You're still pissed off, aren't you?'

'What's that mean?'

'You didn't get your own way with the script, so now you have to go another route.'

He flung the half-smoked cigar out of the open side window. The blood was climbing from his neck to his face. 'Well, let me remind you of something, I'm producing this half-arsed picture. You wouldn't be sitting here if it wasn't for me. They'd have slung it out of the window weeks back.'

'Yes,' I said. 'No one's disputing that, what's that got to do with it? They didn't throw it out, I'm suitably grateful, and we are sitting here. And if we're going to have a stand-up fight, I'd rather it was now than later.'

'Who's talking about a stand-up fight? We're discussing one lousy actor.'

'The one lousy actor, as you call him, happens to be playing the leading role. If you're such a great spotter of talent why didn't you get your much-quoted gut reaction when I first mentioned his name?'

'I never wanted him.'

'Who did you want?'

'I gave you some names and you threw them out.'

'You gave me the name of one American star whom I happen to think is too intelligent to have accepted the role had we been misguided enough to offer it to him. But that's all history, I don't want to get into that. What I want to know is how far you're going to go.'

Outside the truck I could see faces turned towards us. George was hovering and looking at his watch, but he had enough experience not to call me back on the set at that moment.

'I've told you what I'm going to do. I'm going to send the stuff to New York. Let them decide.'

'That's a new one for you, isn't it? Being the office boy for New York. That's what you call producing, is it?'

'Kitty warned me about you.'

'Kitty did?'

'Yeah.'

'Well, neither of us expects any loyalty from Kitty, do we? What sort of gut reaction did you have when you married her?' I said, and got to my feet. I was just about to lose my temper completely, and I knew myself well enough to avoid that. I was no match for Raven in a straight shouting bout, and I was desperate not to give the crew any real inkling of what was going on. In addition I knew that the emotional damage it would do to me would be reflected in the rest of the day's work. 'I'm wanted back on the set,' I said. 'They're waiting for me. I have to direct another dull scene.'

But news travels fast on a film set and by the time I had my eye to the viewfinder, I could hear the whispers in the background. Raven was the natural enemy by long tradition and the particular circumstances of his personality. He knew none of the crew by name, except possibly the cameraman, and could never be bothered to indulge in any small-chat which British technicians regard as the prerequisite before accepting any outsider.

Somebody once likened the role of the film director to that of a benevolent dictator and it's true that during the actual shooting period of a film the unit exists in an isolated and insulated world, expected to perform the impossible, taking orders from one man whose every eccentricity must be satisfied without question. Only a few of those present are aware of the strategy, the rest accept the abnormal working conditions and sometimes incomprehensible decisions with bemused tolerance, concerned only with their own narrow horizons. The slightest hesitation on the part of the director is immediately interpreted as weakness. But when the unit is threatened from outside, the ranks close, loyalty is near absolute.

A few minutes after leaving Raven, by a conscious effort, I had blotted him out and was once again involved with the scene I had to shoot.

When Nethercott and Monika came on the set to rehearse it was immediately obvious to me that rumours of a sort had already reached them. I often think that film technicians would make superb intelligence officers in time of war.

'Is our gifted producer still around?' Nethercott asked.

'I don't know where he is,' I said.

'He's left,' George said. 'I think he's gone to put his name down for an Academy Award.'

'What was his news?' Monika said.

'Nothing much.'

'Had he seen the stuff?' Nethercott said.

'Yes, he's seen what we've done up to date.'

'And?'

'I'm encouraged by the fact he's got reservations about it.'

I gave a look in George's direction, and he picked up the cue. 'Right, let's have a red light,' he said. He raised his voice. 'Now, quiet, let's have you first time.' The rehearsal bell sounded and the noise died away to a murmur.

George took this as a personal affront. 'Now, don't drop me in it, boys. When I say Quiet, I mean QU—IET!' He waited. 'That's better.' He turned to one of his assistants. 'Get outside the door and tell everybody out there to hold their breath.'

I excused the stand-ins and the principals took their places. We started rehearsing the dialogue with camera, making last-minute adjustments, improving, and smoothing, stopping to argue a particular piece of business. I watched a couple of full rehearsals through camera, operating it myself, then handed it back to the actual operator, Mike, and took up the position I would occupy during the actual shooting. The chaos of a film set has to be gradually tidied up before each and every new scene—the technicians, who in the first instance appear to be the dominant figures, withdrawing farther and farther into the background, performing their many and various tasks by a combination of sign language and instinct, until they become anonymous and the actors, exposed and vulnerable, are left to occupy the lighted areas of the stage alone.

The director must judge when that vital moment has been reached—that no-man's-land between reality and artifice, that strange country to which few passports are granted in perpetuity.

I had a peculiar problem in the scenes between Monika and Nethercott. She invariably benefited from long and repeated rehearsals, whereas he reached the peak of his performance much earlier. It was my task to decide what was early enough for her and not too late for him.

Raven's destructive criticism of the boy had no substance in fact. He took direction easily, but on the actual take would always give something beyond the evidence, and he constantly had the ability to surprise me by his invention, which he used with true skill—sufficient for me to note with silent pleasure during the time the cameras were rolling, but not so different from the last rehearsal as to throw Monika. Every new day we worked together I became more and more conscious that he would ultimately surprise everybody.

We worked steadily the rest of that morning, though the pace had slackened, some of the concentration having departed with Raven. I heard myself getting edgy for no good reason on two or three occasions, and, probably coincidentally, minor things started to go wrong. A light bulb exploded during the middle of one take, aircraft noise completely ruined two others, and finally the film jammed in the camera. By then it was time to break for lunch and the natives were getting restless. I asked the union shop stewards if we could continue beyond the allotted time, and for the first time since we had started working I was given a glimpse of those other forces which determine our destinies. Two of the shop stewards agreed, but the man representing a third union held out. We broke for lunch, the scene left in an unfinished state.

Monika, Nethercott and Toller, who had arrived just as we broke, joined me for a rather gloomy meal during which Toller monopolised the conversation. He had apparently just arranged a commercial tie-up with a popular brand of shampoo, and in return for sponsoring the product Monika was to receive several thousand pounds, but more importantly, Herr Toller was to become the proud owner of a new Rolls-Royce.

'But I never use that shampoo,' Monika protested. 'It rots the hair.'

'Who said you had to use it? All you have to do is say you use it.'

'But that's dishonest!'

Toller shrugged. 'Dishonest, dishonest! For a new Rolls-Royce I'd drink the stuff twice nightly on television if they asked me.'

'Why don't you do that, you might start a new fashion.'

He reverted to German for the next exchange and at the end of it she remained silent. I saw Nethercott give him a look, but before the situation could develop, Stan knocked at the door.

'Can I see you a second?' he said to me.

I got up from the table and went outside.

'What's wrong?'

'Nothing. No panic. I just came from the production office. There was a call for you. From Spain.'

'Spain?' I said.

'Yes, were you expecting a call?'

'No, not that I know of. Did they give a name?'

He shook his head. 'I said you weren't available and they were going to try it again in half an hour. Least, I think that's what they said, it was a very bad line.'

'Have you got a car?'

'Yes, I've got mine outside.'

We drove the short distance to the production office.

'Did you get that shot before lunch?'

'No,' I said. 'You're sure it was from Spain?'

'Definitely. How long d'you reckon after lunch?'

'A good hour. One of the stewards was bolshie, otherwise I'd have got it.'

'Which one?'

'The red-haired character, what's his name? Archie.'

'I'll watch him.'

I ran up the stairs to the office and the two girls who worked there left me alone. I studied the progress reports while waiting, but for once the telephone operators were as good as their word and the phone went just as the half hour expired. It was my call coming through again. I listened to a lot of peculiar Spanish noises and then a voice told me to speak up. I said Hello a few times, but nothing happened. I had a feeling of dread.

Then a very faint voice said, 'Darling?'

'Alison?'

'Yes, can you hear me?'

'Just about.'

'Is it a terrible time to call you?' she said.

'No, of course not. It's so marvellous to hear you. Nothing wrong is there?'

'What?'

'I said, nothing wrong?'

'No. He's gone to Madrid for the day. Urgent business or something, so I'm on my own.'

'Are you all right?'

'I miss you.'

Her voice kept coming and going and I could hear other voices cutting across our conversation.

'I miss you too,' I shouted.

It was her turn to ask for a repeat.

'I said I miss you too.'

'You sound a long way away.'

'I am a long way away,' I said.

'I've waited four hours for this call.'

'Well, I'm glad you got through. Did you get my letter?'

'Yes, I collected it yesterday. It isn't easy.'

'No, I'm sure. I haven't had anything from you.'

'I haven't written. Did you hear that? Well, I have written, but I haven't posted anything. I'm hopeless at writing.'

'Doesn't matter,' I said.

The other voices swamped us then for a few seconds and we appeared to be on a totally crossed line. When we made contact again, I shouted, conscious that I could be overheard.

'When are you coming back, d'you know yet?'

'No, we may stay on a bit.' She faded again, then came back and I heard the word 'business' in isolation.

'Darling,' I said, 'can you hear me?' Her voice, when it finally penetrated, seemed to be in an echo chamber. I heard her say 'I love you,' and then the babble of voices swamped everything again and shortly afterwards we were disconnected. I flashed for the operator and explained the situation.

'Well, it's still open at this end,' the girl said, 'we haven't disconnected you. Who's making the call?'

'They are,' I said.

'Oh, well, you'll have to wait for them to ring you back.'

But I couldn't wait. I left the office and told the girls that if the call came through again to explain that I was no longer available.

'Can we give a message, Mr Warren?'

'No, it's just a friend who's in Spain,' I said lamely. 'We'd more or less finished, but we got cut off before we could say goodbye.'

Stan drove me back to the location. Even though I am sure he suspected the source of the phone call, he gave no indication.

'Has Raven asked you to ship any material to New York?'

'Not yet.'

'He will. Let me know immediately he does, will you?'

'How was he this morning?'

'Flexing his muscles. He wants me to get rid of the boy.'

'You're joking?'

'No,' I said. I jumped out of the car the moment we arrived and found George waiting for me on the steps.

'All ready, governor,' he said. 'They've had a dry run with camera while you were away, so they're all set. And by the way, I had a little dicky bird with our union friend. That won't happen again.'

But there was a tenseness on the set that we hadn't had before, and it took me three quarters of an hour before I got the first satisfactory take. I printed it. The actors, thinking the worst was finally over, relaxed, but before they could step outside the scene completely I called them back. I invented some doubt about my own work, looked through the camera again and then announced that I wanted to make a couple of small changes and shoot again. I asked Monika to cut one line of dialogue and varied the camera action slightly. The ruse, an old director's trick, had the desired effect. Actors are creatures of habit and the tiny variations I had asked for put Monika and Nethercott back on their mettle. I didn't rehearse again, but went straight into it and the scene came to life for the first time. I cancelled the first print and made the last take the only one.

The tension disappeared completely during the rest of the afternoon and progress was smooth. I concentrated on Nethercott quite deliberately, telling Monika that I wanted to save her close-ups until the following morning. Actresses never mind waiting for their own perfection.

Now that Raven had tipped me off to his next move I was determined to prove him wrong.

As I pushed Nethercott to extend his performance, he seemed to become me. The direction I gave him and which he translated into images of pain and despair stemmed from the poignancy of my own situation rather than just the script he was required to speak. Every line of dialogue had a double meaning for me, and my invention was fluid. Does it sound false to say that I transformed my own happiness into the sadness that the scene demanded—is that a paradox too obscure? The single hidden fact of my life—that somewhere, in some remote hotel phone booth, Alison had sought me out to confirm her love—became, during the course of that afternoon, part of an actor's performance trapped on the emulsion. There was something doubly satisfying in the process: not only was I able to capitalise on my own secret emotions, I was able to voice them in public without anybody being aware. Alison became the girl that Nethercott was addressing, Nethercott became me, the shutter opened and closed twenty-four times a second, and I photographed my love before strangers.

CHAPTER FIFTY

Before strangers. When I wrote that I little thought that I would become one of them. That afternoon was a long time ago and the memory of it too cruel. I thought the effort of describing it would somehow remove an old pain, but it was not to be. There's been a gap since I last picked up my pen. Like an amputee I have delayed looking under the bandages. I have become the stranger.

Last night the film was shown on television here. It was widely advertised in the papers, but I couldn't bring myself to stay in and watch it. Instead I drove around aimlessly until time had run out. Even so, the past tracked me down and this morning a friend who should have known better phoned to say that he had watched it. 'You ought to sue them,' he said, 'they'd cut it so much, it didn't make any sense.'

But that isn't the story I set out to write. The failure of the film is something else.

That afternoon is a long time ago. The house near Regent's Park, has, I understand, been demolished to make way for a block of flats. I was right about Nethercott, he did have that special talent that separates the actors from the stars. Monika is still making the front covers, and only recently she was persuaded to pose nude for the centre page spread in one of the girlie maga-zines. Herr Toller, who is no longer married to her, was, I am sure, suitably impressed. Looking at her nude body I realised how far I had come from peace.

Last night apparently, they cut deeper. But that isn't, as I said, the story I want to tell. The real story will never be edited to make room for the commercials. Real stories seldom are. If I compel myself to tell what remains, you must read between the lines to discover the happiness.

Raven was cleverer than I gave him credit for. He didn't send the first week's work to New York, he worked on Toller instead. I was so busy watching Raven, I had forgotten that Toller even existed.

Nothing happened at all for at least a week. The shooting con-tinued to go well and Raven kept away. It was one of the happiest periods in my whole life. I worked hard, I slept well, and I was in love. I wrote to Alison between takes, concealing the letters within the pages of my script. She was never able to phone me again, but she did send one unsigned postcard. It was a pathetic attempt at code, like something a schoolgirl tortuously devises to conceal a crush from adult eyes. '*Wish I was still on a diet*' was heavily underlined, as though she had had doubts that I would ever crack the code without help. 'Home soon,' she had written, 'can't wait to get back to my basement flat. Didn't realise how much I missed it.'

Hogarth paid us a couple of visits, and on the second occasion he brought Susan with him and we all had lunch together. Her own film was still grinding on, but she got some time off. They were still arguing whether to take the beach scenes to California, but I was too involved with my own problems to be greatly con-cerned as to the eventual outcome.

Hogarth went out of his way to be complimentary about the results he had seen on the screen. I told him what Raven thought about the boy. 'I think he's wrong,' he said. He was very confident and relaxed, and confided that he expected to go to Hollywood very shortly.

'There's a good chance,' he said, 'that I shall eventually take over out there.'

'Would you like that?'

'I think so. This country's dead. You must find that.'

'What about Audrey?'

'Well, she doesn't want to live there.'

'So what will you do?'

'Oh, I daresay it'll work out.'

The day they came to lunch Toller didn't show up for once. I offered to give Monika a lift back when shooting finished, but she said she had a dress fitting and would take a unit car. I thought nothing of it at the time.

Toller rang me at the hotel that evening. I was in the middle of dinner and had intended to go straight to bed.

'I want to see you,' he said in his usual charmless manner.

'Won't it wait until to-morrow?'

'No, it won't.'

'And you don't want to tell me what it's about over the phone?'

'No.'

'Tell him you're going to bed,' Susan said.

I put my hand over the receiver. 'Be worse if I have to see him during shooting.' I told him to come round to the hotel and put the phone down.

'Well, I'm going to bed,' Susan said. 'So get him to take his jackboots off, and for goodness' sake get rid of him quickly.'

I don't think a director is ever completely free of the fear of surprise attack. You learn, very early on in the game, never to turn your back. The assassins are everywhere and I have noticed that some of my colleagues, mostly the talented ones, have developed a morbid fatalism which makes them uneasy in company: their eyes wander when you talk to them at a cocktail party.

So I was not unprepared for Toller; it was just a matter of trying to guess what weapon he would use.

He declined the drink I offered, but accepted a cup of coffee.

'What did you have to see me about so urgently?'

'You can't guess?'

'I suppose I could, but it's a bit late in the day for guessing games. Suppose you tell me.'

'You're throwing the whole picture to the boy.'

I decided not to answer immediately. He had obviously prepared his speech on the way over and it seemed a shame to deny him the centre of the stage.

'This is obviously a situation which I cannot allow to continue, and I want to know why it is that you have deliberately chosen to destroy Miss Lehmann's performance. She is the star of the picture and she must be treated as such. And if you think, if you make the mistake of thinking that nothing is going to be done until it's too late, then you have another think coming.'

It was a long speech for him and he was flushed at the end of it. I still said nothing.

'I notice you don't deny it.'

'Are you any good at predicting Derby winners as well?'

'I beg your pardon? I don't understand what you mean.'

'Well, apparently, after only three weeks shooting, roughly a quarter of the way in, you've got what nobody else has got. You know what the picture's going to be like.'

'I didn't say that.'

'I'm sorry, I must have misunderstood you. I thought you said I was throwing the whole film to the boy.'

'That's right.'

Perhaps I should have cut it short then, because Toller had no real courage: the shampoo people could have bought him for much less than a Rolls-Royce.

'How do you know?' I said.

'I know because I've seen the film.'

'You mean you've seen what I've shot so far.'

'That's right.'

'And you've also read the script, I presume?'

'Naturally.'

'Then you also know that most of the early part of the film, which I'm shooting more or less in straight continuity, is slanted towards the boy. Monika's big scenes don't come until later.'

'All right, let me tell you this, I'm not alone. Other people agree with me.'

'What other people?'

'Mr Raven, he agrees with me.'

'Oh, you've discussed it with Mr Raven, have you?'

'We've talked about it, yes.'

'Did you talk about it to him, or did he come to you?'

'It was something we both felt very strongly about.'

I poured myself another cup of coffee. 'And what d'you want me to do about it?'

'I insist that you reshoot these early scenes and take advantage of Miss Lehmann's star quality.'

'Don't use the word insist,' I said.

'*Bitte?*'

'Insist. Don't use that word. And let me ask you something. Is Miss Lehmann aware that you've come to see me?'

'I have told her I'm coming to see you.'

'And she knows what it's about?'

'She knows I'm here.'

'That wasn't what I asked you.'

'Look, Mr Warren, I am the one who takes the decisions for Miss Lehmann. She does what I tell her. She goes into the films I put her in, she wears the clothes I choose, she acts the way I tell her to.'

'But more attractively,' I said.

'*Bitte?*'

'Well, fine,' I said. 'You've made your little speech, earned your ninety per cent, and now I'm going to bed.'

I started to turn out a few lights around the room.

'I'm sorry,' I said, 'if you want to stay and have some more coffee, please do. I don't suppose you have to get up too early in the morning.'

'I'm not leaving here until you give me an answer.'

'Oh, well, that's simple,' I said. 'The answer is that you're a total jerk. If that's too colloquial for you, how about prick? Ask Mr Raven about that, too. It's a word he's familiar with. In fact, curiously enough, when he and I first talked about you it was the only complimentary word he used.'

I walked into the bedroom and locked the door. Susan was still awake, and I put my fingers to my lips. We listened to him banging about for a few moments, and then we heard the door slam.

'What was all that about?' Susan said.

I started to undress. We carried on the conversation through the open bathroom door.

'Oh, nothing,' I said. 'The usual.' I gave her a brief summary of Toller's complaint.

'Do you think she put him up to it?'

'No, I honestly don't think this came from her.'

'What will you do?'

'Nothing.'

'You'll have to do something.'

I finished brushing my teeth, climbed into bed, set the alarm clock, and turned out the lights.

'Won't you?' Susan said. 'You can't just ignore it.'

She wasn't being a wife at that moment. She was being an actress enjoying any drama which affected another leading lady. She put a hand out and stroked my forehead.

'Poor darling,' she said. 'You're so trusting where women are concerned.'

CHAPTER FIFTY-ONE

I didn't have long to wait for the next development. The moment I arrived on the location the following morning George and Gladys the Wardrobe Mistress came to see me. George raised his eyes and handed me a hot cup of coffee.

'I think we need your help, Governor.'

'What's wrong?'

'It's Miss Lehmann, sir,' Gladys said.

'Yes, well, okay, don't make a big mystery about it. What's the matter?'

'She seems a bit poorly this morning, sir.'

'Where is she, in make-up?'

'No, she's still in her room.'

I started up the stairs. George followed. He had his script open. 'I wondered if you'd like to give me an alternative we could be working on,' he said. 'You might have a bit of trouble starting as arranged.'

I paused on the stairs. 'What has happened?' George looked around before answering.

'Well, I haven't been in myself, Governor, but according to Gladys, she stopped one last night. I gather you won't be able to shoot on her.'

'Anybody else on call?'

'The Police Inspector is on a stand-by.'

'Well, get him in. We'll shoot his entrance. Bill knows the set-up.'

'Matter of fact, I've already taken the liberty. He's already on his way.' George grinned at me. 'We'll be ready when you are, Mr de Mille.'

He disappeared downstairs again as I made my way to Monika's dressing-room, which was merely a converted bedroom at the top of the house. I knocked on the door.

'Who is it?'

'Me,' I said. 'Dick.'

'Oh, come in.'

She was sitting in an arm-chair with her back to the light when I entered and appeared quite normal. I noticed that she hadn't changed, but was still in her everyday clothes and wearing a mink coat over them.

'Lock the door,' she said.

I locked it and then went across to her. I bent to kiss her on the forehead, and then I saw what it was all about. She had a large bruise under one eye. She started to cry.

'What did you do?'

I knelt by the side of the chair and she clutched at me. I let her cry for a few moments.

'Don't worry. Just tell me.'

'I've let you down,' she said.

'Don't worry about that, just tell me what happened.'

I reached for some tissues to give her. I could see her face more clearly now and there was obviously no hope of photographing for two or three days.

'Did Toller hit you?'

She nodded. 'After he came to see you.'

'You knew he was coming to see me?'

261

'Yes, I begged him not to. It wasn't me, I didn't want him to come.'

I got to my feet again. 'Well, look, the first thing we've got to do is get you to a doctor.'

'No, I don't want to see a doctor.'

'Well, you must get it seen to.'

'No, I don't want a doctor.'

She fumbled for a cigarette. I lit one for her. I went towards the door.

'Where're you going?' she said.

'Nowhere.'

I unlocked the door and looked outside. Gladys was on the next landing down. 'Gladys,' I said, 'would you get a couple of cups of fresh coffee and some aspirins. And ask the prop boys to give you something, will you?'

I came inside the room again and relocked the door.

'Have I ruined everything for you?' Monika said.

'Stop worrying about all that. That'll take care of itself. The important thing is we've got to get you right.'

She looked at herself in the mirror and touched the bruise. 'They could perhaps make up over it.'

'Did he hit you anywhere else?'

Tears rolled down her cheeks again.

'Show me.'

She shook her head. 'I can't.'

'Show me.'

I turned her round and slipped the mink coat off her shoulders. She was wearing a man's shirt underneath which was open at the neck. I could see the beginning of another bruise across one shoulder blade.

'You'd better let me see,' I said.

She undid the buttons of the shirt and slipped it off her shoulders. She was bruised and marked around the neck, and there was also a red weal across one breast.

'He's quite a brave character, your husband,' I said.

'Oh, they're nothing, it's just my face I'm worried about.'

'Where is he at the moment?'

'Back at the apartment.'

There was a knock at the door, and I covered Monika with her shirt again and went to open it. I took the coffee and aspirins from Gladys. She also handed me a bottle of brandy.

'Tell George to have a car standing by, and tell him to get Stan here.'

I relocked the door again and then laced one cup of coffee with brandy. I took it to Monika, together with three aspirins.

'Take these,' I said. I held the cup for her as she sipped at it and grimaced. 'What's in it?' she said.

'Just a little brandy. Go on, it won't hurt you, and you're not going to work to-day.'

'But what will you do without me?'

'I'll find something, that's my worry. Now listen, you must see a doctor . . .' She started to protest again, and I don't quite know why, but I leant forward and kissed her. 'You trust me, don't you?' She nodded. I kissed her again gently. 'I shall talk to the doctor first and he won't ask any questions. We'll just say you had a bad fall on the set. But you must get your face seen to. I don't think it's that serious, if it's looked after. Then we must think where you're going to stay.'

She sipped the coffee and seemed calmer.

'Has he done this before?'

'Not recently.'

I held her hand and we sat talking until Stan arrived. I went out of the room and told Gladys to take care of her.

I gave Stan and George the essential details, and told Stan which doctor to ring.

'I suppose we ought to notify the insurance people,' Stan said.

'They don't pay out for the first forty-eight hours,' I said, 'so let's get our own opinion first. I'll talk to the doctor, he's an old friend. Then when you've done that, reschedule me for the rest of the week, just to make sure. We've also got to get her in somewhere. Not a hotel, we don't want a front page story.'

'Well, she's welcome to stay at my place, if you think it's good enough,' Stan said. 'I can always find somewhere to kip for a few days.' He went slightly red and avoided looking me straight in the eyes.

'Who'd look after her?'

'Gladys would,' George said. 'She's already mentioned it.'

'Has Gladys got a place?'

'Yes, that's an idea.'

'Not turning down your offer, Stan,' I said, 'but she'd probably be better off with Gladys.'

'Yes, fine. You know, just a suggestion.'

'I've been thinking, Governor,' George said. 'How about the Gestapo chief—who's dealing with him?'

'We'll deal with him later.'

'I mean, I can get a few of the stunt boys to lean on him. They'd do it nicely.'

'It's a sweet thought, George, but perhaps not, eh? What I do think would be useful, is have you got any chums in the Law?'

'Yeah. Course.'

'Well, I think that might be a better idea. A little visit from the Law and a friendly warning might work wonders. But let me know first. None of this must leak out.'

'What're we telling everybody?' Stan said.

'The unit, you mean, or outsiders?'

'Both.'

'Hopefully, it won't get any farther than the unit, but we'd better have one story and stick to it. Is Second-hand Sam around, by the way?'

'Bit early for him,' George said.

'Don't you say anything to him, send him to me.'

'Say she slipped on the stairs during rehearsals,' Stan said. 'After all, we're shooting a lot of stuff on the stairs.'

I thought about that. 'Yes,' I said, 'that's simple and could be true. The less complicated the story the better. Don't think there's anything else, do you? Not for the moment.'

'No, I'll get on to the doctor.'

'Car's downstairs waiting,' George said. 'And I take it that if her next of kin should enquire, we don't know nothing, we don't know where she is?'

'You don't know where she is,' I said.

I went back into the room and had a few words with Gladys who readily agreed to the arrangement. I have always found that

Wardrobe Mistresses and theatrical dressers are the most dependable people around in a crisis. I told her to wait downstairs in the car and to go with Monika to the doctor. Monika had listened to everything without comment.

'I haven't got anything with me,' was all she said.

'Gladys'll buy you what you want, toothbrushes and stuff, and anything else in fact.'

'You are sweet,' she said.

'No, I'm not. I'm just angry.'

'Do you always act so nice when you're angry?'

'Always.'

She stood up and put her arms round me.

'I'm sorry I did this to you.'

'You didn't.'

'I never said anything about John. I like John, and he's in love with me.'

'Yes, I can believe that. Are you in love with him?'

'No, I'd destroy him. But I like him very much. I wouldn't do anything to hurt him, not that way, not the way Kurt told you.'

If anybody had come into the room at that moment they might have thought we were lovers. I remember Alison asking, 'Do you find her sexy?' and the answer I had given then. She kissed me and I tasted the brandy on her tongue. I felt very sorry for her. I felt sorry for all of us.

CHAPTER FIFTY-TWO

All things considered, we managed to sit on the story fairly successfully. The *Daily Express* got on to the fact that Monika was away sick and made a routine enquiry which we were able to deal with, and the small paragraph they printed killed the story for the rest of Fleet Street.

My doctor, who never minded visiting actresses as pretty as Monika, treated the case like an unauthorised heart transplant and did his stuff brilliantly. The crew, even if they suspected the truth, behaved admirably and in fact, led by the clapper boy, passed the hat round to send her flowers and a Get Well card. Even Grotefend resisted the worst excesses of his unhappy profession.

We lost a little time, of course, but not as much as I had at first feared. Raven was told the facts, and was visibly, and perhaps understandably, shaken by them. He was chained to the conspiracy by his own guilt and the not-too-subtle hint from me that if the true story ever leaked out he might be given a featured role.

Toller we took care of in a different way. I left that part to George and his friends, who duly paid him a visit.

'From what I could gather,' George said, with a straight face, 'they didn't think his passport photo was up to date. So I think they suggested it might be a good idea if he went home and had a couple of Polaroids taken.'

'There wasn't any strong-arm stuff, was there, George?'

'No, Governor. Please! He thought our police were wonderful. On my life, they never so much as flicked the ash off his jacket. No, that's very how's-your-father these days.'

At all events, Herr Toller gave us no more trouble and forty-eight hours after he left London Airport to attend to some urgent business in Munich.

The night after it happened I paid Monika a visit in Gladys's apartment. I found her with the cat on her lap, surrounded by flowers and enjoying life. I think even in that short space of time she had begun to realise that life without Herr Toller had much to commend it. The bruise on her face had begun to fade and she had lost the tautness that fear brings around the mouth.

'Isn't he sweet?' she said, stroking the fat old neutered Tom. 'He won't leave me. And look at all these beautiful flowers. Thank you for yours, by the way, and thank the boys, too. I have written, but thank them again.'

'And what do you think of our National Health Service?'

'Your doctor? Oh, he's so nice. You know he bathed my face for over an hour? Am I looking better? Gladys has taken all the mirrors out.'

'I told her to. Where is Gladys?'

'She's gone shopping. Did you know she's a great cook?'

'I can believe that Gladys is great at a number of things. There's nothing you want then?'

'All I want to do is get back on the film. John's coming round later. To rehearse.'

'Did you hear from Kurt?'

'No. Nothing.'

'No, well he hasn't got this number, but I was just checking. If there's anything you want me to tell him, I'll pass the message.'

'I don't think so,' she said.

Gladys returned at that moment with a full shopping bag and I excused myself and left. When I got back to the hotel Susan had already started dinner.

'What kept you?' she said.

I told her. I had, of course, told Susan the events of the day before, suitably edited, but women have a limited amount of sympathy for their own sex. She listened with feigned interest.

'Well, I've got some news, too,' she said. 'We're definitely finishing the picture back in California.'

'When?'

'They want me to fly out at the week-end.'

'That soon?'

Now that the moment had arrived I greeted it with mixed

feelings. We are never so lacking in confidence as when we get what we think we want.

'It'll seem funny to be in London without you,' I said.

'Well, we haven't seen much of each other anyway.'

'Still . . .'

'Will you miss me?'

'You know I will.'

Her question took me by surprise. I remembered how I had felt when I came to London this time, the pain that her indifference had caused, the long drive from the airport with Grotefend, the nothingness of her greeting. Now it was Susan who spoke my lines, the disease had been passed on.

CHAPTER FIFTY-THREE

I visited Monika again the following evening after shooting. The change in her was even more pronounced: not so much physical, although the bruise had all but disappeared—but seemed to stem from a gaiety she had never revealed before. She had sent Gladys out to buy some new clothes and was excited because she had managed to wash her hair herself. 'It took me ages,' she said. 'She hasn't got a shower, so I had to keep pouring cups and cups of water over it to get the soap out.' It occurred to me that she probably hadn't done her own hair since she was a teenager: people like Monika were shielded from mundane things, they only had time to live with the abnormal.

'You should wear it like that in the film,' I said. 'It suits you.'

'I shall be able to come back to-morrow.'

'You'll come back when the doctor says so.'

'But he'll say anything I ask him.'

'I don't want you back to-morrow.'

'Why do you say that?'

'Because I don't. I've got plenty to do to-morrow.'

'Is it going all right?'

'Not too bad. Where does Gladys disappear to all the time?'

'Gladys is . . . what d'you call it? very tactful. She always goes out. Except when the doctor is here.'

'Is John coming round to-night?'

'I don't know. Maybe.'

'You heard the news about your husband, did you? Did Stan come after lunch and tell you?'

'Yes.'

'So if you wanted to, you could move back to the apartment.'

'No, I prefer it here. Gladys and I talk about you all. It's company, it's like home. I used to talk to my mother like that.'

'What d'you think you'll do about Kurt?'

'Who knows? For the time being I'm enjoying not thinking about him. It's a strange feeling for me. You see, I've never been on my own before. I sometimes think I've been married all my life.'

'It's a very common feeling,' I said.

'Can I offer you a drink? Gladys drinks stout. Stout. It's a funny name for a drink.'

'When I was in Germany just after the war, we drank U Boat fuel.'

'U Boat fuel?'

'That's what we called it. It was black market gin, but you could run a car on it.'

'Where in Germany?'

'Hamburg.'

'My mother came from Hamburg.'

I watched her as she moved across the room to pour me a drink. She had nothing on her feet and she reminded me of the young girls who used to wait on us in the officers' mess, the girls we bought with cigarettes and bars of Bournville chocolate.

'I meant what I said about your hair,' I said. 'You should have it like that for the scene in the church.'

She handed me my drink. 'You really like it that much?' She turned to study it in a hand mirror she picked up off the mantelpiece. 'I told you John's in love with me, didn't I?'

269

The sudden switch of thought took me unawares. She remained by the mantelpiece with her back to me.

'Since this all happened,' she said, 'he wants me to divorce Kurt and marry him.'

'Is that why you did your hair?'

'No, I did it for you,' she said.

In the pause the neutered cat walked very slowly across the room and arched his back against her bare legs. His purr intensified the silence.

'Well, I'm flattered,' I said finally.

She turned to face me.

'You know what I'm saying, don't you?'

'Yes, but I'd rather you didn't say it.'

'I could fall in love with you so easily,' she said.

'That's just because I was nice to you.' She shook her head. The cat remained between us, desperate for attention, but we ignored it. 'You can do better than me,' I said. I swallowed half my drink.

'Don't you find me attractive?'

'Yes. Very.'

'And are you going to tell me you're happy as you are?'

'My dear,' I said, 'you've been reading too many film scripts.' She came and stood in front of me and lifted her face to be kissed. I did nothing. She put her hands behind my head and drew my face down until our lips touched. I still did nothing. 'It wouldn't hurt to kiss me,' she said. 'You kissed me before.'

'That was different,' I said. 'You were crying then.'

'Please kiss me.'

'If I kiss you now, it'd be for the wrong reasons. And that wouldn't be fair to you.'

She pressed her lips against mine and I felt them open. There was something absurd about the whole situation, something I could never explain, for there was no morality in my reticence, none of the standard reasons applied. I responded gently, with a closed mouth and then I took her hands away. The sound of the cat came back.

'You're making him jealous,' I said.

'Do you think I'm awful, because we're both married, is that why?'

'No. If I told you the real reason you wouldn't believe me, but it's got nothing to do with you. I'm not good luck at the moment. But I shall always remember what you said, and how you said it, and the way you looked when you said it.' She stared at me, and I might have weakened and given Susan some truth to live by, but at that moment the doorbell went. I finished the rest of my drink and went to open it. It was Nethercott, and I recognised in his shiny expectancy something I had lost many years ago.

'Ah!' I said, 'the unknown warrior himself.' He looked past me into the room and saw only what he wanted to see.

'How's the patient?' he said.

'Worth all the trouble you're going to take,' I said, and stepped out into the corridor and closed the door on them.

CHAPTER FIFTY-FOUR

It took six hours to say good-bye to Susan at London Airport that following Sunday. We seemed to spend the whole day buying magazines and drinking free coffee in the Hospitality Lounge while a series of conflicting excuses were relayed to us, with less and less conviction, by the apologetic airline staff. First the plane was late arriving from Frankfurt, or somewhere, then they were going to switch aircraft, then that aircraft developed trouble in one engine—something which always inspires confidence—and when that had been investigated it was decided that it was now worth waiting for the missing original which, once on the ground, proved to have an under-carriage fault. We were only lacking a bomb scare. 'It's nothing serious about the under-carriage,' they told us, 'and you should be boarding within the hour.'

'You go, darling,' Susan said, 'you've been here all day.'

It was true that I now felt in need of a second shave, but airports have a fatal fascination for me: once I am there my senses become numbed. I am prepared to believe every story about metal fatigue, I dread the actual moment when one finally steps aboard the aircraft and the doors close, and take-off renders me dumb and rigid—and yet I can never find enough courage to leave. If I go to see anybody off, my own fears are transferred to them, and I don't walk away until I have watched the plane out of sight and even then, on the way back to the car park, I listen for distant explosions and the wail of sirens. And, of course, I fly all the time.

'No, I'll wait,' I said. 'I've stayed this long.'

'But you're making me nervous now.'

'Am I? I didn't mean to. I'm sure you'll get off this time. What time will you get in?'

'I don't know, I can never work it out.'

'Perhaps you can take a pill, when they've given you dinner.'

'It's supposed to be breakfast first on this flight, then lunch, then tea.'

'D'you think they know?' I said.

'No, I'm sure they took it all on board in Frankfurt, and we shall have a large German breakfast at tea time, an even larger and tireder German lunch at midnight and be woken for German tea just as we land in L.A.'

Two or three of the other hapless passengers in the lounge looked up uneasily as we laughed: delays, like Test Match scores when England is in danger, are meant to be taken seriously.

'Let's see, you've got ten hours, that means you'll just be landing as I get up. Will you ring me?'

'If I have the strength. But don't worry, no news is good news.'

She used the fragment of married code, and it took me back to days when a parting had been a kind of death. I took her hand and it was cold.

'You're not wearing your wedding ring,' I said. 'Are you hoping to get off in the plane?'

'Yes, who do you think is going to be the lucky man?' We both had a quick look round the room and started to giggle, sharing, as of old, a sense of inspired improbability.

'Briefcase and Hitler moustache,' I said. 'Definitely.'

'Oh, no. Too obviously sexy. I think Miami Beach with third degree burns on nose.'

She fished around in her shoulder bag and found the ring. 'My fingers were swollen or something. I couldn't get it on this morning.'

'You mean this morning this morning?'

'Whenever. How long have we been here?'

'Six hours.'

'Do go. You'll be worn out to-morrow. Have you got a heavy day?'

'Average, I suppose. We get Monika back to-morrow.'

'Oh, well that'll be nice for you.'

Was there any edge to her voice? I couldn't be certain. Just then a new stewardess arrived and announced that the flight was finally boarding. 'We shall be serving a combined breakfast and lunch immediately after take-off,' she said.

'You were nearly right,' I said.

I walked with her through a series of dispirited Pakistani tea parties to Passport Control, and there we said good-bye.

'I shall wait until you're in the air,' I said.

'Oh, darling, you don't have to.'

'I know I don't have to, but that's the way I'm made. Take care.'

'You too.' We kissed. She was wearing a scent I had always liked. 'I'm sorry,' she said.

'What're you sorry about?'

'Oh, things. You know what I mean.'

The Stewardess was hovering, trying to give the impression that the entire delay was due to us alone.

'I shall think of you by the pool in all that sunshine.'

'All that smog you mean.'

'Well, I shall think of you anyway.'

She kissed me again, then she picked up her hand luggage and went through the barrier, and the Stewardess blocked my last view of her.

I walked down the wide stairs to the ground floor and by the time I was outside I found I was crying. I crossed over to the multi-story car park and took the elevator to the roof. The sky was overcast and the wind provided an excuse for my wet eyes. I stood by the rail and watched the planes take off. Half an hour later the plane I thought contained Susan strained to reach the low clouds. At one point I imagined that it had stopped, for it seemed to make no progress at all, and then suddenly it had disappeared for good. I waited a few more minutes, then walked down to the floor where I had left my car, and spiralled to the exit.

I drove slowly round the obstacle course and was halted at the lights alongside a Rolls-Royce. The chauffeur's face was vaguely familiar and when the lights changed I was about to drive straight ahead when the penny dropped. He had turned off and was heading for the European Arrivals Buildings, and I cut across the traffic to follow him. I passed him when he pulled in, and this time I was certain. I parked again some distance away and kept him in view in my rear mirror.

I suppose roughly fifteen minutes later he got out of the car and greeted Osmond. Alison and the child came out then, and they waited in a group on the pavement until the luggage arrived. At one point the child let go of Alison's hand and walked off the kerb to retrieve some fallen holiday memento. Osmond dashed to pick her up. She clung round his neck and he kissed her before handing her back to her mother. They looked tanned and happy, the ad-man's conception of the perfect upper-bracket family. Alison and the child got inside the Rolls as Osmond tipped the porters. It pulled away immediately and glided past me, as I bent, like an assassin, to hide from myself as much as from them.

CHAPTER FIFTY-FIVE

I waited for Alison to contact me, which is difficult to explain now but seemed possible at the time, and it was ten days from that Sunday before I heard her voice. Ten days, twenty-two minutes of film in the can, eighty-three separate camera positions, thirty pages of script—the heart stood still, but everything went on as normal.

I say 'as normal' but in reality nothing was ever the same again. Monika returned to the film and we picked up the action where we had left off: the continuity girl and the prop man were, as usual, faultless, but there was nobody to warn me what happened next. On the face of it we were the same people and the work went well, but there was nothing beyond the work.

Susan arrived safely and cabled me HAVE A GERMAN DINNER FOR BREAKFAST IF YOU WANT TO STAY YOUNG AND LIVE LONGER HOPE FILM IS GOING WELL WE START WEDNESDAY DON'T WORRY BE HAPPY LOVE SUSAN, and I cabled back MESSAGE RECEIVED TRYING HARD YOU BE HAPPY FOR ME LOVE RICHARD.

Months afterwards, clearing out the contents of a hotel drawer, I came across her cable again and studied it afresh. Messages, in film parlance, are always for Western Union, but I wondered in view of what happened subsequently if she had intended any hidden meaning.

If Raven, on the other hand, was still plotting at that time, then he concealed it brilliantly, or else I no longer cared. Hogarth came to say good-bye and then took the Jumbo to catch up with his idea of the future. 'Give Audrey a ring,' he said, 'you're both on your own,' as though bequeathing the panacea for loneliness, but there was nobody with whom to share the joke.

I didn't go out at night, but took all my meals in the hotel, preferring to eat in my rooms after long and sybaritic baths. I indulged myself with a bottle of vintage wine every evening, and the combination of the enervating bath and the claret usually ensured a good night's sleep. I caught up with some reading, but I found that fiction failed to hold my attention and I picked up a copy of *The Oxford Dictionary of English Christian Names*. The name Richard, I discovered, has maintained its position as one of the half-dozen favourite men's names with singularly little fluctuation of fashion. The entry for Susan was somewhat cursory and dull, which disappointed me, but I came across a footnote to the description of Alison which, aided by the claret, seemed to have some special significance. The *locus classicus*, I read, is the Middle English poem with the refrain 'From alle wymmen my love is lent, Ant lyth on Alisoun.'

If I had lent my own love, it was returned with a lie. When Alison finally phoned me I had just finished my solitary dinner. The call no longer had any danger, and yet I can remember so clearly the familiar panic when the connection was made.

'We've just got back,' she said.

'Literally?'

'No, but this was the first chance I had to call you. I had to wait until I was alone in the house. I knew you were on your own, because I read in the papers that . . . that your wife had gone back to America.'

'Did you have a great holiday?'

'Some of the time. How are you?'

'I'm just the same,' I said. 'I got your postcard.'

'Aren't I awful? I'm so awful at writing. Thank you for your letters. They were lovely.'

'Tokens of my esteem.'

'Your what?'

'Just a joke. When will I see you?'

'Well, I can make it more or less any time during the days.'

'Yes, the boot's on the other foot now, I'm afraid. I'm working every day, except the week-ends. You still there?'

'Course. I'm thinking.'

'Is it going to be possible?'

'At week-ends?'

'Or the evening. I always dine alone.'

'You mean in the hotel?'

'Yes. You could smuggle yourself up in the service lift.'

'I'd be too scared to come to the hotel.'

'Then it'll have to be the week-end,' I said.

'You sound cross. I can't help it.'

'I didn't mean to sound cross. I suppose when you're on your own you tend to live with great expectations. I just want to see you.'

'Well, I want to see you, too, it's just a question of arranging it. Where would we meet then?'

'Like your postcard said? At the flat?'

'Will that be all right?'

'I'll make it all right,' I said. 'Saturday?'

'Yes, but I won't be able to stay for long. He plays golf on Saturday afternoon, but he's always home for tea.'

'I'll be there from lunch-time onwards,' I said, 'and expect you when I see you.'

'All right,' she said, but it was like a bank manager agreeing to a request for an overdraft without security and it wasn't until after we had hung up that I realised the only thing we hadn't negotiated was the trust that went with it.

CHAPTER FIFTY-SIX

I was there long before lunch-time and spent the time like a proud housewife putting everything in order. I had gone to Harrods first thing after breakfast and bought flowers, smoked salmon, and Dom Perignon, and a small bottle of her favourite perfume—choosing from caution and not meanness. I had forgiven her the lie and I was sick with expectation. I promised myself that if I could have the realness of her love on any terms, then I could believe again in the body and the blood. As I prepared the meal and the gift, I found the prayer that seemed to embrace us all: Give me some part of her, and I'll never betray You again.

I arranged and rearranged the room a dozen times, trying to see it with her eyes, and then I sat down to wait. I listened for the remembered note of her car, but absence had made caution stronger for her, too, and she parked two or three blocks away. I had been there three hours when the small knock at the door took me by surprise.

Telling the story, or rather this part of the story, from this distance of time I find there is no confusion like the remembered confusion of a single event. I had it all sorted out once, or thought I had, and it made a kind of sense to me, but the film has gone through the projector too many times, like love it doesn't last for ever and I can't be sure any more that every frame is still intact.

I can remember her standing just inside the room, looking past me to the carefully turned down bed, and I remember kissing her before she took her coat off. She folded it neatly, that much I recall, and laid it across the back of a chair, and later, when she undressed completely, everything was put tidily to hand, as though from the beginning she didn't expect to stay long and wanted to make sure that nothing hindered her departure. That's the impression I have now, but probably the significance was never there—with a woman's intuition it could well have been that she only wanted to preserve the order I had introduced into Stan's room.

We seemed to have little to say to each other before the act: it was as if she had only come to keep her side of the bargain, with just enough tolerance to last until the ritual of tea claimed her back and she was safe again. There again, perhaps I only believe that now. At the time, in the first shock of loving her, I could have believed that she never existed away from me. She had come as she had promised and I didn't question her lateness—relief was too welcome, relief blotted out the past and future pain. For weeks my lidded thoughts at night had begun and ended with her, and now as our naked bodies slid together in that perfect dovetail, the warmth of her sex against me was more exquisitely unbearable than anything the mind could dream in absence. Her skin had a kind of creamy duskiness where the month of sun and oil had smoothed it, faintly cold to my lips as I traced old patterns to her breasts. Her hand clutched at my head, moving backwards and forwards, and then was still as the first moment came with the claiming of my mouth. Hope was there between my lips and her salt, swimming moistness and I dimly heard that familiar sad cry that only human loneliness brings forth. And later when hope was shared I was conscious only of the soft, warm astonishment we can never remember completely.

Then she began to cry with the utter helplessness of someone worn out, but with hardly any sound so that for one brief moment I mistook her anguish for that other pain that pleasure sometimes imitates. I raised myself above her, too astounded to speak, while she stared past me, her eyes wide open, letting the tears fall helplessly down her face. I bent to kiss her lips, but it was like kissing a statue in the rain. She lay perfectly still and our bodies grew cold together.

I tried asking her the reason, whispering the words close to her ear, talking as one sometimes does to a lost child. For a long time she made no response, then she turned her head away from me, towards the curtained window. I waited. It was so still in that small room, it was like being in a cell listening for the

279

footsteps before the door opened for the last time.

When at last she answered her words had no meaning for me.

'We must never see each other again,' she said. 'It's all hopeless, it's like a death,' and an old echo came back.

I tried to turn her head towards me, but she resisted.

'No,' she said, 'it can never be what we want, not what we talked about, that can't ever happen, so it's best we don't pretend any more.'

'Were we pretending just now?'

'That's the easiest part, it's living afterwards, all that living you have to do alone.'

'It doesn't have to be like that.'

She let me see her face then. Tears had marked it, just as Toller had marked Monika—pain is like a transfer that anybody can use.

'You'll see,' I said, 'it doesn't have to always be like that.'

'Don't make me any more promises, not promises I can't let you keep.'

'But why now? Why suddenly, when we were so happy?'

'Isn't that the best time, while it's all intact? Don't you always want to end things when you're happiest?'

'No,' I said. 'Nobody believes the end of anything like that.'

'I do. I have to, there's no choice any more.'

'But something must have happened to make you think like that? Something you haven't told me.'

She shook her head violently.

'Did you decide all this while you were away?' Even then I would have settled for that false hope that lives in explanation. 'When you phoned that day, you wanted me then. It must have happened since then. Nothing else has changed. I haven't changed.'

'Perhaps you didn't have to change,' she said.

'But it was you, in that restaurant, at the start of it all, and later you said you didn't want to share me with anybody. Well, I kept my side of the bargain, but I'm willing to share you now, to go on sharing you if it means I can still see you.'

She just looked at me. 'But it can't end now, not like this, not after what we've just done. Anything's better than that. I'd rather you hate me. Give me something to hate.'

'There's nothing to give you,' she said, 'unless you can hate a child.'

'Children grow up. They leave you and start loving somebody else.'

'I know,' she said. 'You don't have to tell me.'

'So it's going to be like the first time? Not hate, just nothing, just an end, just another useless end. Doesn't love count for anything? Why did we bother? We could have just slept together between golf and tea.'

'No, that would never have happened. There had to be love. There had to be too much love, that was always our trouble.'

'I don't understand you, I don't understand anything any more.'

'Poor darling,' she said, 'it was you who said it. You said you can never go back. I tried, but it didn't work. It worked in bed, but not anywhere else.'

She searched my face and she might have been taking a close look at a stranger. Her composure terrified me more than her tears. 'Nothing's your fault. Nothing.' She got up from the bed and went to the chair she had put her clothes on. I had the feeling that if I lay very still I could believe I was just waking from some nightmare and that when I opened my eyes she would just be coming into the room, and we'd make love and everything would come right. I opened my eyes again at the sound of the door, but the room was empty, neat and empty.

CHAPTER FIFTY-SEVEN

Human experience is only understandable as a state of transition. Once we have consented to be always ill at ease, we can find life tolerable—how could it be otherwise? When I started this book, I thought I had a personal motive, hoping that in the telling of it I would come to understand myself. Most of all I hoped that certainty could be brought back from these retold promiscuities, so that 'the much life and the little art' could be made comprehensible. For in the days that followed after Alison had left me, there was little enough comprehension. At night I was glad enough, like the poisoned cat, to drag myself off alone to await the death of the heart, but for five days a week, from eight in the morning until nine at night the fiction of my own life had to be enlarged into screen fact. There was no escape from human contact. No release from love, for the clay I worked had to be fashioned into images of truth that I did not share. To stand outside, to direct, if you will, those actors playing out aspects of my dead love, was I suppose my one chance of survival—for the writer, the artist enjoys the sweetest of our more pensive pleasures in that he can ultimately turn every experience, good, bad or more often than not, indifferent, to his own lonely advantage.

The film took from me such strength as I had. I greeted each new day with that particular pang of remorse that sleep has smothered for a few hours. Curiously my wounding dreams, and there were plenty of those, were never concerned with Alison, only with Susan far away and out of reach.

If I did not believe in myself I began to believe passionately in the quality of the film. It seemed that whereas in life I could do nothing right, in my work I seldom faltered. I put all this down, not from conceit, because I have made one mediocre and some average films in my time, but because I owe it to others as well as myself. Nethercott's performance built day by day into something quite unique: he knew it and I knew it and there was no need of a mutual-admiration society, or a press agent. He has been praised more flamboyantly since in lesser roles and lesser performances, but that is the luck of the game. He was in full possession of accumulated resources, the existence of which I sometimes had the happy privilege of bringing to his attention. I will take the credit for casting him and for writing him a good role, and I made sure that what he had other people were made aware of, but the final credit is his. It's lonely out there in front of the cameras at eight in the morning, and if you haven't got it the camera won't photograph it.

As for Monika, well, she was outdistanced but she stayed in the race. In the end she gave what I still believe is her one and only true performance, and she looked beautiful. Things were never the same between us, of course, but I had helped her see that life could hold something more than a Kurt Toller, and she had a kind of bloom to her which even now I can never think of without a stab of regret. She kissed me once again, at the end-of-picture party, that improbable event which tradition demands shall mark the passing of most of the captains and the kings. It's difficult to describe to an outsider the atmosphere that comes about at the demise of a shooting unit. It's something between a working-class wake and a society wedding, with everybody sharing the same catering firm and premises. Wives are invited, and the friends of the actors, and the numbers usually defeat analysis. Strangers wander up on a first-name basis and volunteer drunken opinions on a film they haven't yet seen which are sometimes offensive, often obscene, occasionally perceptive. Like the captain of a sinking ship, the director is required to stay until the end, sharing the last bottle of champagne with two or three sodden technicians who invariably relate long and maudlin anecdotes about the great directors they have worked with in the past, whose likes they will never look upon again.

They are sad occasions for me, and for the actors, and I walk into the cleared canteen with a sense of loss, for whatever the fate of the finished product there was some pleasurable pain in the making of it.

The aftermath is an equally strange period. Another set of

characters come out from the small back rooms to begin that tortuous maze of trial and error known as editing the film. One has mixed all the paints, as it were, and now one has to put them on the canvas, ready for varnishing day.

Raven relinquished the role of producer almost before I had printed the last take. At the time his indifference wounded me more than his expected opposition. I was tired, I suppose, and a little complacent at having come out in one piece at the other end, otherwise I might have guessed at the true reason for his absence from the cutting rooms. He was 'setting up other deals,' he was in the process of shifting the burden of his expense account to another group of shoulders, he was too busy to look at the rough-cut and sent Gerry Blechman instead. That great referee of taste left a cow-pat of chewing gum under his seat in the viewing theatre, pronounced the film 'sort of, you know, meaningful,' and departed. We went back to the moviola, smoked more cigarettes, drank more coffee and wondered what in fact we had made.

I was in the middle of recording the music when the news that Norbert Quarry had sold his interest reached our less than stunned ears. He and Raven were rationalising their common interests and devoting all their creative energies to the coming world of videocasettes. 'We're moving into the twenty-first century ahead of schedule,' Mr Quarry was reported as saying. The company which now owned the negative of my film had appointed three new executives who immediately announced that movies, properly handled, still had a great future, even though their inaugural photograph suggested that they had yet to lose their past, for they had second-hand car salesmen stamped indelibly into their waxwork faces. Their spokesman, the smallest of three dwarfs, lost no time in making his philosophy known. 'This industry is up to here in geniuses,' he said, barely reaching the microphone. 'What we need now is some good old-fashioned showmanship, and that means we're going to be calling the shots.' He couldn't actually get anybody to print his speech, so he paid for full page ads in all the Trade papers and had it reproduced verbatim. The following day the same papers carried further full page ads of congratulatory telegrams from some of his fellow mental cripples. A good time was had by all.

We recorded the music and put it on to the film, and then we started dubbing, and still nobody came near us. The lack of interest could have been a portent of riches to come, but we knew better. We sat in the dubbing theatre putting the film to bed, as the term is used, reel by reel—dedicated madmen working in total isolation, for you need a little madness to survive. It was a good film. Not a great film, for they are few and far between, but it had something to say and it said it intelligently, with a little wit, and much compassion. At the core it had Nethercott's hard and many-faceted performance which the more perceptive critics might have taken note of. It was imaginatively photographed, you could hear every word and the music score complemented the whole. I was proud of it.

Eventually, because life has to go on, I forced my new employers to acknowledge that the film existed. They pleaded pressure of business, which merely meant that they had been going through the books to see how much they could hide before stealing the rest. They promised, in cables of alarming length, to fly to London *en masse* at the earliest opportunity.

It was a further three weeks before they finally arrived. And one thing I will say for them, they knew how to use knives, if not forks.

They flew overnight from New York and viewed the film four hours after arrival. One of the trio fell asleep immediately and noisily. The other two, sitting in front of me, succeeded in staying awake but otherwise betrayed no sign of life. When the house lights came up it was eleven o'clock on Armistice Day. I sat with my editor and waited. The senior member of the trio took out a large silk handkerchief and wiped his palms. Perhaps the slight disturbance of air that this gesture produced affected the metabolism of his sleeping colleague: he revived, got up and went straight to the toilet.

I waited.

The senior member turned to face me.

'How much did it cost?' he said.

'Counting the studio overhead, three million eight.'

'Is that a British actor?' his companion said.

'Yes.'

'They won't understand him.'

'Where?' I said, but this was ignored. My editor left the theatre quietly. He told me afterwards he went to be sick.

'How long does it run?'

'One hour fifty-nine exactly.'

'And that's it, finished, is it?'

'That's how I see it,' I said.

'Well, Charlie,' the other man said, 'we gotta go to that meeting. D'you have a john around here?'

'Yes. That door. But your friend's using it.'

'Well, nice meeting you, Mr Warren.' He held out his hand. He needed to wipe it again.

'What did you think of the film?' I said.

'I think we've got problems.'

The sleeper came out of the toilet.

'We all through?' he said.

'Yeah. Let's go.'

The other two nodded to me as they passed up the aisle. All three filed out of the theatre to vanish back into the vast obscurity of their lives.

I sat for a while in the empty theatre, staring at the blank screen where for the last two hours my shadows had performed. Then the curtains closed by remote control and it was time to leave.

On the way out I stopped by the projection box and gave the man a tip. After all, he'd shown the reels in the right order.

CHAPTER FIFTY-EIGHT

To the best of my knowledge the film was never screened anywhere again until it suddenly appeared on television.

I stayed on in London for another two weeks, and my agent took me out to lunch and made sympathetic noises, but his loyalties were already shifting: failure, like a terminal illness, embarrasses some people.

I had a farewell dinner with Stan in his basement flat, but we were both too drunk to get drunk. I thought about driving home via Hampstead, but it was late and I was catching the morning Polar flight.

When I got back to the hotel there was one letter waiting for me. It was post-marked Los Angeles and the envelope was handwritten. I read it in the elevator on the way up to my room. It was from Kitty. She had taken the trouble to write and tell me that Susan had filed papers for divorce. She was going to name Monika Lehmann as co-respondent, and she intended to marry Robin Hogarth as soon as they were both free.

I cleaned my teeth with the electric toothbrush, but the batteries were dead again, and I went to sleep feeling sorry for myself.

In the morning I found Grotefend waiting for me in the lobby, and he drove me to the airport and his driving took my mind off the coming flight. We arrived in plenty of time and the plane was on schedule.

When we shook hands at the barrier he was quite emotional.

'I wanted to see you off,' he said. 'You've always treated me like a friend.'

'Why, Sam,' I said, 'coming from you that really means something.'